RAFFERTY
TO FIND A KILLER
Lionel White

Introduction by George Kelley

Stark House Press • Eureka California

RAFFERTY / TO FIND A KILLER

Published by Stark House Press
1315 H Street
Eureka, CA 95501, USA
griffinskye3@sbcglobal.net
www.starkhousepress.com

RAFFERTY
Originally published by E. P. Dutton & Co, Inc., New York, and copyright © 1959 by Lionel White. Reprinted in paperback by Bantam Books, New York, 1960. Copyright renewed January 9, 1987 by Hedy White.

TO FIND A KILLER
Originally published by E. P. Dutton & Co, Inc., New York, and copyright © 1954 by Lionel White. Reprinted in paperback by Tower Books, New York, as *Before I Die*, 1964. A condensed version published by *Blue Book*, July 1954, as "Sorry, Your Party Doesn't Answer." Copyright renewed May 4, 1981 by Lionel White.

Reprinted by permission of the Estate of Lionel White. All rights reserved under International and Pan-American Copyright Conventions.

"My Correspondence With Lionel White" copyright © 2023 by George Kelley

ISBN: 979-8-88601-016-9

Book design by Mark Shepard, shepgraphics.com
Proofreading by Bill Kelly
Cover art by James Heimer, jamesheimer.com.

PUBLISHER'S NOTE
This is a work of fiction. Names, characters, places and incidents are either the products of the author's imagination or used fictionally, and any resemblance to actual persons, living or dead, events or locales, is entirely coincidental. Without limiting the rights under copyright reserved above, no part of this publication may be reproduced, stored, or introduced into a retrieval system or transmitted in any form or by any means (electronic, mechanical, photocopying, recording or otherwise) without the prior written permission of both the copyright owner and the above publisher of the book.

First Stark House Press Edition: February 2023

RAFFERTY

They all trust Jack Rafferty. His wife Martha never questions him. Jill, his mistress, is completely charmed by him. Even gangster Tommy Faricetti knows that Rafferty will always do right by him. But Rafferty has dedicated himself to making organized labor his career—by whatever means necessary—and his only real loyalty is to himself. Now a Congressional Committee has got him on the witness stand, asking him questions about his past, probing the secrets that his friends and loved ones trust him with. He knows that the union is behind him. But he also knows the only person who can save Jack Rafferty is Rafferty himself.

TO FIND A KILLER

Lt. Marty Ferris is the kind of cop who sees things in black and white. He's a good cop but has no patience for human failings. So when he begins to suspect that his wife is seeing someone on the side, he has her investigated, and finds out that she has a criminal past. Love turns to hate, and Ferris begins to plan his revenge. So when nightclub singer Billy Chamlers is found murdered, he decides to set up one of the suspects. Sam Duffy, her seedy agent, seems a good fit. But ex-con Willy Holiday is even better. It doesn't take much to badger them both into submission. In Ferris' world, they're *all* guilty... and one of them is going to murder his wife.

LIONEL WHITE BIBLIOGRAPHY (1905-1985)

Fiction
Seven Hungry Men (1952; revised as *Run, Killer, Run!*, 1959)
The Snatchers (1953)
To Find a Killer (1954; reprinted as *Before I Die*, 1964)
Clean Break (1955; reprinted as *The Killing*, 1956)
Flight Into Terror (1955)
Love Trap (1955; reprinted in UK as *Right for Murder*, 1957)
The Big Caper (1955)
Operation—Murder (1956)
The House Next Door (1956; first published in *Cosmopolitan*, Aug 1956)
Hostage for a Hood (1957)
Death Takes the Bus (1957)
Invitation to Violence (1958)
Too Young to Die (1958)
Coffin for a Hood (1958)
Rafferty (1959)
Run, Killer, Run! (1959; re-write of *Seven Hungry Men*, 1952)
The Merriweather File (1959)
Lament for a Virgin (1960)
Marilyn K. (1960)
Steal Big (1960)
The Time of Terror (1960)
A Death at Sea (1961)
A Grave Undertaking (1961)
Obsession (1962) [screenplay published as *Pierrot le Fou: A Film*, 1969]
The Money Trap (1963)
The Ransomed Madonna (1964)
The House on K Street (1965)
A Party to Murder (1966)
The Mind Poisoners (1966; as Nick Carter, written with Valerie Moolman)
The Crimshaw Memorandum (1967)
The Night of the Rape (1967; reprinted as *Death of a City*, 1970)
Hijack (1969)
A Rich and Dangerous Game (1974)
Mexico Run (1974)
Jailbreak (1976; reprinted as *The Walled Yard*, 1978)

As L. W. Blanco
Spykill (1966)

Short Stories
Purely Personal (*Bluebook*, May 1953)
Night Riders of the Florida Swamps (*Bluebook*, Jan 1954)
"Sorry—Your Party Doesn't Answer" (*Bluebook*, July 1954)
The Picture Window Murder (*Cosmopolitan*, Aug 1956; condensed version of *The House Next Door*)
To Kill a Wife (*Murder*, Sept 1956)
Invitation to Violence (*Alfred Hitchcock's Mystery Magazine*, May 1957; condensed version of novel)
Death of a City (*Argosy*, Jan 1971; condensed version of novel)

Non-Fiction
Sports Aren't for Sissies! (*Bluebook*, May 1953; article)
Stocks: America's Fastest Growing Sport (*Bluebook*, Nov 1952; article)
Protect Yourself, Your Family, and Your Property in an Unsafe World (1974)

7

My Correspondence
With Lionel White
by George Kelley

13

Rafferty
by Lionel White

213

To Find A Killer
by Lionel White

My Correspondence with Lionel White
- - - - - - -
George Kelley

3/5/79

Paperback Quarterly,
  Someone in New York said you wanted to get in touch. I'll be glad to hear from you.

Regards,
Lionel White

Back in 1979, I was planning to write an article on one of my favorite writers: Lionel White. I had read many of Lionel White's caper novels and thought writing an article about Lionel White's clever books would appeal to the readers of *Paperback Quarterly,* edited by Billy Lee and Bill Crider, since many of White's books were paperback originals.

I sent a letter to Dutton Books in New York City, who had published some of Lionel White's hardcover books, asking if I could contact him for information that I would include in my article.

Weeks went by and then I received the handwritten note on LIONEL WHITE custom stationery that appears above.

I quickly sent a letter to Lionel White's address outlining my proposed *Paperback Quarterly* article celebrating his work over three decades. Facts about Lionel White's background were hard to find so I asked if he could tell me a bit about how he became a writer. I also took the bold step to ask if I could borrow copies of the few Lionel White books I hadn't been able to buy from bookdealers. Here's Lionel White's response:

March fifteenth

Dear Mr. Kelley–

Appreciate your letter and your interest in what I might laughingly refer to as "my work." That last is a word I despise and an activity I avoid whenever possible. I am sending along, under separate cover, copies of the books you say you are missing and another you haven't mentioned as well as a little stinker called SPYKILL, written under the name "L. W. BLANCO." (That took real imagination, right?)

I am virtually illiterate on the typewriter so trust you will overlook misspelling etc. I'll try to fill you in on a bit of the sordid details of my misspent life but suggest if there is anything in particular you would like to know, ask away or check local police files.

I made it through grammar school (a small miracle) started working on newspapers as police reporter (*Cleveland Press* and some fifteen others in and about the country and finally New York). Born Buffalo, N.Y. July 9, 1905. Brought up in Stockton, Calif. Published my first magazine (*World Famous Kidnappings*) a one shot, after covering the Lindberg Case. Went on to publish *Short Shorts*, a monthly, for the next few years. Brought out my first book, *Logical Nonsense,* a definitive collection of Lewis Carroll, (Putnams) 1934. Another collection of short stories (Putnams) about the same time and I have neither a copy nor can I remember the title. Probably not worth remembering.

Around 1940 started a publishing company, bringing out a monthly called *World at War* and later changed to *WORLD.* Also a string of fact detective monthly magazine which if nothing else made a nice hunk of money and allowed me to form a taste for Jack Daniels and afford a twin engine deep sea fishing toy. Wrote my first novel *(Seven Hungry Men)* in 1952. When I managed to palm it off on a publisher who at least had money if no taste, I went into a state of mild shock and at once abandoned the publishing racket to spend more time fishing the Florida Keys and eventually moving in the Easter Shore of Maryland where I continued living until 1970 at which time I married my current wife and checked into southern California, the land of pleasant dying. I have more or less been turning out these novels for a living off and one since the first disaster.

I've one son who lives on the Chesapeake and builds ocean going cruising yachts and had enough sense not to become a writer. Current wife busy getter her doctorate in Archeology at Claremont Graduate

School. She had previously been an acquisition editor with several New York publishers (if you can't sell 'em, marry 'em.)

Nothing much else except I am falling to pieces and gradually fighting my way down to the poverty line.

I have a suitcase full of old clippings, book reviews and all that shit, but hardly think it would be worth looking through. My books have been published in some thirteen foreign countries and have been made into a half dozen or more pictures as well as having had the basic plots stolen by most of the better tv shows.

I trust you to return the books I am sending as in several cases they are my only copies.

Look forward to hearing from you again.

Lionel

As I was processing all the information Lionel White provided, I received this brief letter from him:

4/5/79

Dear Mr. Kelley,
 Couple of things—one important.
 Have a producer out here who is interested in buying picture rights of the *Grave Undertaking* and he has misplaced the copy I gave to him god knows how long ago. The only other copy I had I sent along to you and would like back as soon as possible and I will shoot along a Xerox if you still want to read the thing. This could mean some much needed loot for me.
 Another thing: You didn't acknowledge receipt of those books I sent you. Hope you got them all right.

Regards,
Lionel White

Of course, I immediately mailed *Grave Undertaking* back to Lionel White. And, I read the novels White sent me in preparation to sending them back to him promptly. A few days later, I received this letter:

4/11/79

Dear Brother Kelley:
 I appreciate your alacrity in returning the copy of *Grave Undertaking*. I too hope to hell my producer friend gets off his prosperous ass and purchases the picture rights.

As to your letter, no I haven't as yet seen a copy of *Paperback Q*. As for your questions. Let me say to begin with that from your letters I get the impression that you are so thoroughly a proper and dignified young gentleman that I find I face certain inhibitions in freely expressing myself for fear I might either shock, offend, disillusion/disgust you with my offhand, but I hope quick frank answers. In any case—

About my writing habits: Absolutely atrocious. I have always tried never to make habits out of virtues.

I do not write daily. I write when the fucking bills pile up so high I can't get out to the booze shop.

I don't start with a plot. I start with an idea that I have to make a buck and then try to get a point of view which I want the story to express. In short, I plan a perfect caper (that's a crime, citizen) every thing goes according to the plan, it can fail—but because of the flaws in the characters involved—well, it does. Next step, Locale, characters, time period, the crime or what ever it is all about. In short we are now in the planning stage. Next and extremely important—the demands of the market, the possible reaction of the first editor, who may be reading it, and last, and most important, the possible reaction of the audience we are aiming at. Then we do the "cris-cross word puzzle" and figure out where to start, how to construct, build up to a climax and finally get the god damned thing over with.

At this point we put a piece of paper in the typewriter.

At about now, I get off my can and sit at either the typewriter or grab a tape recorder. My system used to be to take my boat out into Long Island Sound or the Chesapeake Bay (wherever I happened to be at the time) drop a hook, get bored for a few days and then write myself back home.

Otherwise, I would check into a motel where I had never been before, tell them to throw out the fucking tv, cut off the phone, get rid of every piece of reading material including the Gideon Bible, and after staring blankly at the wall and realizing it was costing me good money to stay "in jail," I would finally get stared and write myself free.

I'll check in with a carton of cigarettes, a few cans of canned soup, some instant coffee, and a hot plate.

Eventually, out of loneliness and desperation, I'd finish the book and buy my pardon.

It's a hard way to make a living. I would rather have owned a gas station or married a school teacher.

Anything else?

> Take care and good luck,
> Lionel

Sadly, that's the last letter from Lionel White. I worked my article for *Paperback Quarterly* but Life intruded. I left Madison, Wisconsin where I was working on my doctorate to move back to Western New York where I became a college professor. Lionel White died in 1985.

Rafferty runs in two different modes. The first is a Congressional hearing on unions where John Carroll Rafferty, President of Local 702 of the International Shipment Union (ISU) is set to testify. His testimony could bring down Rafferty's associate, Tommy Faricetti, a gangster who used the beautiful showgirl, Jill Hart, to gain leverage over Rafferty despite Rafferty's love for his wife and three children. Rafferty's life spirals out of control. A Soviet film based on Lionel White's *Rafferty* can be seen as a critique of American unions and government investigations:
https://en.wikipedia.org/wiki/Rafferty_(film)

To Find a Killer (aka *Before I Die*) revolves around police Lieutenant Marty Ferris's suspicions that his wife, Fern, is cheating on him. Ferris plans the perfect murder using the murder of sexy nightclub singer, Billy Chalmers to advance his schemes.

Both novels display Lionel White's ability to pressure characters to extreme actions and to disrupt careful plans with extreme measures. You can count on Lionel White's work to be chilling and menacing to the last word.

—November 2022

RAFFERTY
Lionel White

For January and Helaine

CHAPTER ONE

The senior senator from the great Northwestern industrial state was the only one not in his seat at the committee table when the chairman, Senator Ormand Fellows, finished his short introductory speech—dry, provident in choice of words and purposely undramatic in quality—and announced that the next witness to take the stand would be John Carroll Rafferty.

That the old gentleman, Senator Hartwell Early, saw fit to absent himself at this particular time was certainly indicative of his exalted stature, both as one of the oldest members of the upper house and as a man with a long and consistent reputation for integrity and dynamic progressiveness in his legislative thinking. He was a Republican, always had been a Republican, and always would be. Unlike many of his colleagues, he prided himself on being an old-fashioned, dyed-in-the-wool liberal. A self-made man inclined to boast of his lack of formal education, in his early years he had been a carpenter by trade. He also had been, at one time, a minor union official. To this day he still carried a card, of which he was inordinately proud, and paid his dues religiously.

There is no possibility the Senator could have been unaware that young George Morris Ames, Chief Counsel for the Investigating Committee, was planning to call Jack Rafferty to the stand on this particular morning. None at all. The press, radio, and television had been predicting the event for the last week and even newspapers in such far-flung cities as London and Paris and Brussels had headlined the information.

And there was not a single person in that great chamber who failed to realize that the Joint Legislative Committee for the Inquiry into Labor Practices, immediately referred to by the press as the Rackets Committee, was out to "get" Jack Rafferty.

The bulk of the testimony, recorded during the past fortnight, was merely a prelude to this dramatic moment; everything which the extraordinarily brilliant staff of investigators—ex-G-men, accountants, attorneys, and professional snoopers—had been establishing and attempting to prove, led up to it. The long list of previous witnesses had been brought before the Committee to lay the background for what was to come.

And what was to come was Rafferty himself.

Getting Rafferty, of course, was not the essential purpose for which the Committee was appointed. The Government of the United States is not prone to appoint legislative committees for the sole function of prosecuting individuals, no matter how much those individuals may need prosecution. Nevertheless, it was a firmly established fact that in this particular case, the entire investigation was aimed exclusively at the lone figure of one individual—and that individual was John Carroll Rafferty.

Yes, Senator Early must have been fully aware that Rafferty was finally due to take the stand. And, like all of those who jammed the chamber on that Monday morning, like each of the more than million members in Rafferty's union, the ISU (International Shipment Union), like the unnumbered other millions who had been following the investigation on television and in print, the Senator knew that Jack Rafferty himself could be expected to do what so many of the others had done. He would take the Fifth Amendment and refuse to talk.

There was no question about it, no question at all. Even if there had been, it had with certainty been settled when old Sam Farrow had faced the Committee some days previously and had himself established the precedent and set the pattern. Farrow had unhesitatingly taken the Fifth. Had sat there stony-visaged and cold-voiced for two solid days, giving back stare for stare to the members of that august but red-faced and annoyed body as their bright young Chief of Counsel spelled out those embarrassing and compromising questions.

Simple, concise, perfectly proper under the terms of the Fifth Amendment. Your name, your address and then that nice, easy-sounding phrase. You deny nothing and you admit nothing. You may not look awfully good, but at least no one has ever been put in jail for not looking good.

So the Senator was absent, lying in bed in his Washington, D.C., home, which was a suite on the sixth floor of the Mayflower Hotel. He was slowly sipping a glass of warm orange juice through twin plastic straws. Propped up on three extra pillows so that he might watch the television set which had been rolled up to within a few feet of the end of the bed, he lay stretched out under the thin cotton blanket. The Senator didn't actually have to see the screen to know what Rafferty would look like. Rafferty was an acquaintance of the Senator's, a friend. Not a long-standing friend, such as old Sam Farrow, the President of the ISU, but still and all a friend. The Senator knew exactly what Rafferty looked like and he knew what Rafferty was going to say. Rafferty was going to say the only thing possible. He was going to say nothing.

For a moment, as he lowered the glass of juice, the Senator was lost in reflection, a reflection not without a certain bitterness. It was ironic that in taking the Fifth, Sam Farrow, who in truth was a very good friend, had without question ended his career as a prominent union official and national figure. He had absolutely and irrevocably condemned himself to oblivion. (He had also, of course, possibly saved himself a term in prison.) But Rafferty, even though taking the Fifth, would probably succeed to the presidency of the ISU.

Senator Early belched and put the empty glass on the night table at the side of the bed. He sighed gently and closed his eyes. Well, that was the way it went. The King was dead; long live the King. Youth must be served. Sam Farrow was seventy-three years old; Jack Rafferty was forty-one. Hartwell Early himself was sixty-nine.

For a brief moment the Senator thought ahead, thought of the elections coming up next fall in his own state. He shook his head angrily and, opening his eyes, stared defiantly at the ceiling. Well, at least he had nothing to worry about. He'd die in office. They—the Republican State Committee back home—they'd never have the audacity, the courage, to put up a younger man while he was still around. He was a statesman—even the opposition in recent years had admitted as much—but he was still a damned good practical politician. He encouraged the younger men, liked to give them a helping hand and bring them along, but he was a lot too smart to kill his own goose tit-feeding a possible successor.

He was very tired; that poker game last night had lasted too long and he'd both drunk and smoked too much, far too much for a man of his age. He lifted the wide, once massive shoulders from the pillow, reached over and clicked off the remote control button on the television set. He was tired. He knew what was coming. The hell with it. Right now he just wanted a little rest, a little sleep.

Thus, confident that Jack Rafferty would take the Fifth, the Senator remained in bed.

No one else who was connected with the investigation, even in the most remote capacity, was absent on that Monday morning. And the entire chamber on the second floor of the great granite and marble building was filled to overflowing by as many of the casually curious as were able to bribe or bluff their way in; extra police had been called out to hold back the overflow crowds. This, in spite of the sure knowledge Rafferty would not talk.

Jack Rafferty was news. Saying nothing, admitting nothing, he was still the star of the show. And, he was going to be the next President of the ISU, come the elections in the fall, just two months off. Despite the United States Senate, despite an almost uniformly unsympathetic press, despite a half a dozen criminal indictments and charges still pending—he was going to be President. As such he would be one of the most important and powerful labor leaders in the entire country, on a par with men like Reuther and Meany. And whereas the ISU was certainly neither as large nor as powerful as certain other labor organizations, he would actually outshine many bigger men because of the peculiarly strategic and significant part his union played in controlling the traffic and communication upon which all other industries depend.

There was a sudden stirring at the back of the chamber, near the door leading into the anteroom which had been reserved for witnesses and their attorneys. Senator Ormand Fellows leaned forward where he sat behind the long mahogany table in the center of the raised dais, slouching just slightly to the left to favor his shoulder, which was bothering him again.

His eyes moved quickly over to the left, conscious suddenly that Representative Mahoney had shifted in his seat and was whispering to young Ames, who himself was busy shuffling papers and apparently paying no attention to the husky rasping words of the gentleman from the Midwest.

Fellows frowned, his heavy, gray-shot eyebrows hoisting in that odd way they had, the right one raising at an angle and the left one following it a split second later. His thin-lipped mouth under the straight, almost delicate nose, drew down at one corner and he quickly turned back, noticing at the same time that the television camera at his right had swung now and was aimed to the rear of the room where the sergeants-at-arms were pushing and shoving to make a path for the two men slowly making their way to the front.

The frown faded and Senator Fellows half nodded, in a satisfied way. Well, that was one argument he had won. Of course, as Chairman, he had every right to win it. But old Early had been very difficult. He suddenly looked around and for the first time noticed that the Senator from the Northwest was absent.

Senator Early had not approved of television. Well, that was easy enough to understand. Early didn't need television. He didn't, in fact, need publicity. His, Senator Early's, position was secure. He didn't have problems back home. Early had the perfect parlay; he was an ex-labor man, a Republican, and he ran in an industrial state.

Ormand Fellows believed himself to be as fair and as honest as any man alive. He didn't question his own integrity and he didn't expect others to question it. Good God, his record—

But after all, he was a realist. His position was far different from that of Early. He had to go out and get the votes if he wanted to remain in office. And there was no reason why the people back home shouldn't know and understand what he was doing while he was representing them down in Washington. No reason at all. Millions of people were interested in this investigation, millions; not only laboring men and women, but consumers and management as well. They had a right to know what was taking place. Early was an old fool. But then, of course, Early as an ex-union man might feel that the less the public learned about what went on behind the scenes, the better.

But was that fair? Was he being honest? Early was something of a windbag and it is true he had come up from nothing. Nevertheless, he was, in spite of being a Republican, an honest and decent man. Hell, when he, Fellows, had wanted that amendment to the Conservation Bill put through hadn't Early gone along? Hadn't Early ...

But that was all beside the point. The point was he had won out with the other members of the Committee, and television cameras had been allowed to record the proceedings. And now, at this very minute, the camera which was stationed at his right and slightly behind him, was focusing on the next witness as he made his way slowly through the crowds toward the table standing directly in front of the dais and some twelve feet away.

Jack Rafferty was followed by his attorney, or a man whom Fellows took to be his attorney, an almost bald, thin-boned man with an oddly unlined, round, baby face. Next to Rafferty, his small figure looked like that of a child. Rafferty was not, however, an unusually big man himself. It was only the great breadth of those shoulders which made him appear so, as he moved slowly through the curious-eyed, jostling crowd.

Cartwright Minton, a permanent member of the AP Washington staff, lifted his long bony face and with his left hand pulled the heavy horn-rimmed glasses down from his forehead to rest on the high bridge of his patrician nose. He stared for a moment and then turned to his companion.

"I see that Senator Early hasn't shown up yet," he said. Unconsciously his right hand reached for the folded blank copy paper lying in front of him on the press table.

Jake Meadow shrugged. Jake was small and swarthy and dressed beautifully, spending, it was rumored, at least a hundred and fifty dollars for his suits. He was a general assignment man for a New York tabloid and frequently covered spot stories in Washington.

"So what?" Jake said. "The old boy probably got laid last night and is taking a day or so to get back his breath." He smiled, his dark cynical eyes unamused.

Carl Hazzlet of the *Times* looked up, annoyed, and then quickly shifted his eyes to follow Rafferty's progress.

Boscum—no one ever did learn his first name—a Chicago photographer believed to be attached to the *Tribune*, but actually a freelancer who'd gotten in on a fake pass, stood up to see over the heads of the people standing in front of him.

"Who's that with him?" he asked, at large. "His mouthpiece?"

Jake laughed shortly, raising his eyebrows to look at Minton and winking. "Mouthpiece," he said. "My God." He lifted a beautifully manicured hand and tugged at Boscom's tweed jacket.

"That's Rafferty's lawyer," he said. "Mort Kauffman. Take his picture. He *likes* to have his picture taken. In fact, if you take a real nice one, emphasizing that high, intelligent, but balding brow, he will probably send you a bottle of Scotch. He might even arrange to get you screwed—or buy you a new box Brownie."

Boscum looked down, perplexed, and Hazzlet said something under his breath, his expression registering disapproval. "He's going to need a lawyer," Minton said.

"The hell he is." Robert Sherman, labor expert for the *Star*, shook his big shaggy head, looking not unlike a slightly aging sheep dog. "Rafferty has never needed a lawyer. He's been through so many investigations, he can handle them in his sleep."

"He'll probably have to," Jake said. "He certainly didn't get any last night—sleep that is. Were you at the party over at the Shoreham? The goddamnedest brawl I've seen in years. Everybody drunk, broads all over the place, and Rafferty the drunkest."

Hazzlet looked up quickly.

"Do you mean to say that Rafferty got …"

Jake looked at the *Times* man with pity.

"You could call it that," he said. "You should have been there. You could have got your wick …"

"Cut it, Jake," Minton said. "Mort Kauffman isn't representing the union, is he?" he asked, changing the subject. "Is he Rafferty's private boy or did the ISU …"

"Rafferty's own," Jake said. "The rank and file will pay—of that you can be sure—but Rafferty isn't using any regular ISU lawyer on this deal. Mort Kauffman is about as smart as …"

Bogardus, a new man recently sent down to the capital by one of the weekly news magazines, interrupted.

"I don't see why they go to all the bother of putting him on the stand," he said. "Hell, they know he isn't going to say anything!"

Jake looked at him pityingly.

"Of course he isn't going to say anything. What do you expect him to do? You think he's going to open his mouth and make a full confession? You think he's going to tell us all about how he done it? How he's muscled in and taken over—aw for Christ's sake!" He turned away in disgust.

"They're putting him on the stand so he won't talk," he continued. "They don't give a damn whether he talks or not. What they want to do is get the questions into the record. And more important than that, they want to get them before the television audience. They want to prove, or at least give the impression they are proving, that they really have the lowdown on what's been happening. Christ, this Committee has spent a quarter of a million-dollar appropriation already and soon they'll be out to get another quarter of a million. They've got to come up with something for the people back home. It doesn't matter if Rafferty doesn't talk. The committee is going to get its publicity anyway."

He stopped, suddenly, as Boscum brushed the side of his head, lifting his camera up to aim it.

"Jesus Christ almighty," Jake said, "get that goddamned thing out of here. Go over with the rest of the photographers and take your pictures. This is supposed to be a press box, not a ferking candid camera contest!"

Mary Ellen Henshaw, columnist and radio commentator, sniffed and lifted her chin daintily.

"Really," she said.

"I apologize for the goddamn," Jake said.

Miss Henshaw ignored his remark and turned to the middle-aged woman sitting next to her.

"I say," she said, half rising in her seat and pointing across the room with a complete lack of either embarrassment or self-consciousness. "I say, isn't that the Hart girl? Jill Hart, Rafferty's mistress?"

Miss Henshaw's voice, clear, high-pitched, and ringing despite that odd, rather whining note which made it so easily identifiable over the air waves, reached the ears of half of the room and a good many persons looked up, taking their eyes from Rafferty's progress.

Rafferty himself probably heard her question, but if he did, nothing showed in his completely expressionless face.

She dropped her hand and fell back into her seat.

"It's her all right," she said. "God, I can't understand what men find in those cheap, oversexed ..."

"I will be glad to explain to you," Jake Meadow began, his brown sleepy eyes slowly dropping from Mary Ellen's chin to her flat sterile bosom, "Yes, I ..."

"Lay off her, Jake," Minton said, leaning toward Jake and intercepting his vision of Miss Henshaw. "Lay off, kid. That gal's dynamite and when she explodes someone always gets hurt. Anyway, shut up. I want to hear what's going on."

CHAPTER TWO

From where he sat just behind the long table reserved for Committee members and the Chief Counsel, Chester Danial, Chief Investigator for the Committee (on loan temporarily from the Treasury Department) observed Rafferty as he slowly approached.

He had to admire the man's control, his utter lack of any sign of nerves. Of course, Danial reflected, Rafferty had no way of knowing the vast amount of damaging material he and his staff had been able to compile, had no knowledge of those tape recordings they'd borrowed from the New York people, no suspicion of the documents from the Chicago offices, the bank records and those hundred and one other items of more or less deadly significance. Rafferty couldn't know ...

But quickly Danial shook his head, his investigative mind at once rejecting his own conjectures. Wasn't that the mistake they had made before? Wasn't that the mistake they had been making all along? Figuring what Rafferty knew and what he didn't know? Wasn't that the reason Rafferty had beaten them in court when they'd thought they had him absolutely cold? Underestimating him. Not giving him credit for the highly unusual intelligence that he did have.

In a sense it was a shame that Rafferty would be hiding behind the Fifth Amendment. Danial would have taken a good deal of pleasure in just sitting there and watching and listening as Rafferty attempted to answer some of those questions which he and members of his staff had so carefully collected. Yes, Rafferty would have made a truly noble opponent. He wouldn't be a pushover by any means. Danial had read the testimony of previous investigations, when Rafferty had talked, and he'd had to admit that for a crude unlettered man Jack Rafferty had a magic tongue. A magic tongue and a bright razor-sharp mind which put the proper words in his mouth, although they might as often as not be mispronounced.

Rafferty had intelligence and guts and, yes—a certain amount of definite charm. He'd certainly needed all of them to come along as far as he had come. All of them and other things besides.

For a fleeting second, Danial felt himself envying Jack Rafferty. Not for what he was, but for what he had. The good schools for his children, those fabulous private bank accounts in his wife's name, his chauffeur-driven Cadillacs and Lincolns (tax-free of course and supplied by a grateful union membership), even the extracurricular pleasures which Danial would not admit that he envied.

Danial was a long-time civil servant, looking forward to a modest government pension. *His* children attended the public schools, not by choice, but by necessity.

His eyes went back to the long table in front of the dais and he saw that Rafferty had pulled out a chair and was sitting down, his attorney had put his briefcase on the table and was seated next to him. Rafferty himself had carried a large attaché case into the room and had placed it on the floor.

Danial was a little surprised. He wondered what could possibly be in it.

Probably, he speculated, a couple of bottles of bourbon. For as much as Rafferty was going to say, or admit to, he wouldn't need a four-cent envelope to hold his notes, let alone an attaché case. He wouldn't, in fact, even need the lawyer. There was no doubt but what Mort Kauffman had already briefed him. It wouldn't take Rafferty long to have memorized the words.

"I respectfully decline to answer on the grounds that to do so ..." etc.

Mort Kauffman shadowed his mouth with the palm of his fat, almost infantile right hand.

"Remember," he said, his voice a low, oddly husky whisper, "remember, just the name and your address. Not your occupation. You have to stop short of the occupation, otherwise ..."

Rafferty shook his head with a peculiar, short, jerking motion. He was whispering as he cut in, but the words came out with a sharp, hard, almost threatening sound.

"Jesus Christ, Mort," he said. "Stop trying to advise me. What the hell did I tell you when I hired you? I don't need any goddamned advice—you think I haven't faced these things before? I told you I wanted you here only in case I want to ask you questions. Keep it in mind, will you? When I want you, I'll ask."

He lifted his eyes as he stopped speaking and saw that he was being closely watched by the press and the photographers. Quickly he smiled, reached over and sort of half patted the little attorney's arm.

It was fantastic what that sudden quick smile did to Jack Rafferty's face. His entire expression was totally altered. From a man in his early forties, a sober, serious, dignified man who could have been just about anyone, his face suddenly took on the expression of a young boy. A charming, completely delightful, open-faced boy. The broken nose now gave him a gamine look; the brown eyes were warm and soft and infinitely trusting and sweet. When Jack Rafferty smiled, it was very easy to see why almost everyone who ever had known him trusted and liked him.

"I just thought," Mort Kauffman began.

"Don't think," Rafferty said, still smiling, but being careful not to seem to be mugging for the cameras. The smile was strictly for Mort, strictly between him and his attorney. "Don't think. I do my own thinking. I'll do my own worrying, too. You just sit back and be happy. For a grand a day, you can afford to be happy."

Mort Kauffman smiled back, although his smile was certainly not in the same league as Jack Rafferty's smile. He smiled and nodded his small round head quickly.

"Sure," he said, "sure, Jack."

The son-of-a-bitch, he thought. A real son-of-a-bitch. But my God, I gotta admire him. Here he is, facing just about the biggest and toughest battle of his life, and he's smiling at me and telling me not to worry. And he pays me a thousand dollars a day just to sit here.

Well, I guess he knows what he's doing. He seems to have been right every time so far. He's been through half a dozen of these investigations before, been through a couple of criminal trials, too. And every damned time he's come out stronger than ever.

Any other client told him, Mort Kauffman, to shut up and he'd do his own thinking, he'd have gotten up and walked out on the case. A thousand dollars a day or not, he'd have just gotten up and walked out. He didn't take that sort of crap from any client. Hell, that's what they were paying him for, to do their thinking for them. And if he was going to take their money he wanted to earn it. Also, he wanted to protect his own reputation. He hadn't gotten where he was by letting his clients do their own thinking. Not by one hell of a long shot.

For just a moment he wondered just why he didn't get up and walk out.

But Jack Rafferty wasn't just any client. Maybe he was only the President of a Los Angeles local right now and the Chairman of a district conference, but he was going to be the next President of the ISU. Jack Rafferty was the man who, in a couple of months, was going to be one of the biggest shots in organized labor.

Kauffman wasn't walking out on that. You could damn well bet he wasn't. He might hate to admit it, but there was also no doubt but what Rafferty was fully capable of doing his own thinking.

Tommy Faricetti carefully patted the talcum powder on the blue-black flesh of his freshly shaved jowls, staring hard at his reflection in the bathroom mirror. His hands were firm and steady and his eyes (looking into the eyes which unwaveringly regarded their own image) were clear, unaffected by the whisky or the lack of sleep. He called through the half-opened bathroom doorway.

"He coming on yet, Francis?"

"In a minute now," Francis MacNammera said. "In a minute. The newspaper boys are taking flashes."

Faricetti quickly finished his toilet. He adjusted his tie, took the well-tailored jacket from the wooden hanger and put it on, and then left the bathroom, not bothering to turn off the light.

"This place is a goddamned mess," he said, looking around the expensive hotel suite, his eyes taking in the half-empty whisky glasses, the overflowing ashtrays, the unmade double bed to be seen through the door leading into the second room. "Girls gone?"

"They're gone," MacNammera said. "I sent 'em back to New York. That big blonde wanted ..."

"The hell with her," Faricetti cut in. "Just so they are gone. Jesus," he sighed, pulling up a chair so that he faced the television set. "Jesus, I don't envy Jack. Not after what I had to go through last week. Boy, what they did to me."

"They'd have done a lot more if you'd answered those questions," MacNammera said.

"More? What more could they a done? Christ, that goddamned Ames. Called me a thug, a muscle man. Asked me, asked *me*, for Christ's sake, how I felt while I was beating up that garage guy. And I had to sit there and refuse to answer. Mac, you know damned well I haven't beaten up anybody, personally, in at least twenty years. That son-of-a-bitch knew it, too. But he had me; knew I couldn't answer him."

"Of course you couldn't answer," MacNammera said. "I know it made you look bad, but there was nothing else you could do, Tommy." The lawyer looked over at him, his face serious, "Tommy, you might as well realize it. You're facing a stretch in the can. You're out on bail right now. If they'd have got you started talking, you wouldn't have been able to stop. And before you were through, you'd have said enough to have put you away for the rest of your life. All you need is this one more fall."

"Where the hell do you suppose they got all of that stuff?"

"It doesn't matter," MacNammera said. "It doesn't matter where they got it. The point is—they got it. And you are far from out of the woods yet."

Faricetti reached for a cigarette, lighted it from the flame of a solid gold Dunhill, and shook his head in irritation.

"They should be getting along. What the hell are they stalling for?" he asked, looking at the television screen.

"Listen," MacNammera said, "don't be in such a hurry. And don't worry about Jack Rafferty. You got your own worries, Tommy."

"As long as Jack is behind me, I got no worries," Faricetti said. "Don't ever forget that. They won't pin him, they'll never pin him. He's beaten these things plenty of times before. In another couple of months, he's going to take Sam Farrow's place and then no one can touch him."

"A lot can happen in two months."

Faricetti looked up at the attorney, his face flushing.

"What the hell does that mean?" he asked. "What could happen? Christ, Jack's got it cold. He's got the delegates behind him; he's got the locals. The votes are already in, in and counted. Even if the convention hasn't been held yet."

MacNammera shook his head.

"Rafferty still has to get through this hearing," he said. "You want to keep one thing in mind. If he takes the Fifth and refuses to talk—and I can't see how he can do anything else—there's the matter of public opinion ..."

"Public opinion, balls! Public opinion don't elect the President of the ISU!"

"True," MacNammera said. "But you want to remember the Federation has gone on record. Any union official who takes the Fifth automatically is barred from holding office. When Rafferty takes the Fifth, he as much as says he is willing to have the ISU tossed out of the Federation."

"So what? So we get tossed out. The Federation needs the ISU a hell of a lot more than the ISU needs the Federation. You aren't suggesting that Jack would hesitate—that he'd let himself open to questions which could ..."

"I'm only saying he's been up before these hearings in the past. He's never yet taken the Fifth Amendment."

"For Christ's sake," Faricetti said, "Sam Farrow took it. I took it. All of us took it. It was Jack himself who planned that strategy. Now are you trying to say ..."

"I'm only saying this. After all, Tommy, I'm your lawyer, not Rafferty's. I'm only saying that if he takes the Fifth, he's going to jeopardize his own position. He's going to sell himself short in the eyes of the membership and in the eyes of the public. He may have to do it. All right—he does have to. But it's a calculated risk. Certainly, after what's been going on these last few weeks down here, Jack realizes that the Committee has plenty of stuff. You should be able to tell that from the things they dug up when they had you on the stand. They have plenty, and right at this point they may be doing a little guesswork here and there, putting two and two together to get four, but they know what's been going on."

"Sure they know," Faricetti said. "But what the hell good's it doing them? They know—but can they prove anything? We set up a few paper locals. So what? Some of the boys got greedy and put their hands out. Again, so what? These things been going on as long as there's been unions."

He was standing now, pacing the room, and he turned and went over to the window and pulled one of the curtains aside to look out.

"He's just taking the oath," MacNammera said. "Come on back and sit down."

"... and nothing but the truth. So help you God."

Senator Fellows kept his right elbow bent, his arm half raised as he finished speaking. He stood, listing just noticeably to the left (favoring the pain which persisted in his shoulder and had by now spread down into the chest cavity), his eyes steady and devoid of any trace of expression, his face unmoving except for his lips. He looked directly at the man standing some ten or twelve feet away, facing him squarely.

Jack Rafferty said, "I do."

He nodded, imperceptibly, slowly lowered his own hand and reached behind himself blindly to find the edge of the chair. He bent his knees and carefully settled back into it. Hitching the chair an inch or two forward so that he was resting his folded arms on the top of the table, he kept his eyes on the Chairman. Unwavering, serious eyes. His complexion was ruddy, giving him the appearance of blushing, but the color was natural, a result of recent weeks in Miami. His blond skin burned, but never tanned. His face was clear, unmarked by lines or shadows. There was nothing tense about his expression; he had the appearance of a man who was seriously interested, paying strict attention to what was happening, or was about to happen. A man with an interest in coming events; not a man who was to be a participant in those events.

Senator Fellows found his own seat. He waited a moment, pulling a sheaf of papers forward so that he could see them by looking down and barely bending his neck. For a moment his eyes lifted and he glanced briefly at young Ames, the Chief Counsel, bent over his own collection of data. Then once more he looked at the witness.

"Your name?"

"John Carroll Rafferty."

"Place of residence?"

"Los Angeles, California."

"Occupation?"

Rafferty didn't hesitate. Even as he opened his lips to speak, he was aware of the sudden stir in the room; aware of Mort Kauffman at his side, looking up at him. Aware that Senator Fellows and the other members of the Committee all had their eyes on him.

"I am the President of Local 702, International Shipment …"

The quick, persistent tugging at his elbow as Mort Kauffman reached up and jerked his sleeve, made him halt for the briefest of moments and it was during this sudden forced interruption that the room came to life. It was a sound like the faint, unidentifiable rustlings before a storm; the whisper of excited voices, the movement of restless bodies as the spectators in the room shifted and moved about nervously, unexpectedly.

Senator Fellows rapped quickly with the gavel; rapped again as the whispers, the squeaking of chairs, and the wave of sudden sound engulfed the room.

He rapped a third time, half rising in his seat.

"No. No, Jack, for God's sake," Mort Kauffman said. His voice was urgent and his face paled as he tugged at Rafferty's sleeve.

Almost with indifference, as though he were tossing off the hand of a beggar, Rafferty shook off his attorney. He continued, not waiting for the room to once more grow silent.

"… International Shipment Union of Los Angeles, California," he said. "I am also Chairman of the Western Conference of the ISU and a sixth Vice-President of the National ISU."

In the sudden shocked silence as Rafferty finished the sentence, a silence deeper and more profound than any silence had a right to be, coming as it did after the initial whirring of sound, the voice of Jake Meadows came clearly and defined from the press table.

"Christ, he's blown his lines!"

Senator Fellows again rapped sharply with the gavel, staring angrily across at the press.

"This room will be cleared if there is any further disturbance," he said.

"Mr. Chairman." Rafferty spoke from his seat, "Mr. Chairman, I request permission to make a short introductory statement and ask that the same be read into the minutes of this hearing."

CHAPTER THREE

Ann Rafferty moved her legs—long, slender, little-girl legs, escaping from the frayed edges of denim shorts. She moved them from the arm of the old-fashioned, overstuffed chair and leaned forward to twist the dial of the television set to increase the volume. A pretty girl, with her mother's auburn hair (but worn in a short pageboy, not in a bun), she had also her mother's azure-green eyes, delicate bone formation, and clear, fine-grained skin. She had all her mother's physical features; from her father she had inherited expression. She had that same odd characteristic of appearing completely poised, even indifferent, and then by suddenly smiling, showing infinite charm.

Ann, at sixteen, was still growing and her fine slender shape was rapidly taking on the formations of full maturity. Beneath the rolled-up sleeves of her cotton shirt—borrowed without his knowledge from her brother Eddy—her arms extended, slender and rounded and soft. Under that same cotton shirt, which she wore during these hot summer months without underwear or brassiere, her small, pear-shaped breasts had filled out, the nipples were evident under the thin fabric.

Above the sudden crescendo of the sound track, she called out through the open door to the kitchen.

"Ma," she said, "hey, Ma. Dad's on. And he's going to talk. He just asked permission ..."

Martha Rafferty spoke from the sink over which she stood doing the breakfast dishes.

"I can't hear a thing you say, dear," she said. "Not with all that noise. You'll have to come in here if you want ..."

Ann reached forward a second time, cutting the volume. At the same time she again shifted and climbed out of the chair. Crossing the room, she poked her head in through the doorway.

"I said, Dad's on. He's going to talk."

Her mother rinsed her hands and reached for a towel. She turned and spoke as she dried her hands.

"And why shouldn't your father talk?" she asked. "Is there any reason that— Ann, are you looking at television?"

Ann shrugged.

"Sure. Why not? It isn't every day that a girl gets to see her own father …"

"Ann, I told you Daddy asked particularly that you children didn't tune in on those hearings. When he called last night, he made a special point of telling me he didn't want any of you to turn the set on while he …"

"Oh mother, for goodness sake!" Ann drew up her shoulders and threw out her hands. "I'm not a child you know. After all. Really! I certainly have every right to know what …"

Martha Rafferty shrugged helplessly.

"I'm only telling you what your father …"

"But Dad's in Washington," Ann said, rather pointlessly. "I can't see why, with all of the publicity he's been getting, I shouldn't know …"

"I'm telling you what he asked," her mother interrupted.

"Listen, Mother," Ann said, "after all, I have to see the other kids. They're all talking about it. All of them. Saying Daddy was going to take the Fifth Amendment and if I'm going to answer them, going to defend my own father, then I certainly ought to know …"

"Defend your own father? Now see here, young lady, you don't have to defend your father or anybody else. Nobody has ever had to defend Jack Rafferty. Why if he could hear his own flesh and blood talking about him this way—" she stopped, her eyes going to the ceiling beseechingly.

"I only know what everybody's been saying about him, Mom," Ann said. "You must know what's been going on. You must know that Daddy is …"

"I don't know anything of the kind," Martha Rafferty said sternly, not waiting for her daughter to tell her *what* everyone was saying and *what* had been going on. "I stopped worrying about your father's business more than a dozen years ago. I only know that whatever he does or may have done, it is all right. And I certainly wouldn't start worrying about what the neighbors say. But that isn't the point—not the point at all. You were told not to listen in on television and I want you to obey Daddy's orders."

"Orders, shmorders," Ann said. "For goodness' sake. At least you might be a little interested yourself. He's just asked that Senator down there if he can make a statement. I should think you would be at least interested in hearing what your own husband has to say—in front of the United States Senate."

Martha brushed past her child and entered the living room. She walked directly to the television set and reached down, seeking the knob which turned the set off. As she did, her eyes quite unconsciously went to the screen and she saw the image of her husband as he opened his mouth and began to speak. It was almost as though he were staring directly into her own eyes, talking to her and her alone.

Her fingers hesitated on the knob and she stood there then, straining her eyes as she watched the picture from a bad angle and much too close up. She stood motionless and silent, listening to the words.

Ann Rafferty crossed behind her mother and slumped into a chair, sitting off at an angle, several yards away from the set. Her face was serious, with the strange, remote seriousness of a child, and as she watched the screen and listened, her lips half opened.

Martha Rafferty didn't sit down; at the moment she had no idea she would be spending a good many hours, during the next three days, staring at the screen of that television set.

With experience which only long practice could have given him, Jack Rafferty pulled the portable table microphone closer, so that when he spoke his mouth was approximately a foot and a half away from it. He looked directly at Senator Fellows. He was opening his mouth, preparing to speak, when Mort Kauffman jumped to his feet.

"Senator," Kauffman said, in a surprisingly deep and full voice for so small a man, "Senator, I would like to ask this Committee for time to consult with my client."

Rafferty turned a cold eye on his attorney, started to speak, but was cut off by the Chairman.

"You are Mr. Rafferty's attorney?"

Kauffman, this time ignoring his client, answered quickly. "I am, sir."

"In that case please give the Committee your name and your address."

"My name is Morton Kauffman, of Cline, Benhardt, and Kauffman. West 44th Street, New York City. I ..."

"You may have time to consult with your client."

Senator Fellows banged his gavel, needlessly, and turned to his right to whisper with George Morris Ames. The two conferred in low tones, now and then looking up to watch Jack Rafferty and Mort Kauffman.

"Jack—for the love of Christ!" Mort said. "What in the name of God are you doing? I thought ..."

"I know what I'm doing," Rafferty said, his voice low and angry. He didn't forget to put his hand over the mike as he spoke. "God damn it, leave me alone. I know what I'm doing!"

"I thought you were going to take the Fifth. I thought everybody said … what … how …"

"I can't help what you thought and I can't help what everybody said. I'm doing what I have to do."

"But why the hell didn't you tell me? Why didn't …"

"If I were going to take the Fifth, there would be no point telling you. No point even having you here. Christ, I could have used MacNammera, or Levy or anyone, if that's what I was going to do. That's why you're here. I wanted my own …"

"But Jesus, you should have warned me. Let me prepare …"

"I didn't want you to prepare. I didn't want anyone to prepare. You or the other boys or the members of this Committee. Now damn it, just sit back and take it easy. Listen and shut up. When the time comes—and it will—then I'll ask you. I'll be asking plenty before this is over."

Mort Kauffman shrugged, the startled expression still on his face.

"Sam Farrow will be having kittens," he said.

A grim smile passed over Rafferty's face.

"I wouldn't be surprised," he said. He turned back to the Committee and saw that Senator Fellows was watching him. The Senator, seeing he was ready, again banged the gavel. Rafferty cleared his throat. He remained seated as he spoke.

"Mr. Chairman—members of this Committee"—his voice was rather low but thoroughly distinct, "I should like to say the following few words for the record."

He hesitated, looking slowly from one member of the Committee to another. He had their attention; he had the attention of every single person in the room. He had the attention of several million people who were not in the room.

"For some twenty-odd years, since the week I took my first job in a slaughterhouse in Los Angeles, California, I have been a union man. During most of those years I have been a union organizer and have served as an official in the ISU. For the last thirteen years, I have been President of Local 702 of the ISU. When I took over that position, we had approximately four hundred members—and there wasn't a dime in the treasury. Today," he paused, turning to stare into the lenses of the TV camera, "today, Local 702 has more than twelve thousand members and there is more than a million and two hundred thousand dollars in its treasury. It has one of the finest welfare and retirement programs of any local in this country or in the world."

Again he hesitated, not for dramatic effect, not theatrically. He merely wanted the facts to sink in.

"For twenty-four years I have fought for the rights of the workingman. I have fought against communism in and out of organized labor and I have fought crooked and unfair practices by management where I have found them to exist.

"I am not a rich man—I live in the same six-room house which my wife and I purchased seventeen years ago. There is still a mortgage on that house. My wife does not keep a servant and she does the laundry for ourselves and our three children. We own a secondhand Buick.

"I have a criminal record. At one time I was arrested more than twenty-two times within a twenty-four-hour period—while I was on a picket line fighting company-employed strong-arm thugs in Stockton, California. I have been charged with, and convicted of, picketing unlawfully, assault and battery, carrying concealed weapons, and numerous other charges—each and every one in connection with my organizing activities. I have had my face beaten in by company goons, have had my nose broken by deputy sheriffs in the employ of private industry, have been kicked, assaulted, and threatened. My car has been bombed and I have been ordered out of more towns than I care to remember.

"I have fought the fight of organized labor all of my life and I shall go right on fighting so long as I may live and breathe."

This time when he hesitated, he reached down and lifted the water pitcher on the table and poured a glass three quarters full. He did not, however, lift it to his lips.

The room remained in complete silence as he continued.

"I did not ask to come before this Committee. I came in answer to a subpoena. I do not approve of what this Committee is doing or the tactics used by its Counsel in questioning witnesses. As an officer of the ISU, I am automatically a member of the official family of the Federation. The Federation has gone on record as condemning the taking of the Fifth Amendment by labor officials. I voted against that decision and I am still against it. I firmly believe that the constitutional guarantees handed down by our forefathers should be freely available to any citizen of this country, irrespective of what his position may be in private life.

"A number of witnesses before this Committee, within the past weeks, have taken either the First or the Fifth Amendment. Despite the decision of the Federation, I feel that they were thoroughly entitled to do so. Were I to feel that in answering any question this Committee might ask me, I would be tending to incriminate myself—or offering testimony against myself for use in some possible future criminal or civil proceedings—I too should feel thoroughly free to take advantage of either the First or Fifth Amendments, as provided by the Constitution of the United States of America.

"I may say now, in finishing this statement, that there is no possible question which can be asked and which I shall answer, that could possibly tend to incriminate me. I come here against my wishes, not believing that this Committee is performing its proper legislative function, but I am now prepared to take the stand and answer each and every question put to me to the very best of my ability, in full honesty and with complete confidence that there is nothing I have to conceal, or ever shall have to conceal. Let the chips fall where they may. I thank you, gentlemen."

Phillip Hunt pursed his narrow bloodless lips and spoke the words in a bitter monotone, his inordinately sharp voice as colorless as the polished rimless glasses which he wore high on his bony nose.

"Let the chips fall where they may!"

He turned from the window, a window which reached from the deeply carpeted floor of the room to the fourteen-foot ceiling and which was covered with heavy, lined velvet drapes. The drapes and the carpet were, like the rest of the room, expensive, in excellent taste, but obviously the taste of a professional decorator. The room itself was typical of the building, which was also expensive.

When Sam Farrow had decided to move the headquarters of his union—and it had been thought of as "his union" for a good many years now—he had felt that the nation's capital would make a suitable and proper location. This building, in a way, was a monument to himself, a three-million-dollar monument, and he was as proud of it as though he had personally built it.

Hunt, Secretary and Treasurer of the national ISU, nervously picked an invisible thread from the sleeve of his dark, conservative tailor-made suit. He returned to the chair facing the couch.

"Let the chips fall where they may," he repeated. "Has he completely lost his mind? Has he ..."

Sam Farrow lifted a gnarled, old man's hand. A huge hand crippled with arthritis but a hand which, in its day, had been as heavy as a small ham and as strong as steel.

"All right, Phillip," he said. "All right. I heard it."

"He must be crazy," Hunt said. "Did you have any idea about this, Sam?"

Sam Farrow lifted his eyes and looked at the younger man.

"The boy probably knows what he's doing, Phillip," he said. "Jack wouldn't do anything that he thinks might hurt …"

"Sam! Sam, you heard him. He's going to talk. After his advice to you and the others. What's he trying to do, anyway? Is he going out of his way to wreck everything?"

"Don't say that, Phillip," Farrow said. "Why I know Jack Rafferty better than I know my own son. He's closer to me than my own boy. For eighteen years—" he hesitated, thinking back. "Maybe he should have taken me into his confidence—but, then, maybe he just didn't want to give me any more troubles. But one thing I'm sure about, just as sure as I'm sitting here in this room—I'm sure Jack is doing what he thinks best. And if he thinks so, why then it is best."

"Best for whom, Sam?" Hunt said. "Best for Jack Rafferty?"

Farrow stirred restlessly and looked up, the old fire once more in his eyes.

"What's best for Rafferty is best for the union; best for me too. I'm not letting you sit there and say anything against the boy."

Hunt shrugged helplessly.

"Sam," he said, "are you forgetting that you refused to talk? Are you forgetting that you took the Fifth? Are you forgetting the trouble you're in—that we're all in?"

"I'm not forgetting anything," Farrow said. But his voice, once so booming and strong and dynamic, was weak and thin. He was an old, old man and a worn-out old man, and he sounded like it.

"Sit back and be quiet," he said. "I want to hear what's going on. And draw that curtain—it's hard for me to see the picture unless the room's dark."

Hunt got up and pulled the heavy drapes over the high wide window.

He's lost it, he thought. Yes, the old man's lost it. God, it was a tragedy, a real tragedy. Sam Farrow, the strong man. The man who for more than fifty years had been the personification of a great union leader. A man who had fought all the way down the line. Fought and won.

It was six months now, six months since the first of the charges had been lodged against him. The things which had happened afterward, bad as they were, could be nothing but an anticlimax. The new troubles with the tax people, the accusation that he had borrowed union funds without security and without paying interest, the phony real estate deals and all of the rest of it, smelled to high heaven, but essentially they weren't what bothered Sam Farrow. Not even the fact that almost overnight he had changed from a millionaire to a relatively poor man had bothered him. No, it was that other thing, the turndown from the administration after the initial investigation into his income taxes.

Up until then old Sam had believed he had the Cabinet position in his lap. Hell, wasn't he a personal friend of the President; a pal of countless Senators and Representatives? Wasn't he that peculiar paradox, an old-time union man and organizer—and a close friend and confidant of management?

A year ago, less than a year ago, there had been no question about it in any man's mind, least of all in Sam Farrow's. He was a shoo-in to be named Secretary of Labor and it was the one thing which would crown his remarkable career. It was really something, a poor, uneducated laborer, a one-time IWW radical, a simple man of the working classes, fighting his way up to the very top.

Yes, there'd been no question. There were those dinners with top party leaders, the big brass of both parties. The predictions of the *Wall Street Journal*, the daily press, and the columnists, who were supposedly in the know. And then, on the very eve of the appointment, when it seemed that nothing could possibly happen, the business about the income tax frauds came out.

The administration might make some pretty sad errors of judgment, but they weren't going to back any man who was facing that kind of trouble. And so the whole thing had fallen apart and here was Sam, a year ago one of the greats and now nothing but a broken, tired old man.

Three blocks away, facing the Joint Legislative Investigating Committee, was Jack Rafferty, the man whom Sam had personally selected to follow him into office when he retired. The man whom Sam had made his crown prince. The man who meant more than a son to him.

Hunt had never particularly liked Rafferty, but in fairness he had to admit it was probably a matter of envy as much as anything else. What had happened to him, Phillip Hunt, couldn't really be blamed entirely on Rafferty. It couldn't be blamed entirely on Farrow, either. But it was Farrow who had broken the news to him; told him how he stood. He remembered the incident only too well. It was only three or four months ago.

There had just been the two of them, he and the old man, and they were having lunch at the Waldorf in New York. A dinner Farrow had purposely arranged. It was then that Sam had told him he was planning to retire.

"I've had it, Phillip," Farrow said. "All these troubles, these Investigations and everything. Not feeling like I used to. Next fall, when we have the convention, I'm not going up again for the presidency."

Hunt looked at him, unbelieving.

"Not going ..."

"That's right, Phillip," Sam said. "I'm retiring. Just getting too old to take another stretch. I've got to quit sometime, I guess. Everybody does. I hate to think about it, but...."

Hunt thought of the fifty thousand a year Farrow would draw as a pension, and couldn't feel too sorry. He knew even then that it wasn't entirely a case of Sam Farrow's making his own decision. The Federation, the big men in organized labor, were disillusioned with Farrow after what had been happening. There had been pressure.

"And that brings up who is going to succeed me," Farrow said. "I guess you know that I'll have something to say about it."

Hunt had looked up at him quickly. He felt a sudden tightness in his throat, as the idea came to him. So that was it? That was the reason for the lunch, the private, intimate conversation. Well, what could be more logical? Why not himself? He was Secretary already, Secretary and Treasurer. In point of years with the union, one of its oldest active officers. What could be more logical than that Sam would reward him for those years of hard and loyal work?

"We need youth," Sam said. "I'm too old." He hesitated, playing with his fork. "I'm too old and Fellows, out in the Middle West, who might logically follow me, is also an old man. Furthermore, he's having plenty of trouble right now with local investigations."

"Of course there's Messini, in Chicago," Hunt said, knowing of course how Farrow felt about him.

"Messini? That wop! Not, by God, while I still have anything to say," Farrow said. "Are you forgetting that he fought me during the last election? No, Messini isn't the man I have in mind. I want someone who's been with me all the way through. Hennessy, of the Northwest Conference, might do, but he's had his second heart attack and he'd never be able to take on the work."

Hunt nodded, sagely. He wished the old bastard wouldn't play with him, wouldn't kid around with this cat-and-mouse game. That he'd come right out and say it. Well, he was grateful enough, he knew what he was being handed.

"No," Sam said, "none of those. The guy I have in mind—well, I think Rafferty is the right man."

It was just as though he'd been smashed with a fist between the eyes.

It took every bit of Hunt's self-control just to hold himself in, to sit there, pale and shaken and wanting to vomit, and not show it. He would have liked to have been able to get up and spit in the old man's evil filthy face. He could, for one moment then, have killed him without compunction or any feeling but happiness.

He wanted to say something, knew that he must say something, but he was unable to get a word past his drawn, white lips. He looked up, helpless.

Farrow wasn't even watching him.

"Yes, Jack Rafferty," Farrow said. "He's the boy, the one I think …"

"Rafferty?"

The single word came out, a harsh whisper.

Sam quickly looked at him then.

"That's right," he said. "Jack Rafferty in Los Angeles. Seems to me …"

He stopped suddenly. He couldn't help reading the expression on Hunt's face.

"Oh," he said. "I see."

He leaned across the table and put a hand on Hunt's arm.

"I guess I know what you're thinking, Phillip," he said. "Yes, I guess I know. You want to know why not you?"

Hunt didn't say anything, he didn't dare speak. If he had, he knew that his voice would break, that the—

"There's nobody I'd rather see follow me," Sam said. "Nobody."

"Then why?"

Farrow shrugged.

"Phillip, you've been around long enough to know why. You have to look at these things realistically. I know you've been with me for a long time, know that you are competent and loyal. Never been any doubt about it. But Phillip, you're a white-collar man; always have been. When you came into the movement, you started out as a bookkeeper. You never drove a truck, never worked as a hunky, never were a linesman or an operator. You were always an office man—a white-collar man, as I said. You've never organized, never been on a picket line in your life. You've never been one of the boys. Oh, I know," he held up his hand as Hunt started to interrupt, "I know you've worked like a horse, always had the welfare of the union in your mind. But you have to face it. From the standpoint of the members, the workingman who makes up the membership of the ISU, you've never been anything but an employee. A good one and a valuable one, everybody will admit. But you're just not a workingman and never have been."

"A union executive in these days," Hunt began, but once more the old man interrupted him.

"Goddamn it, I know all about today's crop of union executives. Most of 'em look more like company presidents than a General Motors' board member does. Hell's bells, ain't I a millionaire myself? Aren't some of my best friends so-called capitalists? But I wasn't always. Look at these hands."

He held up those great, massive, hamlike fists.

"These are the hands of a workingman. And when the membership of this union votes for their next President, they are going to want to vote for a workingman, or anyway, what they think is a workingman."

"But Rafferty ..."

"Rafferty was a day laborer when I first found him. He's been in jail, been beaten up, kicked around. He's what they mean when they say a 'hero of the picket lines.' And the goddamned membership knows it. They got confidence in a guy like Jack Rafferty, same's they have in me."

"I didn't know that it was up to the membership ..." Hunt was unable to keep the bitter sarcasm out of his voice.

Sam Farrow looked at him, slight disappointment in his face.

"Of course it's up to the membership," he said. "For Christ's sake, they vote, don't they? Or at least they elect delegates who do vote."

"Well, you control the dele—"

"Sure, I control a lot of them. I'll continue to, just so long as I back the right man. Rafferty controls delegates, too. So does Messini and so do a lot of the other local presidents and conference chairmen. How many do you control, Phillip?"

"I'm a national officer," Hunt said, weakly. "I couldn't be expected ..."

Once more Farrow reached over and took his arm.

"I know how you feel, Phillip," he said. "I don't blame you. Not one damned bit. But let me ask you one question. You know this organization just as well as I do. Do you honestly think, that if I backed you to the hilt, you'd have a chance in hell of making it?"

Hunt didn't really have to think; he knew the old man was right. He, Phillip Hunt, was not the man for the job. Never would be the man.

"Well," he said weakly. "I guess you're right. But Rafferty? Isn't he a little young? And you know how they've been bearing down on him. The way they've been investigating ..."

"Sure I know," Farrow said. "That's why I want him. He's a fighter. A fighter who wins his fights."

"Yes, he's that all right. But the people he's been mixed up with. Faricetti, for instance. Ex-bootlegger, extortionist, a thug who has been convicted of murder, of ..."

"For Christ's sake, Phillip, I don't care who he's been mixed up with. You think you go out and break strikes, fight company hired goons who carry deputy sheriff badges—and use a bunch of goddamn fairies to do it? You think you can go into a company town, where they've got professional killers scabbing for them, and organize if you don't have tough people yourself. How the hell do you think we got more than a million members into the ISU? You think those bums just wanted to come in? You think because Roosevelt said 'Let there be unions' that was all there was to it?

"It took men like Rafferty, and like the men he brought in with him. If you're going to fight some bastard who wants to break your head with a blackjack, you don't do it with a writ or a pamphlet. You get a blackjack of your own."

"I know, Sam," Hunt said. "I understand. But I just thought, with all the bad publicity ..."

"The publicity that Rafferty is getting shows that he's a fighter. It shows what he's done for the workingman. If we've got to have men like Faricetti and his kind around, it's a damned sight better we have them organizing for us than working for the bosses. I don't expect those holier-than-thou social workers to see it; I don't expect a bunch of damned socialists and reformers to see it. But you should realize that. The membership of this union understands it. It's why they've always backed me and it's why they'll back Rafferty. Nobody can say that Jack Rafferty hasn't always had the welfare of the union membership next to his heart."

CHAPTER FOUR

George Morris Ames, the thirty-six-year-old Chief Counsel for the Investigating Committee, looked down at the notes lying on the desk and then spoke. His voice was soft and he pronounced his words with a faint Boston accent. A cultured voice; a meticulous voice.

"And this company, Mr. Rafferty? This M-D Warehouse Disbursement Company, Incorporated?" He spoke the word incorporated so that each syllable had a distinct accent, giving it an almost snide connotation. "This company in which you say your wife owns 75 per cent of the stock under her maiden name. Does this company employ union labor?"

"I don't know what kind of labor it employs."

"But Mr. Rafferty," Ames said, "this company is owned by your wife …"

"My wife owns 75 per cent of the shares in the M-D Disbursement Company, but …"

"As I said, Mr. Rafferty," Ames interrupted, "as I said, this company, owned by your wife and the wife of Peter Gannon, a Vice-President of Local 702, ISU, both holding the stock in their maiden names, does this company employ union labor?"

Rafferty stared at him, unperturbed.

"I have answered the question, Counselor."

"And then you mean to say you have no knowledge of the …"

"That is what I mean to say."

"In that case, Mr. Rafferty," Ames said, "who does have a knowledge? Does Mrs. Rafferty …"

"Mrs. Rafferty merely owns some stock. She bought and paid for that stock. She has no idea at all about the company or even what it does. I suppose that there is a working manager …"

"There is indeed, Mr. Rafferty. A Mr. Steven Deheny. Do you know Mr. Deheny?"

"I do."

"And who is Mr. Deheny, Mr. Rafferty?"

"Steve Deheny is my wife's brother."

George Morris Ames nodded.

"Yes," he said. "I know. It might interest you, Mr. Rafferty, as a union official, to know that Mr. Deheny does not employ union labor. That the company which Mr. Deheny manages, and which is owned by your wife and the wife of one of your vice-presidents, is the only firm which is permitted to operate in its locality, by the ISU, without employing union labor."

"Is that a question?"

"It is."

"All right, it interests me very much."

"Would you like to see union labor employed by the M-D Disbursement Company?"

"I'd like to see union labor employed by every company."

"And would you term the M-D Disbursement Company a 'scab company' because it does not employ union labor."

"I very definitely would."

"Now Mr. Rafferty, how does it happen that you, being an official of the union, have made no effort to see that the shop which your wife owns, does employ union labor?"

"The M-D Disbursement Company is located in Seattle, Washington. Seattle is not in my jurisdiction. I have, as a local President, no authority over the affairs of the Seattle locals."

"I see. And so," Ames smiled thinly, "and so then we can assume that you are not interested in what takes place …"

"I didn't say that, Mr. Ames," Rafferty interrupted. "I said I had no authority. I have a great deal of interest in any place—city, village, or town—where there are local branches of the ISU, or where there should be branches." He reached for the glass of water and took a sip, shifting in his seat to make himself comfortable. His face remained bland, but there was a slightly satisfied expression around his mouth.

Ames again shuffled his papers and finally found the one he was looking for.

"Can you tell me the amount of money the M-D Disbursement Company earned during the last fiscal year?"

"Are you referring to the gross or the net?" Rafferty asked, looking at Ames as though the other man were a not too bright student in an economics class.

"The net profit," Ames said, patiently.

"I cannot."

"Can you tell me the net profit made by the firm over the last five years?"

"I cannot."

"Can you give me an approximate figure?"

Rafferty looked up at the ceiling, cocking his head.

"Well," he hesitated, "well, I am disinclined to make guesses, but I should say there was a profit."

Ames looked at him quizzically.

"And that is all you would say?"

"That is all."

"Mr. Rafferty," Ames said, "does your wife take you into her confidence?"

Rafferty looked startled, his face slowly flushing, and Mort Kauffman quickly leaned toward him, covering his mouth with his hand as he whispered. Rafferty nodded and Kauffman turned back to Ames and started to speak.

Before he got more than a word out, however, Ames quickly spoke up himself.

"I will withdraw that question," he said. He looked down at the paper he held in his hand. "Mr. Rafferty, according to the figures which our investigators were able to compile after checking the books of the M-D Disbursement Company, the firm netted fifty-six thousand dollars last year, after paying all taxes. During the last five years, the firm has netted just over two hundred thousand dollars, also after paying taxes. Now Mr. Rafferty, do these figures surprise you?"

"Nothing surprises me," Rafferty said.

"When Mrs. Rafferty, using her maiden name, Martha Deheny, purchased the stock she owns in the M-D Disbursement Company, some five years ago (the company being called the West Coast Processing Company at that time) do you remember the size of her investment?"

"I wouldn't know," Rafferty said.

"Do you remember how she paid for that stock?"

"How?"

"Yes. How she paid. Was it by check, or bank draft, or cash or just what?"

"I wouldn't remember."

"I see. Well the records of the stock transfer show that she paid a total of six thousand dollars for her 75 per cent interest in the firm. In short, on a six-thousand-dollar investment, she has made a net profit of a little more than a hundred and fifty thousand dollars within five years. Does this news startle you at all, Mr. Rafferty?"

"It pleases me," Rafferty said and smiled.

"It should. Now I would like to ask you if you are familiar with the

Continental Harvester Company?"

"I am."

"And does the ISU have a contract with the Continental Harvester Company?"

"It does."

"Do you recall when the Continental Harvester Company contract was negotiated?"

Again Rafferty hesitated before answering. "Well," he said, "I can't give you exact dates. I should say, though, that that contract is, like most of our contracts, a two-year agreement. It probably comes up for negotiating periodically and ..."

"Let me rephrase the question, Mr. Rafferty," Ames said. "I am trying to find out if you remember when the contract was first put into effect between the ISU, which represented some seven thousand men employed by Continental, and the Company?"

Rafferty slowly shook his head, pursing his lips.

"As near as I can remember, the contract has been in effect several years. Perhaps five or six."

"And who negotiated that contract?"

"A committee representing ..."

"Were you a member of that committee, Mr. Rafferty?"

"I was."

"Were you the chairman?"

"I believe so."

"And who else was on that committee?"

"Well, right off I can't exactly remember. However I will be glad to check our records and ..."

"Perhaps I can save you the trouble," Ames said. "There were three members. Yourself, a Mr. Peter Gannon, and a Mr. James A. Farmer. Mr. Gannon is the husband of Jeanne Gannon, who, under her maiden name, owns the other 25 per cent of the M-D Disbursement Company. Does this information help you to recall?"

Rafferty nodded.

"It does."

"Now Mr. Rafferty—" Ames dropped the papers he was holding, "now Mr. Rafferty, what is the relationship between the Continental Harvester Corporation and the M-D Disbursement Company?"

Rafferty didn't hesitate. If he was supposed to be startled by the question, he certainly showed no indication of being aware of it.

"The M-D Disbursement Company has a contract to do work for

Continental," he said. "That is, I believe, the function of the firm—the M-D firm, that is. The assuming of subcontracts to move and handle ..."

Ames interrupted.

"Exactly," he said. "And isn't the contract which the M-D Disbursement Company has with Continental its sole and exclusive contract to do work in that field? In other words, does the M-D Disbursement Company have contracts with any other firms aside from Continental?"

"I wouldn't know."

"Would you know how often the ISU contract with Continental has come up for renegotiating?"

"I am not sure. Perhaps two or three times."

Ames looked down again at his notes.

"It has come up three times," he said. "Do you recall having had any difficulty with Continental in renegotiating its contract?"

"I cannot recall anything in particular. After all, I negotiate and renegotiate contracts a hundred times a year with various firms—well, perhaps fifty times a year."

"Again perhaps I may refresh your memory. Each time the Continental contract came up for renegotiating, the original basic contract was renewed, without changes and without additional benefits. Does that often happen, Mr. Rafferty? In other cases where contracts are renegotiated?"

"It can happen. If workers are getting what they should get, if there are no grievances, if conditions and wages and hours ..."

Ames raised his hand to stop the onslaught of words.

"I agree with you," he said, "that it can happen and sometimes does. But also let me assure you that it is a very rare and exceptional case when a contract is renegotiated that the union is not granted certain additional advantages. And now ..."

He hesitated, looking over at Senator Fellows, who was trying to attract his attention.

"Representative Ellison would like to ask the witness a question," Senator Fellows said, "Representative Harvey Ellison."

Representative Ellison pushed his glasses up on his brow and leaned forward, putting his elbows on the table. He spoke in a deep, rather theatrical voice.

"Just let me get this clear, Mr. Rafferty," he said. "Are you telling us that you acted in the capacity of a union representative and negotiator, between a firm owned by yourself and the Continental Harvester Company?"

Senator Fellows looked down at his fellow member and he was unable to keep the annoyance out of his expression.

That's the trouble with these damned joint committees, he reflected. It wasn't bad enough to have to put up with his fellow Senators; he had to cope with the members from the lower house as well. Not of course, that there weren't intelligent men in that body. But this man Ellison—

He shrugged. Well, what could you expect? But it was a damned shame the man didn't take the time to go over the material in advance, or at least listen to the testimony as it was being given. It would certainly make things a lot easier.

He saw that young Ames had quickly leaned down and was whispering into the Representative's ear.

"I certainly did not act as ..."

Representative Ellison interrupted Rafferty, at the same time nodding to Ames.

"Let me rephrase my question," he said. "What I mean is are you telling me that you negotiated a contract between union employees and the Continental Harvester Company and at the same time owned a firm which had an exclusive contract to do work for Continental?"

"I do not own any firm which has a contract with Continental."

Representative Ellison looked baffled for a moment and then pulled his glasses down on his nose and merely seemed annoyed. "All right," he said. "All right. That your wife owns?"

"Is that a question?"

"It is."

"All right then. The answer is yes."

"And do you think, Mr. Rafferty, that you can do a fair and decent job for the members of your union if a company that you own—that your wife owns—is doing business and making profits out of a contract with the firm which you, as a representative ..."

The man from the lower house hesitated, realizing again that he was getting lost in a cloud of verbiage.

Rafferty came to his rescue.

"Certainly," he said. "One has nothing to do with the other."

"But Mr. Rafferty," Ellison said, still not giving up his brief moment in the limelight. "But Mr. Rafferty, are you a union man or a businessman? I thought ..."

"I am both a union man and a businessman," Rafferty said. "A union executive who fails to understand business certainly would be in no position to negotiate with business. However, let me make my answer clear. In regards to the M-D Disbursement Company, I am not a businessman. I do not own or run that business. However, I make every effort to understand and sympathize with business in general. As a realistic union leader, with the welfare of my union members solely as my goal, I know that management and labor must have mutual understanding—a mutual partnership, so to speak, if this country is to be and remain truly great."

"Thank you, Mr. Rafferty," Representative Ellison said.

Senator Fellows banged the gavel on the oak block.

"You may proceed, Counsel," he said.

God damn it, he thought. That fool Ellison! Here he's gone and undone just about all the good we have accomplished. In making his grandstand play, he has merely succeeded in giving Rafferty a chance to give a nice little propaganda speech—a speech justifying his position and taking the curse off everything we have been bringing out. The infuriating part was that Ellison was sitting back complacently, happy in the illusion that he had offered a truly significant contribution to the proceedings.

"At this time," Ames said. "I would like to enter certain documents ..."

He looked over and saw that Senator Fellows was trying to get his eye.

"One minute, please."

Ames leaned down and the Senator whispered something to him and he nodded.

Senator Fellows stood up, banging the gavel.

"It is after twelve o'clock," he said. "This Committee will stand adjourned during the lunch period. The witness will please return at one-forty-five this afternoon when we will resume these hearings."

He turned away from the table, and as he did he observed Hartwell Early, the senior Senator from the Northwestern industrial state, pushing his way toward the committee table. He could see that the old gentleman had a slightly baffled expression on his gaunt, worn face. He was obviously annoyed that he had not been present during the beginning of Rafferty's testimony; he was also obviously not aware that the hearings had been adjourned until that afternoon.

CHAPTER FIVE

With the adjournment, Jake Meadows, realizing in advance that Rafferty would neither talk nor make himself available, set about to corner Mort Kauffman. Minton, the AP man, headed directly for Senator Fellows. Sherman, the *Star's* labor expert, concentrated his attention on George Morris Ames, figuring he would have an inside track. Ames had been a Harvard classmate.

Mary Ellen Henshaw ignored both the members of the Committee and the principals to make a beeline for Jill Hart. Her audience would be looking for the personal sidelights—the human-interest angles—not the political or economic implications.

Carl Hazzlet of the *Times*, however, made no attempt to see anyone who had been in the room. He left the chamber and headed for the University Club, where he was to keep a luncheon appointment he had arranged several days previously. The appointment was with Phillip Hunt.

Hazzlet had already filled himself in on the superficial information concerning Rafferty. He knew about the recent affairs of both the man and the ISU. He had talked briefly with Rafferty himself, getting nowhere much, and had checked and rechecked a good many facts and figures. What he needed now was background, and he wanted to get it from a man who had nothing to gain or to lose because of his relationship with Rafferty. He wanted a man who had known Rafferty for a long time, from the very first days when he had become active in organized labor, but a man who had never been too closely identified with him.

Hunt, as Secretary and Treasurer of the national organization, was such a man.

Hunt, in accepting his invitation, somewhat hesitantly it must be admitted, had made one provision. "You must promise me that you will not mention my meeting you. This is not to be construed as an interview and anything I may or may not say will have to be off the record. I am not anxious to have other executives in my organization know that I am seeing members of the press …"

His voice had trailed off and Hazzlet knew exactly what was in back of his mind. The *Times*, like every other major newspaper in the country, had blasted Sam Farrow for not taking the stand and talking.

They'd called for his retirement from organized labor. More conservative than many other papers, the *Times* hadn't quite come out and called him a thief, but the implication had been there. Farrow, like other union officials under fire, was not friendly with the press. This was one reason Hazzlet had suggested the lunch be held at the University Club. He was pretty sure that no one from the other papers would be there and he was very sure none of Hunt's friends or associates would be around.

Phillip Hunt was already waiting at the table, off in a secluded corner of the dining room, which Hazzlet had reserved in advance, when the *Times* man arrived.

They ordered a drink and Hazzlet was careful to keep the conversation on generalities until after they'd had time to get settled. Later, seeing Hunt hesitating over the menu, Hazzlet suggested the lamb chops, and Hunt was happy to let him order for both of them. Neither man mentioned the hearings, and it wasn't until the coffee came that Hazzlet got down to business.

"You've known Jack Rafferty for a long time," he said, making it more or less of a question.

Hunt looked up quickly, and then smiled dryly.

"Now it's coming, I guess," he said.

Hazzlet also smiled.

"Well, yes. You could put it that way. I'll be frank with you. I want to talk about Rafferty; or rather, I want you to talk about him. I am anxious ..."

"Mr. Hazzlet," Hunt interrupted, not unpleasantly, "let me set you straight on one thing. Jack Rafferty is an official in the ISU and so am I. Brother officials, so to speak. Don't expect me to say anything ..."

Hazzlet put up a hand in mock indignation, smiling.

"Please," he said. "Let *me* get something straight. I'm not going to ask for any secrets; I'm not looking for any scandals; I am not curious about the inside workings of ISU politics. Nor am I interested in anything derogatory concerning Rafferty. I merely am interested in the man's history—where he came from, what sort of family he has, how he first got interested in the labor movement. What sort of person he was twenty years ago. I want to know what makes him tick, but in order to know that, I think an understanding of his early years, of his ..."

Hunt interrupted, cocking one eyebrow, thereby giving his rather studious, austere face a faintly disreputable look.

"What makes him tick? Mr. Hazzlet, you don't know quite what you are asking. That's something a good many people would like to know, including myself. Sometimes I wonder if Jack Rafferty himself knows."

Hazzlet nodded.

"I realize that, of course," he said. "But I still think that given certain knowledge, certain facts, one might draw conclusions. Which, of course, is the reason I am interested in collecting as many facts as I can. Suppose we were to start at the beginning. When and where did you first run into Rafferty? Was it after he got into the union? After …"

The reporter hesitated, seeing the look come over Hunt's face. The silence lasted a long time, and while it lasted, Hazzlet, careful not to disturb his companion's mood, beckoned to the waiter and not speaking, pointed to his empty coffee cup and then held up two fingers.

Finally, when Hunt began to speak, his voice was soft and almost nostalgic.

"As I remember, the first time I came across Jack Rafferty was back in the days of the Roosevelt administration. Probably sometime in the late thirties. Sam Farrow and I had stopped off in Los Angeles where a new local had recently been chartered. Nothing particular, just a sort of routine check as I recall. I have forgotten who was running things out there at the time, but I do remember meeting Rafferty. You know," he hesitated, looking down at his fingernails as though he had suddenly thought of something, "you know, it's a funny thing, but it seems to me now that Rafferty looked exactly the same twenty years ago as he does today.

"Younger, of course—he would have had to be. But the same expression on his face, the same tough, Irish good looks. Not handsome, understand, certainly not what you would have called a pretty boy. But a good deal of charm. A very intelligent, alert face."

Hazzlet nodded, but remained silent.

"Anyway, there really wasn't much about that first meeting to make a lasting impression. He was a member of the new local and had done some excellent work in bringing in members. Also, as I recall, he already had a reputation as a tough fighter on the picket lines. At that time he was a minor officer of the local and was about to quit his regular job to become a full-time paid organizer. I can remember Sam Farrow remarking something about his being the sort of fellow we needed.

"About his earlier years, his family and so forth, I know very little. I believe his father and mother died while he was still a child and he was brought up by a Catholic orphanage somewhere in the Far West. In any case, I know that he still pays lip service to the Catholic Church. He's not what might be considered a really solid communicant, but at least he professes to be a Catholic and I know that he is raising his children in the Catholic faith. He married a Catholic girl, you know."

"I didn't ..."

"Yes—old James Deheny's daughter. The old man was a disbeliever and a heretic; one of the old-time anarchists. I'll tell you about him sometime. He was a fascinating character. Anyway, he raised his daughter, Martha, as a Catholic, in spite of his own heresy. But to get back. One thing you must understand. A lot of people believe that because the Roosevelt administration was pro-labor, the unions had a field day back then. It wasn't quite so. Actually, big business was fighting harder than ever before to keep from being organized. Those were the really tough years. Not only sit-down strikes, but bloody, deadly battles between union men and company thugs. The depression was at its height and there were plenty of men around, jobless and willing to take any kind of work at any kind of pay. The administration might have favored unions and organized labor, but the hard realistic facts were that it was just about the toughest possible time to bring men—the rank and file—into organized labor. Too many people out of jobs and too few jobs to go around.

"Anyway, that's the way it was. And as you know, a lot of pretty strange fish began to be interested in unions. There were the old-time socialists, the Wobblies—IWW graduates, professional revolutionaries and radicals in the tradition of Big Bill Hayward, Tom Mooney, and men of that type. These were the dedicated men, the fanatics if you wish, who'd been fighting all of their lives in the labor movement. Well, Jack Rafferty wasn't of that breed. I doubt if he even knew who Eugene Debs was. He probably didn't know the difference between Karl Marx and Harpo Marx.

"No, Jack Rafferty was no radical, no starry-eyed dreamer or egghead. He went through that early period, when Commies and all sorts of freaks were getting into unions and trying to take over control, and he never got mixed up with any of them. As a matter of fact, later on when he did learn what a Communist was, he fought them all the way down the line."

The waiter brought the fresh coffee and Hazzlet asked Hunt if he'd care for some brandy on the side.

Hunt shook his head, a little sadly.

"I'd like some," he said, "but it wouldn't like me. Gives me heartburn."

He stirred his coffee and Hazzlet waited, not wanting to prompt him.

"In recent years," he continued at last, "Rafferty has been accused of playing footsie with a number of racket boys, ex-bootleggers and professional extortionists and the like, who crept into the unions. Whether he has or not, I will have to leave to your own judgment. But I can say this. When I first became aware of him, first met him and knew him, Rafferty was certainly no racketeer. I think Sam Farrow was the one to spot him for what he really was—a dedicated, union career man.

"In those early days he gave every promise of becoming what he has turned into—a big man in the labor movement. Let me explain. Had Jack Rafferty had a formal education and a normal, middle-class background, he might very probably have gone in for some sort of government work. And he would have been a success. Had he had a good technical education, say in engineering or something of the sort, he'd have started out with one of the big firms and become a career man in that field. And again, I say, he would have become a success.

"But he was an orphan, lacking in technical skills as well as in formal education and he was thrown on his own very early in life. He became first a laborer and then a skilled laborer—not a craftsman, understand; and he became a union organizer. Not because he was a 'bleeding heart' for the downtrodden working man or because of lofty principles—but for a very practical reason; to improve his own economic position. In doing this, he found his métier. He became a professional union man, a career man in organized labor.

"As I remember, it was old Deheny who first brought him into the movement. I've forgotten the details—I think he roomed in Deheny's house or something. In any case, it wasn't long before he began to make something of a reputation for himself. Seems to me, as I recall it, there was something about a strike he organized—that was before the local was affiliated with the national union—a strike of some eight or ten slaughterhouse workers. Rafferty waited for the strategic moment, when a new shipment was coming in and the company just had to get the stock moving. He was making around three dollars a day at the time. Anyway, the story was that he organized this strike singlehandedly, formed his own little group, and they went out. They won, too, and it broke the open shop setup in the slaughterhouses out there. Shortly after that the group became an ISU local and Rafferty was made an officer—Recording Secretary or something."

Once more Hunt hesitated. He lifted the coffee cup and saw that he had already emptied it.

"You know," he said, "I think I'll take a chance on that brandy, after all. Except, without the coffee."

Hazzlet called the waiter. He ordered brandy for his guest and took a B and B for himself.

"It was after Rafferty became a full-time organizer that he really started being noticed. In the first place, he had quit his job, at a definite sacrifice in salary, to take on union work. And he was fearless. Management, in those days, didn't handle their labor problems with kid gloves. They went out and hired thugs, professional muscle men and goons, to do their dirty work. If they couldn't buy off the organizers, or frame them, then they'd have them beaten up and crippled. Well, Rafferty wasn't the kind of boy they could buy off. I still don't think he is, in spite of all of these recent scandals. But in any case, he certainly wasn't during the early days. He fought them right down the line. I can still remember vouchers coming into national headquarters for bail money and fines for him. He was tough, all right. The men liked him and respected him. And they still do. No matter what comes out at these hearings, one thing you want to remember—the rank-and-file think Rafferty is a great guy.

"Pretty soon we began to hear more and more about him. By this time Sam Farrow had become pretty important in the national union and Sam always took a big interest in the locals. Sam had a twofold interest. He wanted a strong national union and he also wanted men in key spots, on whom he could depend. You are familiar with union politics—locals electing the delegates who, at the national conventions, elect the officers and so forth. Anyway, before long, Rafferty was a big man out on the Coast. It wasn't long after that that he began to spread out.

"We have, as you know, conferences made up of all the locals in certain geographic areas. Los Angeles is in the Western Conference and Rafferty began to make his influence felt in conference circles. It was only to be expected. He was an organizer and a fighter and he was also a very smart Irish politician. He knew how to do favors and who to do favors for. Also, by this time, he had become a friend, or perhaps I should say, a sort of protégé, of Sam Farrow's.

"Rafferty thought like Sam thinks. Unions were a business as far as he was concerned. And he wanted to make them a paying business. The only way he could see to do it was to deliver benefits to the membership—get them better wages, shorter hours, health and insurance benefits, security. He wasn't interested in socialism, didn't have any wild theories about the 'laboring man owning the means of production' and so on. He just wanted to see that the workingman got a fair share of the profits—and he had the sense to realize there had to be a profit before the workingman could. So he tried as best he could to get along with management.

"It was a tough fight—all the way down the line. When Rafferty wasn't fighting with management, he was fighting factions within his own organization. Fighting the radicals and the dreamers and the Commies. Fighting infringement from other unions. Fighting just about everyone. And, all the time, he kept his eye on one single goal. He wanted to become a big, if not the biggest, man in organized labor. He was, in a sense, a dedicated man. Dedicated to making organized labor his career. Of course, to do this, he's probably had to do a lot of other things which may look a little odd; had to form friendships and associations which may be questioned and which, in fact, are being questioned."

Hazzlet shifted in his chair, surreptitiously looked at his wristwatch. He wanted Hunt to keep on talking, but at the same time, he also wanted to be sure to return in time for the hearings.

"Yes," Hazzlet said, "a lot of things he has done are being questioned. One thing interests me, Mr. Hunt. You say that Rafferty had to do a lot of things. That as a labor leader, fighting for the cause of labor, he made certain friends, did certain things—well I guess you know what I mean. Now take yourself. You've been in the labor movement all of your life, and meaning no disrespect, it's been a lot longer life than Rafferty's. You are Treasurer and Secretary of the national organization. And yet from your record, it is quite apparent that you yourself have not had to do these things—make these certain friendships."

Hunt looked at the newspaperman and nodded, an amused expression on his face.

"You know," he said, "it's a little odd. But just this morning I was thinking about a conversation I had with Sam Farrow. He said almost the same thing—but in a slightly different way and in relation to a completely different matter.

"There's a big difference between a man like Rafferty and myself. Rafferty is really going places—or at least he seems to be, if he can live down this latest investigation. It is true that I'm an official in the union. But the real fact is, I don't amount to a great deal so far as having any power is concerned. My position in the union is about the same as would be that of our accountant, or our attorney. I do more or less technical, clerical work. No one particularly wants my job—it only pays fifteen thousand a year and the hours are hard and long—and the job itself has little glory and little power. I have nothing to do with forming policy, nothing to do with the real inner organization. You could almost classify me as a sort of high-class clerk. In any case, that's the way Sam Farrow probably thinks of me."

Hunt was unable to keep a trace of bitterness out of his voice as he spoke and Hazzlet looked up at him sharply.

"A lot of people have accused Farrow of being money hungry. He's reputed to be a millionaire—a couple of times over," Hazzlet said. "Do you feel ..."

"I'm not going to discuss Sam Farrow," Hunt said. He smiled a little, to soften the words, but it was obvious that he wasn't going to be led into any criticism of his boss.

"What I was going to ask," Hazzlet said, "was whether you feel that this is another characteristic which Rafferty and Farrow have in common? In short, just how ..."

"I can tell you this," Hunt said. "Rafferty started out as a poor boy. He came from nothing and he had nothing. During his early years with the union, I doubt if he ever made more than seventy-five dollars a week. During all the investigations, the grand jury hearing and so forth, no one has ever accused him of shaking anyone down or stealing. As he said this morning he lives in the same modest house he's lived in most of his married life. That he ..."

"His youngsters go to private schools," Hazzlet said. "I know that ..."

"That can be explained," Hunt interrupted. "Rafferty, at least in recent years, has been very much in the public eye. He's been the target of a hundred attacks. Both by the press and in a much more direct sense. His home has been bombed twice and someone planted explosives beneath the hood of his car. I feel sure that the only reason his children are in private schools is because he wants to protect them from the sort of snide and vicious remarks that they would be subjected to from other children, who get their ideas from their parents. After all, in Los Angeles, Rafferty's name is almost a byword."

"Then you feel that private schools offer an immunity to ..."

"The youngsters—there's a girl of around fifteen or sixteen and twin boys a year or so older—go to eastern schools. It isn't likely they would come up against any particular problems. If I were in Rafferty's position and had children, I'd do the same thing."

Hazzlet nodded.

"I see what you mean," he said. "But why, with the money he is supposed to have made, the high salary and expenses he draws, does he continue to live ..."

"You're missing the point," Hunt said. "Rafferty, in living in the same low-priced house, in the same section of the city, is identifying himself with the rank and file who keep him in office. One of his great strengths, at least within the union, is the fact that the membership considers him 'one of the boys.' And it isn't merely a pose. To this day he still goes out on a picket line when the occasion arises. If Jack Rafferty has put away any money—and that's something that only Rafferty himself can tell you—he doesn't throw it around living ostentatiously."

The newspaperman nodded and reached for a cigarette.

"There have been stories about certain young women," he said. "Showgirls and so forth. Just what sort of woman is Mrs. Rafferty?"

Hunt shook his head, looking at Hazzlet with a trace of disappointment.

"We agreed that we wouldn't dig for dirt," he said. "I've probably told you a lot of things already that are none of my business and certainly none of anyone else's. Don't expect me to speculate about Rafferty's private life. Mrs. Rafferty, well, as I remember her, she is a rather plain simple woman. A housewife and a mother. Seems to me that she's a year or so older than Rafferty. As near as I know they are happily married and always have been. She isn't the sort to interest herself in her husband's affairs. I've probably only seen her two or three times, if that. I can tell you one thing, though. Despite the rumors about Jack Rafferty's private life, he has never been proved anything but a good husband and father and a reliable family man."

This time it was Hunt who looked at his wristwatch.

"It's getting along," he said. "Anyway, I've talked too much. You'll probably want to be getting back to the hearings, and I should be pushing off myself." He pushed his chair out.

"It's been a pleasure," Hazzlet said. "And I don't have to tell you everything you have said will be kept in the strictest confidence. Thank you for giving me your time."

"No trouble at all," Hunt said. "I enjoyed the lunch."

Hazzlet leaned over the table and signed the check, adding on a proper amount for the tip. He followed Hunt out of the dining room.

They stopped just outside the building and shook hands.

"Mr. Hunt," Hazzlet said, "I would like to ask you one final question. Your answer will never go any further and I will forget it immediately after you tell me. I'd like to know what you—you yourself as an individual and not as a union executive or fellow worker—think of Jack Rafferty."

Phillip Hunt looked at Hazzlet for several seconds, his face still and expressionless.

"What I think?" he said, at last, speaking the words softly.

"Exactly. What you think?"

Hunt nodded his head, still without expression. "I think he's a first-class, dyed-in-the-wool son-of-a-bitch," he said. "I will add that I also think the only man in the world who will ever prove it is Jack Rafferty himself."

He turned then, still unsmiling, and walked rapidly off without looking back.

CHAPTER SIX

Martha Rafferty sat in front of the television set mesmerized by the sight of her husband's face and the sound of his voice as he phlegmatically answered one question after another. She was not aware of Ann's sudden movement as she got up and left the room, slamming the door so that the whole house shook. She was unaware of anything but the tableau taking place on the screen in front of her, an electronic marvel which, had she thought at all about it, would not have baffled her quite as much as the marvel of hearing her husband promptly and fully replying to those dozens and dozens of questions put to him by a man who could have been nothing but a complete stranger.

He's answered more questions this morning, she thought, than he has answered, to me at least, during the last fifteen years. She wondered if perhaps her technique had been at fault.

He was by nature a secretive man, a man who resented anyone asking him anything. He had always had one stock answer for her, don't worry yourself about it; if I told you it would only confuse you. God knows she hadn't wanted to be confused; this marriage of hers had confused her enough without her attempting to compound the chaos.

Her attention returned to the television screen and she saw that the hearing was apparently over, at least for the time being. A news commentator had come on and was doing a recapitulation of the morning's testimony.

She reached over and turned the set off, but she didn't get up. Instead, she sat back on the broken springs of the old, upholstered chair, thinking.

Martha Rafferty was not a stupid woman, but the fact is, the actual questions and answers hadn't made a great deal of sense to her. It is true that she was considerably surprised to learn that she was, apparently, the owner of a block of stock in a company which she had never known existed. She was equally surprised to learn that her brother Steve (whom she had always considered a ne'er-do-well with an unfortunate taste for hard liquor and the horses, neither of which he could possibly afford) was the manager of that company.

Actually, she didn't pay a great deal of attention to either fact. She was surprised, but that was all. After thinking about it for a moment or so, she realized it must be another one of Jack's deals. Jack was always making deals, always having her sign this or that paper.

"Nothing important," he would explain, "just need your signature. You don't have to bother reading it."

She knew that because of his position in the union, it was best if certain things were done in her name. It didn't make any difference to her, one way or the other, Jack always knew what was best.

The fact that the company had made something like a quarter of a million dollars, however, did interest her. She wondered what had happened to it.

Looking around the room, at the threadbare carpet, the old-fashioned furniture, the worn, almost shoddy, lower middle-class respectability and poverty of the place, she thought that a certain amount of it certainly could have been put to good use right here in the house.

It was no wonder young Eddy wouldn't bring his fiancée home to visit. Eddy was in his second year in Dartmouth and he was engaged to a very pretty girl from Boston. Carol Wilson was the daughter of a lawyer and was a freshman in Radcliffe. Martha had never met her and although the girl and Eddy had been going together for more than a year now, Eddy had always evaded her suggestion that he bring her out to the Coast for a visit. He'd never said as much, but Martha knew he was ashamed of the small house, ashamed of the neighborhood in which they lived.

It wasn't that Eddy hadn't been able to keep up, didn't have enough money. Why just this year Jack had let him have a new Ford, had in fact given it to him for Christmas. Jack always saw to it that the children had good clothes and plenty of spending money. It was only about the house that he was peculiar.

Not of course that Martha herself minded. The house was plenty good enough for her, and as far as Jack himself was concerned—well, if he was home on an average of one day a week, it was something.

No, she herself was satisfied. She had been living in the same house and in the same neighborhood most of her married life and she neither knew nor wanted anything different. Most of the year the children were away at their schools, going around with nice friends and visiting at those friends' homes. She hadn't really thought of it before, but now she remembered that none of the children ever brought their friends home.

She decided that the next time Jack returned she'd mention it to him. That was one thing she must say for him; he was always very generous about money. Especially during these last few years, when money had been a lot easier and when they really hadn't had any problems about that, at least. It hadn't always been like this, however.

Lord, how the time did fly. Why it seemed like only yesterday when she and Jack were getting married and settling down to a home of their own. She smiled a little and remembered back to the very first time she had met Jack Rafferty.

A lot of people had considered old James Deheny pretty much of an eccentric, if not a downright nut, but no one ever could accuse him of not being a good father. And it hadn't been easy. His wife had died in her early thirties, leaving him two youngsters to raise. Somehow or other he managed, in spite of grinding poverty and the trouble he always seemed to find. He was an iron-molder, a good workman, but a man who found it exceptionally difficult to hold jobs. An uneducated man who had never finished grammar school, he had a passion for reading and studying. Early in life he had parted from his church and become what in those days was considered a radical and freethinker. The fact was that all of his life he had been a rebel, a nonconformist. He was a moderate man, however, so far as his personal habits were concerned. He drank only mildly and he had a generous kindly nature. But he hated the Church (the opiate of the people), hated the bosses (Wall Street bloodsuckers), distrusted politicians of all parties (the last resort of scoundrels), and loved his fellow man. He also loved his children and made as good a home for them as possible.

In spite of his own distrust of religion, paradoxically, he sent his daughter, Martha, to a convent and his son, Steven, to a parochial school. He probably did so out of respect for the memory of his dead wife, whom he had also loved in his wild and violent way, and who had remained a good churchgoing Catholic all of her life.

Martha finished what was the equivalent of four years of high school and then came home to keep house for her father. Her brother, three years her senior, had joined the Navy, thus escaping a sentence in reform school, in which direction he was definitely headed had the parole officer not been a man of kind and understanding disposition. The house itself was a tiny bungalow, not three blocks from where Martha and Jack Rafferty bought their first and only home.

Deheny was a man who loved to talk. On a Saturday afternoon, he would wander down to Pershing Square in the center of the City and gather a crowd around him and harangue them. He'd join picket lines, just for the sake of lending moral aid to anyone who was striking against anything. He frequently got into trouble, but being essentially a man who didn't believe in fighting or bloodshed, he avoided getting arrested on any major charge. One result, however, of his activities, was that he was forever bringing home strange and outlandish characters. He'd find them on park benches, in workingmen's barrooms, on picket lines, almost anywhere. Drunks, hobos, the down-and-outers, and the misbegotten. He found them all, and more often than not he'd bring them along home for a square meal and a bed and, if they were the kind who were interested, long hours of discussion and talk. It is true, however, that he himself did most of the talking.

Martha quickly became used to the routine, and although she was unable to generate any particular enthusiasm for the stray cats her father dragged in, at least she was courteous and tolerant about it. She only insisted that they not make a mess and that they clean up the bathroom after themselves. Now and then one would offer to help her with the dishes, or do some little thing around the place to give her a hand. Mostly she rejected these offers and was glad to be left alone to do the chores herself.

Few of these men paid much attention to her. She was a rather plain girl, neither good-looking nor ugly, and she dressed simply and without charm or taste. However, at eighteen, no girl, unless she is a complete gargoyle, can be without a certain appeal and Martha, with her slender, well-proportioned body and her clear, unblemished skin and really fine eyes, was as attractive as most. The fact that James Deheny's friends, his strays and outcasts, saw fit to ignore her wasn't as much her fault as it was the fault of the people who came to the house.

They had, almost without exception, long ago lost interest in women and sex, and, in fact, in just about everything but a hot meal and a place to sleep. Even had any of them any desire, and been willing to violate Deheny's kindness and hospitality (which would not have been likely as everyone recognized the essential "goodness" in the old fellow), it is doubtful if they would have made any overt passes. Martha's own indifference would have been enough to have discouraged it. And certainly it cannot be said that she possessed that fatal type of beauty which is believed to drive men to do insane and unpredictable things.

And so, for the most part, her father and the strangers would sit around, sipping coffee and discussing Robert Ingersoll, or the civil war in Spain, or possibly Hindu philosophy or foreign exchange, and Martha would sit by reading (she was crazy about romantic novels in those years) or just sewing on a new dress and not even listening to what was being said. She loved and adored her father, thought he was a very brilliant man but felt he talked an awful lot of nonsense.

It was on the night of her twentieth birthday that James Deheny brought Jack Rafferty out to the little cottage in the Huntington Park district where they lived. She would never, never as long as she lived, forget that night. And not because it was the first time she was to meet the man who was so soon to become her husband.

She knew the very minute she looked out the window and saw the taxi pull up and stop in front of the house that something must be wrong. Actually, she had been looking out the window for more than two hours, off and on. Her father had promised to be home early (it was during one of his jobless periods, but he went downtown every morning religiously, immediately after breakfast, ostensibly to look for work but more often than not to meet with his cronies at the square);

she knew he was planning to dip into his slender bank account to get her a birthday gift and she'd prepared a special dinner, or supper as they called it, for the occasion.

That was the kind of neighborhood in which they lived; a taxicab was almost a sure sign of something amiss; either the man of the house was drunk or important guests were arriving. It was the same with a Western Union boy; he could only mean one thing, a sudden death in the family.

The driver got down from his seat and opened the rear door and a moment later a stranger, a slender, hatless boy, climbed out. The two of them, the boy and the driver, helped her father to the street. She could see the blood on his face, the red splotches splattered down his white shirt and darkening the fabric of his trousers, and she knew that he had been injured.

She was at the door, pale and frightened, when they brought him in. The boy took some money from his pocket and wordlessly paid the driver, who turned quickly and left. Her father looked at her with unseeing eyes and she didn't waste time asking questions. She got her shoulder under one arm and the two of them took him into the living room and put him on the couch.

"Get a doctor," the boy said. "Hurry up—you must know a doctor around here."

She nodded, dumbly, and hurried out of the house. There was a doctor a block away and she was lucky and found him in.

That was the first time that Jack Rafferty had ever given her an order. She had accepted it and done his bidding, blindly and without question, knowing that what he asked was right.

Later, after the neighborhood doctor had cleansed the deep gash in her father's head, pulled the lips of the wound together and sewed them tight and given the old man a sedative, he turned to the boy, who was also bleeding. Someone had smashed a blackjack across his nose and it was broken. There wasn't much that the doctor could do about it, but he did what he could.

Later she was in the kitchen, making coffee, and he was standing in the doorway, watching her.

"What happened?" she asked, listlessly. "Where did you ..."

"You're his daughter?"

"Yes, I'm his daughter."

"He said he had a daughter," he said. "My name's Rafferty—John Carroll Rafferty," he added.

"What happened?" she turned, looking at him now and repeating the question, anger in her voice. "What happened to him?"

"There was a demonstration," he said. "Down in the square. The unemployed were holding a rally and the police came and broke it up. I was there and so was your father. But he really didn't have anything to do with it. I was talking, making a sort of speech, and the police came. They were mounted and swinging clubs. Two of them had me cornered and were starting on me, when your father interfered. So they let us both have it."

She continued to stare at him, not seeing him at all as a person; not seeing him except as someone who had gotten her father into trouble.

"Demonstrations," she said, her voice bitter with scorn. "I should think ..."

"He's going to be all right," Rafferty said. "The doctor said he'll be all right. I guess I'd better go now, and ..."

"You might as well stay and have coffee—have something to eat as long as you're here. The dinner is spoiled now anyway." She shrugged, but the anger had died out.

"No," he said. "Thank you very much, ma'am, but I guess ..."

"You don't have to call me 'ma'am,'" she said. "My name's Martha. And take off that bloody jacket and wash up a little. The doctor said you were to take it easy if you don't want to start that bleeding again. So just wash up and I'll put the food on."

"I could eat," he said, and he smiled and for the first time she really noticed him. Noticed that he was very young, probably not as old as she was. That he had nice eyes and very square, white teeth. His hair, which badly needed cutting, was jet black, growing low on his forehead, but his eyes were a soft brown and his skin was not dark, as might be expected because of the hair, but extremely fine and very white, touched only with color over the cheekbones.

He stayed for dinner and later, after James Deheny sat up to take a bowl of soup, the old man persuaded him to spend the night. It turned out that Rafferty had no place to sleep in any case, having been evicted only that morning from his furnished room. And so he not only stayed that night, but he continued to stay, using the room young Steve had vacated when he joined the Navy.

Two days later Deheny got a job as a night watchman and within a week, Rafferty was back at the house again badly beaten and with his eyes blackened and missing a tooth. He'd been in another demonstration.

Martha was alone when he came home and this time the neighborhood doctor wasn't in and he wouldn't let her call anyone else. And so she put him to bed herself, helped him to take off his clothes and washed and bandaged him and sat at the side of his bed, holding warm compresses on his swollen forehead. She cried a little and later, after he'd fallen into a deep, exhausted sleep, she sat by the side of the bed and watched him. She felt an almost unbearable sense of tenderness and love. But was it really love?

Years later, in remembering it, she would wonder. One time, during her fourteenth or fifteenth year, she'd found an alley cat in the street which had been struck and run over by a car. She'd taken it home and nursed it, sitting up nights with it and feeding it warmed milk and taking care of its wounds. It was an ugly cat, a thoroughly disreputable and ungrateful animal, yellow streaked, red of eye and with a mean, spitting disposition.

She'd felt that same tenderness and love for the cat, however, that same protective possessiveness. Was that love too? What, really, was love?

She remembered sitting there at the side of the bed, watching his still face as he lay with his eyes closed, breathing deeply and regularly. She had moved her hand unconsciously, laid it, palm outward, against the bruised cheek and she'd again felt the waves of tenderness and compassion. He wasn't ugly and hateful, as the cat had been, but there was that same feeling.

The wounds had healed quickly and she soon forgot her own emotional stirrings on that long, lonely night when she'd nursed him and watched over him. He was up within a few days, and a week or so later had taken the job in the slaughterhouse. But he continued living with the Dehenys, now as a paying boarder, and he had his breakfast and dinner with her and the old man and she'd pack a box lunch for him to take when he went to work.

Within four months they were married.

It, the marriage of Martha Deheny and John Carroll Rafferty, was probably the one major event in Rafferty's life, aside from the deaths of his parents and his years in the orphanage, which happened completely independently of his own planning and his own contriving. Martha herself had very little to do with it, as it turned out.

Old James Deheny, working on his new job as night watchman, left the house at six-thirty and worked a straight twelve-hour shift, returning well after daybreak the following morning. As a result,

Martha and Rafferty were alone in the place during the long evenings.

Rafferty himself put in a long day, but he started early in the morning and was back by five in the afternoon. The three of them, the girl and her father and the young boarder, would have dinner together and then Deheny would get up and put on his windbreaker and cap and kiss his daughter goodbye. Martha would clear the table and do the dishes.

Before long Rafferty began helping her, wiping the plates and silverware as she washed and cleaned up. Later, he'd either go out for a while, or would go into the parlor and read. Sometimes they'd sit opposite each other at the dinner table and play casino or two-handed rummy.

Rafferty had been in the house about a month when the incident took place.

Deheny had already left for work and he was helping Martha with the dishes. Both of them were feeling good and there had been a lot of kidding during the dinner. The thing began innocently enough. Rafferty was reaching for the dish towel to start on the silverware, and Martha quickly grabbed it from the rack before he could take it.

"You go on in and sit down," she said. "I'll do them alone tonight."

He'd laughed and put out his hand to take the towel from her and she'd quickly put her own hand behind her.

"Come on," he said, "let me have it."

"Just try and get it," she said.

He laughed again and made a grab for her and she skipped away, circling the table.

He started to chase her and a moment later they were wrestling together.

Martha was a tall girl, as tall as Rafferty himself, but she was fine-boned and slender and no match for him. She managed, however, to break loose, and, hair tossing and breathless, she ran laughing into the parlor.

He followed her and backed her against the couch, still trying to take the dish towel from her. His arms were around her waist now and he was pushing his body against her and she fell back on the couch. He fell on top of her, still struggling with her. A second later and she lay still, half under him, staring up into his face.

He too suddenly became still, his body pressing down on hers. He felt the soft warmth of her through her thin dress and lifting his head, he looked down into her face. His hands were pressed down on the couch, one on each side of her shoulders.

Her lips were parted slightly and her face was hot and flushed. Before he knew what he was doing, he lowered his face and his mouth crushed against her opened lips. For a second or two she just lay there and then her arms went around him and she pulled him tight against her.

They didn't do anything that night, just kissed each other and held each other. But it was the beginning. After that he couldn't wait to get home in the evenings, couldn't wait for the old man to leave.

For a while it would start the way it had in the beginning, the roughhousing and the games and the wrestling. But soon they gave up all pretensions and the moment old Deheny left the house, they would fall into each other's arms. Neither had had any experience and neither was quite sure what was happening to them. But it wasn't long before they were going well beyond the kissing stage. He started by feeling her breasts, and then he'd become bolder and as he would lie on her, both fully clothed, he'd put his hands under her blouse and against the softness of her bare flesh. She liked what he was doing (although she was sure that it was wrong and that both of them were sinning) but she never got really excited the way he did. She didn't care for it so much when he would force her mouth open as he kissed her and several times she made him stop when his hands would press too hard on the round softness of her breasts and he would hurt her.

They barely spoke to each other, hardly talked at all, during these long evenings as they lay together, fondling and kissing each other. Once he tried to put his hand up under her skirt and she let him get as far as caressing the inside of her thigh, but she quickly stopped him when his nervous, taut fingers moved and found the soft, protective down which guarded her vagina.

He would lie on her, pinning her down and his own hard body would jerk and move and she knew that something was happening. After a while, after he'd become wild and crazy with excitement and his body heaved and writhed in contortions, something would happen and then he would lie still and exhausted.

This went on for three or four weeks and it was on a Thursday night while they were lying together on the couch in the darkened room, around ten o'clock at night, that old Deheny returned unexpectedly. (He'd left his post to attend a meeting of the Agnostic Society and had been found out and immediately fired.)

Climbing up the steps to the porch, Deheny had noticed the house was dark and he assumed that the children—as he thought of Martha and young Rafferty—had either gone to bed or possibly left to take in a movie.

He wasn't trying to be particularly quiet, but he was always a gentle man and walked softly. He let himself in through the front door and walking on the thin carpet, entered the parlor and snapped on the light.

For a moment, as the two of them looked up at him with frightened faces, frozen there in each other's arms, he just stared. Then, carefully, he put his lunch pail on the library table at the side of the door.

"You had better go to your room, Martha," he said, his voice flat.

She got up from the couch, her face as red as fire, and quickly went upstairs.

Rafferty sat on the edge of the couch, surreptitiously pulling his clothes together.

Old Deheny walked into the room and took off his cap, dropping it on a chair. He looked at the youth but didn't say anything for a moment. When he did speak, there was no anger in his voice.

"Well, son," he said at last.

Rafferty looked up at the older man, his own face brick red with embarrassment.

"I'm sorry, Mr. Deheny," he said. He had always called the old man mister and he continued to do so after he and Martha were married and until Deheny finally died in the late forties.

"I guess I had better go," he said.

Deheny sat down.

"Do you want to go?" he asked.

Rafferty looked up at him quickly, surprised.

"Why—why, no," he said. "That is ..."

"You haven't been trying to make a fool of my girl, have you?" Deheny asked, the soft voice suddenly hard and cold.

"No sir," Rafferty spoke up quickly. "Why, no sir. We—I guess we love ..." he probably didn't really know what he was saying—he just knew he had to say something.

"All right then, son," Deheny said. "I know that Martha is no slut. She's a good girl and always has been a good girl. Like her mother, and God bless me, a finer woman never lived. When are you planning the wedding?"

The words came out softly, but Deheny's normally warm, calm eyes were sharp and wary.

And that was the way it was. The wedding took place a couple of months later and despite the three children and her more than two decades of married life, Martha Rafferty never experienced quite the same sense of sexual thrill from her husband as she had in those first few weeks before she actually lost her virginity.

The sharp, insistent sound of the telephone ringing interrupted her reverie to bring her mind suddenly back to the present.

She stirred, her eyes going to the clock on the mantelpiece and she saw with a shock that it was already almost eleven o'clock. Good Lord, she'd sat there and wasted the whole morning! And with a million and one things to do.

The phone rang again and she jumped to her feet, but before she'd taken two steps she heard Ann answering it out in the hallway. She moved into the kitchen then, to prepare an early lunch for herself and her daughter—the boys being away and just the two of them there to eat together. She heard Ann's voice as the girl spoke over the phone and was vaguely conscious of her hanging up the receiver a moment or so later. She called in to the hallway.

"Ann—who was it, Ann?"

The girl didn't answer and she shook her head in irritation as she heard the retreating footsteps.

She left the sliced bread which she'd been buttering for sandwiches and went to the foot of the stairs.

"Ann," she said.

She knew that her daughter heard her, but the girl remained silent. She sighed and started up the stairs.

Ann was lying sprawled on her back in the bed, staring up at the ceiling. She gave no notice of being aware of her mother's entrance into the room.

"Ann!" Martha said. "What in the world is the matter with you, child? Didn't you hear me ask you who that was on the phone?"

Ann turned her large azure eyes on her mother and stared at her coldly.

"It was Bud," she said.

"Bud? You mean Buddy Abbot? I thought that you weren't seeing him any …"

"He wants to go for a ride. He's got a new rod. He's going to pick me up in a half hour."

Martha threw up her hands in exasperation.

"Ann," she said, "I can't understand you. I simply can't understand you at all. After what you told me about Bud, that business about his getting fresh with you and everything, to still want to see him …"

Ann sat up suddenly on the bed and looked at her mother, her face furious.

"I guess you'd rather I saw my *nice* friends, I suppose," she said. "Like the kind I know in school. The people who live on the right side of the tracks."

Martha looked at her daughter open-mouthed.

"Now what in the world has gotten into you?" she asked. "Just why shouldn't you see …"

"I'll tell you why," Ann said, raising her voice until she was almost screaming. "I'll tell you. It's because I'm ashamed, that's why. Ashamed. Ashamed of this ghastly neighborhood and this ghastly house. We don't have to live here. I know we don't have to. I heard what Daddy said on television. About that company you own and all that money you've been making. And yet we keep living in this sewer. In this terrible, old, broken-down shanty. It's no wonder that Daddy almost never comes home anymore. I wouldn't blame him if he never came home."

"Ann, for goodness sake, *what* are you talking about, child? What has this house …"

Ann climbed off the bed and fighting back tears of anger, ran toward the bathroom, speaking over her shoulder.

"Oh forget it, Mother," she said. "Never mind, just forget it. Buddy's going to be here in a few minutes and I want to get changed and ready."

She slammed the bathroom door and a moment later Martha heard the water running in the sink.

What in the world had gotten into the child? Where did she get her ideas from anyway? And seeing that Abbot boy. It wasn't as though Ann didn't know what sort of boy he was. Didn't know that a young girl was bound to get into trouble…. If her father heard she was going out with him in his new hot rod or whatever he called it….

She hesitated, halfway down the stairs.

She suddenly remembered what Ann had said about Jack not coming home much anymore. And then she remembered the other things the girl had said—that business about the house and about the money she was supposed to have made in that company and everything.

Martha stood quite still, and for the first time thought seriously of the things she had heard over the television set that morning as Jack Rafferty had answered the questions put to him by the Joint Legislative Committee.

CHAPTER SEVEN

Senator Hamilton Tilden had been elected to office by a solid Republican majority from his home state on the eastern seaboard for seven consecutive times. A tall, heavyset man in his mid-sixties, with snow-white hair and a ruddy healthy complexion, he looked every inch the conservative machine politician that he was. He liked being referred to in the press as one of the last of the old guard; he was proud of the label "Hoover Republican." His seniority had been responsible for his appointment to the committee, but he had been more than anxious to be selected—even before he had realized the publicity possibilities of the appointment.

The Senator was anti-labor and made no effort to conceal the fact. He was anti-labor not only because he believed, albeit erroneously, that his constituency was anti-labor, but also because of personal convictions. Perhaps it would be better to say Senator Tilden was anti-organized labor. The Senator was willing to admit that there was a need and a place for labor; he merely objected to unions on principle, feeling they were in their own fashion as much of a monopoly as those giants of industry which had been legislated under control and government supervision during the early part of the century by the Walsh Act, the creation of the Securities and Exchange Commission, and the other devices he termed "interference by acts of Congress."

Despite a certain pompousness and a tendency to express himself in trite and meaningless platitudes, the Senator was no fool. He had the strength of a man who entertains blind, undeviating convictions and his mentality was first-rate, even though he had ceased to nourish it with new ideas for more than a score of years. He still had the capacity of a good realistic politician to compromise when compromise was necessary.

Unlike several other members of the Committee, the Senator was thoroughly conversant with the background of the investigation; he had gone to great effort to study the work done by the professional investigators and had frequently consulted with the Chief Counsel.

He realized that the work of the Committee presented an excellent opportunity to castigate organized labor, by playing up the only too obvious abuses by some of the very top men in union affairs. He also realized, of course, the sword cut two ways. That all too frequently management as well as labor had much to answer for.

Knowing full well that other members of the Committee, and especially Senator Early who had come up from the ranks of organized labor himself, would be making every effort to protect the good name of labor, Senator Tilden was going to see to it that management and big business were protected. He had respect for Early, in fact liked him in spite of the differences in their basic political beliefs, but he wanted to be sure that the Senator from the Northwest didn't interfere with the work of young Ames in bringing out every bit of malpractice and corruption which the investigators had turned up.

During the months he spent in the Capitol each year, the Senator, whenever possible, made it a practice to have lunch at Harvey's, where they invariably kept a table in reserve for him. He enjoyed a double bourbon and water before his lunch and usually ate rather heavily, in spite of a tricky digestive system which double-crossed him more often than not.

But on this particular day the Senator passed up his after-lunch brandy and ate sparsely. He didn't wish to risk the inevitable aftereffects of a heavy midday meal and thus jeopardize his being present at the afternoon session of the hearings. Also, he wanted to return a little early and have a chance to corner both the Chairman and young Ames. As a result, he was the first member to return to the anteroom, where he had to wait impatiently for at least twenty-five minutes before the others began to drift in.

Fortunately George Morris Ames and Senator Fellows were the first to return and thus he was able to pin down his two men before any of the others arrived. He greeted them perfunctorily and wasted no time in opening up the subject which was closest to his heart.

"A most surprising turn of events," Senator Tilden said. "Most surprising."

"Quite," Senator Fellows said, but not looking particularly concerned.

"Nothing ever surprises me with that man," Ames spoke up, a note of smugness in his voice. As usual the Chief Prosecutor's precise diction struck Senator Tilden as supercilious, but he swallowed his irritation.

"Naturally," he said, "we will have to alter our overall plan of ..."

George Morris Ames interrupted before he had finished the sentence.

"Not at all, Senator," he said. "Not at all. The mere fact that Rafferty sees fit ..."

"Now see here, my boy," Senator Tilden said quickly, making a very conscious effort to keep his tone friendly, "you must understand that this changes the situation entirely. With Rafferty talking we have the opportunity to get a good many questions answered which those other fellows refused to answer. After all, he is just about the first labor man who has shown a willingness to cooperate. I feel that we should, in view of his desire to answer questions, concentrate on those questions concerning union activities and practices. A certain amount of the material which you have gathered, and I must say gathered with extreme competence, is essentially irrelevant. It was, if I am not mistaken, to be used largely because we didn't expect Rafferty to answer any questions. Going into the man's various associations with certain business and industrial people, seems, at least now, rather a waste of time. It would appear to me that so long as he is going to answer questions, we should concentrate our efforts on learning about those things in which Rafferty has been most vitally and essentially involved."

"We certainly intend to," Ames said. "That is, if I am not mistaken, the function of this Committee. But I see no reason to soft-pedal ..."

"I am sure Senator Tilden wasn't suggesting that we soft-pedal any phase of this investigation," Senator Fellows interrupted. "However," he turned to his associate and smiled rather wanly, "however, I am inclined to agree with young Ames here. I think we should follow the strategy we have already outlined. The fact that Rafferty is willing to answer questions should not of necessity change our own plan of procedure."

Senator Tilden coughed and his face reddened.

"I was not necessarily suggesting we soft-pedal anything," he said rather huffily. "But the fact is that this fellow Rafferty is nothing but a cheap agitator and a crook. Any testimony he offers concerning his relations with management is bound to be prejudiced and irresponsible. He's a union leader and I merely am suggesting that we concentrate our questions on those matters which are germane to union affairs."

"We shall certainly go into them and in detail," Ames said. "On the other hand, where Rafferty's interests and activities have involved management, that too will be gone into. Exactly as we have planned."

Senator Fellows, sensing the antagonism between the two and anxious to keep harmony, nodded imperceptibly at Ames, indicating that he wished him to end the conversation. He turned to his colleague and took him by the arm.

"Hamilton," he said. "I know that you trust me, both as Chairman of the Committee and as a long-standing friend and colleague, to be completely fair. But in all frankness, I do feel we should progress along the lines which we have planned. Certainly we intend to go into every phase of Rafferty's activities so far as union and labor affairs are concerned. But the fact that the man is prepared to answer our questions is no reason to ignore his business relationships. We have certainly turned up enough evidence that Rafferty and certain unethical businessmen have collaborated to …"

"Yes—yes," Tilden interrupted. "I'm quite confident, Ormand, that you have the situation well under control. And equally confident that you will be eminently fair. I was merely suggesting, that in view of Rafferty's sudden switch about …"

His voice dwindled off and once more he coughed, looking a little more apoplectic than usual. He realized he was getting nowhere and he didn't wish to lose face in front of young Ames, whom he considered more or less of a pipsqueak, although undoubtedly a very bright pipsqueak and a boy who was destined to go places.

For a moment he was secretly glad that Counsel for the Committee came from Massachusetts and not from his own state. He knew that as soon as the hearings were over, Ames would be planning the next step in his career and that step would without doubt be a bid for either a governorship or a seat in the United States Senate. Ames would make a formidable candidate and Tilden was glad he would never have to face him.

But he was still annoyed. And he decided that the minute the investigation looked as though it would be getting off its main track, which he considered to be strictly the inquiry into unethical union practices, he would take a hand.

Several other members of the Committee had drifted into the room. Senator Fellows turned toward the door leading into the main chamber where the press and the public were already jostling for seats. He was reflecting that his colleague, Senator Tilden, would probably drop dead one of these days. A man with obvious high blood pressure and a tendency to overindulge.

John Carroll Rafferty looked as though he had enjoyed his lunch. He sat back in his chair, facing the Committee members, his eyes alert, but his body relaxed and comfortable. He looked like a man without a care in the world. The fact is, however, that he had missed lunch completely. There hadn't been time for it. He'd spent the entire interlude while the Committee was in recess on the telephone. Talking to New York, to Cleveland, to Chicago. He had also spoken briefly with Sam Farrow. At one point, while he was waiting for a free trunk line to Denver, he had vaguely considered calling his home. That testimony concerning the M-D Disbursement Company and its affairs had distressed him a little and he knew that sooner or later Martha would hear about it. But he quickly dismissed the matter from his mind. There'd be no point in talking with his house; he'd explain everything to her when he was back in L.A. the next time. The stories in the papers wouldn't mean anything to her, even if they were brought to her attention. She never paid any mind to what the press said about him in any case.

It never occurred to him that she might have listened in to the testimony on television.

Chairman Fellows rapped sharply with his gavel and the room became silent except for a few isolated coughs and the rattling of paper at the press table. He waited a moment and then reached over to take a folder which Ames was holding out to him.

His other hand went to his breast pocket and found a pair of horn-rimmed glasses, which he put on carelessly so that they were halfway down his patrician nose as he slowly opened the folder and looked at its contents.

"I have here," he said, "a number of checks. Some twenty in all. They range in sums from five thousand dollars to ten thousand, five hundred dollars. They are drawn on banks in New York, San Francisco, Miami, Los Angeles, and Denver. They are all drawn to John Carroll Rafferty and are all signed by Haddon Bosworth. They are dated over a period of three years, ending some nine months ago. They have all been cashed. I should now like to submit them to the witness for examination."

He leaned across the table, holding out the folder and it was taken by a court attaché, who in turn handed it to Rafferty. Mort Kauffman leaned forward, looking over his client's shoulder as Rafferty carefully took each check and examined it.

It was obvious at once that the move came as a surprise, but it was equally obvious that Rafferty was thoroughly familiar with the vouchers. Nevertheless he lingered over each separate piece of paper and the experts who sat in the press box realized he was stalling for time. Once he turned toward Kauffman, and putting his hand over the microphone, whispered for several moments. Kauffman was seen to shake his head vigorously. At last Rafferty looked up.

"I recognize them," he said.

"And will you tell the Committee what they are?"

"They are checks, made out by Haddon Bosworth and payable to me," Rafferty said in a neutral voice.

Senator Fellows nodded.

"They will be entered as exhibit number—" he hesitated, turning to whisper to Ames—"as exhibit number sixty-nine," he said.

The clerk retrieved the checks and returned them to the counsel table.

George Morris Ames stood up.

"The checks which you have just examined total in amount one hundred and thirty-two thousand dollars," he said, speaking slowly and emphasizing the figure at the end of the sentence. "Now Mr. Rafferty, would you tell this Committee exactly who Mr. Haddon Bosworth is?"

Rafferty smiled bleakly.

"I am sure the Committee is aware of who Mr. Bosworth is," he said. "Particularly in view of the fact that he spent more than two days testifying before this body only last week."

"Please answer the question, Mr. Rafferty."

Rafferty shrugged.

"Sure—sure," he said, as though he were pampering a petulant child. "Haddon Bosworth is an insurance broker and a businessman. His firm has handled and invested ISU welfare and pension funds. He has offices in New York and ..."

Ames interrupted, holding up his hand.

"And these checks, made out by Mr. Bosworth and payable to you? Exactly what do they represent?"

"The Los Angeles Grand Jury has already gone into that," he said wearily. "The story's been in the papers a dozen times. I can't see what's to be gained ..."

"Please just answer the questions, Mr. Rafferty."

Mort Kauffman started to raise his hand but Rafferty spoke to him quickly in an inaudible voice, and then answered.

"They represent loans, made to me by Mr. Bosworth, over a certain period of time."

"And what was the purpose of these loans?"

"The purpose?"

"Exactly. The purpose of the loans. Just why did Mr. Bosworth lend you a matter of some hundred-odd thousand dollars …"

"He loaned me various sums at different times when I needed money for one purpose or another."

"For what purpose, Mr. Rafferty?"

"Why because I asked him to loan me the money. Probably to go into various business ventures."

"Would you name some of these various business ventures?"

Rafferty didn't hesitate, but the quality of his voice showed his annoyance when he spoke.

"I don't recall exactly what and at what time," he began. Ames was quick to interrupt him.

"Would one of the business adventures have been the Tri-State Exploration Company?"

"It could have."

"And what was the function of the Tri-State firm?"

"Exploring for oil. And I might add," Rafferty said with a wry grin, "that we never found any oil."

Ames smiled also as there was a titter throughout the room.

"Who else was involved in the ownership of Tri-State?"

"Mr. Bosworth, myself, and Sidney Fields."

"That would be the Mr. Fields with whom you were also involved in the ownership of the Moore City Trotting Association?"

"It would."

"Was Mr. Bosworth also interested in the race track?"

"I wouldn't know. I merely owned stock in the track."

"Did the stock ever pay you dividends?"

"It did not. The oil wells didn't produce and the track went broke. We were unable to get a parimutuel license."

"What other business did you invest money in—with money borrowed from Mr. Bosworth?"

Rafferty looked at the ceiling for a moment and scratched his chin reflectively.

"Well there was a laundry chain."

"The Do-Rite Laundry in California?"

"That's right."

"Did the laundry have a contract with the ISU?"

"I believe that there was such a contract."

"And did the laundry make money?"

"I believe that it did and still does. My accountant would know and I am sure that your staff knows. They have gone over the books."

"Does Mr. Bosworth have an interest in the laundry chain?"

"I do not think so."

Ames cleared his throat and laid the papers in his hand back on the table.

"Now tell me, Mr. Rafferty. Have you repaid the monies loaned you by Mr. Bosworth and represented by the checks you have just examined?"

"I have."

"How did you pay these loans?"

"How?"

"Yes. How? By check, by bank draft, by ..."

"I paid them in cash."

"Do you have any record of these payments?"

"I have a record in my mind."

"Mr. Rafferty—" Ames lowered his voice, making it friendly and almost confidential. "Mr. Rafferty, please explain to the Committee how you are able to keep track of these payments—in your mind as you say."

Rafferty looked annoyed, but quickly controlled himself.

"When I borrow money—and I often do as you no doubt have found out—I remember it," he said. "I usually borrow only from close friends. And remembering the loans, I also remember to repay the loans."

"Do you always conduct your business by cash?"

"I don't believe I understand the question."

"You say you repaid the loans in cash. All I am trying to find out is if you always use cash in conducting your business?"

"Generally, yes. I don't even have a personal checking account."

"I see. Don't you trust banks, Mr. Rafferty?"

Rafferty's face flushed but again he made a conscious effort to control his temper.

"Of course I trust banks," he said. "As you probably know I'm on the board of directors of the First National Citizens Bank of ..."

"We know, Mr. Rafferty," Ames said. "Now let me ask you this. In conducting union business, you do use banks, don't you?"

"I certainly do."

"But you don't use banks in conducting your private business affairs. Why is that, Mr. Rafferty? Do you feel that banks are less reliable when it comes to …"

"I don't know what you're trying to get at," Rafferty said, this time outwardly showing his irritation. "Of course I use banks for the union business. And I trust them completely, otherwise I wouldn't use them. However, so far as my own business ventures are concerned, I have found it more convenient to handle matters on a cash basis. I …"

"We should imagine you do, Mr. Rafferty," Ames said, sarcasm heavy in his voice. "Now tell me this, do you feel a deeper sense of responsibility toward union funds than you do in relation to your own funds?"

Kauffman was pulling at Rafferty's sleeve and he leaned down to listen to the whispered words of his attorney before answering.

"He's baiting you, Jack," Kauffman said. "Trying to throw you off guard; get your goat. Good Lord, if you have any proof that you repaid those loans, this is the time to bring it up. This sort of testimony is damning."

"Listen," Rafferty said, careful to cover the mike with his hand, "I don't need proof. My word—and Bosworth's word—are proof enough. I said that I paid the money back—Bosworth has admitted I did. That should be proof enough. And don't worry about his baiting me. I understand what's going on."

"But Jack, it looks bad, not having any record …"

"Don't you be a prosecutor, too," Rafferty said shortly.

He turned back to Ames and when he spoke, his voice was once more suave and the crimson had faded from his neck. His tone matched that of Ames in smoothness if not in the perfection of its diction.

"I feel a complete sense of responsibility so far as union funds are concerned," he said. "I also feel a complete sense of responsibility so far as my own funds are concerned. The fact is I never formed the habit of using a checking account. I don't have large sums of money liquid and have never found a need for a checking account. I like to pay my bills in cash and I have always done so. I am quite sure it is all perfectly proper and legal."

"I'm quite sure it is," Ames said. "But to continue. Did you pay any interest on these loans you made from Mr. Bosworth and which you say you repaid?"

"I not only say I repaid them; I did repay them. Mr. Bosworth himself has so testified before this body only last week. And as Mr. Bosworth also testified, I did not pay any interest."

"Did you put up any security?"

"The very best security, Mr. Ames," Rafferty said. "My word."

Ames nodded quickly.

"Of course, your word," he said. "But no other security? Nothing more tangible. Nothing that a bank would accept as security?"

"As I told you Mr. Ames, I don't deal through banks in conducting my private business. And so far as I am concerned, and my creditors are concerned, there is no more reliable security than my word."

Ames shook his head and sighed.

"Could you tell this Committee if Mr. Bosworth has borrowed any monies from Local 702 of the ISU during the past five years?"

"I believe he has."

"Some two hundred and fifty thousand dollars, to be exact, isn't it, Mr. Rafferty?"

For a moment Rafferty hesitated, and then spoke.

"I believe that is the sum."

"The loan was made from the local's welfare fund, was it not?"

"It was. At 6½ per cent interest."

"And what security did Mr. Bosworth offer for this loan?"

"I believe he put up certain stocks and bonds."

"Stocks in the Tri-State Exploration Company and the Moore City Trotting Association?"

"It could very likely be."

"And those two firms are broke and their stock is worthless? Is that right, Mr. Rafferty?"

"They were not broke and their stock was not worthless at the time Mr. Bosworth offered them as security. What their exact status is at this time, I am not prepared to say."

"Quite, Mr. Rafferty. Now let me ask you this. Were you the union official, the officer of Local 702, who endorsed the loan to Mr. Bosworth and arranged for it?"

Rafferty shook his head vehemently.

"I was not. No single official of a local ever makes or okays a loan. The loan was made by the financial committee."

"And did you, as President of the local, appoint the members of that committee?"

"I did."

"In other words then, Mr. Rafferty, the committee members were your creatures, so to speak?"

Kauffman again started to get to his feet, but Rafferty waved him back. He turned and spoke directly to Senator Ormand Fellows.

"I resent the use of the word 'creatures' and its implication," he said. "The men I appoint to a committee are no more my 'creatures' than Mr. Ames is the 'creature' of the man who appointed him to his position on this Investigating Committee."

There was a stir in the room and the Chairman banged twice with his gavel.

"I am sure Mr. Ames meant no offense," he said in a smooth voice. "Perhaps Counsel will rephrase his question."

Ames smiled thinly and half nodded.

"Did you have control over the members of Local 702's financial committee?"

"I did not and do not. I control no member of any committee of either Local 702 or any other local in the Southwestern Conference or in the national body of the ISU."

Ames again smiled and there was another stir in the audience. Someone in the back of the room laughed and once more Fellows banged the oak table with the gavel.

"Does Mr. Bosworth still owe this money to the union?" Ames asked.

"I believe that he does."

"And the security that he has put up as collateral for this loan is worthless, is that right, Mr. Rafferty?"

"I didn't say that it is worthless," Rafferty said quickly. "I said ..."

"But Mr. Rafferty," Morris interrupted, "isn't it true that it was a short-term loan, that is now overdue and that it hasn't been paid?"

"I wouldn't know," Rafferty said. "That is a matter which lies entirely within the province of the financial committee."

"Would you know if any suit has been instigated, or any action taken, to collect on this loan?"

"I would not know."

"All right, Mr. Rafferty. Let us go on then. Mr. Bosworth is, I believe you said, the broker who handles the insurance policies of the membership of Local 702? Is that right?"

"That is right."

"And as the broker, he collects a substantial fee?"

Rafferty again looked annoyed.

"I have no idea what his fee is. The fee is paid to Mr. Bosworth by the insurance firms he represents. I assume—in fact I am positive—that whatever fee he collects is the standard fee which all brokers collect."

"I believe that you assume correctly," Ames said. "And for your information, I can assure you that it is a substantial fee. But now let us return to the checks which were previously offered in evidence. These checks, you say, represent monies loaned to you by Mr. Bosworth. Money which you tell us you have paid back. But you have no documentary evidence that you actually paid back those monies. And when our examiners went over Mr. Bosworth's books, they failed to find any …"

This time Mort Kauffman succeeded in getting to his feet, crying out, "I object. Mr. Chairman, I object to the line of …"

Senator Fellows turned to the attorney.

"The chair recognizes the witness's attorney," he said.

"I wish to object to the inference drawn by Counsel for this Committee," Kauffman said. "This is not a criminal trial nor is it a civil trial. But if it were, such tactics would never be permitted in any court in the land. If the Counsel wishes to bring out evidence to establish some point he may be attempting to prove, certainly he is aware of the proper procedure …"

"Counsel will be very glad to withdraw the last question," Ames said smoothly.

"This entire line of questioning is such," Kauffman began, but was interrupted by Senator Fellows before getting any further.

"The question has been withdrawn, Counselor," Senator Fellows said. "You may proceed, Mr. Ames."

Kauffman, disgruntled, slowly sat down.

"Whether or not the loan was paid back, Mr. Rafferty," Ames continued, "doesn't it strike you as highly unusual that a businessman would lend you a large sum of money, more than a hundred thousand dollars, without security and without interest?"

"This Committee is aware of the fact that I have borrowed substantial sums of money from a number of personal friends, on numerous occasions in the past," Rafferty said. "I have never had any difficulty …"

"That we can completely understand, Mr. Rafferty," Ames said, cutting in. "We know that you have borrowed money—from close personal friends, many of whom are connected in one way or another with the ISU. However, that is not the case in this instance. Mr.

Bosworth was before this Committee last week and testified, under oath, that you and he were merely casual business acquaintances. He testified that he has known you a matter of five or six years and that he first met you while you were both visiting a boys' private school where you had entered your sons. Is that not so?"

"I have no particular knowledge of what testimony Mr. Bosworth gave or what he did not give. I merely said that I have frequently borrowed money from close personal friends."

"And you consider Mr. Bosworth a close personal friend?"

"I do."

"On the basis of the fact that you met him less than half a dozen years ago while ..."

"If Counsel will be good enough to let me—" Rafferty began, but stopped when he saw Senator Fellows rising to his feet. The Chairman of the Committee banged the gavel sharply on the table twice and spoke.

"I am sorry to interrupt at this time," he said, "but word has just reached me that there is a vote being taken on the floor of the Senate. This Committee will stand temporarily adjourned while its Senatorial members have the opportunity to retire long enough to cast their ballots."

CHAPTER EIGHT

Haddon Bosworth lifted his lean, well-knit body out of the heavy red leather armchair. Moving slowly, like a man half drugged, he crossed the room and reached down to turn off the sound on the portable television set, leaving just the picture. He hesitated a moment, staring at the picture, and then went back to the chair behind the large, quarter grained oak desk. He noticed that the red bulb on the intercom had lighted up, indicating that the girl at the switchboard was attempting to get through to him. He flicked the switch and spoke into the box in a low tired voice.

"I thought I told you, Miss Drubbin," he began, but he hesitated as she interrupted him.

"It was Mrs. Bosworth," Miss Drubbin's voice said over the intercom. "The third time she's called this afternoon and she said it was very important."

"Call her back," he said. "Tell her that I phoned in and asked you to telephone. Tell her that I will be in touch with her sometime early this evening. That I will be unable to be home for dinner. Tell her not to worry."

"Tell her not to …"

He quickly shook his head back and forth as though to clear his mind. He realized that he was talking out of character and he made an effort to gather himself together.

"Not to worry about reaching me," he said. "Just explain that I will be home late. And if that's all, you might as well …"

"There have been a half dozen other calls, Mr. Bosworth. Would you like the other messages?"

"No—no thank you, Miss Drubbin. Just call Mrs. Bosworth and then you might as well close up the office and go home. It's after four anyway and …"

"I would just as soon stay on, Mr. Bosworth, if you …"

"No—no, that won't be necessary. Just call Mrs. Bosworth and then you can leave. I'll be here for a while, working. But don't bother to plug a trunk line through. I don't want to be bothered with the telephone."

"Well, all right, Mr. Bosworth, if you say so."

"Thank you, Miss Drubbin. And good night."

He flicked off the intercom switch and the red bulb went out. For a long moment he stared at the box and then he closed his eyes and ran a long-fingered, nervous hand through hair which had become noticeably gray during recent weeks.

After a moment or so, he reopened his eyes and stared at the picture on the television tube. But actually he was seeing right through it. He was seeing nothing at all.

Sitting there, staring into space, Haddon Bosworth was reviewing the ruin of his life.

The ruin of his life. The phrase went through his mind and it suddenly occurred to him that he had come full circle. His life had started as a ruin and now it was ending as one. Or almost ending. Once more his eyes focused, seeing the screen this time and looking for Rafferty's face. The face wasn't there but he didn't really have to see it.

Opening his lips he spoke in a low whisper, as though he were confiding to someone sitting in the room alongside him.

"You wouldn't do it," he said. "You wouldn't do it to me, Jack."

But even as he spoke the words, tried to reassure himself, he didn't believe them. He didn't believe them for a moment. He had known

Jack Rafferty for too many years ever to believe them.

Slumping back in the big leather chair, he stared at the television set, waiting for the hearing to resume. And while he sat and waited, he thought of John Carroll Rafferty.

He could remember, even now, the first time he had laid eyes on young Rafferty.

He must have been sixteen at the time, because it had been during his last year at the orphanage. He hadn't been an Episcopalian then; he'd been a Catholic. And his name hadn't been Haddon Bosworth. It had been Paul Cook. It was a long time ago, more than thirty-two years, and the things he had accomplished during those years had been phenomenal. He had, in more ways than one, done everything he had set out to do. Very early he had started making the money which he had wanted and needed. He had married exceptionally well, and in that marriage he'd been doubly fortunate. He'd not only found a wife who came from the society he'd always envied and admired—Grace Ridpath was from one of the finest families in the country—but he'd found a wife with whom he was completely in love and who loved him in return.

In the course of their years together he had told her only one lie and that was the initial lie—the big one. The lie about his background and his family and his religion and his name.

He'd fathered two fine children, children which any man could be proud of. He'd lived well, joined the best clubs, enjoyed the best there was of life. He'd been a success almost from the very beginning. And now he was coming full circle.

It had started when he'd met Jack Rafferty for the second time in his life, less than six and a half years ago.

But what he was remembering now was their first meeting, the day when Rafferty had first entered his life, back in the Home of St. Theresa in the little town outside of San Diego, California, those more than thirty years ago.

The sister had brought him in while he, Paul, was alone in the large square room which he shared with the three younger boys who were his charges. Alone studying during his free hours, as he always studied, because even then he knew what he wanted and he had already set out to get it.

"Paul," the sister had said—and it was odd that he couldn't remember her name, because she had always been good to him. He had loved her and remembered her for years, although she was an old woman then and must have been dead for a score of years by now—"Paul, this is John Rafferty, a new boy. He will be in your room. And John, this is Paul, who is to be your monitor and who will look after you."

He had stood up when the sister entered the barracks-like room, and now he looked down and saw the alert, half frightened, half wary face of the nine-year-old whom she held by the hand. An odd, almost tough little face, with the soft brown-black eyes denying the toughness, but with the square chin set and hard under the trembling lips. Black tousled hair, badly in need of a combing and the short, too thin little body already dressed in the gray, formless, depressing uniform of the orphanage.

He stood there, wordlessly, his sturdy legs spread and his feet firm on the floor; stood there as though he were half expecting a blow and was prepared for it.

Paul had smiled, held out his hand and the sister had had to prompt the child, but finally he too put out his own hand.

"I'll take care of him," Paul had said and the sister again smiled and nodded and turned and left the room. And he had taken care of him; taken care of him during the last year that he himself had spent at the orphanage and, in a way, taken care of him for several more years, after he'd left the orphanage and Jack Rafferty had stayed on at the home, growing into adolescence.

It was odd, that attachment Paul formed with the younger boy. Odd because although he felt a deep sympathy with all of the younger children in the home, he felt something special for Rafferty. And Rafferty, of all of them, probably needed sympathy and understanding the least. From the very beginning he was sufficient unto himself. He was the only child who never cried for his parents, never seemed to remember or miss the life that he had had before coming to the orphanage.

Paul himself had been in the orphanage since the age of twelve and because he had come when he was older than most of them, it had been a lot harder for him to make the adjustment. But that was only the lesser of the reasons it had been hard for him, much harder than for the others. The thing which had made it so terrible during those first years at St. Theresa was the thing which had happened to send him there. Because Paul was different from the others. It wasn't only that he was an orphan; it was what had caused him to be an orphan.

Paul Cook had left the orphanage on his seventeenth birthday. He had gone up to San Francisco and taken a job at nights, working in a bakery where he wrapped bread. He finished out his last year of high school in a parochial school and during the year he often used his weekends to visit young Rafferty at the orphanage.

From San Francisco he had gone to Canada, where he entered McGill University. He chose McGill because he wanted to get away from the States, away from any place where anyone might have remembered his name and remembered the thing which had made him an orphan.

He'd had only a few dollars that he had saved up while he worked at the bakery, to start out, but he took a night job, this time in a laundry, to earn part of his tuition. He was a popular boy and made friends easily and it was as well that he did, because he was soon invited into a fraternity and it was only thanks to the job in the frat house, cleaning up and working as a waiter, that he was able to augment his slender earnings sufficiently to put himself through school. In the summers he doubled up, working nights in the laundry and daytimes as a bookkeeper for an insurance firm.

It was during his last two years at McGill that he began to sell insurance on the side and he made an immediate success of it. His ability to make friends easily was a part of it, but the important thing was the driving ambition which motivated him.

During these years he kept in touch with the orphanage and kept in touch with Rafferty, whom he considered almost in the light of a protégé.

By the time he had graduated from McGill, he'd managed to save more than fifteen hundred dollars.

And that's when he came to New York.

He'd been planning the move for a long time and he'd planned carefully and well. The fifteen hundred dollars was enough to see those plans through.

Paul Cook died the day that he stepped off the Montrealer in Pennsylvania station and Haddon Bosworth was born. He took a room at the University Club, showing his diploma with the forged name, as a reference. Within a week he had obtained a job with a Wall Street insurance firm, starling out as a salesman. It hadn't been difficult. The job paid commissions against a minute drawing account; insurance companies in those years found very few newly matriculated college men who wanted to begin as salesmen.

The past was dead and the orphanage and the college years were something which had never existed. Haddon Bosworth never discussed his background, except to imply that his parents were dead and that he'd come from England via Canada, where he had obtained his major education. He joined the Episcopal Church, and became a member of the Downtown Athletic Club. And he worked.

From the very beginning he was successful. He knew that success depended not only on effort but on contacts as well. He set out to make these contacts. He joined a country club and then, a little later, a yacht club. For business and for social reasons. He bought a Star and began sailing in amateur races. He played golf like a pro, but was careful not to let himself become a money player.

Four years after coming to New York he was making fifteen thousand dollars a year and was firmly established. He was beginning to be invited to parties on the north shore of Long Island and in the better homes in Westchester and Connecticut. He was young, handsome, and intelligent. And he was popular. He was smart enough to be neither a pusher nor an obvious climber. Jack Rafferty, of course, had been buried along with the other memories of his youth.

Grace Ridpath and Haddon Bosworth were married in the fall of the year in which they had met at a tennis party at Newport. It was one of the social events of the season. The marriage was a success from its very inception. Grace soon learned that her husband didn't wish to talk about his youth and she believed it was probably because it had been unhappy and so she quickly learned to control any curiosity she might have. In any case, she was too happy and too busy really to think about it very much.

By now they were living in a house in Greenwich (which Bosworth had drained his savings to purchase) and first the boy and then the girl had been born. They belonged to the best clubs and traveled in the best circles.

Haddon Bosworth had a bad time when the war started, for he was theoretically not a citizen. But when he went down and tried to enlist he discovered, much to his astonishment, that he had a tricky heartbeat which the army doctors believed might have been caused by overexercise; it confused them to the extent of rejecting him, and that solved the problem.

Of course there had been other near disasters, such as the time he had run into two old school friends from McGill at the University Club. They greeted him hilariously, having lunched on an exclusive diet of Martinis, and he'd had a difficult moment or so in convincing them that they had made a mistake in identity. But finally a man he knew well had come by and called him by name and they had shaken their heads and reluctantly turned away, muttering about the amazing coincidence of two men looking so much alike.

Aside from that he had never encountered anyone from his past life—until the day six years ago when Jack Rafferty had walked into his office down on Wall Street.

The moment his secretary brought the card in, he knew that he would have to see him.

He wouldn't have needed the card, in spite of the more than twenty-five years which had elapsed. He hadn't seen Jack since that last visit at the orphanage when Rafferty must have been eleven or twelve, but he recognized him immediately. And he knew that Rafferty recognized him as well.

Rafferty had waited until the door closed behind his back, waited until he was sure they were alone together in the room, and then he had smiled, looking more than ever like the boy he had been back in San Diego. He crossed the room and held out his hand.

"Hello, Paul," he said.

Haddon Bosworth slowly stood up and unconsciously his hand went out. For one brief second he almost decided to brazen the thing out, but immediately he rejected the idea. He knew that it would be useless.

"Jack," he said. "Jack."

Rafferty's smile spread wide and he took another step forward and grasped his hand and shook it vigorously.

"Sit down, Paul," he said. "Sit down, boy, and take it easy. And Paul, I'm not a ghost."

He pulled a chair next to the desk and sat down himself and looked at Bosworth intently. Quickly he spoke up.

"Paul," he said. "Before you say a word. Before you say anything, let me make something clear. I'm not here to cause you any trouble. No trouble at all. I don't want anything and I don't want to embarrass you. But I just had to come and say hello—for old times' sake."

Haddon Bosworth nodded, dumbly, not knowing what to say. Not knowing what to do.

"Jack," he'd said at last. "Jack Rafferty. Well …"

"Catch your breath, Paul," Rafferty said. "And Paul, if you'd rather, I can call you Haddon. It's a little clumsy, but I guess I can handle it all right if it will make you any more comfortable."

Bosworth had nodded dumbly, still trying to collect himself.

They were silent for several moments, mutually and covetously inspecting each other. What Bosworth saw was a well-set-up man, broad of shoulder and slightly stocky, in his late thirties and looking younger. He still had the jet-black hair, the soft brown eyes and the broken, tough-looking gamin's face.

But the suit was tailor-made, in excellent taste, and the shirt was Irish linen. He wore a conservatively striped tie and his hands were a little too well manicured.

"I've known who you were for a number of years, Paul," Rafferty said at last. "Please don't worry about it, boy. It means nothing to me, nothing at all. I know that you must have had a good reason for changing your name."

Once more Bosworth had nodded, looking stupid and still a little dazed. Yes, he'd had a good reason. And Jack Rafferty certainly knew what the reason was.

In an effort to get over the first few minutes, Bosworth had picked up the card and again looked at it, seeing nothing but the bare name, John Carroll Rafferty. He said, more to kill time than anything else, "Jack. Well, Jack Rafferty. And what in the world have you been doing with yourself these last twenty or more years?"

Rafferty smiled once more, unable to keep a certain smugness out of the smile when he spoke.

"Well Paul—or Haddon, if you prefer—well, I'm still out in California. Live in Los Angeles. Married and have three youngsters. I've been in union work for the last twenty years. I'm president of Local 702 of the ISU out there and head up the Southwestern Conference."

"Jack, that's fine," Haddon said. "I always knew that you'd make it, fellow."

"You seem to have made out pretty well yourself, boy," Rafferty said. Bosworth looked up at him closely for a second, but saw nothing in the other man's face other than kindly interest.

"Oh, I've done fair enough," Bosworth said. "But Jack, tell me about yourself. How did you ever happen to get into labor work? What ..."

And so they had talked, each man about his own career and his own life, neither one actually saying a great deal but merely skimming the surface of the years. It was a clumsy conversation, a little embarrassing and a little forced. But it went on for the better part of an hour. Finally Rafferty sighed and reached for the hat he had put on the floor at the side of the chair.

"Well, boy, it's been good to see you," he said. "Maybe I could talk you into having lunch?" His eyes went to his wristwatch.

Bosworth started to shake his head and then suddenly it came to him. This visit was not an accident, not a mere caprice on Rafferty's part. Rafferty had come with some definite thought in the back of his mind.

For a moment he looked at the other man intently and then he spoke, this time his voice devoid of its former forced good humor. This time in a voice devoid of all emotion or feeling.

"Jack," he said, "exactly why did you happen to drop in on me today?"

Rafferty stared at him for a second and then once more smiled.

"O.K., boy, I guess I'd better tell you," he said. "But please take that worried expression off of your face. I'm not here to cause you any trouble or any embarrassment. It's just this. I happened to be reading the sports pages this morning and I saw where your boy—Haddon Bosworth, Jr., is your boy, isn't he?—well, I saw where he was appointed captain of the football team up at St. Matthew's Academy."

Once more Bosworth looked sharply at the other man. His face began to redden and he started to speak, but Rafferty quickly cut him off.

"You see, fellow," Rafferty said, "I happen to have two boys of my own. Twins. And they're damned fine boys, too, I can tell you. Anyway, I've been thinking about a prep school for them and then, when I saw that item about your son, it just occurred to me that there probably isn't a better school in the country than St. Matthew's."

"It is a fine school," Bosworth said, his voice guarded.

"Exactly," Rafferty said. "Well, I'd like to get my boys in, but I'm realistic about it. Oh I have the money all right. That's no problem. But I know that it's a tough school to get into and I knew that the boy who does enter has to come with top recommendations. Not that I have to worry about my kids so far as their school work or their records go. Eddy's captain of his school's basketball team and editor of the school paper, and Martin was voted the most popular kid in his entire school last year. Both fine, bright boys. But I know that they won't have a chance in hell of making a real first-class prep school unless they come with the proper recommendations."

"Now, Jack," Bosworth said, "that isn't quite true. You are a man who's come a long way and …"

"Being a big shot in the labor racket isn't the sort of background that gets your kids into good schools," Rafferty said. "There's no use kidding me about it, Paul—Haddon. I know what the score is. What my boys need is the proper introduction and the proper recommendations. And I just thought, for old time's sake, maybe you'd be good enough …"

"Why Jack," Bosworth said quickly, "of course. Of course, I'll do anything I can. I'm damned sure any kids of yours are the best and deserve the best."

The funny thing was that he was sincere. He really meant it. He would have been only too glad to have helped Rafferty. He still felt that old kinship, that old feeling left over from their days together in the orphanage.

This time Rafferty did stand up.

"Haddon—I'm going to call you Haddon from now on—I want you to know I appreciate this. I'm going to bring my boys into town within the next few days and I want you to meet them and get to know them. I want you to feel really sure you're doing the right thing if you decide to give them a hand. And another thing—" this time he hesitated for several seconds, staring directly into Bosworth's eyes, "another thing. I'm not a man who doesn't appreciate favors. I appreciate them and I return them. You're in the insurance business, aren't you, boy? Well, I want you to know that I have the complete control over a welfare fund of better than a million and a half dollars, which is invested with insurance companies. I also want you to know that I handle the pension funds of more than thirty-five thousand union men."

And that was the way it had started. That's the way it started, but that isn't the way it ended.

Rafferty's boys were, in due time, entered in St. Matthew's and Haddon Bosworth had to admit that he never once regretted having recommended them. Rafferty had been right about part of it at least. They were fine boys and they were a credit to the school. Haddon Bosworth's own son became their closest friend and frequently invited them home for weekends during the vacation periods.

And Rafferty had been as good as his word. He threw a certain amount of business Bosworth's way. Later on, he gave him a great deal more and it was only natural, when he came to Bosworth and needed a quick loan, that Bosworth obliged him. It wasn't until Rafferty had borrowed more than fifty thousand dollars that Bosworth suddenly realized the loans were that in name only. Rafferty was accepting the money as a gratuity, which he seemed to feel he was due as a result of the very profitable business he threw into his old friend's lap.

It is quite true that the business actually brought in more money than Rafferty borrowed; the only trouble was that Bosworth had to pay an income tax on his profits from the business and was unable to deduct the rising amount of the loans he made to Rafferty as bad debts.

When the sum reached seventy-five thousand dollars, Bosworth felt the time had arrived when he must bring the matter to Rafferty's attention. And that was when Rafferty told him about the Tri-State Exploration Company.

"Forget the loans, kid," he said. "They're peanuts after all. I'm going to let you cut into something that's really good."

Bosworth believed him. He knew by this time that Jack Rafferty was a man with vast and important financial connections. He went into Tri-State and later on he went into the race track venture. And in the meantime the personal loans to Rafferty continued to mount. By this time Bosworth knew that he had no intention of ever paying back the money. The collapse had come suddenly and with devastating swiftness. Bosworth overextended himself to invest in Rafferty's enterprises and when both the Tri-State firm and the race track went against the wall, he was caught hopelessly short. About this time the Joint Legislative Committee opened its investigation.

He'd called Rafferty, but Rafferty had put him off with vague promises. And then he himself had been subpoenaed by the Committee. The one lie he'd been forced to tell had been about the monies he'd loaned Rafferty. He'd told the Committee that Rafferty had paid him back in cash. He'd had to tell them that and not only because Rafferty had asked him to do so. To admit that Rafferty had not paid back the loans would have been tantamount to admitting that he'd been bribing Rafferty for throwing the union business his way.

Well, it was over now. Over and done with. His desire for easy money, his desire to protect himself and his family, had finally destroyed him. He was broke—dead broke and in debt. And in the meantime, Jack Rafferty was testifying in front of the very same Investigating Committee which he himself had faced less than two weeks ago.

Haddon Bosworth was suddenly aware that the Committee was

once again sitting in session. Quickly he stood up and crossed the room and turned up the sound on the television set. George Morris Ames was standing up to take up again the questioning of the principal witness, John Carroll Rafferty.

"All right, Mr. Rafferty, to get back to where we left off when we recessed," the Counsel for the Committee said. "You had explained that you frequently borrowed money from close personal friends and furthermore that you considered Mr. Haddon Bosworth to be a close personal friend of yours. Now what I had asked when we were interrupted and what you did not have time to answer was this: Do you consider the fact that you have known Mr. Bosworth solely in a business relationship these past five or six years sufficient justification for calling him a close personal friend?"

Rafferty cleared his throat and half nodded.

"I have known Mr. Bosworth for more than thirty-five years," he said.

Once more there was a sudden stir in the room and Senator Hamilton Tilden quickly lifted his head and stared at Rafferty, not quite sure that he had heard him right.

Ames himself looked at the witness and was unable to conceal his surprise.

"Did you say that you have known Mr. Bosworth for thirty-five years?"

"I did."

"But Mr. Bosworth himself testified only last week ..." Ames began.

"I am not responsible for any other witness's testimony but my own," Rafferty said. "You have brought me here—against my wishes, I might add—to ask me certain questions. I have sworn to tell the truth and that is exactly what I am doing and what I shall continue to do."

Ames leaned over and whispered for a moment with Chairman Fellows and then quickly turned back to face the witness.

"Then you are telling the Committee that you have had other than a purely business relationship with Mr. Bosworth?"

"I am."

"Would you please explain that relationship?"

Rafferty took his eyes from Ames and turned to the Chairman of the Committee.

"Senator," he said, and his voice was deep with sincerity, "Senator, I don't believe that going into my personal relationship with Mr. Bosworth is or can be of any possible help to this investigation. I have testified that we have known each other for a good many years—that we were long-time personal friends. Delving further in that relationship can in no possible way hurt me, but it may very well hurt other people. I would prefer not to ..."

"Mr. Rafferty," Senator Fellows interrupted, "I would like to remind you that Mr. Bosworth himself only last week denied a personal friendship. That he said you have known each other for a matter of five or six years, not thirty-five. Either you or Mr. Bosworth has committed perjury in front of this Investigating Committee. As a result, I feel that it is essential that we pursue the matter at hand. You may proceed, Mr. Ames."

"I will again ask that the witness explain his relationship with Mr. Bosworth," Ames said.

Kauffman leaned over and spoke in an undertone to his client.

"You'll have to answer," he said. "It's either you or Bosworth, Jack. They know one of you is lying and I only hope ..."

"I'm not lying," Rafferty said quickly, speaking only so that his words reached Kauffman. "I just don't want to put an innocent man on the spot."

"Don't put yourself on the spot."

For a long moment Rafferty hesitated and then, looking at an invisible point just above the Chief Counsel's head he spoke, his voice coming out clipped and precise.

"Haddon Bosworth and I were both inmates of St. Theresa's Orphanage, in San Diego, California, when we were children," he said.

This time Senator Tilden not only looked at the witness; he cleared his throat and spoke before Ames had a chance to ask a further question.

"Do you mean to tell this Committee," he roared, "that Haddon Bosworth was in a California orphanage with you?"

Tilden was a long-time friend of both Grace Bosworth and her husband and he refused to believe that he was hearing correctly. Senator Fellows pounded his gavel on the table.

"Senator Tilden has the floor," he said.

Rafferty turned toward the table behind which Hamilton Tilden sat, leaning forward apoplectically, in his seat.

"That is right, sir. Only his name wasn't Haddon Bosworth then. It was Paul Cook."

"What, what did you say? Explain yourself, man."

"I said," Rafferty repeated, "that his name was Paul Cook. We were in St. Theresa's Orphanage together and I knew him then. I knew him later while he was attending McGill University in Canada. We frequently saw each other and we corresponded. Later on, Paul went to New York and changed his name to Haddon Bosworth. He became an insurance broker and a few years back we renewed our childhood friendship and also began doing business together. As I say, we are old personal friends."

Senator Tilden half rose to his feet.

"What do you mean, he changed his name?"

"Exactly what I say. He changed his name from Paul Cook to Haddon Bosworth."

"And just why would he want to do that?" Tilden asked, disbelief and anger in his voice.

"I would prefer not to answer that question."

Tilden smashed his closed fist down on the table.

"I demand that the witness answer the question," he said. "Not that I believe a word of it, but I demand that the witness answer my question."

"I would still prefer not to ..." Rafferty began.

Senator Fellows interrupted, his voice a neutral monotone.

"The witness is instructed to answer the question," he said.

For a second Rafferty hesitated and then spoke.

"Paul Cook probably changed his name for the same reason that he was in the orphanage. Because when Paul was twelve, his father had murdered his mother and, as a consequence, was sent to San Quentin Prison to serve out the remainder of his life."

For a moment there was a dead silence in the courtroom as mouths fell open and every eye in the place stared at Jack Rafferty.

Mary Ellen Henshaw's voice was the first to break the stillness, before the sudden bedlam, and fortunately her words reached only a few ears close by.

"Good God," she said. "Grace Ridpath Bosworth's child the granddaughter of a murderer!"

Jake Meadows was halfway out of the room by the time Senator Ormand Fellows had begun pounding the table with his gavel to bring back order.

He didn't stop in the lobby to telephone his office—he knew they would have received the news over television. Instead, he grabbed a cab and went directly to the airport. He wanted to get to New York as fast as he could.

But Jake Meadows was wasting his time. Even as he stepped aboard the plane, Haddon Bosworth had already taken the bottle of sleeping tablets from the bathroom cabinet in his office.

He wanted to write a last note to his wife, but there really was nothing to say. Nothing at all.

CHAPTER NINE

"I've know Jack Rafferty for twenty years," Robert Sherman, the *Star* labor expert said, "and I still can't figure what makes him tick. But I am sure of one thing—he is sincerely dedicated to the interests of organized labor. Do you agree with me, Cart?"

He turned sidewise so that he faced Cartwright Minton across the table in the dining room of the National Press Club, where they were having lunch on the day following Rafferty's testimony about Haddon Bosworth. Minton looked around at the other two who made up the foursome, and shrugged.

"Hell," he said, "I'm not a labor man. The AP usually keeps me pretty close to the White House. And I don't really know Rafferty at all. But from the things which have come out at this hearing, I can't say that I would completely agree to that premise."

"Well from what I can see," Claude Braden, the NBC newscaster began, but Jake Meadows quickly cut in.

"Bob," Jake said. "I realize that we are your guests, but I think you're nuts. You are either stupid or blind or crazy. I don't know Rafferty, but I've known thieves all my life and …"

"Slow down, Jake," Sherman said. "I didn't say that Rafferty was decent or ethical or kind or generous or anything else. All I said was that he was devoted to the cause of organized labor."

"A matter of semantics," Jake said. "He's devoted to the cause of Jack Rafferty. Perhaps it's a simple case of confused identification, but …"

"The thing I can't understand," Braden said, "is why he put Bosworth on the spot. Why he …"

Jake turned to the news commentator and looked at him sadly, shaking his head.

"Tell me, son," he asked, "what were you doing for NBC before they sent you down here to cover this hearing?"

"Why, I did the five o'clock sports roundup and then again at ten …"

"I thought so," Jake said. "Good God!" He turned back to Sherman. "Explain to the boy why Rafferty put Bosworth on the spot," he said.

Minton looked at Jake disapprovingly.

"The fact is," he said, "he didn't. The Committee itself did."

Jake threw up his hands.

"Oh God," he said. "Did you fall for that too? Bob, you should know better. That is exactly what Rafferty wanted the public to think. That the Committee dragged those answers out of him."

He turned back to Braden.

"Order the next drink," he said, "and I'll explain the facts of life to you. You won't use them—I don't think your network would let you—but I'll explain anyway. Rafferty was in trouble. They had proved that he borrowed large sums of money from Bosworth. Rafferty said he had paid it back, but he couldn't prove it. Bosworth also said the money was repaid, but Bosworth couldn't help himself. He'd have had to say so in any case. But it doesn't really matter. The whole situation made Rafferty look bad. Made him look like he was getting kickbacks for giving Bosworth ISU business and lending him union funds. And incidentally, I don't believe Bosworth ever saw a hell of a lot of the money he himself was supposed to have borrowed from the union. In any case, Rafferty had no documentary evidence of repaying his own loans. He was in a corner and he knew it. He had to do something."

Jake hesitated for a second to get his breath. He caught the sleeve of a passing waiter and said, "Another round of drinks, *garçon*. My rich friend from the ether waves is buying."

He lighted a cigarette and continued.

"Anyway, he was in a spot. And Rafferty is a very smart cookie, especially publicity-wise. He could see the headlines in the paper this morning and he knew what they would be. He didn't like what they would be. And so he deliberately set up a smoke screen. He deliberately created a new headline. Created a story which would be so sensational that the public would forget all about …"

"Oh now see here, Jake," Minton said. "You aren't trying to tell us Rafferty made that orphanage bit up out of whole cloth."

"Certainly not. He didn't have to make it up. It was true."

"Well, then you aren't telling us that Rafferty figured Bosworth would commit suicide, are you?"

Jake looked at the ceiling and cocked one eyebrow.

"Who can tell?" he said. "Maybe he did and maybe he didn't. It really didn't matter though. Once Rafferty spilled his guts, brought out the fact Bosworth had been an inmate of an orphanage and that his father was a convicted murderer, he had already accomplished his purpose. Bosworth's suicide was an aftermath, a little additional fillip, so to speak. The big news, the news which would overshadow the hearing and anything Rafferty had said during the hearing, was the fact that Grace Ridpath Bosworth was married to the son of a murderer. That Haddon Bosworth was a phony and that his whole life had been phony. That was the news and that was the smoke screen Rafferty needed."

Cartwright Minton shook his head.

"I find it hard to believe that anyone would deliberately wreck a man's life, wreck his wife's life and his children's lives, merely to escape the sort of innuendo …"

"You just find it hard to believe Rafferty," Jake said. "I do myself. He has never seemed quite human and maybe he isn't. But I can assure you that is exactly what he did. And he was very clever about it. He did it under protest and with reluctance. Made it appear that the Committee, that young Ames, was dragging the facts out of him. And the result? Simple. Public opinion—and in particular the opinion of the laboring man—is that Rafferty did his best to protect his friend and that the heartless Investigating Committee deliberately destroyed a man. Even Bob Sherman here believes it. Swallows it whole."

Sherman at once protested.

"Not quite whole," he said. "The only thing I feel is that Rafferty must have had some other motive. Maybe he hated Bosworth; maybe Bosworth had done him some sort of injury in the past, maybe …"

"Not an injury," Jake said quickly. "Much more likely to have been a favor. Men like Rafferty, strong, ambitious, power-seeking men, can't stand it when people do them favors. They haven't the humility to be obligated."

"God, Jake," Minton said, "you *are* a cynical bastard."

"Cynical my ass," Jake said. "The trouble with people like you, Cart, is you hate the truth. And when someone tells it to you, and especially if the truth happens to be unpleasant, well then you just blandly accuse him of cynicism."

"Maybe I do," Minton said. "But how do you account for Rafferty's friends? For the hundreds of people who swear by him? For the …"

"Rafferty's friends may be divided into two distinct groups," Jake said. "The people who fear him and the people who have something to gain from him. They have one great thing in common. They all hate him. Secretly or otherwise—they hate him."

"And Rafferty? Does he hate them?" Braden asked.

"Hell, no," Jake said. "He doesn't hate anyone. He just uses people and despises them."

Minton started to push his chair back, waving at the waiter for the check.

"You're wrong about one thing, Jake," he said. "He loves those kids of his, especially the girl. He loves the kids and he's loyal to old Sam Farrow. He's even loyal to Tommy Faricetti, although he knows Tommy is a cheap hood. No, I don't think you have him figured at all, Jake. Anyway, I want to get back before the afternoon hearings start and talk with Ames. Rafferty's been before the Committee for a day and a half now and I still haven't had a decent news break. My outfit likes the 'exclusive angles.'"

Bob Sherman looked at his wristwatch.

"I'll stay around for another quick one," he said. "How about you boys?"

"I don't ever want to leave," Jake said. "And Claude here has to stay; he came to pump me about what this shindig is all about and I have promised to give him a little background material. But, Bob, you're the labor expert, maybe you better answer the questions. My specialty is people, not organizations."

Claude Braden looked over at Sherman a little shyly.

"You see," he said, "this whole thing is really out of my line. I don't know why the office decided to send me down, but they have, and I just thought ..."

"Just what *is* it that you would like to know?" Sherman asked.

"Well, all this talk about paper locals. I find it confusing. That business about captive unions, about dishwashers, toy stuffers, salesgirls, and God only knows what being forced into the ISU. It's a little over my head."

Bob Sherman smiled.

"Mine too at times. But let me try and explain. You see ..."

"Listen," Jake interrupted, "maybe you better let me explain after all."

He turned to Braden. "The trouble is," he said, "Bob here is a goddamned expert. If he starts talking to you he'll only get you confused. Anyway, he's pro-union—and I'm unprejudiced. I'm so damned unprejudiced that most of the time I'm anti-union."

"Aw now listen, Jake," Sherman said, "you're a Guild member, aren't you? Weren't you one of the boys who organized the Newspaper Guild? Didn't you ..."

"Sure," Jake said. "And I'm proud of it. But let me add this. No one told me I *had* to join the Guild. No goon came around and made me join. No publisher, at that time, said that unless I joined I couldn't work."

"And then you think it is O.K. for you guys who do belong to fight for better wages and conditions and have some other guy come along and refuse to join and pay dues and get the benefits?" Sherman asked.

"Why not?" Jake said. "The Guild—or union or whatever you want to call it—makes a contract between its members and management. If some other guy doesn't belong, let him make his own contract. And if it's a lousier contract, that's his own lookout. I just say I think he should not be forced to join and by the same token, he shouldn't be refused membership in case he wants to join. And right here I would also like to add that today there is probably a bigger problem as a result of the closed unions not letting the working man join than there is in getting men to join who don't want to. But anyway, the hell with all that. We could argue the subject endlessly. Claude here is trying to find out what this particular investigation is all about."

"You've been attending all of the hearings?" Sherman asked.

"No, I just came down a week ago," Braden said. "I have a pretty good idea, but what has confused me is this business of paper locals and the granting of charters to operations that seem to have nothing whatsoever to do with the ISU or Rafferty or ..."

"Let me give you a little background," Sherman said. "You see in the early days of organized labor, when the American Federation of Labor was in its prime, most unions were strictly craft unions. Railway conductors had their union, carpenters had theirs, plasterers and plumbers each had theirs. Probably the typographical union was as typical as any. It was a union exclusively designed for men who did a certain kind of work. And then, as unions became more widespread and more and more workers joined, two things occurred. First, unions began raiding each other's membership. The teamsters took in warehouse workers, bricklayers took in stonemasons and various groups absorbed other groups in kindred or closely allied lines of work. The second thing which happened was the forming of the industrial union—a union which in every sense was industry-wide.

"The United Auto Workers is typical of this kind of union. It includes not only machinists but body painters, tinsmiths, iron-molders or whoever might be employed in a specific plant or industry. The CIO was formed by unions which believed in the theory of industrial units as opposed to purely craft units.

"The result of this was that there has been an ever-increasing tendency for any union to seek members at large. John L. Lewis' Local 57 which was formed as a sort of catchall, was typical. This was a local of the United Mine Workers, but actually it covered people as far apart as farmers, office clerks, and God only knows what.

"It soon became an established practice for a professional labor organizer first to seek a charter from any recognized union which would grant him one and to go out and organize any random group of workers who were not already organized. Possibly more than any other, Jack Rafferty's ISU operated in this manner. That's the background and the reason I've taken so long to explain is that I want you to understand about the paper locals."

"It really isn't necessary that he understand," Jake said. "Hell, he's a news commentator and a news commentator should never know any more than his audience knows, otherwise the audience won't know what the hell he's talking about. Anyway, let's have another round. This is a signally dry conversation."

He waved to a waiter and ordered three drinks despite the protestations of both Sherman and Braden.

Braden fingered his drink when it came. He looked up at Sherman and said, "But these so-called paper locals ..."

"A paper local," Jake said, "is a strictly phony union local. What happens is that a man like Rafferty, or one of Rafferty's stooges, grants a local charter to someone like Tommy Faricetti, or any one of hundreds of the type of hoodlums who were on the stand last week taking the Fifth Amendment. These men in turn, not yet having an actual union or any membership, go out and start organizing. They organize anywhere or any place they can. It can be a one-man garage, or a lower East Side sweatshop; or a garbage collector with two trucks. It doesn't matter. Sometimes, if it's a regular business employing several people, they'll make a deal with the boss, who tells the employees they either join up or they lose their jobs. And then the worker is forced to pay weekly or monthly dues to the man who has the charter and is the self-appointed president or treasurer or secretary. It's a straight out and out shakedown and the hoodlum collects more often than not from both ends. From the worker by getting the dues from his pay check before he even sees it, and from the crooked boss who is guaranteed that he'll have no labor troubles. That's what they call a 'sweetheart contract.' The boss sometimes benefits, at least for a short while. The worker never does." Braden nodded.

"That part I understand. The testimony last week made it pretty clear. But what I can't understand is Rafferty's interest. Why is the Committee getting into that phase of the operation? What has Rafferty to gain?"

Jake looked at him pityingly and turned to Bob Sherman. "Tell him," he said.

"Well," Sherman said, "I'm not prepared to say whether this is true. But the theory is that Rafferty is aiming for Sam Farrow's job; for the presidency of the ISU. The job pays a hundred thousand a year incidentally, and it has made a millionaire out of Farrow. In any case, Rafferty is known to want the job. Personally I think it is the power that appeals to him more than the money.

"The national ISU convention comes up this fall. The idea is that members of each local elect delegates who attend the convention and select the national officers. Rafferty has a hell of a lot of strength, but it isn't going to be a cinch. And so, if Rafferty can charter enough locals—whether these locals have members or not—he'll have enough votes. What the Committee is out to prove is that Rafferty, using Tommy Faricetti as his front man, has lined up dozens or perhaps even hundreds of professional hoodlums and muscle men to form various locals, which in turn will cast their ballots in his favor. Isn't that the way you see it, Jake?" Sherman asked, turning to Meadows.

"That's the way everyone sees it," Jake said. "I think even old man Farrow, blind as he is, is beginning to get the picture. And there is no doubt that the government knows what's going on!"

"And then, you feel," Braden began, but Jake had already pushed his chair back.

"I feel I better get the hell back to those hearings if I want to hold my job," he said.

Sherman looked at his watch in sudden alarm and also quickly rose. He muttered something and started for the door.

"You get the check," Jake said to Braden as he walked after the other man. "I'll straighten it out with you later."

Jack Rafferty lay flat on the bedspread. He stared up at the ceiling and when he spoke, he didn't bother to turn toward his companion.

"All right," he said, "just order anything you want for yourself. I'm not hungry; tell 'em to send up a bucket of ice cubes and some soda. We've still got Scotch, haven't we?"

"Plenty," Mort Kauffman said.

"Good, then just cubes and soda. And tell that damned girl on the switchboard that I don't want any more calls put through. I don't care who it is, I don't want to talk to anyone."

"That last call was from your wife," Kauffman said. "She wants you to call back as soon ..."

"I've nothing to say to her," Rafferty said. "I've nothing to say to anyone. I just want to lie here and think."

Kauffman looked over at his client and there was a worried, almost perplexed expression on his face.

"Listen, Jack," he said. "Are you sure you aren't making a mistake? Maybe it would be better to see these people, or at least talk to them over the phone."

"I haven't anything to say to them," Rafferty said shortly. "Christ, I have my own troubles, don't I?"

"Sure, Jack. I understand. I can see why you might not want to bother with Faricetti or some of the others. But Sam Farrow! You should at least talk to the old man. He's worried. Plenty worried."

Rafferty bent one knee, pulling his foot up so that his shoe rested flat on the counterpane. He frowned and wiped a trace of sweat from his forehead and hitched around to make himself more comfortable.

"He's got plenty to worry about," he said. "Anything that I could tell him at this point would only add to it."

Kauffman nodded.

"Sure," he agreed. "But still and all, he'll rest easier if you talk to him. Let him know just what you plan ..."

Rafferty turned to his attorney and stared at him coldly.

"Goddamn it," he said, "how the hell do I know what I plan to do or say? How can I set his mind at rest? A lot of this stuff that's coming out is as big a surprise to me as it is to anyone else. I thought I had it figured as to what Ames and the Committee had. I thought I knew what they would be asking. But apparently those snoops have dug into a lot of things I don't know anything about. I just have to play it by ear. That's all I can do. And there's no point in having a lot of palaver with anyone else—not at least until I know where I stand myself."

"Well, I hate to remind you," Kauffman said, "but when you didn't take the Fifth …"

"This is no time for Monday morning quarterbacking," Rafferty said. "I knew what I was doing—I still know what I'm doing. I'm doing the only thing I can do. Take the questions as they come and answer them to the best of my ability."

"Sure," Kauffman said. "I understand. But what happens when they start throwing questions you can't answer? What …"

Rafferty quickly turned and sat up on the side of the bed. He stared at the little man opposite him with a cold eye.

"There are no questions I can't answer. Get that through your head, Mort. No questions I can't answer. I'm not going to volunteer anything, but at the same time, I'm not out to perjure myself."

Kauffman slowly shook his head.

"Of course you realize, Jack," he said, "that a lot of people may get hurt. May get hurt badly."

Rafferty's face was grim when he answered.

"Sure," he said. "Of course someone may be hurt. I can be hurt myself, can't I? Well, that's a calculated risk. Bosworth took that risk and although I feel sorry as hell about him, I refuse to accept any blame. When he decided to kick in with me, to accept favors and money and business deals, he knew what he was doing. This thing isn't a one-way street. Everyone has to take risks. I don't want anyone hurt, but my God, I can't go around being a babysitter for every person I've ever done favors for. I don't kid people and I try not to kid myself. In fact, you can bet that I don't kid myself. I knew this thing was going to be no picnic. And so should the rest of them. So far as talking to them, holding their goddamned hands, the hell with it. Right now I'm the boy who is on the spot. I'm the one they're out to get. And I've got plenty enough troubles worrying about myself without worrying about anyone else. Anyway, you better call room service if you want anything to eat today. And even if you don't, I still want a drink and I don't want it straight."

He waited until Kauffman had put in the call and then stood up and stretched and once more spoke, this time his voice more friendly.

"But stop worrying about it, Mort," he said. "That was Bosworth's trouble and Sam's trouble and the trouble with all of them. They sat around worrying instead of doing something. Me, I'm going to do something. I don't know what until the questions come, but whatever it is, it won't be worrying. I didn't get where I am by sitting around worrying. This is no different than any other fight. The tougher the opponents get, the tougher you have to get yourself. It's as simple as that."

There was a knock on the door and Kauffman sighed and turned to open it.

"Sure, sure, Jack," he said. "Except that there is one little difference this time. Instead of the opposition getting hurt, it may very well be your friends who are axed."

"There are always innocent bystanders," Rafferty said, almost casually.

CHAPTER TEN

Senator Early departed from his usual custom of dining in the Senate's private dining room. He didn't want to risk interruptions while he and his two luncheon guests held the discussion which he felt was rather vital at this point in the proceedings. And so he reserved a table in the Mayflower and arranged with the headwaiter to place them in a more or less secluded corner where they would be guaranteed a certain amount of privacy.

Ormand Fellows had tried to avoid the invitation. He rarely had more than a glass of milk at midday; besides, he had a feeling that Early wanted something of him. But Early had been insistent and Fellows had weakened and come along in spite of his foreboding. He knew very well that he would probably be tempted to eat more than he should, but he was quite sure he would not be tempted, despite Early's persuasions, to deviate in the slightest from the procedures he had decided to follow as Chairman of the Investigating Committee.

Senator Early's second guest was Representative Harvey Ellison.

"... and I have to agree," Senator Early was saying, "that his methods have certainly been neither legal nor ethical. But the thing we have to keep in mind, as I see it, is that organized labor itself is not given a black eye."

"No question about it, Senator," Ormand Fellows said. "No question at all. But it is still necessary to root out the black sheep. In doing so, in bringing the bright light of publicity to bear on men like Rafferty and his ilk, we are doing an invaluable service to labor and legitimate unions as a whole."

"True enough," Early said. "But that is all the more reason it should be very clearly pointed out to the public that the renegades, the crooks, and the chiselers and opportunists are the exceptions rather than the rule. So far as Rafferty himself is concerned, I am still inclined to believe he was tempted too much to let the ends justify the means. That essentially ..."

"Oh now, Senator," Ellison interrupted. "You're not questioning the material our investigators have turned up, are you?"

"Not at all. And I will be the first to admit that much of it came to me as a complete and shocking surprise. After all I've known Jack Rafferty for a number of years; known Sam Farrow even longer. Of course I still consider Sam an honest union official. I am willing to admit that many things he has done are questionable, but I think he has been honest according to his own lights. I only wish I could say as much for Rafferty."

"Farrow has cheated on his income taxes, he's milked his membership for hundreds of thousands of dollars," Ellison said acidly. "He'll be very lucky if he doesn't end up in prison."

Senator Early turned to the member of the House and coldly stared at him.

"I don't believe you understand Sam Farrow," he said. "Farrow has probably done more for the members of his union than any other single labor leader in the country. Why I can remember back when Henry Ford instituted the five dollar a day wage for his employees. It was an unheard of and radical gesture for the time and the period. The result was that the plain everyday workingman made more money a day than he'd ever made before in his life. And Henry Ford made millions. Hundreds of millions.

"No one complained about it and for a brief time Ford was considered a champion of labor. Certainly no one begrudged him his fortune. Well, Sam Farrow took his union membership from thirty-five cents an hour to an average of two dollars and eighty-five cents an hour. He got them the eight-hour day and the five-day week. He got them pensions and health insurance. And perhaps, somewhere along the line, he picked up a million dollars for himself. It probably prorates out at a dollar per member, if that. I think he well earned it."

"You're evading the issue, Senator," Ellison said. "I'm not questioning whether he earned it or not; I'm merely questioning the methods by which he got it. In the case of Rafferty, I more than question his methods—I condemn them. Men like Reuther, Lewis, Meany, Green,

Dubinsky—I could name dozens of them—have done fine work in the labor movement. Some of them have made excellent salaries and managed to establish personal fortunes—but they did not use the techniques which Farrow developed and which Rafferty has apparently perfected."

"I am not defending Rafferty," Early said, "but I still say that this investigation shouldn't turn out to be a witch hunt, that its results should not be a reflection on or end in the condemnation of, legitimate unionism."

"I don't believe there is an issue on that score, Senator," Ormand Fellows said. "Certainly no one can accuse me of being anti-labor. Nor any other member of our Committee. But racketeers and gangsters, personal opportunists and chiselers must be forced out of labor's ranks."

"I realize that, sir," Early said. "But I feel that there is a tendency on our part to concentrate too heavily on the man's personal life and personal business transactions. The whole thing about his wife, about Bosworth, the material we have dug up concerning Miss Hart ..."

"Senator," Fellows again interrupted, "I think you are overlooking one point. All these matters vitally concern Rafferty's own relationship with both his union and with organized labor as such. You see, I can't help but feel that Rafferty, like all other labor leaders is, in a broad sense, filling a public office. He has been selected to represent his fellow workers. As a responsible official, as a person who to a certain extent is in a position of public trust, his own life and his own activities should be above suspicion."

"Men of Rafferty's type should be driven out of organized labor," Ellison said.

Early stared at the younger man icily.

"It is my understanding that the purpose of this investigation is to seek information which will determine whether legislative action is needed so far as the activities of labor and management are concerned," he said. "We are neither a court nor a prosecuting body. We were merely an investigative body."

Ormand Fellows looked at his colleague speculatively. He's a damned old windbag, Fellows thought to himself. And a bit of a hypocrite as well. The only reason he wanted to get on the Committee in the first place was to be sure that Congress doesn't pass any legislation affecting labor. He knows about the abuses as well as I do, and he knows about Rafferty and Rafferty's type of union official. But he's purposely blinding himself.

And Ellison? Ellison is even worse. He's in the thing purely for the personal publicity he may receive. That's why he is playing hot and cold. He was as willing to make a hero of Rafferty as he is to make a criminal of him. He just wants to be sure to follow the most popular line of thinking.

For a moment Ormand Fellows stopped and wondered just what his own aims and ambitions were. There was no reason he shouldn't be as suspect as any of the others. It was true that he welcomed publicity of the right sort. It was true that he wanted the people back home, the people who had elevated him to office and kept him in office, to know that he was doing a good and a competent job. Yes, even he was out for a certain type of glory. It was foolish to criticize the others. Early had a right to want to protect labor, the same as Tilden had a right to protect management. The thing to do was be as fair as possible, perform a conscientious job.

"... and don't you agree with me, Senator?" he heard Ellison say. He looked up and realized he was being addressed.

"Sorry," he said, "sorry—my mind—what was it you asked, Harvey?"

"I asked if you didn't agree that Rafferty is almost bound to commit perjury if he answers certain questions which Ames is bound to ask before this hearing is over? I can't see how the man can give truthful answers without hopelessly damning himself, not only with the American public, but with the members of his own union."

"Well," Senator Fellows mused, "up to this point he seems to have succeeded in damning almost everyone else but himself. He is not only an extremely clever man, but he is an extremely cautious one. Of course I don't know how he can answer certain questions. But he has gone through this sort of thing before, and rather magically come out scot-free. I should be inclined to withhold any opinions until after we hear what he has to say. But I seriously doubt if Rafferty will commit perjury. He is much more inclined to pull off some such feat as he managed when we went into the Bosworth loans. In any case, it's getting late and I guess we'd better be getting back. That's the best way to find out what he intends to do."

Tommy Faricetti drank his lunch. It consisted of a double rye and water, without ice, and he took it in the glass which had held his toothbrush. Early that morning he'd left the hotel and checked into a tourist camp across the river on the edge of Alexandria, Virginia. He checked in under the name of Anthony Ranger and he arrived in a rented car, a black sedan also taken out under the same name. He had thoughtfully provided himself with a forged driver's license as well as sundry other identification papers. He arrived with a single suitcase—which contained one clean shirt, a change of linen, his shaving kit, and several bottles of whisky. The second piece of luggage he carried was a portable television set. Scotch-taped to the inside of the back of the set were eight one-thousand-dollar bills.

Francis MacNammera had advised the move. MacNammera believed that the police would be picking Tommy up any moment now and he doubted very much that he could arrange bail this time in case Tommy were arrested. MacNammera himself arrived at the tourist camp in the middle of the morning, while Tommy was listening to Rafferty's testimony coming over the television set. He stayed on during the luncheon recess, not because he wanted to, but because Faricetti wanted to talk.

"I can't understand why Jack doesn't call," Faricetti complained. "He knows where I am—you got word to him, didn't you?"

"Certainly I got word to him," the attorney said. "He knows where you are all right."

"Then why don't he call? Why don't he get in touch with me? I wanna know what to do. Wanna know ..."

"Listen, Tommy," MacNammera said, "Rafferty's got his own problems right now. He's got plenty to think about without worrying over ..."

"He's got me to think about," Faricetti said. "He told me he'd keep in touch. Told me not to worry. Said that he'd let me know ..."

"He told a lot of people a lot of things," MacNammera said. "He probably told Bosworth not to worry, also."

Tommy looked up sharply.

"What do you mean by that?"

"I mean that he probably told him not to worry—and then he dumped him. Cut him down and dumped him. Maybe he's planning to do the same thing—"

Faricetti stood up and threw his half empty glass across the room.

"You're crazy, Francis," he said. "What the hell are you saying anyway? Look—Bosworth was nothing but a stiff. Jack knew it and we all knew it. Nothing but a stiff."

"Bosworth was one of Rafferty's oldest friends," MacNammera said. "They went to the same school, didn't they?" he added, his voice sarcastic. "They knew each other when they were kids. But it didn't keep him from throwing him to the wolves."

"That's different," Faricetti said. "Bosworth wasn't one of the boys."

"Kid, I got news for you," MacNammera said. "I know you swear by him, but Jack isn't one of the boys either. You might just as well stop kidding yourself. He's not one of anything. He's Jack Rafferty and he's for Jack Rafferty first, last, and always."

"You may be a good mouthpiece, Francis," Faricetti said. "But you got a lot to learn about people. Jack don't throw his real friends over. Not in a million years. Why I know a dozen guys would lay down their life for him."

"Bosworth laid down his life."

"Jesus, get off that kick, will you?" Faricetti said. He crossed the small room and lifted the whisky bottle and took a slug, wiping his mouth with the back of his hand and making a wry face. "Get off that kick. I tell you Jack is loyal. He'll stick by me. He has to. Hell, I know enough about him that if I wanted to talk, they could throw the key away."

"He knows enough about you that they'd send you to the chair," MacNammera said.

Tommy swung around and stared at the other man.

"I say you're wrong," he said quietly, after a full minute. "Wrong. He'll stick by me all right. And he can do it, too. He's got the influence and he's got the connections."

"I don't want to upset you, Tommy," MacNammera said, "but you are my client and I might as well lay it on the line. Jack Rafferty is going to need every bit of his influence and every one of his connections to clear himself. He isn't going to have a lot left over."

"Listen," Faricetti said, "you don't know him. Don't know how he operates. Listen, I been in hotel rooms with Jack when he sent a state senator out as an errand boy—to pick up half a dozen condoms at a drugstore. I heard him bawl out a district court judge for being five minutes late for an appointment. I seen one of the most influential men in Washington hold his coat for ten minutes while Jack kidded with a phone operator. He's got connections and the right connections."

MacNammera sighed.

"Sure kid," he said, "but he didn't have enough connections to keep you from being indicted. He didn't have enough connections, even in his own organization, to keep those local charters for you, did he? He didn't have enough connections to keep somebody from ratting to the

FBI about that deal in New York. The one that may put you away for the rest of your life."

Tommy sniffed and shrugged his shoulders. He slumped into a chair and frowned, looking down at his boot tops. "Somebody ratted, sure," he said. "Somebody tipped off the FBI. But my God, Jack couldn't have foreseen that. You can't blame him for that, can you? And he's promised to get the fix in, hasn't he? He's said that I don't have to worry. That he can get it squared away. So what are you worrying about?"

"You're the one who's worrying. You're the one who wonders why he doesn't call. You're the one who can't understand why he denied being a personal friend of yours at the hearing this morning. Oh, don't misunderstand me; of course I'm worrying too. You're my client and it's my job to keep you out of jail and in the clear. I'm going to do it too, if I possibly can. The truth is, I worry plenty. I worry about the way Rafferty has been putting everyone else in the middle in order to protect himself. I even worry about the way he's indicated that you're Sam Farrow's responsibility rather than his.

"Yes, I don't blame you for worrying," MacNammera continued. "But worry about the right thing. He hasn't reached us either because he's too busy or else because he's being watched too closely. That doesn't worry me. What does is the fact that he decided to talk at all. It's been my experience that when someone starts talking, they don't know when to stop. And when you start talking in front of an investigating committee, you can't stop, even if you should want to. I'm not at all sure Rafferty will want to."

Faricetti was silent for a long time. At last he looked up, his expression thoughtful.

"Francis," he said, "you don't think, everything being equal, and if Jack for some reason or other can't help me out—you don't think I'm going to be able to beat this rap, do you?"

MacNammera sat on the edge of the bed and ran a hand through his hair. He didn't look at his client but spoke softly, staring at his feet.

"You haven't one chance in a million. Not one. And I'll tell you why, boy.

"It isn't that the case itself is so tough. It isn't that everything else being equal, I might not be able to beat it, it's because somewhere along the line you've managed to get yourself really fouled up. The New York police want you and the Federal people want you. You're the patsy. Maybe it's the old record, maybe it's all the publicity you've been getting. I don't know. But I have a feeling in my bones, that you're being elected. I have a feeling that if they take you, it's going to be for good. You've had your three felonies in New York State and we both know that one more means the book.

"I'm not worrying about that New York business only; I'm not worried about the Federals only. I'm worried because I think that they're all working together on this thing and that they'll throw you to the wolves. You see, the way I got it figured is like this. Sam Farrow is through. They'll get him for income tax evasion and maybe for fraud. Nothing too serious—except he is in his seventies. They'll send a half a dozen of the little guys away—guys like Camenetti, Sammy Cone, Richards, Goldman, and punks like that. They may indict some of the Los Angeles and Chicago crowd. And they'll do everything they can to pin enough on Rafferty so he won't have a hope of making the presidency of the ISU. That's about all they can hope for as far as he's concerned. But you—you're to be it. They need one big name, one big straw man that they can really make a showing with. If a guy like Anastasia had been mixed up in the ISU instead of with the dock workers, they'd have probably elected him. But you're the one mixed up with the ISU and that's the outfit they are interested in at this time. And so I think you're the guy who's elected."

Faricetti stared at his lawyer and his mouth dropped half open. He shook his head and blew out his breath.

"But Francis, I don't get it," he said. "I been careful. Very careful. I never stepped out a line; did only what Jack agreed I should do. I followed his directions—you know that. He wouldn't have let me get fouled up."

"He *has* let you get fouled up," MacNammera said. "Get that through your head. He *has* let you. It's a case now of whether or not he can get you unfouled. Up until yesterday morning, when he decided to talk instead of taking the Fifth Amendment, I was sure that he could swing it for you. I was sure that you'd end up in the clear. Right now I'm not at all sure. Not one damned bit."

"Why? Why—what's changed? What's his talking ..."

"Just this, Tommy," MacNammera said. "He's open to charges of perjury if he should lie. And if he doesn't lie—and lie like hell—well."

MacNammera stopped talking and Tommy Faricetti was silent for a long time. At last he looked up, shrugged, and threw his hands out.

"So what?" he asked. "So what am I supposed to do?"

"You're supposed to sit tight and see what happens. See what Jack says when he gets in touch with you. See what happens during the next day or two at the hearings. But I'd be a damned poor lawyer, and a worse friend, if I didn't tell you to get set for the worst. It can happen."

"And if the worst happens?"

"Blow. Get out of the country. Go to Cuba, or Mexico, or back to Italy. But blow."

Faricetti stood up and again crossed the room. He picked up the bottle and brought it back, but didn't uncap it, merely sat holding it between his knees. He didn't look at MacNammera when he spoke.

"No," he said. "No. I don't blow."

Watching him as he sat there it occurred to MacNammera for the first time that Tommy Faricetti was an old man.

"I'm fifty-seven," Faricetti said, as though he'd read the lawyer's thoughts. "Fifty-seven, Francis. I'm too old to start running. Too old to go to Cuba or Mexico or Italy. Too old to start all over. I got a wife and I got kids. A family. I gotta house in Brooklyn, a flower shop, an interest in a dry-cleaning company. I'm not blowing. I can't. It's too late for that."

MacNammera shook his head.

"Then ..."

"So I wait. I wait until I hear from Jack. Wait until he tells me what to do. Until he gets the fix in. I trust him—he's my friend. I *have* to trust him. I've done too many things for him, been with him too long, not to trust him. I don't give a damn what he does with the others, don't care about Bosworth or even Farrow. It's me that counts now. And he ain't going to let me down. Just remember it, Francis—*he ain't going to let me down.*"

He lifted the bottle and uncapped it and took a long drink.

"Turn the set back on," he said. "It's two o'clock and they should be getting back." He sighed. "Boy, you sure get a lousy picture with these portable antennas."

Young Eddy Rafferty looked up at his sister as she walked into the room and flung herself into the rattan Morris chair with the broken springs—the one he and his twin brother Marty always fought about when they happened to be home at the same time and sharing the joint bedroom.

"Sickening," Ann said, curling her under lip in a pout. "Positively sickening. Treats me like a child."

Eddy shrugged and turned back to his packing. He had his own problems.

"So what's the matter with you?" he grumbled.

"You'd think I didn't know the facts of life," his sister said, ignoring his question. She sighed deeply. "Let me have a cigarette," she demanded.

"A cigarette?" Eddy looked up again. "You know very well you're not supposed …"

"Yes, yes, yes, yes, yes," Ann said. "I know. I'm not supposed to smoke. And mother just sent me upstairs because I'm not supposed to watch television. And I'm not supposed …"

"You've been watching it for two days," Eddy said. "I should think you would have had a bellyful by this time."

"Well, I haven't," Ann said. "And anyway, that Hart woman is just coming on and I want to hear …"

"I don't know about you," her brother said, "but as far as I'm concerned, I've heard plenty already. More than plenty. I don't want to see any more television, I don't want to read any more about it. I don't want even to think …"

"Say," Ann interrupted, looking up at him and suddenly sitting erect in the old chair. "Say, just what do you think you are doing?"

For the first time she noticed that he had spread a suitcase open on the bed and was packing it haphazardly with clothes he was pulling from the opened bureau drawers.

He didn't bother to look up when he answered, and he half mumbled the words, not caring whether she heard him or not. "I'm packing," he said. "Packing and getting out!"

For a moment she just stared at him, looking at him almost as though he were a stranger. It was a funny thing, Eddy and Marty were twins, but they were nothing alike. Marty had always been her favorite, Marty who was a dead ringer for his father. Eddy was tall and thin and although he had a face which was as Irish as Paddy's pig, he had a reddish tint to his hair and his mother's features. Eddy had a quick temper, but it wasn't offset by his brother's capacity for humor. Eddy took everything dead seriously. Yes, in a lot of ways he was a stranger. It wasn't that she didn't love him, of course, it was just that he was different. Not like Marty. Marty, who reminded her so much of her father.

She felt terribly sorry for Marty; she knew what he must be going through. Marty had been spending the summer at camp with his very best friend, Had Bosworth, when the story had broken about the senior Bosworth's suicide. He'd called last night and said he was quitting the camp for the summer, coming home. He hadn't given any details, but they'd all known how upset he was.

Ann suddenly reacted to what Eddy had just said.

"Say, what do you mean?" she asked. "Packing and getting out. What in the world …"

"Just that," Eddy said. "I've had it. Fed up. I'm getting out. I'm sick of this house and everything about it. And I'm not going back to school, either. I'm going to enlist. I have to do my time anyway sooner or later and this is about as good a time as any."

Ann shook her head.

"Say, what's come over you and Marty anyway?" she asked. "Have you both gone a little batty or something? Here he is, quitting camp just because Had's dad—well, you know. I don't know why Marty should take it so hard. After all, Had Bosworth is the one who should have gone to pieces. Not Marty. It wasn't *our* father who did it. Marty doesn't have to feel ashamed …"

"He doesn't?"

Eddy swung on his sister and glared at her.

"You are a little fool," he said bitterly. "Really, Ann, sometimes I wonder if you …"

"Don't you call me a little fool," Ann said. She stood up, her hands on her small hips, and glared back at her brother.

"You may think I'm pretty dumb, but I'm not so dumb that I don't know what the score is. Had Bosworth's dad committed suicide because he lost all of his money and it turned out that he was brought up in an orphanage. So what? Daddy was brought up in the same orphanage and instead of being ashamed of it, he's always been proud of it. I can't see why …"

Eddy shrugged his shoulders and turned back to his packing.

"There are a lot of things you can't see, Sis," he said. "A lot of things. It wasn't that business about the orphanage that bothered him so much—it was how he happened to be in the orphanage. It was because of that, what happened a long time ago with his father and mother. He wanted to keep it a secret. And so what happens? Nothing, except his son's best friend's father—a man who was supposed to be one of *his* best friends—tells the story to the whole world. I can just imagine how Marty must be feeling."

"Daddy was under oath and he had to answer the questions he was asked," Ann said, defensively. "You know very well that ..."

"Sure—sure," Eddy said. "I know all about it. And he's still under oath and he's probably answering all the questions—and truthfully I don't doubt—about that Jill Hart. Why do you suppose mother sent you upstairs—unless it was so you can't hear those answers?"

Ann blushed.

"Are you trying to tell me that Daddy and that woman ..."

"I'm not trying to tell you anything," Eddy said. "I'm not going to tell anybody anything at all. I don't even want to know anything myself. All I want to do is pack and get out of here. I want to get as far away from this house and from this town, as I can." He hesitated a second and then reached into his pocket and took out a crumpled pack of cigarettes. He tossed them across to Ann.

"Here," he said. "Here's a cigarette. But for God's sake get out now and let me finish what I'm doing."

Ann stared at him for a second, holding the cigarette in her hand.

"But Eddy," she said, "you mean you are just going off and join the army? Not going back to school or anything? How about Carol? Aren't you going to ..."

"I'll write her," Eddy said shortly. "Not," he added, his voice bitter, "that she will probably care, after what she's been hearing about this family the last few days. It's been bad enough, her having to explain to her family that her fiancé's father is a union leader—but how's she going to explain that he's the kind who is mixed up with racketeers and loose women. How ..."

"Daddy just does what he ..."

"Sure, go ahead and defend him," Eddy said. "You should. You're just the same as he is. Always doing just what you want to do and the hell with everyone else. O.K. But go on, just run along now. And Sis," he added, more kindly, "don't say anything to mother about my going. I'll call her later. She's got enough worries just now."

Martha Rafferty suddenly put her head into the doorway.

"What's all this about my having enough worries, Eddy?" she asked. "What in the world are you two children talking about, anyway? A nice day like this, you should be out somewhere. I can't understand ..." She stopped talking as she suddenly saw that Eddy had his suitcase on the bed and was packing it.

"Eddy, what are you ..."

Her son turned to her and shrugged his shoulders resignedly.

"I'm packing," he said. "Packing and leaving. I've decided that I'm going to go into the army. I have to do it sometime and now seems about as good a time as any."

Ann Rafferty started edging toward the door and her mother quickly reached out and took her arm.

"You stay right here," she said, her voice suddenly shrill. "Eddy—" she turned back to her son, "Eddy, have you lost your mind? What do you mean, 'joining the army'! Have you gone completely out of your head? How about school? Do you mean you don't want to go back east this fall and finish …"

"I can always finish school. Maybe later, on a G.I. Bill of …"

Martha threw her hands in the air and went over to the bed and sat on the edge of it.

"What's happened to everyone?" she asked, staring around the room. "What's come over this family? Not going back to school indeed! Why, what do you think your father would say? And a G.I. Bill and so forth! Are you being purposely silly? You know that your father would never in the world permit …"

"I know that my father probably has enough to think about right now not to care what I'm going to do," Eddy said. "Anyway, I'm sorry, but that's how it is. I'm old enough to decide a few things for myself. And I've decided that the thing I want most right now is to get away from this house and this family. I've had just about all …"

"What's wrong with this family, young man?" Martha said sharply. "What exactly …"

"What's wrong? Well, Mother, just keep on listening to television for the next day or so, and I think you'll have the answer to that. Anyway, don't worry about me. Worry about Ann here and that Abbot punk that she's running around with. I can take care of myself."

"You just leave Buddy out of this," Ann said furiously. "He's no more of a punk than you or that snotty Boston girl of yours …"

"Children, children," Martha said. "Now both of you—stop this at once. Why, if your father …"

Her voice died out in midsentence.

Sitting there on the side of the bed and looking at her offspring, she felt a sudden sense of helplessness. Helplessness and defeat.

CHAPTER ELEVEN

"And will you tell the Committee, Mr. Rafferty, how long you have known Miss Hart?"

Quite unconsciously, as he finished asking the question, George Morris Ames looked over the head of the witness, his eyes going to where he knew Jill Hart was sitting. With the exception of Senator Fellows, virtually every other person in the room, except the witness himself, followed the direction of his gaze.

Jill Hart sat straight in her chair and looked at nothing. Her large blue-gray eyes were wide open and she was staring at a point slightly above the prosecutor's left ear, but she was seeing nothing at all.

"Approximately ten years," Rafferty said.

"And what has been the relationship between yourself and Miss Hart?"

Kauffman leaned toward his client, but Rafferty answered quickly, before his attorney had a chance to say anything.

"We have been business acquaintances," he said. "I would say that the relationship was one of employer and employee."

"Through whom did you meet Miss Hart?"

"I don't remember. It's been a long ..."

"Was it through Tommy Faricetti?"

Rafferty's mouth tightened and he spoke up quickly.

"I do not think so. I am not sure I even knew who Faricetti was at the time. I ..."

Yes, she thought, employer and employee. He was right. He was telling the truth. That's what they had been. That and so many, many other things.

She thought: It's odd. It really is. I am probably the only person in the whole world who has both known him and loved him. Several people have probably loved him. Maybe his wife, certainly his children. Maybe even Tommy Faricetti. And certainly many people have known him. Bosworth did. Maybe even Sam Farrow does—that is, really knows him. But I am unique. I am the only one who has managed to do both. Know him and love him.

"—Miss Hart's name at the time was Kaffov, Jane Kaffov, I believe?"

"That is right."

"And Miss Hart was employed as a chorus girl?"

"That is also correct."

"What qualifications did you find in Miss Kaffov—or Miss Hart as she calls herself, to make her a suitable employee for work in a union organization?"

"Miss Hart did not immediately become an employee. It wasn't until …"

She sat there, coldly aloof, indifferent to the stares, indifferent to those around her, looking straight ahead, her eyes always on Ames as he shot out the questions. Her expression never changed. Her face, still beautiful and unlined at thirty, was almost classical in its perfection. The fine-grained skin was pale beneath the carefully applied makeup and although she must have been aware of the frequent mutterings and the attention of those around her, she never blushed, never showed in any way that the questions and answers were reaching her.

It was almost as though she had two minds, two mentalities. She sat there, hearing those same questions which had been asked of her only the week previously—when frozen and monosyllabic in the witness box she had taken the Fifth Amendment on everything but her name and address—she heard the questions and she heard Rafferty's answers and they registered on one distinct segment of her brain. But there was a second part of her brain that was a thousand miles away. A part which was reviewing those last ten years during which she had known Jack Rafferty, as well as those even earlier years, before he had come into her life.

The ten years with Jack Rafferty were the important years, but then again all of the years were important years.

Jane Kaffov. Yes, that had been her name. It was a coincidence that she had become Jill Hart almost at the same time she had first met Rafferty; the change had, actually, nothing to do with Rafferty at all, but in a way it was an omen of the changes that were to take place and the things which were to happen. Because Jane Kaffov and Jill Hart were two completely different persons and the girl who became Jill Hart really, in many ways, shared nothing with the girl who had been Jane Kaffov except the same physical being.

Jane Kaffov, to all intents and purposes, had been dead for ten years, but now as she listened to those questions which involved Jill Hart, she once more became alive, and that part of her mentality which was not occupied with what was happening in the room around her was again buried in the past.

She had been told that she was born in the bedroom of the railway flat up on East 102nd Street in New York City and so she knew it to be true. But when she first became conscious of the dismal shabbiness of that wretched cold-water flat she was unable to remember.

Since she had become Jill Hart, she had consciously attempted to erase all memories of those early years from her mind. It wasn't that she had objected to her childhood. It was only in retrospect that it seemed sordid and undesirable. At the time during which she was passing through it, it had seemed only normal and natural.

Her father was dead now, had died when she was fourteen, and she remembered him only as a dour, bitterly disappointed man who worked as a janitor and handy man around the row of tenements in which they had lived. He'd never managed to forget that he'd been a minor bank official in Europe before he had come to America where he had been unable to adjust to the new language and the new world. He had been inclined to blame all of his troubles on his wife, whose own life was a long discouraging routine of childbearing, poverty, and hard work. Jane Kaffov had never loved her father and she had little affection for her four brothers, cast as they were in the same mold, but tougher, harder, and far more able to cope with the realities of the new world.

Her mother was still alive, living out in Queens now with Jill's oldest brother and raising his three motherless children. Her brother was a longshoreman, a great hulking brute of a man, who when he thought of her at all, criticized everything she was and did. As a result she rarely saw either of them. Her mother never missed her; they'd had little in common and what little natural affection Julia Kaffov had had for her children had been too sparsely dispersed among them to have meant much.

The one thing which Jane Kaffov's background gave her, however, at a very early age, was an essential understanding of the harsh realities of life; that and an almost animal instinct for self-preservation. She understood about money and the value of money long before most youngsters of her age. And she also knew all about sex at about the time when other girls were not even sure of the basic difference between themselves and boys.

By the time she was nine years old she had understood the

significance of the creaking springs of the broken old iron bed in her parents' room, a room she and the next youngest child had shared with them until they were four and five respectively and had been moved into the small alcove off the other bedroom. She knew that her father would come home at night, drunk on cheap whisky, falsely and temporarily gay, and would drag her mother off to the bedroom in spite of protestations. They would stay outside, she and the other children, sometimes slyly looking at each other but for the most part pretending to ignore what was taking place, as the sounds from behind the door reached them. She knew that what was happening was something her father wanted but that her mother hated and fought against.

She matured early. By the time she was fourteen she still had a couple of inches to grow and several pounds of additional weight to put on, but to all intents and purposes she was already a woman. It was as well that it was so because it was during that year that she was to lose her virginity. It happened to her the way it happened to so many pretty girls brought up in the tenement districts of large cities; she was raped, violently and brutally.

Like most of the children among whom she lived, Jane Kaffov at fourteen was already earning small sums of money. Two or three nights a week she would babysit, receiving fifty cents an hour. Her best customer was a family which lived in the same tenement house, on the floor above that where she lived. The woman was a trained nurse who frequently worked nights and her husband was a butcher, a barrel-chested, truncated man in his late forties with a waxlike complexion and colorless lips. He was an immaculate dresser, who, each Sunday, took his two roly-poly infants across town to play in Central Park. He had no friends in the neighborhood, but was always very polite when he would pass his neighbors in the hallways or on the street. On those nights when his wife worked, he would stay home and tend the children. Once or twice a week, however, Jane would go up and babysit for two or three hours while he went out.

It was two weeks after the death of her father that the incident took place. Phil, her oldest brother, was still home on the temporary leave granted by the Army so he could attend the funeral, and Jane hadn't wanted to go upstairs and sit, but he'd insisted. It had already been agreed that they would stay on in the flat, that the next two oldest boys, who were still in high school, would help their mother take care of the janitoring work.

"We all gotta pitch in," was the way Phil explained it. "An' it don't matter how you feel, Janie. The guy wants you to babysit, you sit. And tell him he don't have to get home at eleven o'clock or any particular time. You'll stay as long as he wants you to. We need the money. We're gonna need every dime we can get. If the old man hadn't been too cheap to take out some kinda insurance...."

So she had gone upstairs and told the butcher she'd stay with his children and not to hurry back, even if it was a school night. She was allowed to sit as late as he wanted her to.

He'd nodded to her and muttered a few words about the death of her father. And then he'd kissed his children and gone out. He came back sometime after one o'clock and his clothes were rumpled and he looked as though he'd fallen. The knife-sharp trousers were torn and his tie and hat were missing. His light blue eyes were bloodshot and Jane knew at once that he was drunk.

He'd hardly looked at her when he came into the apartment and slammed the door behind himself.

She'd spent the evening listening to the radio and had fallen asleep in a large overstuffed chair. She was wearing a sweater, a short skirt, and saddle shoes without stockings. She'd tossed off her shoes sometime during the evening. Awakened when she heard his key in the door, she was still sprawled out in the chair, rubbing her eyes with a slightly dirty fist, when he came in. She got up and stretched and then went over and cut off the set.

"You find the cokes in the refrigerator?" he called in from the other room.

"Yeah," she said. "Thanks."

"Any left?"

"I think so."

"Well, would you get me one while I get your money for you? And have another yourself," he said. His voice was thick.

She went into the kitchen and opened two cokes. When she returned to the living room, he was there, standing in his stocking feet. He'd taken off his stained coat and his shirt and was in his undershirt. His belt was loosened and as she walked toward him she noticed, almost unconsciously, that several buttons of his fly were open. It neither shocked nor alarmed her. She knew that he'd come home half drunk, knew that he'd probably gone at once to the bathroom. It was the way she'd been used to seeing her father and her brothers walking around the house for years.

She handed him his coke, yawned, and started to drink her own. She noticed that he didn't bother to drink from the bottle she'd given him, but put it down on the table and just stood watching her.

She finished her drink.

"Money's on the dresser," he said, after a moment. "You go in and count out what I owe you. I'm a little foggy."

She shrugged and walked past him into the bedroom.

She saw that the little boy, who was five, was awake and sitting up in his crib. The girl, a couple of years younger, still slept. She also saw the money on the dresser and was walking over to pick it up when she heard the door slam behind her back.

He grabbed her from behind as she started to swing around.

Not once during those next ten or twelve minutes did she utter a sound. Aside from the whimpering of the child and the man's heavy, tortured breathing, the scuffling noises, and that old familiar sexual crying out of the mattress springs, there were no words, no cries. The battle was short and brief, fought in wordless vacuum.

Somehow or other he'd managed to drop his trousers and underwear so that he'd been naked from the waist down when he'd followed her into the room. Coming up behind her, he'd put one hand over her mouth and even as he lifted her and carried her to the bed, his other hand had torn the short skirt loose.

She fought hard, trying to scratch his eyes, trying to knee him, but he was far too strong and heavy for her. As he fell on top of her, her small square teeth sank into his shoulder. His flesh had a salty, bitter taste and it repelled her so that instinctively she released her hold even as he cuffed the side of her head.

She kept on struggling and fighting through it all and even when the sharp agonizing pain came, she was hardly aware of it. It wasn't until he was through, lying still and panting and exhausted himself, that she managed to squirm from under his heavy body.

The strange part was that at no time had she been really frightened. Shocked, repelled—yes. But not frightened. She'd known at once what he wanted, known what he would do. It was the thing that boys and men always wanted to do.

Her ears rang from the blow he had struck when she bit him, and every bone in her body was sore. She knew that she was bleeding and could feel the warm blood as it trickled down the soft inside of her thigh. But still she wasn't frightened.

She crossed the room and pulled on her skirt. The first words she said, without looking at him, were, "You dirty fat son-of-a-bitch, you tore my skirt."

He sat on the edge of the bed and he had modestly pulled the dirty gray sheet across his nakedness. He didn't look at her but stared blindly at the floor.

"Take the money," he said. "All of it. You buy yourself some new skirts." He looked up at her then, his eyes vacant. The younger child was awake now and also crying.

"There's forty bucks or more," he said. "Take it all."

She swung to the dresser. There were three tens, a five and several ones. She didn't bother to figure out what he owed her for babysitting, but snatched up the five. Her hand swept the rest to the floor.

"Pig! Pig! Pig!" she said as she swung to the door. A moment later and she'd found her saddle shoes, but she rushed out of the apartment without putting them on.

Phil sat at the table in the kitchen when she entered her own apartment a few seconds later. There were half a dozen empty bottles of beer on the table and he was listening to the radio. He'd taken off his army shirt.

He hardly looked at her when she came in.

She walked over and snapped off the music and then she sat down opposite him, still dry-eyed, and told him what had happened.

He didn't say a word as the words rushed out; didn't speak until she was all through.

"Are you hurt?" he finally asked.

"I don't know."

He didn't look at her, but sat dead quiet, staring at the floor. "Well, do you think he got you knocked up? Was he using …" She blushed.

"I don't know," she said. "It all happened so fast."

His hand reached out and he knocked a half-empty bottle of beer off the table, rising quickly to his feet.

"The bastard," he said. "The dirty bastard."

He looked at her, his face grim, staring into her face as though he hated her.

"Get into bed," he said. "Go on—get into your bed." He started for the door.

"Phil," she said. "Phil, what are you going to …"

"I said get to bed," he growled.

A second later the door slammed and she heard his heavy boots on the bare boards of the hallway as he began mounting the stairs.

For the first time she began to cry, sitting on at the table and looking at the door, her face almost without expression, but tears streaking down her pale smudged cheeks.

He was gone a long time. Once or twice she thought she heard noises from the apartment above, but she couldn't be sure. She wanted to go upstairs and stand outside the door and listen, but she was afraid.

She was still there a half hour later when Phil returned. He came in, his face more grim and dour than ever. He had a handful of bills in his fist and he jammed it into his pocket as he entered the room.

He stopped and stared hard at her.

"I thought I told you to get to bed," he said.

"Phil," she said. "Phil what ..."

"If he got you pregnant," he said shortly, "at least I got the dough to pay for the doctor. Now go on—get to bed. And another thing—keep quiet about this. Don't you peep a word to anyone. Not mother or the boys or anyone. Understand? You're not to talk."

She looked at him, bewildered.

"Shouldn't the police ..."

He stepped over to her quickly and grabbed her by the shoulders, his face hard and bitter.

"You hear me," he said, his fingers biting into her soft flesh. "Ain't you caused enough trouble all ready? What the hell you want? I said get to bed. You ain't hurt. Understand that—you ain't hurt. And you're gonna keep your yap shut about this. I don't care what else you do. You can go back up there and babysit if you want—but you're to keep your mouth shut. If anything happens, if you get knocked up, I'll see that you get taken care of. Outside of that—just keep your mouth shut."

He swung her around and shoved her toward the door. "Now get the hell to bed before you wake up the old lady," he said.

She cried herself to sleep. She cried because of the pain and the fatigue which her slender body had suffered under the brutal treatment of the man who had raped her. And she cried because she knew that her brother had taken money from the butcher, had taken the money and would let it go at that—was even willing that she go back to the man again.

Shortly after her fifteenth birthday, Jane Kaffov quit school to take a full-time job. She worked in a small parts assembly factory for several months, making good wages and bringing money home to her mother each week. By now she was going steady with a boy in the neighborhood and, fearful that he would find out she was not a virgin, insisted that he go "only so far" in their lovemaking.

Within the next couple of years she had a number of jobs—as a receptionist, working behind the counter in Woolworth's, as a dentist's assistant (the dentist having been willing to overlook her lack of practical experience because of the startling beauty of her face and body) and for a short time as telephone operator (after the dentist had attempted to do to her what the butcher had done, but without success as by this time she knew all of the tricks when it came to protecting herself in the clinches).

She no longer lived at home, but roomed with two other girls down on East Eleventh Street, sending a small sum uptown to her mother every payday. One of the girls was a model and that is how she herself happened to become one. She still had a lot to learn about how to dress, how to use makeup and how to do the small amount of acting necessary in order to pose for photographers, but she worked for free lancers who did mostly cheesecake for detective and true confession magazines and it wasn't long before she caught on. Finally she connected with a good agency and started to do fashion work, getting increasingly higher fees. She learned a lot during this time of her life.

She learned to stay away from the men who made a practice of seeking out good-looking girls and trying to turn them into professional call girls; she also learned to avoid the nice boys who had neither money to spend nor serious intentions but were merely marking time until they grew up and married girls in their own social circle.

She learned how to wear and to buy the right kind of clothes, how to keep her face and her body looking their best, even how to talk so that the people she met and did business with would have no idea of her sordid tenement background.

But more important than anything else, she learned that the most important thing in life was to better herself and to have some destination. She wanted to become an actress, wanted fame and position and everything that they would mean. She went to an acting school and really worked in an attempt to master the techniques they taught. After a year, she managed to get a job in the chorus of a musical, and she had no illusions about the job. They hired her because of her freshness and her youth and her beautiful woman's body—not because of any great Thespian talent. But it was a beginning.

That was when she first met Tommy Faricetti. Tommy made a practice of hanging around backstage and he was friendly with both the cast and the management. It was understood that he had a small interest in the show and it was also known that he had a very dubious reputation. He was supposed to be an ex-gangster and it was said that he was mixed up in a protection racket. She had, of course, run into plenty of racketeers and mobsters before, small-time, strong-arm men and hoodlums who hung around the fringes of show business. But Faricetti was different. He was older and quieter and everyone liked him. He wasn't always on the make for one or another of the girls; he wasn't a pimp or a drug pusher as were most of the other shady characters who were perpetual hangers-on. He dressed well and conservatively, spoke in a low polite voice and didn't throw his weight around.

When he asked her to go out after a rehearsal and have dinner with him, she didn't hesitate. He was forty-eight but by this time she had learned that age wasn't a factor. The older ones were often the nicest and certainly they were the easiest to handle. Also, they could afford the good restaurants and the best shows.

Tommy took her out three or four times and then he made his pitch. By then she knew that he liked her a lot—had a yen for her as he expressed it—and wasn't surprised. The only thing that did amaze her slightly was the cold-turkey way he put it. They were sitting across from each other at a small table in a dimly lighted nightclub, and he'd leaned over and picked up her hand, looking directly into her eyes. Until then he hadn't made the slightest overture.

"You like me, kid?" he asked.

She looked at him, unblinking, without expression. He was a tall man, still slender and well kept, with dark hair, slightly gray at the temples, a sharp, narrow, olive face with very black eyes. He had a slightly crooked nose and she could see the thin white lines of old scars over both eyebrows. He was rather good-looking.

"Sure," she said, "sure I like you, Tommy."

He nodded, smiling and exposing two rows of very white teeth.

"I like you," he said. "I like you a lot, kid." He dropped her hand and stared off over her shoulder. "I guess you know I'm married," he said.

"I guessed that you were."

"That's right. Married and got kids. In fact, I'm a grandfather. Got a home over in Brooklyn and I live there—a lot of the time. I like it that way and I'm not going to change it."

"That's nice," she said.

"I just wanted to get straightened around on that," he said. "Another thing. I don't play around much. Sometimes—sure. If the right one comes along and I feel like it. But nothing serious and I never let anything interfere with my family life. I don't go for just any broad and I don't go for the pros. I'm not saying I'm the cleanest living guy in the world or that I'll get a medal from the Boy Scouts, but I ain't no chaser."

She nodded, still looked at him, not too interested and not quite knowing what he was getting at.

"Yeah," he said, "that's the way it is. Now I don't know you too well and don't know too much about you. But I know a couple of things. You ain't a bum, of that I'm sure. You're not on the make. Tell me— you got a steady boyfriend?"

She shook her head.

"I haven't time for boyfriends," she said.

He grunted.

"Good," he said. "So—I'm making you a proposition." He looked at her and smiled and she looked back at him, one eyebrow raised quizzically.

"As I say, I like you. I'm not nuts over you, or flipping, or anything like that, but I like you. In some ways you're like my own kid—" and this time he half laughed "—except now and then I think of you in ways I swear to God I never think of my daughter. I wanta take you some place and get into bed with you. I guess most guys feel that way about you."

She nodded again, soberly.

"Most of them do, I guess."

He bit his lower lip, shaking his head.

"Natch," he said. "So here it is. Suppose you let me set you up in an apartment. You can keep on working or not, just as you like. I'll see you got plenty of loose dough and I'll pay the bills. Sometimes I'll stay with you, sometimes not. That part will be up to you—at least the part about staying with you. You won't owe me nothing. Only thing is, I don't want no one else …"

She reached across the table and this time took his hand.

"What you mean, Tommy," she said, "is you want to keep me on the side and at the same time keep things going on over in Brooklyn just as they are now. Is that right?"

"That's about the size of it, kid."

For several moments she looked at him thoughtfully and finally she spoke.

"Thanks," she said, "and I really mean it. I'm not being sarcastic. But let me explain the way I feel about it. You said that you knew I wasn't any tramp or professional. That you don't go for pros. Well, this is the way I see it. If I let you get me an apartment and let you pay the bills, it's the same as taking money from you. And you are going to expect me to sleep with you. So—what am I? I'm taking your money and in return I'm letting you take me. What does that make me? And what does it make you?"

He shrugged and smiled.

"It's a little different," he said. "As I told you, I really like you. I don't know how you feel about it, of course, but hell, I'm not a bad guy. And it isn't as though …"

"Tommy," she said, "don't kid me and don't kid yourself. If I sleep with you for money—let you keep me—I'm no better or worse than any other whore. I don't want to be a whore and I don't want to feel like one. I don't want anybody keeping me—not until the right guy comes along who is so much in love with me that I'm the only woman in his life. I don't want to take money for something I might not want to do, and I certainly don't want to take money for something that I might like to do. I know you mean right, but that's the way I feel. Anyway, I want a career. I want to be an actress if I can, and if I can't do that, then I want to be in show business somehow or other. I know that you'd be good to me and take care of me, but right now I don't want to be taken care of. I want to take care of myself."

He looked at her for a long time, speculatively, after she finished speaking. Finally he again shrugged and smiled.

"O.K., kid," he said. "That's O.K. I don't blame you a bit. And I hope you make it—I sure hope you make it. No hard feelings. We're still friends?"

"Sure we're still friends."

They stayed on until the place closed and for the first time in her life she had more than a half dozen drinks in one evening. She got a little tight, but not too much so. When they left, she let Tommy take her to a hotel and get a room and she spent the night with him. He surprised her a great deal by his gentleness and consideration, but somehow or other he failed to arouse her. She had had a number of sexual experiences in the past and knew what to do, but she was unable to respond to his body despite his own passion. She had never experienced any particularly wild ecstasies in her affairs with other men but there had always been some sensation of pleasure, even if only vicarious, but with Tommy Faricetti she felt nothing but lassitude verging on boredom. It amazed her slightly and she secretly wondered if there might be something wrong with her. If she might be frigid or cold.

In the morning when she started to get out of bed, he pulled her back and she dutifully allowed him to kiss and caress her, but he understood how she felt and so he released her, neither angry nor bitter.

"Not your type, kid, I guess," he said. "I suppose it's just one of those things. Anyway, you're a doll and thanks for everything. And if you can't be my girl, well at least you're my friend and I'm going to keep an eye on you."

When she arrived at the theater that night there were a couple of dozen roses waiting for her and a small slender box from Black Starr & Gorham. It contained a platinum wristwatch.

That was the way their friendship began and that was the way it remained. He was, in many ways, almost a father to her. He never tried to take her to bed again and made no demands, but he would take her to dinner and to nightclubs, to hockey games and the race track.

Several times he asked her to go to parties with him, parties mostly attended by politicians and businessmen and once or twice he asked her as a favor to go out with some other man on a blind date—but always when he was along.

"You don't have to do anything," he'd explain. "Just be nice to the bastard and let him think he's getting places if he wants to. The guy's important to me, but you don't have to worry. I'll see that nothing happens to you and that you get away O.K."

She'd been glad to do it; glad to be able to return some of the many favors he'd shown her.

And that was how she happened to meet Jack Rafferty.

CHAPTER TWELVE

From where she sat, midway between the exit doors and the witness stand, Jill Hart had a perfect view of Rafferty as he monotonously answered the questions, leaning a little forward on one elbow and keeping his eyes always directly on the Counsel for the Committee. She could see the white linen collar of the imported, handmade shirt rising above the smoothness of the two-hundred-dollar suit which she knew he'd had made by Curtiz. She knew that he was wearing a twelve-dollar necktie from Sulka's and that it would be conservative and in good taste; knew that his trousers were held up by suspenders and not a belt, that there were the right number of buttons on the single-breasted suit; she knew that the one-hundred-and-ten-dollar cordovans which encased his feet had been made to his own last by a famous house in London. His hair above the collar of his suit was neatly trimmed and she was positive that his smooth face was perfectly shaved and that he had not been too lavish with after-shaving powder.

His voice was low and steady and smooth as he answered one question after another, and only now and then did he make a grammatical slip. Ten years. His figure was still the same, rather short, heavy without being stout. The face had remained unwrinkled and even the small lines which had developed around the eyes were barely visible. The hair was as dark as ever, still parted on the right side, and had barely receded over the rather narrow brow. The hands, well-manicured as they were, remained the hands of a day laborer. Ten years hadn't aged him, had brought about very few physical changes. And he still had that oddly provincial look. But the man who sat facing the Committee was a different man from the one she had met a decade ago. A far different man. They may have looked the same—although certainly the clothes were different and the manner was different and even the voice was different—yes, they may have looked the same, this Jack Rafferty and the Jack Rafferty of ten years back—but they were not the same. They weren't the same man at all. Why even now she could remember almost every detail, every ...

Tommy had telephoned her at the theater during the intermission. The show had only been open a week and she had her first singing part. It was a musical and it looked as though it might be a hit and she had already got over her first feeling of fear and worry. She knew that her voice wasn't much, but the audience—and more important, the producer—had seemed to like her and she was feeling fine. They had changed her name to Jill Hart before the show opened and that was the way she was billed. Not on the marquee, of course, but at least on the program. A specialty number by Jill Hart.

The assistant stage manager had told her she was wanted on the phone and she'd taken the call in the booth over near the exit door.

"Hi kid," Tommy said. "How's it going?"

"Great," she said. "Just great, Tommy."

"Fine, kid," he said. "Listen. You got anything on for after the show?"

She hesitated a moment. She'd half made a date with two of the girls in the chorus to go over to Lindy's.

"Listen," he said, not waiting for her to answer. "Whatever it is, can you call it off? I gotta favor I want you should do me."

She hesitated another moment and then shrugged. Tommy had gotten her her present part in the show. It had been his idea that she change her name, make a sort of fresh start with her first real part.

"Anything, Tommy," she said. "You know that, anything at all."

"Well, it's kind of important, kid," he said. "I got a guy in from the Coast, big shot in the union. I wanta throw a little party for him. He caught the show with me last night, and afterward he said he thought you were great and so I thought I'd give him a little surprise. He's an important guy and he really means a lot to me. So I thought maybe you could pick up another babe and we'll stop by and get you when the show's over. Go somewhere and have a late supper and then go on up to your joint and have a few drinks."

She didn't hesitate.

"Of course, Tommy," she said. "Only thing is, I don't want it to be too late or develop into a brawl or anything. I have to be here early in the morning for another rehearsal. They are making a couple of changes in the last …"

"Of course," Tommy cut in. "Of course, kid. It won't be no brawl. Not with Rafferty, you can be sure. So pick up some kid and we'll be by."

"Anyone in particular, Tommy?"

"Hell no, kid. Anyone. She's for me and you're going to be Rafferty's girl on this deal. Just don't make her no pig."

He hung up and she went back to finish her work and forgot all about the call until the final curtain had dropped. She had no trouble finding one of the girls in the chorus to go out on the double date.

They were waiting at the stage door when Jill and her friend, a tall thin blonde named Mavis, left shortly after eleven-thirty. Until the moment Tommy stepped forward, smiling, and introduced the man at his side, she hadn't given him a second thought.

He stood there, under the street light, and she never forgot her first impression of him.

He held his hat in front of him, in both his hands, and he was wearing a dark rumpled suit, scuffed brown shoes, and his blue shirt sleeves hung out at least two inches beyond the cuffs of his coat. He had on a flowered tie, badly knotted, and the uneven ends were pinned to the front of his shirt by a large clip with his initials on it. He needed a haircut, but he'd been freshly shaved. His face was completely expressionless as Tommy introduced them. He looked like every hick she'd ever seen in her life and she half expected him to blush and start stammering. Instead he bowed and said nothing. But she noticed that he never took his dark, rather brooding eyes from her, never looked at Mavis at all.

"Told Jack here we'd see a little of the town," Tommy said, his voice jovial. "I suppose you kids would like to get something to eat, so what do you say? Shall we hit Lindy's, or maybe Sardi's or would you like ..."

"Maybe the Brass Rail," Mavis said, looking at Rafferty.

Tommy gave her a cold look and Jill quickly spoke up. She knew that whoever this man was he was important to Tommy and she wanted to help him out any way she could. She kicked Mavis surreptitiously with the toe of her foot and said, "Any place you say, Tommy. How about you, Mr. Rafferty? Do you have any particular ..."

Rafferty shrugged.

"Tommy's party," he said.

Jill spoke up then, suggesting a steak place over on the East Side. It was a spot famous for its food, but it wasn't patronized by the theatrical crowd and the lights were always shaded so that it was impossible to see far beyond your own table. She wanted to please Tommy, but at the same time she wasn't anxious to be seen with Tommy's friend in any of the better-known places. My God, she'd thought, if the cops should see me with a cornball like him, they'll pick me up for soliciting loose trade at the bus depot.

Tommy called a cab and they started out.

By the time they were seated and Tommy had ordered a bottle of champagne, Mavis cheered up a little and even Jill herself was prepared to spend a pleasant evening. Rafferty spoke barely at all during the dinner. When the check came, Tommy quickly reached for it. He slapped Rafferty across the shoulder as he was waiting for the change.

"We can hit a nightclub," he said, "or, if you'd rather, we can go up to Jane's place and have a few drinks and listen to some music. What do you say, Jack?"

"I'm not much on nightclubs," Rafferty said. "I thought your name was Jill?" He looked over at her unsmiling.

She laughed. "It was Jane until last week. Jane Kaffov. But Tommy here renamed me. Now I'm Jill Hart. He thought it would be better, you know, being in show business and everything. Kaffov isn't much of a name for an actress."

"What am I supposed to call you, Jane or Jill?"

"Call her sweetheart," Tommy said and laughed.

"I guess you better start calling me Jill," she said. "It's going to be my real name from now on. I'm going to have it legally changed."

"O.K., Jill," Rafferty said. "I'll call you Jill."

"Then I'll call you Jack."

Mavis laughed. "That's good," she said. "Jack and Jill. What are you going to do now? Roll down a hill together?"

Jill started to smile and looked up and saw that Rafferty was blushing. When they left the restaurant, he carefully held her arm as they walked out ahead of the others.

It started out as one of the dullest evenings she'd ever spent. Tommy and Mavis danced to the record player and Rafferty sat on the couch, drinking rye and water and saying almost nothing. The liquor seemed to have no effect at all on him and failed to break down his reserve. Jill asked him to dance but he told her he didn't know how. He said he was tired and just liked to sit and listen to the music.

Once while Jill was in the small kitchenette of the apartment, Tommy came out and closed the door.

Jill motioned with her head to the other room.

"What's with him, anyway?" she asked. "You'd think we were holding some kind of wake."

Tommy threw his arm over her shoulder affectionately.

"He's all right," he said in a low voice. "You might not believe it kid, but he's a big man. A real big man. Runs the ISU local out in L.A. One of these days he's going to be one of the biggest guys in the country."

She'd met union officials before, but none of them had been like Rafferty. For the most part they'd been smooth tough Italians or Irishmen who'd been city-wise and Broadway sophisticated. She knew that Tommy was mixed up in union work and although she never asked him questions and he rarely volunteered information, she had a vague idea that unions and rackets were synonymous and that there was something vaguely illegal about them. At least the union leaders Tommy had introduced her to had seemed indistinguishable from gangsters and mobsters.

"Is he always so talkative?" she asked, sarcastically.

He looked at her seriously and shook his head.

"He's one of the smartest cookies I've ever known," he said. "Never kid yourself, baby, Jack Rafferty is smart. He may look like a cornball, but he has a mind like a steel trap. He's a big man and he's going to be bigger. And he can do me a lot of good, a lot of good. That's why I want you to be nice to him, kid."

"I'm being nice," she said. "It's just that I don't know what he wants. He doesn't pay any attention at all to me but just sits there and listens to the music and drinks. I don't think he's said three words to Mavis all evening."

"That's just his way. But he likes you. I can tell. He likes you, kid."

"Well, it's certainly different to be liked his way," she said.

"Look, kid," Tommy said, "this guy means a lot to me. He's important. Very important. In a few minutes I want to push off and I want you to tip Mavis to pull out when I do. Jack may want to stay around a while and if he does, I want you to let him. I want you to be nice ..."

She took a step back and stared up at him.

"What? You mean you are going to blow and leave that creep with me? What is this anyway? I don't want to be left alone ..."

He reached over quickly and took her by the shoulders, at the same time putting a finger to her lips.

"Listen, kid," he said. "He isn't going to try to rape you or anything. He isn't that kind of guy at all. And I just want you should ..."

"I'm not worrying about being raped," she said. "I just worry about being bored to death."

"All right," Tommy said. "All right. Just take it easy." He wasn't smiling any longer. "I said this is important to me. He can do one hell of a lot of good for me and frankly, kid, right now I could have a little done. I want you to do it for me. For some reason or other he seems to like you and I want you should be nice to him. I think maybe the reason he isn't talking much is because me and that other broad are here. These western guys are funny. Anyway, do it for me, eh baby?"

She shrugged.

"Of course, Tommy," she said. "I'll be as nice to him as I know how. But if you want my opinion, all he wants to do is get back to his hotel and go to bed."

She followed him back into the living room and noticed that the music had stopped and that Rafferty was changing records. Catching Mavis' eye, she nodded her head toward the bathroom.

"Tommy wants to blow in a few minutes," she said, "and he wants you to leave with him. O.K.?"

Mavis whistled.

"Sure it's O.K.," she said. "But how about the stiff? Is he staying?"

"Just be a good girl and do what Tommy wants," Jill said.

Mavis hunched her shoulders in a shrug.

"Your friends are my friends, honey," she said.

A half hour later, Tommy drained his glass and stood up and stretched.

"Gotta push off, Jack," he said. "But why don't you hang around for a little while with the girls? They don't hit the deck until dawn anyway."

Rafferty looked up quizzically.

"Well, maybe I better be ..."

"The night's a pup," Jill said, fighting to stifle a yawn. "Come on, hang around for a while. I'll pour you another quick one."

He relinquished his glass and sat back on the couch.

When Jill returned with the drink, Tommy was already gone. Mavis was not in sight.

"She left with Faricetti," Rafferty said, taking the glass. "Said she had to be getting along too and they both said to say good night." He hesitated a minute, looking down at the glass. "You want me to leave too, maybe?"

She stood in front of him, looking down at him and she thought, my God he acts like a little boy. He looked young, true enough, but she guessed that he must be in the mid-thirties at least. He'd have to be, to be the big shot Tommy said he was. For the first time since she had been introduced to him early that evening, she looked into his face and she smiled and then she laughed.

"No, I don't want you to leave too, maybe," she said, flouncing down on the couch next to him. "You sound like a little boy," she said, "who's done something wrong. Say, tell me, are you a little boy?"

He looked back into her eyes and he too smiled for the first time and the smile completely altered the habitual expression on his face. Seemed to completely change his entire character. It gave him charm, lightness, vivacity.

"I'm not a little boy, ma'am," he said. "I'm a big boy."

"Tell me something about yourself," she said.

"Name—Jack Rafferty. I live in Los Angeles, and—" he hesitated for several seconds, staring at her and no longer smiling "—and I am married and have three fine children. I am visiting in New York for a few days. I'm head of a union local. You tell me about yourself."

"Well, I have two names, as you already know. But we'll stick to Jill. I was born in New York, brought up in New York and I love it. I'm free, white, and twenty. In show business. I live here alone and someday, if I can learn to keep my feet from falling all over each other, I'm going to be an actress. A really big actress. If I can learn to sing a little better, I may be a singer. I don't drink much; I have to watch my weight. I don't like sports—except baseball of course—and that's, well, that's about it. But I don't want to talk about me. I want to hear about you. Tell me, how do you like New York? This is your first visit?"

Rafferty put his glass down and turned to face her.

"No," he said. "No, I've been in New York before. Many times. I suppose," and once more he smiled at her and she was again amazed at the difference the smile made in his personality, "—I suppose I *do* look a little like a hick to you," he said. "But the fact is, I spend a day or so in New York every couple of weeks. It's just that I'm always pretty busy. I've never had much time for night life or anything like that."

He edged away an inch or so and turned on the couch so that he was directly facing her. He stared for a moment into her face and she saw that he had a certain tough attractiveness about him. It was a plain face, neither good-looking nor ugly, but the eyes were wide spaced and the slightly crooked nose seemed to lend it a certain peculiar strength. His eyes were very clear and completely guileless. She noticed his hands for the first time. They were large and thick and the nails, immaculately clean, were square cut. They were strong, expressive hands and they never seemed still or at ease. They were the hands of a workingman, but they didn't look as though they had known work for a long time.

"Have you known Faricetti very long?" he asked.

"He's an old friend. Why do you ask?"

Again he hesitated, looking at her quizzically. When he finally spoke, he continued looking into her eyes.

"He told me that if I wanted to, I could sleep with you," he said. "Is that right—can I?"

It was so unexpected that for a moment she just sat there and stared at him. He continued looking into her face, making no move toward her, his own expression enigmatic.

"Well—" she said at last. "Well—I've got news for you, buster. Your friend Tommy Faricetti is just a little mistaken. Whatever makes you think ..."

"I don't think anything," he said. "And you said he was your friend. I'm just telling you what he told me. I saw you last night in that show and I said I thought you were really something. And he said that you were a pal of his and that if I wanted, he could arrange to fix it up for me. I'm just telling you what he told me, so don't get sore at me about it. I thought I'd find out the score."

She was furious with Tommy, but at the same time she was half amused. If this was some new kind of pitch, it certainly was different. She'd half expected a pass of some sort when he'd stayed on; figured she'd have to handle him and that it wouldn't be too tough. But this forthright conversation left her at a loss. The odd part of it was that Rafferty didn't seem in the slightest bit embarrassed about it.

"Tommy should know better," she said. "And so should you. What do you think I am, anyway? Are you one of these characters who think because a girl is in show business that she necessarily has to have round heels? That she's a pushover for any jerk who comes along? Are you one of those ..."

"I'm not a jerk," Rafferty said, his voice still neutral, "and frankly I have no ideas at all about showgirls. You're the first one I ever met. I just told you what Tommy said. If you say he was wrong, well, then, I'll believe you."

"You can believe me all right," she said. "He was wrong. Very much wrong. I can't understand why Tommy would say a thing like ..."

"I can," he interrupted. "I can do Faricetti a lot of good, in certain ways I don't want to go into just now. And so he was trying to do me a favor, or at least what he thought was a favor."

"It's no favor to me," Jill said shortly.

"Oh now—" he laughed but made no attempt to touch her. "Oh now, I'm not that bad, you know."

Suddenly she too laughed.

"I didn't say you were," she said.

"Can I ask you something without you getting sore?"

"Shoot away," she said. "Right now I'm sore at Tommy and I've always found it hard to be mad at two people at the same time."

"Are you Tommy's girl?"

"What do you mean by that?"

"Well, you know …"

She stood up and moved off toward the phonograph.

"No," she said, "I don't know. But let me get you straightened out a little. First about me. I don't go around sleeping with casual strangers; I'm not a hooker, I'm not a party girl, if you know what I mean. I've had boyfriends in the past and I will probably have more in the future. But what my relationship with them has been and will be is strictly my own business. Tommy has never been a boyfriend, but he has been a damned good and loyal companion. He's done a lot for me and been almost—I know this sounds corny—but he's been almost like a father to me. He's certainly made a mistake, so far as you are concerned. I guess you really must be pretty important to him."

The odd part of it was, that even as she spoke, she suddenly realized that if Tommy had told her it was a matter of supreme importance to him, she probably would have slept with this man. But Tommy had no right to go around blandly promising …

"I said I was important to him," Rafferty said. "But let's forget Faricetti. I guess he just made a mistake. Anyway, I'll tell you something. You may think I'm a sap, but I'm glad he did. I'm glad he was wrong. I think you are a nice girl. A hell of a nice girl. And if you will pour me one more drink, I'll drink it and then I'll get out of here and go back and try to get a couple of hours' sleep at the hotel. I gotta meeting at eight sharp in the morning."

"I have a rehearsal at nine," Jill said. "But I'll pour that drink and I'll have a nightcap with you."

Twenty minutes later he found his hat and she walked to the door with him. She noticed then, for the first time, that he was only two or three inches taller than she was and that, if he would ever learn how to buy clothes, he could be rather impressive.

He stood for a second with his hand on the knob, looking at her and then suddenly put out his other hand.

"It's been nice meeting you," he said, and they shook hands. "Good night."

He had a strong firm grip and she felt an odd thrill as he held her hand. A moment later and he was gone and she turned back to the room.

Rafferty was in town for the next six days and he saw her at least once each day. It was the beginning of a strange, bizarre relationship, a relationship that was completely new and unusual to her and which she was unable to define. Even from the very beginning, after that first night, he acted in many ways like a lover. The following morning, when she arrived at the theater, there were a dozen red roses waiting for her backstage. There was a card with nothing on it but "Jack."

He telephoned her that afternoon at the apartment and luckily found her in. He didn't give his name—during the entire ten years of their relationship it was a characteristic of his that he never said who was calling when he phoned, as though it never occurred to him that she could expect a call from anyone else—merely said "Hello."

She said hello and waited and there was a long silence.

"Can I see you after the show tonight?" he asked.

She knew even then who it was although it was the first time she had heard his voice over the phone, but she asked who was calling anyway.

"Why Rafferty," he said, as though surprised that she had to ask.

She thanked him for the flowers and again there was the silence.

"About tonight," he repeated at last.

"I guess so," she said and even as she spoke the words she wondered why. But she said yes without thinking and before she had a chance to change her mind, he said, "Thank you," and hung up.

She thought it was strange that he hadn't told her where he would pick her up, at the theater or at her apartment, and then she wondered how he happened to have her phone number in the first place. Later, after she knew him better, she realized that he had undoubtedly noted it while he'd been in her apartment the previous evening. It was typical of him, noting everything and remembering everything.

He was at the stage door, this time wearing a shiny blue serge suit and the same brown scuffed shoes. He had on a blue shirt again of a slightly different hue. They went to the same steak house they had gone to the night before.

If Rafferty had been dour and silent the previous evening, something certainly had happened to him. This time he talked incessantly. And during those times when he saw her during the following week, he kept on talking. He told her about his family, his wife and daughter and his two sons, he told her about his home life and his work with the union. He talked about his early years and his life in the orphanage.

The odd part of it was that he always talked as though he were speaking of someone else and not himself. He didn't refer to himself in the third person, but she always had the feeling that he was talking about a man who was not present. It was probably because of the way he talked and the things he did say. He gave her facts and dates and places and chronological events, but never once did he allow himself, his feelings and his emotions, to come through. After that first night, he never asked her about herself or her own life. He seemed satisfied merely to be with her, to have her across the table from him in a restaurant, or next to him on the couch in the living room of her apartment.

He sent her flowers each day and when she told him not to, that it was really silly, he laughed and said that he wanted to. Never once did he make the slightest overtures to her, never put the conversation on a personal basis. One night, when she kept a date with someone else, which she had made weeks before, he sounded disappointed and hurt over the phone, but when he saw her the next day, he said nothing about it and asked her no questions.

The night before he was to return to the Coast he mentioned Tommy Faricetti for the first time. They were having an after-theater supper in a small East Side restaurant where she'd had him take her after five consecutive nights at the steak place—by this time she'd come to believe that his diet consisted only of rare steak and French-fried potatoes—and the conversation lagged after he'd said he must return home the next day. Finally he'd looked up at her and smiled.

"I'd sort of like you to do something for me," he said.

She watched him curiously, as she nodded, wondering what was coming.

"It's about Tommy Faricetti," he said.

"Yes?"

"Yeah. I don't think you should see so much of him," he said. "You know he's a hoodlum."

She opened her eyes in surprise.

"I thought you and he did business together?" she said.

"We do. I know a lot of hoodlums. I have to in my work."

"Yes, I understand. But isn't Tommy some sort of union official?"

"Of course he is."

"And isn't that what you are?"

He looked at her with an odd, almost baffled expression.

"That's different," he said. "You wouldn't understand. My job, my work, is my whole life. It's the most important thing in the world to me. I'm no hoodlum, no gangster. You wouldn't understand. It's complicated and would take too long to explain. But a guy like Tommy—sure, he's a nice guy I know," he said as she started to open her mouth to protest "—a guy like Tommy Faricetti, he was a racketeer who *came* into organized labor. I was a workingman; I came up through the ranks. I've never been a crook or anything like that."

It was a peculiar attitude he had, an attitude he explained to her countless times during the next ten years she was to know him, and one on which he never deviated.

"Anyway," he said, "you're a young girl, just starting out, and I think it would be better for you if you didn't hang around with men like Faricetti."

"Well, I like that," she said. "He introduced me to you, didn't he? And anyway, what do you care? What am I to you?"

He stared at her for several moments and then shrugged.

"I don't know," he said. "I don't really know."

That first week set the pattern for the next year. It was as though he were courting her and then again it wasn't. During that entire year, he never tried to make love to her, either physically or verbally. Never even attempted to put their relationship on any basis except casual friendship. And yet, each time he came to New York, he sent her flowers and spent every available free moment with her.

He pursued her with all of the avid passion of a lover, but if it was a romance, it was certainly a weird and unusual one. He never wrote her while he was away, but always the day before he would return, he would wire that he was coming. Once or twice he brought her small, inexpensive gifts, costume jewelry and that sort of thing. He never asked questions about what she did or whom she saw while he was gone, but he was almost insanely jealous of her time while he was in town.

They would go to ball games, and sometimes, but rarely, to the race track. He liked simple pleasures. He liked to take her to Coney Island, or he would rent a car and they'd drive out to Jones Beach. He never went swimming himself—it wasn't until years later that she found out that he'd never learned to swim and was too proud to admit it—but he'd sit on the sand and watch her as she swam. He loved to play skill games, throwing balls at stuffed dolls and that sort of thing, but he was a bad loser and he would sulk when he failed to get some sort of prize.

She thought for a long time that he was lonely away from home, but she gradually began to realize that it wasn't that. He saw countless people during his working hours and she knew, through Faricetti, that he could have had a different girl every night of the week if he had cared about it.

Sometimes he would come to her apartment and she'd make dinner for him—by this time she knew that steak and French fries *were* his favorite dinner and that he ate them five nights out of six—and they would sit around and play records.

He still talked a lot about his children and though she had never met them, she felt that she knew them better than her own brothers.

He mentioned his wife now and then, but when he would talk about her in relationship to himself, it was as though he were discussing some casual acquaintances.

He didn't care for nightclubs and he drank only moderately. She never saw him drunk during the first year—except for the one time late in August, almost a year to the day from the first time they had met, when he flew in unannounced from Los Angeles and came to her apartment at three o'clock in the morning to tell her that he had been elected president of the Southwestern Conference.

That was the night that changed everything; the night which started the new era of their relationship.

CHAPTER THIRTEEN

George Morris Ames again handed a sheaf of papers across the table to Chairman Ormand Fellows, who without bothering to look at them, said:

"Once more I should like to ask the witness to identify the papers which I will now hand him. This batch consists of a number of canceled checks, drawn on the account of the Local 702 of the ISU and signed by the treasurer of that local and countersigned by Mr. Rafferty. They date over a period of several years and are all made out to the AC Realty Company of New York City. They vary in sums of from one hundred and fifty dollars to three hundred and ten. Will the clerk please give the witness these checks for purposes of identification?"

He handed the folder across the desk to the clerk, who in turn gave it to the witness.

Rafferty opened the folder and looked at its contents. He looked at perhaps a dozen checks, reading them carefully, before returning them to the waiting clerk.

"Are those checks familiar to you, Mr. Rafferty?" Fellows asked.

"Vaguely."

"Well, are they or aren't they?"

"I've probably seen some of them. I see a good many checks over a period of several years."

"Is that your signature on those checks?"

"I believe that it is."

Fellows nodded.

"These will be entered as Exhibit number ..." his voice trailed off as he handed them to the clerk and then turned again to the Chief Counsel.

"You may continue, Mr. Ames."

Ames stood up and again faced Rafferty. He held the checks in his hand.

"The AC Realty Company is the landlord of the apartment in which Miss Hart lives, is that right?"

"I believe so."

"And these checks were made out for the rent on that apartment. Is that correct?"

"As near as I know, it is correct."

"In other words, Mr. Rafferty, Local 702 of the ISU of which you are and have been President for the last ten years, has been paying Miss Hart's room rent for at least six of those years. Is that correct?"

"It is."

"And can you explain to me exactly why Local 702 should pay the rent ..."

Rafferty didn't wait for the finish of the question.

"Miss Hart," he said, "was an employee of Local 702. If the local paid her rent, it can be considered to have been a part of her salary."

Ames smiled thinly.

"Is it a practice of a local in Los Angeles to pay the rent of its employees? Is it even a practice of a Los Angeles local to have girl employees in New York City?"

"Which question do you want me to answer first?" Rafferty asked, unperturbed.

"Well, does the union make it a practice to pay the rent of its various employees?"

"Yes. Sometimes. I can assure you that when the rent is paid, such as it apparently was in the case of Miss Hart, the sums are deducted from the total salary."

"And what was Miss Hart being paid this salary for?" Ames asked.

There was a sudden titter in the court and Chairman Fellows rapped sharply with his gavel as half a hundred heads turned and looked at Jill Hart.

"This room will be cleared if there is any further demonstration," he said curtly, observing at the same time that the television cameras had switched from Rafferty and the Counsel and now were trained on the section of the room where the woman sat.

This thing is becoming worse than a damned front page murder trial, Fellows thought regretfully. He was a little sorry that the Committee had agreed to go into the Hart business in the first place. He knew that something like this would happen. But it couldn't be helped. It was all a part of the fabric of the case they were trying to put together.

"Miss Hart held a rather unique position with the union," Rafferty said, his voice calm. "She did organization work—a confidential type of ..."

"I see. And a Los Angeles local hires a New York girl then to do organizational work?"

"I didn't say that Miss Hart worked in New York," Rafferty answered, his voice suddenly sharp. "I merely said she did organizational work. She could do it almost any place, New York, Cleveland, Los Angeles ..."

"Las Vegas, or Miami," Ames finished for him, making no effort now to keep the sneer out of his voice.

Mort Kauffman started to get to his feet, his face flushed, to make an objection, but Rafferty quickly reached over and took his arm, shaking his head.

"I am sure," he said quickly, "that Counsel is not so naive as to believe that a local union's sole activity or responsibilities lie within the confines of the city in which it is located. My local, 702, maintains liaisons with many locals in many cities. As head of the Southwestern Conference, my own interests certainly extend far beyond Los

Angeles. I have sent organizers—loaned them in effect—to many locals around the country. It is a common practice"

"Let us return to Miss Hart," Ames said. "You say she was an employee of Local 702. Was she on the regular payroll?"

"She was not."

"And why not?"

"Miss Hart did confidential work, as I have said. Investigative work, often done prior to regular organizing of workers in various sectors. Frequently it was better if she conducted her activities without them being publicized. Consequently, she was carried in a special account."

"And how was she paid?"

"Sometimes in cash, sometimes by checks."

"And you were in charge of this special account?"

"I was."

Ames hesitated a moment or two and looked over at Fellows. Then he swung back and when he spoke, it was obvious that he was about to drop a bombshell. His voice was suddenly high pitched and angry.

"Isn't it true, Mr. Rafferty, that Jill Hart has been your mistress for the last eight or ten years?"

Kauffman was on his feet before the question was completed, screaming objections, and Fellows was banging wildly with the gavel.

This time it was several minutes before Fellows was able to obtain order. He would have carried out his threat and cleared the room but for the fact that half of the disturbance was coming from the press box.

During the interlude, Rafferty, with his right hand firmly pressed over the microphone, talked hurriedly to his lawyer, who kept shaking his head in disagreement. It was obvious, however, that Rafferty would have his way. He began to speak almost as soon as Fellows had given a second warning to those in the room about any untoward demonstration.

"Let me say first," he said, "that I resent Counsel's question and consider it both out of order and impertinent. However, I certainly will answer it rather than leave any implication in the minds of the Committee or the people who are listening in to these proceedings. Miss Hart is not, has never been and will never be 'my mistress' as you put it. As long as Counsel has sought to introduce this element into these hearings, I should like to qualify further my statement if the Chairman will permit me to do so."

He turned and looked from Ames to Senator Fellows.

"You may," Fellows said. "But please keep it short. We want to get on with this hearing, if we may."

Rafferty nodded.

"Thank you," he said. "Miss Hart did confidential work for the union. Certainly there is nothing unusual about that. Management frequently has confidential employees—even the United States Government does. This Committee itself has hired a number of confidential investigators. The fact that Miss Hart is a New Yorker, was at one time a showgirl and may have received widespread publicity recently, is beside the point. No one thinks it is unusual when a manufacturing firm hires models and showgirls to attend their sales conventions and to entertain their customers and I certainly see nothing unusual in having used the services of Miss Hart. What Miss Hart's personal life is, is her own business. Unfortunately, as a labor official, I have had to deal with many types of people. I am not responsible for either the morals or the private lives of the people who work for us. As this Committee knows, it is possible for gangsters and racketeers, for hoodlums and extortionists, to worm their way into unions. People of this ilk have connected themselves with my own union as they have with almost every union in the country. I can only say that when we find out about them, we get rid of them."

He hesitated a moment, and looked down at his hands.

"I am not, of course, putting Miss Hart in the aforementioned category," he said. "I merely say that I am not personally responsible for each and every person connected with an organization as large and complex as is the ISU. And once more, to answer the Counsel's last question: Miss Hart is, or was, merely an employee. I have had no personal relationship with her whatsoever. I can in all truthfulness say that whenever I have had contact with Miss Hart I have been on union business, that union business was the only thing in my mind and that the duties she performed were to advance the cause of Local 702 or of the Southwestern Conference. She has never meant anything to me but a part of my work and my job."

In the back of the room Jill Hart heard the words and almost unconsciously she nodded her head.

Yes, she thought again, in a way he's really telling the truth. Truth in a broad sense of the word. That is what she had meant to him—a part of his job. She'd been a handmaiden to his driving ambition. It had taken her ten years to find it out, but she should have known that first night when he had broken in on her unannounced nine years ago, when he'd flown to New York after being elected President of the Southwestern Conference.

The moment she opened the door of the apartment and saw him standing there, she knew that something had happened. He wasn't wearing a hat, which in itself was unusual, his brown tweed suit was rumpled and unpressed, and his tie was loose, his collar opened. But it wasn't his disheveled appearance that told her. It was the strange, almost fanatical look in his eyes and a peculiar, arrogant expression around his mouth.

She could tell by his whisky breath and the way he stood there staring at her, that he was drunk, and this in itself was enough normally to have surprised her. But there was something else about him, a tenseness, almost an attitude of semi-hysteria, which communicated itself and let her know that something very unusual had happened.

"Jack," she said. "Why, Jack! What in the world are you doing here? How did you get in anyway? It's after three o'clock."

He started to grin then, not moving.

She reached out and took him by the coat sleeve.

"Come in and close the door," she said. "What is the matter? What's happened to you? Why didn't you tell me you were—"

He was in the room now and she closed and snapped the night lock. As she turned around, he suddenly opened his arms wide and threw them around her.

"Baby," he said. "Oh baby!"

He swung her around in a short step, almost stumbling, and then suddenly he kissed her, full on her half-opened mouth.

She had climbed out of bed, stark naked, when she'd heard the apartment bell ringing and had grabbed a thin, sheer nightgown and pulled it on. His strong arms were around her waist as he bent her back and she could feel the short square fingers of one hand on her bare flesh as he held her. For a second or so as he kissed her, pressing his body tight against her own, she was so completely surprised that she was unable to move. And then she pulled her head away from his and stared at him, still held tight in his arms.

"What in the world has happened to you?" she said, more amazed than angry. "For Lord's sake, loosen up. You're breaking my back."

He released her then and staggered over to the couch, flopping down on it.

"Come 'ere," he said. "Come over here, baby, and let me tell you all about it. I'm drunk," he added as though it were an afterthought.

"I'll get you some coffee …"

"No. No, first come here. I'm not that drunk."

She crossed over and as she started to sit down, he reached up and took her hand, pulling her next to him.

"Baby," he said, "you are now talking to the new President of the Southwestern Conference of the ISU. Get it, the President of the Southwestern Conference. They elected me late yesterday afternoon and I grabbed a plane and came to tell you about it as soon as I could get away."

"You must have grabbed something else too," she said.

He didn't even hear her.

"Don't you understand?" he said. "Don't you get it? Me. The new President of the Conference. I'm on my way at last. This is it—this is what I have been working for, slaving for, and dreaming about. I'm started now, really started. The biggest man in the biggest goddamned union in the West. And it's just the beginning. Just the goddamned beginning. Come here and give me a kiss."

He didn't wait but once more pulled her to him, half across his lap and pressed her mouth against his. It was a clumsy, crude kiss and he hurt her lips, but she didn't protest. For the moment she was still too surprised to see him drunk to do much of anything. She suddenly felt his hand pressing hard on her breast and again she jerked and pulled away.

"My God," she said. "You smell. You smell like every distillery in the world. Jack, it's great about your election and I'm just as pleased as you are. But don't break every bone in my body."

She pulled herself to her feet as he looked up at her, his eyes a little crossed.

"Go in the bathroom," she said, "and rinse your mouth out with some mouthwash or whatever you can find. There's a new toothbrush in a wrapper; brush your teeth, and wash your face with cold water. I'm going in and get you some black coffee."

"Coffee, hell," he said. "I'll wash my mouth out and clean up a little—I guess I had one or so too many—but no coffee. I'm not drunk, or at least too drunk. What I want is a rye and water, or whatever you got around. We aren't going to drink to my success with coffee."

She looked at him closely for a moment and she saw that it was true. He wasn't nearly as tight as he had seemed.

"You may not be drunk," she said, "but you did kiss me. Do you realize that? You kissed me."

"I've been wanting to for a long time," he said. "Don't you think it was about time I did?"

She started for the kitchen.

"Did you have to wait until they elected you President of whatever it is out there to decide?" she said over her shoulder.

She mixed two drinks, not really wanting one herself, but knowing that he would be hurt unless she joined him, and returned to the living room. He was still in the bathroom and she went into the bedroom and found a dressing gown and a pair of mules and then went back and waited. He was gone for a long time and when he finally came back, he'd combed his hair and straightened himself out and he looked cold sober. But he still had a wild expression and she could see that he was still keyed up.

He grabbed the drink and lifted it.

"To your success," she said, lifting her own glass.

He downed his drink in a gulp.

For the next hour he talked incessantly, taking several drinks as he told about the election. It had been close and a very tough fight and up until the last minute he hadn't been at all sure. But now he was in and he felt great. He tried to explain to her in detail just what had happened, the deals that had been made and the delegates that he'd been able to influence and reach, but much of it didn't make sense to her. She would nod and say yes, trying to follow him, but really not caring much. Only glad that something had happened which made him happy.

It was odd, the way he talked about it, not actually boasting, but showing how pleased he was. At once expressing surprise that he had made it, but at the same time, fully accepting what had happened as though it was only just and proper.

While he talked, he held her hand tight in his, only releasing it when he would ask her to pour another drink.

After an hour, he got up and took off his jacket and tie, and she suggested he'd be more comfortable if he kicked off his shoes. She said, "Jack, how come you came here? Why didn't you go home? You could have wired me. I ..."

For a second he stared at her and then spoke slowly. "It seemed this was the natural place to come," he said.

Once more he took both of her hands and this time he pulled her to him, still staring into her face. "The most natural thing. You are the one I wanted to know; the one I wanted to share it with me."

She felt the power in him, felt the strength in his arms and then, before she knew what she was doing, she leaned close to him and this time it was her lips which found his.

That night she slept with him for the first time. Later she had tried to analyze it, probing her feelings and trying to find out what lay behind them. But self-analysis failed to give her an answer. She had responded to his own ardor, his wild, passionate and uncontrollable desires, immediately, and it wasn't until long after that first night that she had come to realize his lack of finesse, his crudeness and impatience. But perhaps these were the very qualities which in some perverse way attracted her. He had been almost brutal in his overwhelming desire to possess her, careless and hurried and yet inexhaustible.

They finally slept and it was long past daybreak when at last they awoke, simultaneously and finding their arms twined around each other still from their last breathless moment of ecstasy.

He had talked to her then and for the first time he talked like a lover. He knew at once that the night had changed things and that from now on their relationship would be on a new and a different plane. He spoke as though he had never known her before, had only that night met her for the first time.

"You're what I've been looking for all of my life," he said, lying on his side, his arms still around her and looking into her face with sober thoughtful eyes.

She smiled at him.

"I guess this is what they mean by love," he said.

"You've never been in love before?" she couldn't help asking.

He knew at once what she meant.

"I've told you about Martha," he answered. "We were kids, and, well, the thing was really pretty much of an accident. If it hadn't been for her old man ..."

"Yes, you've told me," she said. "But it doesn't change things. You're still married to her, you still have the children."

"I'm married to her, yes," he said. "But you have to understand about it. It's habit. Just something that I seem always to have done. We have the children and we have our home—not that I have much of a chance to spend a great deal of time there—but the truth is, we never did mean a great deal to each other. It was never like this—never."

She knew that he was telling the truth, but she couldn't help wondering if the truth applied to Martha Rafferty as well as himself.

"Marriage becomes a habit," he repeated. "Almost like smoking, or drinking coffee. It's something that's there. And the sexual part of marriage also becomes a habit. A custom."

She pulled a little away from him.

"You mean," she said, "that you reach for your wife like you reach for a cigarette?" She couldn't keep a bitter note out of her voice. But if she expected him to protest, she was disappointed.

"Yes," he said. "That *is* what I mean. If you are not in love with your wife—and I know of almost no one who is after a dozen years of marriage, that is exactly what I mean."

He suddenly laughed and reached for her and pulled her to him and kissed her ear.

"The hell with marriage," he said, "and the hell with cigarettes. What I want is you. Now."

She started to protest, to pull away, but she was helpless as his strong hands held her down, one on each arm, and his mouth found hers, smothering the words which she would say. A moment later and she felt all resistance melt and once more she stretched out pulling him to her and entwining her arms and legs around his heaving, frantic body.

Later they showered and she made coffee and toast and orange juice and once more he sat across the table from her, as fresh and alive as the new day. He talked as they ate, again going over the story of the election and his elevation to the presidency, going into details and gleefully explaining the deals and the clever maneuvers which had landed him in the position.

"Things are going to be different now," he said. "Very different. I'll be operating on almost a national scale. And another thing, I'll have more money. A lot more money."

It was strange, but she had never thought about him in connection with money. He'd always seemed to have enough, although he was anything but a spendthrift and she had assumed that he made an adequate salary.

"Not," he hastily added, "that the money is the important thing. The money doesn't mean anything to me. Except a certain convenience. I'd have taken the job with no additional money—God, I'd probably have paid to get it."

She knew what he meant. She'd listened to him long enough, knew him well enough to understand. The union was his work and his life. He had a driving unconquerable ambition to be the biggest man in the entire labor movement. And yet, it wasn't really the workers themselves who interested him. The working man had ceased to be an individual with Rafferty; he'd become merely a symbol. It was the union itself which was important, or perhaps, even more than that, it was his own position in the union which was the paramount thing.

The money would be nice to have; he admitted as much. But what drove him on was his essential need to become the biggest wheel of them all. He was like the schoolboy who tries to get the very highest marks in his class, not because it means that he is smarter or has learned more but because it makes him stand out head and shoulders above his schoolmates.

This she vaguely understood and the fact that even now with the bed they had so recently vacated still damp and warm from their love, he chose to talk of his work, was proof to her of the all-importance of it to him.

"It has been the greatest night of my life," he said at last. "The greatest."

Long afterward when she remembered the remark, she would wonder if he had been referring to their hours of passion, or if he meant his election to the union office. Finally she decided that somehow or other the two things blended together in his mind and had become interchangeable.

They were finishing their second cup of coffee, when he said, not looking at her, "I want to see if you can't get a bigger apartment. This place is cramped. I'm going to have to spend more and more time in New York and ..."

He saw the sudden surprised look on her face and hesitated.

"We're supposed to start living together?" she said, making it a question.

"Well," he said, "you're my girl, aren't you?"

She nodded slowly.

"Yes, Jack," she said. "I guess I'm your girl all right. But aren't you sort of forgetting about Los Angeles?"

He didn't blush, didn't hesitate.

"No," he said. "I'm not forgetting. I never forget. But you have to understand how it is. Hell, I can't get a divorce. Not now I can't. In the first place, it wouldn't look good. It would hurt me in my work. In the second place there are the kids. You know how I feel about them. I can't do anything to hurt them or to upset them. No, things have to remain as they are, at least for a while. These things have to be done gradually. But that shouldn't interfere. You know what my relationship is with Martha. You know how infrequently I get home."

"Yes—I know," she said, unable to keep a thin edge of bitterness out of her voice. "Like a cigarette."

He looked up at her quickly, annoyed. But then suddenly he laughed.

"I don't inhale," he said, "Now come on, snap out of it, kid. Don't spoil things. I feel too good to—"

He jumped up and pulled her to her feet and the minute he grabbed her, pulling her to him and kissing her, she forgot her irritation and anger and succumbed to his own carefree enthusiasm. She decided that things had just happened too fast and that sooner or later they would straighten out. He'd need time; they'd both need time.

He left her that morning before noon, and he tried to talk her into taking a larger apartment, but on that she was adamant. She would stay on where she was. She couldn't afford to pay more rent and when he started to say that he would be glad to help out and that it was only fair that he should—putting it on the basis that now and then he'd like to use the place to entertain business friends—she'd quickly disagreed.

"Let things stay as they are," she told him. "That's what you yourself suggested, you know."

They did stay that way, for more than a year. He would come to New York every two or three weeks and check into a hotel. But he never slept there. He always came to her apartment when he was through working, through with his endless conferences and appointments.

It might have gone on like this indefinitely if it hadn't been for her losing her job simultaneously with a sudden depression in show business. By this time she'd learned that she would never really be a singer; she just didn't have the voice for it. And she had grown lazy and indolent and given up working on dancing and so finally, when she at last found herself out of work and unable to find a part, she'd spent the last of her savings and was becoming desperate for something to do. By then she'd been Rafferty's mistress for more than two years.

Another man would have known about it, have been interested enough to have learned her condition, but Rafferty had never asked her questions and had always taken her work for granted. It wasn't until she told him that she was going to have to give up the apartment that he learned of her circumstances.

"All right," he said. "We'll do what I wanted to do in the beginning. You're going to move. Get a bigger place."

"Great," she said. "I can't pay for this one and so ..."

"There's just the point," he said. "So I'm going to pay the rent—or rather the union is. And you can work for me from now on. I've been telling you for a long time that I need a spot in New York to entertain in. Now that we're trying to get Sam Farrow in as President of the International, it's more important than ever that we have some sort of informal headquarters in New York where we can entertain and confer with certain important people. And so ..."

"And so you think it is a good idea to have it become known that you are using your girl's apartment ..."

"You don't understand," he said. "A lot of things which happen in union politics go on behind the scenes, so to speak. I'm always meeting people, people from all over the country, unofficially and in private. The informality of a private apartment is ideal—a hell of a lot better than a hotel room, which can be bugged and where the phone can be tapped. No, this is what we will do. See if you can't get another apartment in this building—at least two bedrooms, a bigger living room. I'll take care of the rent and all of the expenses. And don't bother anymore about getting a job. I'll have things for you to do. Union work which you can handle confidentially. But your main job will be to keep up the apartment, have it available when I want to use it to bring people in for private talks."

She'd moved at the end of the month to a larger apartment two floors above in the same building. And from that time on Rafferty took care of the rent. Sometimes he gave her cash to pay for it, but more often he sent checks directly to the landlord. It began a new era in her life and a new era in her relationship with Jack Rafferty.

She knew that at least until his children were raised and through school, he would never break up his home. She would have to be content to assume a sort of permanent position as his mistress, secure only in the knowledge that she was the only woman who really meant anything to him. If the thought frequently disturbed her and made her unhappy, at least she took refuge in the belief that she was the only woman he loved and the only woman he slept with. It wasn't everything, but it was something.

Rafferty arranged to give her a hundred dollars a week to live on.

"It's like this," he explained. "I don't want you taking some cheesy job. I'm going to put you on the union payroll; we'll take care of the rent and you'll get a hundred a week. And expenses. It will come out of a special account."

"And just what am I supposed to do for this?" she asked, adding, wickedly, "as though I didn't know, of course."

He looked at her seriously, half shaking his head.

"That you do," he said, "because you are supposed to love me. No, I'll see that you have things to keep you busy. As I say, I'll want the apartment now and then for entertaining. I'll want you too, as a sort of hostess. But there are other things. We have trouble spots, places where we are fighting to get plants and factories organized. You can come in mighty handy. No one is going to know who you are or what your connection is. We'll be able to use you. Send you out where we are having trouble. You can take a temporary job, where it can be arranged, and send us information. Who's fighting to keep the union out, which employees are 'company' men or women, as the case may be. That sort of thing. There will be other things also.

"There will be times when we'll want you to move into a town and get to know certain people. The wives of workers. Wives talk. You can learn a lot which will be valuable to us. Which men are for us and which aren't. That sort of thing."

She nodded, thoughtfully.

"Sort of like a spy?" she said.

He looked at her and shook his head, annoyed.

"No," he said. "No, not like that at all. We have to have confidential agents, the same as management does. We have to know what's what and who is who. There are other things; there will be times when I will want to find out who my own friends are, who is really with me and who is against me. It isn't only the wives who talk; men talk too. And they talk a lot more readily to a beautiful woman than they do to anyone else."

"Isn't it going to make it a little difficult?" she asked, "the fact our names have been linked by newspaper and gossip columnists. That a good many people know already that we are ..."

He shook his head.

"Nobody in the sticks reads the New York gossip mongers. That's where you will be working mostly, outside of New York. No, don't worry about that part of it. A lot of people may have guessed a lot of things about us, but no one, no one but you and myself, really knows how we stand."

It was true to a certain extent. Things had changed a great deal in recent years, but he still played it very cagey. Of course, as Rafferty had matured, had grown more used to being in New York, his own circle of friends had changed to a great extent and so had his habits. She'd managed to get him to go to a good tailor, had taught him how to buy and wear clothes. They no longer only went to the obscure East Side steak house for dinner, but frequently hit the better-known spots. Now they did go to nightclubs and Broadway shows together and the old days of Coney Island and the baseball games were very infrequent now. But rarely were they seen in public alone. Almost always there were two or three other men in their party and frequently another woman or two.

For the first year or so after the new arrangement he frequently gave her jobs to do out of town. They were jobs she always hated, working herself into the confidence of people and then reporting back on their activities. She never complained, but he seemed to understand her distaste for the work and he sensed her discontent. Gradually the assignments became less and less frequent and finally it was only on rare occasions that she left New York.

It was during this period that Farrow became President of the national organization and she knew that Rafferty's support had played a vital role in his elevation to office.

The apartment became an unofficial meeting place for important union men from all over the country and Rafferty entertained constantly when he was in town. Often she would be present and a number of times he had her act as a sort of liaison agent in finding girls to entertain influential friends.

She was widely acquainted with showgirls and models as a result of her work in those fields and never had difficulty in digging up dates for Rafferty's important friends. She knew that often the girls she found for these parties and blind dates were little better than prostitutes and the knowledge frequently upset and bothered her. She protested to Rafferty, but he passed it off casually.

"Listen, honey," he would say, "so what! My God, these guys are only human. If they don't sleep with one girl, they will with another. What's the difference?"

"The difference," she said, "is that I'm being put in the position of a procuress."

"Nuts," he said. "I'm not asking you to go out with them. All I'm asking is that you find the girls. What they do, or what the men do, is their own business. We can't be the moral guardians of the world. Do you think these union guys are any different from anyone else? Hell, half of the big business deals that are made, the heavy contracts and so forth, are arranged because some salesman or company executive gets the right guy laid."

"Well, because big business does something, does that make it okay?" she asked.

He shook his head.

"You don't understand these things," he said. "What do you think a union is? It's big business itself. Anytime an organization has a couple of million dollars, or ten million, or fifty million, it's big business. Anyway, don't let it worry you. This sort of thing happens all the time. Look, you've made dates for union leaders, but don't forget, you've also arranged to get girls for big men in politics—men who sit on legislative councils in Washington. In this life you have to be a realist."

And that's the way it had been.

CHAPTER FOURTEEN

Their affair, over the years, had settled into a steady routine until, in some ways, it was almost like a marriage. He took her for granted and saw her as frequently as he could. His sexual ardor failed to cool with time, but no longer did he mention his wife and his children or any plans for breaking up his marriage. She knew after a while that he never would, that at no time had he ever planned to change that relationship.

When he had to be away from New York for extended periods, such as the time he spent two months in the South, he would have her come out to where he was and check into a hotel. He always arranged that she check in under another name, and the name would be legitimate.

She would be registered as Mrs. John Schmidt, or Mrs. this or that, and there was always a man who would be the other party of the act. A man who was a close friend from some other town. The man would take the room under his name, ostensibly for himself and wife. When she would arrive, she would already be registered, but the man who had made the registration would have disappeared and Rafferty would show up. He usually had a suite in the same hotel and it was a simple case of walking across a hallway or up or down a couple of flights of stairs.

A good many of Rafferty's friends in the union knew of the arrangement; the press itself had hinted of the relationship a hundred times. But there was never anything that could be proved.

It was after Sam Farrow began having his trouble that a subtle change took place in their relationship. Farrow was virtual dictator of the International and Rafferty was closer to him than any other local boss. Rafferty had worked hard to get Farrow the top position and already he was being talked about as the heir apparent. And then, less than a year ago, Farrow had been indicted on income tax fraud. This had been followed by the forming of the so-called Rackets Committee by Congress and the handwriting was on the wall.

Rafferty, pleading the urgency of business, saw her less frequently, but he was constantly in touch with her.

"This is the time I really need you," he would tell her. "Farrow is through, nothing can save him. And it's my chance. My big chance. I've got to line up the locals and the district conferences, get my delegates together. I have strength, strength all over the country, but I have to be sure. You can be a big help."

He started her arranging parties for friends visiting New York, when he himself wasn't present, and soon she found that he expected her to entertain personally certain important men.

"They've heard of you," he would say, "and they want to meet you. You understand how it is, baby. You're a glamorous figure. All you have to do is be nice to them. They won't get rough with you; they know how we stand. But I want you to take them out and be nice."

That was the way she had met Karl Offenback and it wasn't until after her experience with him that she'd finally put her foot down. Finally told Rafferty that she was through; that she'd get a job if she had to, but that from then on, there would be no more entertaining of his friends and business associates unless he was around himself.

Offenback was the President of a southern local of the union. He had never been overly friendly with Rafferty and several times in the past he had fought him. He was a big, red-faced Dutchman who had come up from the rank and file, and he had little liking for friends of Sam Farrow. He had little national importance, but he controlled his own local with an iron hand and also had a great deal of influence with various southern delegates. Rafferty had been trying to get his backing for a long time.

He'd called her from San Francisco about it.

"Want you to go down to New Orleans," he said. "You are going to be checked into the Southern Hotel. Under the name of Mrs. Karl Offenback. Karl's a big man down that way …"

"Yes," she said. "I know. You've told me about him."

"Get a plane out tonight," he said, "so that you'll be there tomorrow. Just check in. I'll be along in the evening sometime. Karl will be there when you arrive. I want you to be nice to him. He's very important to me, so be nice. Understand?"

"Jack," she said, "couldn't we just skip it this time? I've got a tryout for a new show and …"

"We can't skip it, kid," he said. "This guy Offenback is terribly important to me. Klein has been trying to reach him and so have some of the others. Now you do what I say. I want to see you, anyway, and that's the main reason I want you down there. You do what I say. Get in by noon tomorrow. Karl will meet you at the airport and you check in with him and then wait for me."

He hung up as she started to answer.

And so she had shrugged and called the airport for a reservation.

She arrived in New Orleans at ten-thirty the following morning and even as she climbed down the landing ladder, she looked into the faces of the crowd below her and spotted a man who could be no other than the union official. He was watching her with a big smile on his heavy, brick-red face.

Offenback was a man in his fifties, big and beefy. He wore a flowered Hawaiian shirt, open halfway down to his navel to expose a mat of iron-gray hair. His white trousers were held up by a wide belt above white doeskin saddle shoes. He had a fan in one hand and in the other a half-smoked cigar.

Aside from two elderly women who looked as though they might be retired schoolteachers, she was the only other female getting off and he came toward her at once.

Reaching for her arm, he said, "Jill?"

She nodded, smiling up at him. He had very pale, small, faded blue eyes under white eyebrows and she saw that his teeth were yellow and broken and that his face, in spite of its cheerful, good-natured expression, had at some time in the past been badly beaten in and pushed around. His hairy arms were like piano legs and he was a big man, well over six feet tall. His stomach bulged out, but there was nothing soft about his thick hard body.

"Car's over in the lot," he said, gesturing. "Gimme the bag."

He took her suitcase, after putting the cigar stump back in his mouth, and propelled her along, still holding her arm. They didn't speak until they were settled in what was very obviously a rented two-tone convertible.

"Just got in a couple hours ago myself," he said. "I already checked us in at the hotel. What time you expectin' Jack?"

"This evening," she said. "I ..."

"Good, then we got the afternoon to kill. You wanna go out to the track maybe, or would you rather hang around and have a few snorts."

"Why—why I guess by the time we get there I could use a little lunch. Then if you like, the track sounds like a good idea."

"Fine," he said. "Jack said I should take care of you till he gets here." He turned and looked down at her. "An' that will be a pleasure," he said. "A real pleasure, Miss."

She remembered to smile and answered, "Sure. It will be a pleasure for me too."

He didn't stop at the desk, but steered her to the elevator. He already had the key to the room and he allowed her to enter first.

"You get yourself freshened up," he said, "and I'll mix a drink."

He walked ahead of her into the single bedroom and tossed the bag on the bed. Turning he grinned at her and as she passed him, he suddenly reached out and gave her a careless pat on the fanny.

"Need a drink, eh baby?" he said.

She was so surprised that for a second she just stood, too amazed to be indignant.

He ignored her expression and started for the kitchenette off the living room, saying, "After all, you *are* Mrs. Karl Offenback and Mrs. Offenback always has a drink before she does anything." He laughed as he said it.

She closed the door then and shrugged.

Well, she'd met plenty of Jack's friends before and nothing much surprised her. This clown was a little more crude than a lot of them, but he seemed good-natured enough.

They had two drinks at his insistence and then went down to the dining room and ordered lunch. He ate like a man who never again expected to see food. Later, they climbed into the rented car and went out to the track. He drove with one hand, putting his arm over the back of the seat so that it rested gently on her shoulder and when she squirmed a little, he looked down at her, surprised.

"What's a matter," he said, "you itchy?"

She forced a smile.

"No, just a little warm," she said, trying to make her voice friendly. She decided to take things in her stride and be as pleasant as possible. She only had the afternoon to get through and then Jack would be arriving and would take this oaf off of her hands.

Offenback was a heavy better, laying two or three hundred dollars on every race. He had an almost phenomenal ability to pick losers, and despite the fact that several times he laid his bets across the board, he never cashed a winning ticket. Each time he would insist on giving Jill half the tickets he bought and although the afternoon cost him a small fortune, he never lost his good humor.

"Well," he'd say, carelessly tearing up the valueless stubs, "that's me. No luck. It's like the man says, lucky in love, unlucky at cards."

He carried a quart flask with him and openly drank from it during the afternoon, but the liquor didn't seem to have any effect on him. Jill tried to match his gaiety, but refused to drink from the flask, and she found it a little heavy going. He had a crude, boisterous good humor along with an irritating habit of reaching over and pinching her thigh when he'd tell one of his rather dirty and pointless stories. He talked very little about himself and asked her no questions about either herself or Rafferty, but seemed content merely to drink and bet and tell his bad jokes.

They left after the last race and returned to the hotel. She was a little surprised when he rode up in the elevator, and said to him, "Well, I'm sure Jack will be getting in pretty soon now so I guess I'd better excuse myself and go in and take a shower. I feel hot and kind of sticky after that crowd this afternoon."

"I'll come in and we can send down and get some ice and mix and have a decent drink," he said. He still had the key to the room and he opened the door.

She hesitated a moment at the threshold.

"Perhaps a little later," she said. "I would like to rest up now for a bit."

"Now see here," he said, jovially, half pushing her into the room. "See here. We gotta have a drink. Old Jack told me you would sort of entertain me while we were waiting for him and …"

He closed the door behind them and she mentally cursed Rafferty. It was one thing for him to tell her to be nice to Offenback; it was something again telling Offenback that she would "entertain" him.

"Ol' Jack needs me, baby," he said. "And he knows it, too."

For the first time his gruff voice lost some of its jollity and she looked up at him quickly.

He smiled at once.

"Don't you worry about Karl, kitten," he said. "Now you just sit down and take it easy and I'll order up the booze."

He went to the house phone and asked for room service.

Jill looked at her watch and saw that it was after six. He finished putting in his order and then fell onto the couch next to her. As he did, the telephone rang and he motioned to her to answer it.

Rafferty was on the other end.

"Jill?"

"Where are you?" she asked at once. "I just got back from the ..."

"Listen, Jill," Rafferty said. "I've been delayed. I probably won't get in until very late tonight."

"Oh Jack," she started, but he quickly interrupted her.

"Listen," he said. "Did Offenback meet you?"

"Why yes," she said. "He's here now. Do you want ..."

"No—no," he said. "No, but remember what I told you. I want you to be nice to him. If he wants to take you out this evening or do something to kill the time until I get there, I want you to entertain him. Understand, kid? It's very important."

"But Jack ..."

"No buts, honey," he said. "Just do like I say. It means everything to me."

She hunched her shoulders.

"All right," she said. "All right, Jack. But you'll be here tonight for sure ..."

"For sure," he said. And then the line was dead.

Offenback was looking at her, his eyes amused, as she hung up. Later she remembered thinking that it was almost as though he'd been listening in on the conversation.

"It was Jack," she said. "He won't be in until a little later."

"Great," he said. "That's fine. Now I'll tell you what. The booze will be here in a minute—why don't we call back and have the bellhop bring up a menu? You said you're kinda tired and we can just have dinner right here in the room. Nice and cozy like."

She started to protest, but he was already on the phone.

When the whisky and soda and ice arrived she had one drink with him and then excused herself, saying she wanted to wash up before they ate.

"Don't you want to go to your hotel and change?" she asked. He looked at her blankly for a moment and then he laughed.

"Hell," he said, "I'm as clean as I'll ever be. No, you go on in the can and clean up if you want. I'll just have another slug while we're waitin'."

She entered the bedroom and closed the door after herself and as she walked toward the bathroom, she saw for the first time that there was a man's pigskin suitcase on the floor next to the bed. She stopped in shocked surprise and then went over and examined it. There were gold initials on the lock flap—K.O.

Her face was red with fury when she swung open the door of the room.

"Is that your bag in there?" she asked.

He looked up surprised.

"Why sure," he said. "Sure it's my bag. I had to check it, didn't I? You think I could check in without luggage?"

"I understand that," she said coldly, "but haven't you taken another room for yourself? Haven't you ..."

"Listen," he said. "I just done what Jack told me to do. He said check in as Mr. and Mrs. and I did. He told me to wait here and after he gets here I'll change over and take his room and he'll come in here. What's eating you, anyway?"

For a moment more she stared at him. And then she shrugged. She wondered why she had suddenly lost her temper. The man was right. It was the way it was usually arranged. It was just that she'd been disappointed by Jack's calling and saying he would be late.

She forced a smile. After all, it wasn't Offenback's fault. "Oh, all right," she said. "But make me another drink—not too strong. I'll be back in about ten minutes."

This time she went in and quickly stripped down and climbed under the shower. When she got out, she was still hot and quickly put on shorts and a white tailored shirt over her brassiere and panties. She didn't bother with stockings, just thrust her feet into mules. She wouldn't be going out until Jack arrived and she might as well be comfortable.

The drink he handed her tasted like straight whisky, but she made a face and swallowed it. She felt as though she could use a stiff drink. It was going to be a dull, boring evening.

He'd ordered champagne with their dinner and he insisted that she drink along with him. Jill was still tired from her trip and the afternoon, and the wine really hit her. Even before the meal was over, she knew she was a little high.

He didn't talk while they dined, but studiously shoveled food into his face. She wondered where he put it all.

When they had finished eating, he poured two small glasses of liqueur from a flask that he retrieved from his bag in the bedroom.

"Very special," he said. "Creme de menthe. I got it in New York one time. Makes your dinner settle."

She protested, but he insisted and rather than argue, she downed the drink. It had an odd taste which she found rather bitter.

It wasn't until she felt the dizziness coming over her that she realized something was wrong. She felt faint and had trouble focusing her eyes and she only vaguely remembered his saying something to her and then she was staggering into the bedroom. She tossed off her mules and fell on the white counterpane, staring at the ceiling, knowing that she must be drunk.

She heard doors open and close in the other room and the rattle of dishes and realized that the waiter had come to clean up. It was the strangest sensation; she was conscious and knew what was happening, but she felt almost as though she were in a dream.

She must have closed her eyes and fallen asleep because the next thing she knew was that the door had slammed. She looked up weakly and saw Offenback standing there looking down at her.

Without a word he crossed over and pulled down the blinds. She started to get up as he slumped down on the bed next to her.

"Just stay where you are, baby," he said. "You look good just as you are."

She was still weak and dizzy, but she struggled to sit up. He reached over and pushed her back with one hand.

"Look," he said, "what's the matter with you anyway? You think you're too good for me or something? Now you just be a nice little girl and ..."

"Get out," she said. "Get out of here right now. If Jack ..."

"I'm as good a man as Jack ever was, sweetheart," he said. "If you don't think so, well then you got a real nice surprise coming."

"If you don't get out of this room this minute," she said, "I'll call downstairs and have you thrown out."

He laughed.

"Yeah? Listen, you checked in here as my wife, didn't you? What the hell do you think a man and his wife do? Don't you think they know downstairs? Now you just be nice an' ..." He leaned over suddenly, his hand reaching for her shirt.

She tried to sit up but he half slapped her and she fell back, a frightened, startled look on her face.

"I said be nice," he said.

"When Jack gets here," she started, but his harsh laugh interrupted her.

"Screw Jack," he said.

And then suddenly he was on her.

It was like the time it had been with the butcher, when she was a child. He ripped the clothes from her body even as she attempted to struggle and when she scratched at him, he struck her a hard blow in the pit of her stomach with his fist. She doubled up in pain and as she lay there gasping and breathless, he casually took off his own garments.

Only once did she fight back, when he threw himself on her, but again he struck at her, hitting her on the side of the neck. The blow all but paralyzed her. She knew then that fighting him would be meaningless. So she lay and suffered and writhed under his brutality, trying to dull her mind and her senses. She thought of Rafferty and once during the next hour, when he was still and quiet, lying half off of her, she spoke in a whisper. "He'll kill you. You know that, don't you? He'll kill you when he gets here."

He laughed harshly.

"Rafferty won't kill anyone," he said. "But baby with what you got, you'll probably kill me before I let you up."

A hundred times that night she lay there and prayed for Rafferty, but Rafferty never arrived. Somewhere around three o'clock in the morning, Offenback climbed out of bed and got into his clothes. The room was black, but she could hear his movements as he fumbled around and dressed. He left the room after stumbling over a chair and cursed and she could hear the outer door slam behind him.

She was sick in the bathroom for a full half hour before she found strength to stagger out into the other room, and go to the door and snap the burglar lock. And then she sat down on the couch and began to cry.

It wasn't until late afternoon the next day that she heard from Jack Rafferty. Again he telephoned and before she'd even had a chance to more than answer, he said:

"Sorry, Jill about last night. My plane got grounded in Kansas City. I tried to call you but the hotel said no one was answering. Anyway, I just talked to my office and I have to get up to Cleveland at once. Something very important. You go on back to New York and I'll call you there."

"Jack," she said. "Jack, listen. I'm …"

"Do what I say, honey. Get back to New York."

He hung up as she started to cry into the mouthpiece.

She stayed on at the hotel for another twenty-four hours, too sick and weak to move, and then she packed her bag and took a taxi to the airport and returned to the apartment in New York.

It wasn't until three weeks later that she was able to reach Rafferty. He was always out when she called and he never once got in touch with her although she left messages for him each time.

When he finally showed up in New York it took her a long time to tell him what had happened. By then she wanted more than anything else in the world to forget it. He waited until she was all through, sitting grimly listening as she glossed over the details.

"He didn't really hurt you?" he asked at last, when she was finished. "You know—I mean he didn't actually injure you inside or anything, did he?"

She looked at him in amazement.

"Is that all you have to say?"

"What can I say?" he asked. "The man's a sonofabitch. He should be arrested and sent to the pen. But what can we do about it? There's nothing now we can do."

"Well, I should think that you …"

He reached over and took her hand.

"Honey, listen," he said. "It happened. It doesn't make me any happier than it does you. But it was just one of those things. What can I do? Denounce him? And have it turn out I sent you down there to register as his wife? No, I can't do that. You want me to go looking for him with a gun? Well, maybe …"

She looked away from him.

"No," she said. "No, I don't want anything like that. It's just that—" she hesitated and then turned and looked into his face.

"Jack," she said, "you should have come. You should have been there when you said you would be there."

"Look, honey," he said, "you know when I'm on union business my life isn't my own. You know that I can't control my time. That the union comes first, always, and that ..."

Suddenly she was no longer listening, no longer hearing his words as his voice droned on. There was something terribly familiar about those phrases he had used; she seemed to have heard them a hundred times before. Not that he had used them with her—no that wasn't it. And yet they were so familiar. And then she knew why. They were the same words and phrases she had heard him use time after time when he was alibiing to one of his associates. Trying to explain away something which had happened when he had been in the wrong.

For the first time in her entire relationship with him, she suddenly doubted him. Was he telling the truth? Had his plane really been grounded in Kansas City? Had he tried to telephone?

Quickly she shook her head. She was beginning to imagine things. Wasn't this the way he always talked? And it meant nothing that she hadn't been able to reach him for three weeks. That had happened before.

She must be insane to doubt him. She trusted him; she had to trust him. For a moment she was ashamed of herself for her doubts. She thought of the trust and faith which he had in her; thought of the hundred thousand dollars in negotiable securities and cash which he had been keeping in the wall safe in her apartment for more than three years now. The safe to which only she had the combination. Would a man who had that kind of faith in her be likely not to deserve her own complete trust?

No, it was the way he said. He'd missed his plane and missed arriving. He couldn't have known what would happen.

Mort Kauffman stood up and faced Chairman Fellows.

"Senator," he said, "before this wiretapped recording is put into evidence, I should like to object strenuously. The United States Supreme Court has ruled that wiretapping is illegal and that it may not be used in evidence against any ..."

"I would like to remind Counsel," Senator Fellows interrupted, "that this is not a court of law. I should also like to remind Counsel that the recording of this wiretapping was made legally in the State of New York, prior to the time that wiretapping was outlawed and as a result it is perfectly legal. Further that a New York State Grand Jury has admitted this identical wiretap as evidence and that ..."

"But, Senator," Kauffman interrupted, "that decision is under appeal at the present time. Wiretapping has been outlawed by the Federal

Government itself, which this very Committee represents. I cannot stand here and quietly see this recording used against …"

Fellows rapped the table with his gavel.

"If you wish to make an objection, it will be entered in the record."

"I do."

"Objection overruled," Fellows said. "You may proceed, Mr. Ames."

Kauffman flushed and quickly spoke.

"I ask that a ballot be taken by the full Committee membership," he said. "I feel …"

Fellows looked at him disinterestedly.

"A ballot will be taken. Clerk," he said.

There was a huddle at the committee table and after two or three minutes, Senator Fellows again turned to Rafferty's attorney.

"Objection is still overruled," he said. "Proceed, Mr. Ames, if you will."

"I would like to call Detective Sergeant O'Brien to the stand temporarily," Ames said.

"Has Detective O'Brien been sworn in?"

"He has."

"All right. You may proceed." He turned to Rafferty. "It will not be necessary for you to step down," he said. "Detective O'Brien will stand at one side."

Ames turned to a slender stooped man with a fringe of gray hair around the edges of his bald head.

"Your name, please?"

"Detective Sergeant Wallace O'Brien of the New York Police Department."

"What is your job, Mr. O'Brien?"

"I am on the rackets squad."

Ames handed the officer several sheets of typed paper.

"That is a transcription of a wiretap you made a little over a year ago," he said. "I want you to look at it and tell this committee where and under what conditions you made the tap."

The officer barely glanced at the papers in his hand.

"This is a tap I made at the Office of Local 1610, ISU. The tap was made on the telephone of the Secretary, Tommy Faricetti. The voices are those of …"

Morris quickly held up his hand.

"I will ask you to identify the voices after we have heard the recording, Officer," he said. "That will be all for the moment."

He turned again toward Rafferty and spoke, but his words seemed addressed to no one in particular.

"The following tape recording," he said, "speaks for itself. The only changes or deletions which have been made are those occasions when one of the persons talking used language which is unfit to be repeated in a public place. You may now go ahead with the recording."

Rafferty shoved his chair back and quickly got to his feet.

"Mr. Chairman," he said, his voice strained. "Mr. Chairman, I would like to ask a few minutes' recess while I consult with my attorney."

Senator Fellows looked over at Ames, who half nodded.

"You will be granted fifteen minutes," he said. He pounded on the desk with his gavel. "This hearing will be adjourned while the witness has an opportunity to confer with his attorney."

Rafferty took Mort Kauffman by the arm and quickly began pushing his way through the crowd to the back of the chamber, to the small anteroom they had been assigned for conference purposes. He didn't speak until they were inside and had closed and locked the door.

"Mort," he said, "Mort, you've got to stop this. I don't know what that tap is going to be about, but I don't want it on the record. I don't want it made public."

Mort Kauffman looked at his client and slowly shook his head. He realized that for the first time since the hearing had begun Rafferty was losing his air of supreme self-confidence, was beginning to show the strain.

"How can I stop it?" he asked. "You were there—you heard me object. You saw what good it did …"

"Damn it, Mort," Rafferty said, "they can't do this. It isn't legal. Why, Christ Almighty, the Federal Government has indicted me for using a wiretap in my own office—and here they are turning right around and using a wiretap they have made themselves as a weapon against me. I tell you …"

"Not one they made themselves," Kauffman said. "One made by the New York City police. And one made before the use of wiretapping evidence became illegal."

"What the hell's the difference? Where do they get off, indicting me for making a tap, and then turning around and using a tap of their own as evidence …"

"Now, Jack," Mort said, "for God's sake try and look at this realistically. We've objected. Sooner or later we may be able to make that objection stand up. But this isn't a court of law. There isn't a damned thing we can do at this point to stop them. When you decided you would talk, this is the sort of thing you left yourself open to."

"I decided to talk because I wanted to cooperate," Rafferty said. "I never believed that the sons-of-bitches would stoop ..."

"Now listen, Jack," Mort said, putting a hand on Rafferty's shoulder, "listen. Hang on to yourself. This is no time to blow your top. No time to kid yourself. You know why you decided to talk and so do I. You want Farrow's job and to get it you had to talk. You've been the one who has been yakking about calculated risks. Well you took one and things are turning out to be a little tough. If you'd just take me a little more into your confidence, maybe I could help ..."

"Could you keep that wiretap off the record?"

"I didn't say that."

"All right," Rafferty said. "Then skip it. And I'm taking you into my confidence as much as it is necessary to do. I just don't want that tap made public. But if you can't stop it, well then you can't. I still say I have nothing to worry about. This Committee is trying to wreck my personal reputation, to undermine me with my friends and associates. But they won't get away with it. No sir, by God, they won't get away with it, I think that the American public is smart enough to realize what they are up to."

"Sure," Mort Kauffman said. "Sure. But the point is, are your friends and your associates smart enough?"

Rafferty stared at him for a moment, not smiling.

"Come on," he said at last, "let's get back. But Mort, if there are any more of these taps, try and do something about it. Try and keep them off the record, keep that damned Ames from having them read. Do something; make a deal or ..."

Mort Kauffman looked at his client rather sadly.

"You don't make any deals with this bunch, Jack," he said. "You should know that."

Rafferty stalked out ahead of him, ignoring the remark. Five minutes later and they were once again in their seats behind the table and facing the Committee. And once again the hearing resumed.

"You may now go ahead with the recording," Ames repeated.

There was a sudden hush in the vast chamber as the technician worked over his machine. After a moment or so there was a prolonged squeaking and then a woman's voice was heard.

"Yes, Mr. Faricetti?"

"Get me Lake 4-3442 in New Orleans. I wanna talk with Karl Offenback."

"One minute, please."

There was the sound of confused background noises for several moments and then a second woman's voice spoke.

"Lake 4-3442."

"This is New York calling. May we speak with Mr. Karl Offenback, please?"

"One moment, please."

A husky masculine voice now came on.

"Karl Offenback speaking."

"This is Tommy, Karl."

"Who?"

"Tommy. Tommy Faricetti in New York. Is this Karl?"

"This is Karl. How the dash dash dash are you keed?"

"Fine, Karl. An' how's the larceny down your way?"

"Never better, kid. What's up?"

"I got the big guy here. He wants to talk to you."

"Put the dash dash on."

Once more there was a sound of background noise and then a new voice came on.

"Karl?"

"I thought you were out home, boy. What are you doing with that burglar in New York?"

Laughter.

"Karl, I want to find out how it's coming."

"How what's coming?"

"You know. The boys. How does it look? Have we got everything lined up?"

There was a long hesitation.

Then: "You know what I told you. I can't guarantee to deliver …"

"The hell you can't, Karl. I know better than that. You remember what I told you? Old Sam is finished—all washed up. He may not know it, but that's the way it is. And I'm counting on you to come through. What is it you want? Just name it, kid, and it's yours. I need those dash dash delegates and I have to have them. Just tell me what you want."

"You wouldn't give it to me, cousin."

"Listen, Karl, name it and it's yours. You know me, I never yet made a promise that I didn't damn well keep."

"You ain't going to like giving me what I want, cousin."

"I said name it, didn't I?"

"Maybe you can't give it to me."

"What's with you? Of course I can give it to you. What the hell is it you want? You know I need those delegates and you know damned well I'll pay to get them. So stop your stalling. Name it."

"O.K., cousin. Get a grip on yourself. I want that broad of yours."

"You want what?"

"Your broad. Your girl. That's the price, kid!"

"Are you out of your mind? Maybe I didn't hear you right."

"You heard me right, cousin. I said I want your broad. You want my delegates—well, I want your broad. You said I could have what I want, so how about it?"

"Karl, you're kidding."

"I never kid."

"But Karl, even if I was willing. Good Lord, maybe she might have something to say."

"Nuts. She'll do what you tell her to do. It just happens I got a hard on for her and I want her and that's the price, cousin. You ask me, I'm telling you."

Again there was a long pause and then a woman's voice spoke. "Your three minutes are up, sir, and ..."

"Get the hell off this wire."

"Look Karl, even if you are serious, how the hell do you expect me to talk her into anything as crazy ..."

"You don't have to talk her into nothing, Jack. Just send her down. Check her into the Southern Hotel as Mrs. O. Hell, you been using that business with her all over the country. Everyone knows about it. Have her check in and tell her I'm meeting her. Once we get in the room together, you don't have to worry. Just don't show up and don't worry. I can handle things from there on in."

"Karl, you aren't really serious, are you?"

"I was never more serious in my life. You need the delegates and I'm telling you what it will cost you."

Again there was a prolonged pause.

"O.K., Karl. I'll arrange it. You let me know when you want it set up. Call me Tuesday in L.A. I'll arrange it."

"Good boy. And don't worry about my end of it. My boys vote just exactly the way I tell 'em to."

"I'll count on it. But remember one thing, Karl. I'll get her into the hotel, under your name. After that you're on your own."

"Sure, pal. There won't be no difficulty. I'll call you Tuesday. Right?"

"Right."

Ames waited until the recording was finished and immediately had O'Brien identify the voice. He unhesitatingly did so, identifying the first male voice as that of Tommy Faricetti, the second as Karl Offenback and the last one as that of Jack Rafferty. And then he stepped down. Ames again turned to the witness.

"Now, Mr. Rafferty," he said, "do you recall having had that conversation?"

"I do not."

"But you do admit that that was your voice which was heard speaking?"

"I admit no such thing. I don't recall having been in New York last—" he hesitated, looking down at a paper on which he had been scrawling a note "—last August. I cannot at this time say for sure, but when I have a chance to check my old appointment pad, I will be able to do so. In any case, I flatly deny ever having made such a telephone call."

"But you have talked with Mr. Offenback over the telephone?"

"Frequently. I talk to a good many local officials."

"And you have no recollection of this call?"

"Not only no recollection of it—I deny that that was my voice. As Detective O'Brien himself knows, and you have brought him here as an expert on wiretapping, it is never completely possible to identify a voice over the telephone."

Ames shrugged.

"All right, Mr. Rafferty. However, I should like to remind you that our investigators have testified to the fact that Miss Hart was registered in the Southern Hotel in New Orleans under the name of Mrs. Karl Offenback, on September second of last year. She has been identified by a bellboy and a waiter. We have already established that Miss Hart has been registered a number of times in the past in various hotels around the country, under the names of the wives of various union officials. In each case the hotel bill was paid with a check drawn on Local 702 and the checks were signed by yourself. Now do you still deny …"

Rafferty half stood up as he interrupted. His voice was edged, but his temper was still under control.

"I have already stated my position," he said. "Miss Hart's hotel bills were paid on those occasions when she was on union business. If Miss Hart saw fit to register in hotels with various men as their wife, that is a matter of her personal morals or lack of them. And certainly any questions concerning such matters should be asked of Miss Hart and the men involved. As I have already stated, I cannot be held responsible for the private behavior of each and every person who is connected with the ISU. And I will remind this Committee that I have already gone on record of saying that any time I discover the personal activities or behavior of one of my employees reflects on the integrity of the union, I shall do everything in my power to get rid of that person."

As Rafferty relaxed in his seat, Senator Early stood up, looking over at the Chairman for recognition. Senator Fellows said, "Senator Early has the floor."

Early was very obviously annoyed.

"Mr. Rafferty," the Senator said, "Speaking only on behalf of myself, I wish to apologize for the introduction into this investigation of the type of evidence we have been listening to during the last few minutes. It has been my understanding that the sole purpose of this investigation was to seek information concerning any illegal activities of either labor or management which might lead to legislation to correct such evils. This Committee was not formed to castigate labor or to crucify the personal reputation of any particular labor leader."

He hesitated, taking his eyes from Rafferty and staring coldly at George Morris Ames. "It is my suggestion that Counsel for the Committee return to the work in hand."

As he regained his seat, Chairman Fellows looked down at his wristwatch and saw that it was after four o'clock.

He sighed and rapped several times with his gavel, at the same time standing up.

"We shall try to complete the testimony of this witness before adjourning for the weekend," he said, "if it is at all possible to do so. At this time we will take a fifteen-minute recess."

CHAPTER FIFTEEN

There was no sound in the crowded room as Senator Ormand Fellows called the Committee to order and then indicated to his brilliant young Counsel, George Morris Ames, that he was to proceed.

Ames slowly rose to his feet:

"At this time, Mr. Rafferty," he said, "I would like to go into the matter of certain 'paper locals.' I am referring now to those locals which rarely if ever had members and whose officers were almost without exception men with long criminal records. These locals were used either as a means of extorting protection money from legitimate small businesses, under threat of calling strikes; to pay dues from uneducated and unwilling members who were forced to join them but received no benefits; or to send delegates to regional and national ISU conventions who were instructed to vote for certain preselected candidates.

"Now Mr. Rafferty, you have already testified that you have no knowledge of such locals, that you were unaware of the purposes to which they were put and that you had no business dealings with the men—" he hesitated and pointed to a blackboard behind him on which was a long list of names opposite which were various union titles and criminal records "—with the men who received charters from the ISU and were in charge of these racketeering paper locals."

"I have testified that I had no knowledge as to the methods these locals pursued," Rafferty interrupted, his voice cold and unhurried. "I have never said that I had no business with the men who ran these locals. Of course I had business with them. In certain cases I was responsible for granting them charters. I have known some of the officers, met many of them, whose names are on that board in back of you. What ..."

"Then you admit ..."

"I admit nothing. I merely say I have known some of those men. I've known hundreds, thousands, of union members and union officials. When I have discovered that they were violating their trusts, taking advantage of their positions, I have done everything in my power to get rid of them."

"And if they were known hoodlums and ex-criminals ..."

"A man can be an ex-criminal and still be a good union official," Rafferty said. "The law of this country is such that when a man finishes serving his time for having committed a crime, he has paid his debt to society. If on returning to society, he lives a decent, honest life, I believe he is entitled to a fresh start. I will fight to rid organized labor of any known crook or racketeer, but I will also give a break to a man who has reformed."

"I am sure you would, Mr. Rafferty," Ames said, his voice heavy with sarcasm. "And I am sure that you have. However, let us take up the matter of one Tommy Faricetti. Mr. Faricetti is, I believe, the Secretary of Local 1670 of the ISU in New York City."

"He was," Rafferty said, "He no longer is."

"And when did …"

"The charter of Local 1670 was withdrawn some two months ago," Rafferty interrupted. "At that time Mr. Faricetti ceased to function as either an official or a member of the ISU."

"The charter was withdrawn at the time this investigative body began to function, isn't that correct, Mr. Rafferty?"

"It could be. You have the records."

"Quite so. Now Mr. Rafferty, will you explain to the Committee your relationship with Mr. Faricetti."

Ames quickly held up his hand as Rafferty opened his mouth to answer.

"You see," he continued hurriedly, "it is a matter of some importance since this Committee has already developed evidence which establishes that Mr. Faricetti was not only the boss of Local 1670, but was the power behind seven other locals in New York City—all so-called 'paper locals'—as well as the organizer of and undercover boss of a half dozen other assorted locals in New Jersey and Pennsylvania. All these locals, I might add, were chartered by the national body of the ISU."

"What is the question, please?"

"I would like to know exactly what your relationship is and was with Mr. Faricetti?"

Rafferty coughed and took up the glass of water.

"I have known Thomas Faricetti for a number of years. As you know, I have heard the testimony before this Committee and the things which have been said about him. He has been called a criminal, a racketeer, an extortionist, a procurer, and just about everything else in the book. It may be true and it may not. But when I first met Tommy Faricetti, he was the walking delegate for a small local union in Brooklyn, New York, and my impression of him at that time was that he was a dedicated union worker and organizer. It was back in nineteen hundred and forty-five or -six, sometime after the war had ended and …"

Tommy Faricetti, sitting alone in the motel room across the river from Washington, D.C., reached over and turned up the volume of the small portable television set. He hunched his chair a little closer and his eyes concentrated on the screen. He was in his shirt sleeves and he was holding an unlighted cigarette.

Nineteen hundred and forty-five. Yes, that was right. About the time the war ended. Nineteen forty-five. He remembered not only the year but the month and the day. The time, the place and everything else about it. Even the people who had been in the room when Shorty had brought Jack Rafferty in and introduced him.

He even remembered the very words Shorty had used, some ten minutes before Rafferty had been brought in.

"Tommy," Shorty said, "this guy is strictly legit. One of these fanatic-type guys. All for the working stiff and that stuff. But he's important and he's going to be a lot more important. He's a comer and we gotta play ball with him. You'll like him, Tommy, even if he is a square."

Tommy had liked him, from the very first moment that Jack Rafferty had stuck out his hand to shake. Had liked him and known right then, from the very beginning, that Rafferty would someday be a big man in national union affairs. It was written all over him.

"Sam Farrow suggested I look you up when I was in town," Rafferty had said.

"Mr. Farrow sent you?" He knew that Farrow was a big man in the ISU, knew that his power and influence extended well beyond his own district.

"That's right. Told me your outfit has just been granted a charter and said I might stop by and say hello for him. I'm with Local 702, out in Los Angeles."

"That so? Well, grab a seat. Shorty, you go out and get us a couple cold beers."

The room was in back of a candy store, and Tommy had rented it only two weeks previously. It was temporary headquarters but more than adequate for his purposes. At that time his local consisted of no one but himself and four other men, all old pals who had joined him in what was, for Tommy, a new business venture. Tommy had only recently discovered unions.

They were alone, drinking the beer, and Tommy had started the conversation. Somehow or other he knew that unless he did, it probably wouldn't start.

"You a friend of Mr. Farrow?" he asked.

"In a way," Rafferty said. "He's my boss."

"How come he ..."

"Well," Rafferty said, "he just heard around that you people had been granted a charter. I suppose you got it through your district conference?"

"That's right."

"He just wanted to send congratulations along," Rafferty said. "By the way, have you selected your delegate yet?"

"Delegate?" Tommy hadn't known what Rafferty was talking about.

"That's right, delegate. As a local union, you are entitled to a delegate. There's going to be a national convention in the fall and your delegate will attend and vote for district conference and national officers."

"Is that so?" Tommy said. "Well then I guess I'm the delegate."

Rafferty had looked up at him sharply.

"How many members do you …"

"Well, that's kinda hard to say right now," Tommy answered quickly. "You see we just got the charter and the boys are out organizing right this minute, but we expect …"

"Have you pledged yourself to any candidates so far?"

This time it was Tommy who looked at Rafferty sharply. He knew what was coming.

"Well, it's like this," he said. "Katzman got me the charter. I suppose I'll have to go down the line with …"

"Mr. Faricetti," Rafferty said. "Katzman is not very popular right at this time with the big brass. After the next election, I doubt very much if he will have any influence at all."

"Is that so? Well, I'm sorry to hear that. But you see he got me the charter and I wouldn't want anything to happen to it."

"I can promise you that nothing will. Also …"

"Are you promising for yourself or are you promising for Mr. Farrow?"

"Let's just say I am reflecting Mr. Farrow's sentiments. But I can say this. That if you should find it possible to back Mr. Farrow's candidates in the fall election, I can very definitely assure you nothing will happen to your charter."

"That's nice to know," Tommy said.

That was the first time they met but it was far from the last. The friendship, which was to come later on, did not, of course, develop overnight, or even in the first year or two. Rafferty was mostly in the Southwest at that time, building himself and his own local into national prominence. Tommy barely paid lip service to his own private local; he had half a dozen other irons in the fire and the local was merely a sort of side line that brought in a buck now and then. Its real value to him was that it gave him a certain respectable background. As a legitimate union official, he enjoyed a degree of immunity from trouble with the police who had, in recent years, been giving him a lot more attention than he wanted or needed.

It wasn't until two or three years later that he and Rafferty became personal friends. It happened when Tommy stepped over the border and got into the trouble. The trouble wasn't with the police, it was with his own district conference. There had been complaints from workers he'd forced into his union and others from small-time manufacturers whom he'd victimized.

The President of the district conference, a thoroughly honest union man who'd been in the movement from the earliest days, had grown increasingly aware of Tommy's illegal activities and called him in on the carpet. He'd ended up by saying:

"Faricetti, this whole movement would be a lot better off without men like you. I'm going to see what I can do about it."

When Tommy left the meeting, he remembered two things. The local official who had threatened him was a member of a group which opposed both the national leadership and Sam Farrow, and Jack Rafferty had once obliquely asked him a favor.

He called Rafferty in Los Angeles.

Rafferty refused to talk over the telephone but suggested Tommy come out West. He flew out and Rafferty met him in the airport restaurant. Tommy laid his cards on the table.

Rafferty listened until he was finished and then looked up.

"I guess you know you should lose your charter," he said.

Tommy didn't say anything.

There was a long silence and then Rafferty spoke again.

"You probably didn't hear about it," he said, "but I've got my own troubles. A different kind of trouble. We have a big strike going at a shipping company in San Pedro."

"That so?"

"Yes. And it's a tough one. Management has brought in dozens of thugs from Frisco and Seattle. They've been sworn in as deputies and we've had several men badly beaten up. One of our boys, Floyd Cameron, lost an eye and is still on the critical list."

Tommy nodded. He wondered what Rafferty was leading up to.

"We can lose that strike," Rafferty said. "The men who are out aren't fighters. They are mostly guys who hold white-collar jobs. It doesn't take a great deal to discourage them."

Tommy nodded, wondering what all this had to do with him.

"What we need," Rafferty said, "are a few really tough boys, men who know how to use their fists or anything else they may have to use."

"Can't you hire …"

"If I could, I would," Rafferty said, not waiting for the question.

"Well, I could send you along a few boys. Say maybe a dozen. Not many, I'll admit, but my guys wouldn't be afraid of nothing. Nothing at all. They might not be so hot on a picket line, but they'd do what had to be done all right."

Rafferty nodded.

"We can use them," he said.

"Of course they would have to be paid."

"They would get fifteen dollars a day and expenses," Rafferty said. "That's the pay. Fifteen and expenses."

Tommy looked at him, obviously shocked.

"Fifteen? My God, they can do better than that."

Rafferty stood up.

"Well, I just thought I'd mention it. I'm sorry about that business back in New York, but …"

"Wait a second," Tommy said. "Wait a minute. When do you want your men?"

"Right away. As fast as they can get out to the Coast."

"They'll be there. I'll get on the phone within the next half hour. But fifteen bucks a day!" He whistled. "Do they get bail money if they need it?" he asked.

"They'll get bail money. Don't worry. And by the way. About that business of Malley threatening to take your charter away. Forget it. Malley can't take anyone's charter away; as a matter of fact, Malley probably won't be around himself much longer. You go on back to New York and just forget about him."

Tommy nodded his head.

"Well," he said, "that's a relief to know. I wanna thank …"

"Skip it," Rafferty said. "But take a tip from me, will you? Just go a little easy. I don't know what you have been doing back there and, frankly, I don't want to know. But take it easy. We don't care too much about New York, but there are a lot of pretty important people in the ISU who don't like to have a stink. Anywhere."

"You won't have to worry," Tommy said. "And listen, next time you come into town, be sure and look me up. I'd like to take you around and show you the joints."

The next time Rafferty had come to New York, Tommy had

introduced him to Jill Hart.

From that time on Tommy saw more and more of Rafferty. He liked him and he admired him, but he never really understood him. Couldn't figure out what made him tick. It was, in all, a strange sort of friendship that developed between them, a friendship based neither on common interests nor any similarity in character. The cement which held it together was probably an exchange of favors more than anything else, and yet the friendship had certain definite personal qualities.

Rafferty was, to Tommy, a new and strange kind of fish. It was obvious to him from the very first that Rafferty was no hoodlum, no racket guy. He talked and acted like a man who believed thoroughly and wholeheartedly in what he was doing. His conversation was inevitably punctuated by phrases like "welfare of the workers," "benefits," "corrupt management," "contractual negotiations."

Tommy knew that he had innumerable chances to sell out his men and make a killing and that he never did so. He seemed, so far as his job was concerned, incorruptible.

On the other hand, Tommy knew that Rafferty had no illusions about his own operation. He knew Rafferty understood that he, Faricetti, was using the union façade strictly as a racket. He knew Rafferty understood that he victimized both the membership of his local and the small businesses which were dependent on the workers under his control.

He soon learned that he wasn't the only man of his type with whom Rafferty had dealings. Rafferty had connections with ex-criminals, crooked politicians, gamblers and underworld characters in more than a dozen cities. It took Faricetti a long time to realize the answer to this apparent contradiction in Rafferty. But finally he began to understand.

Rafferty was sincerely dedicated to the cause of organized labor, but Rafferty was also a man who believed that any means were justified by the end. To do what he wanted to do, to become what he wanted to become, he had to have power and to gain that power he would hesitate at nothing.

Following the pattern he had set for himself, Rafferty would always need men like Faricetti and Faricetti soon realized this. He had done any number of favors for Rafferty. A dozen times he had framed local elections, stuffed ballot boxes and used threats and coercion to get Rafferty-backed candidates in office. He'd supplied Rafferty with wiretapping equipment when Rafferty wanted to keep track of what went on in his own and other local headquarters. He'd supplied him with strong-arm men, with dynamiters, arsonists, and bodyguards.

And, of course, it was a two-way street. Rafferty had backed Tommy up time after time when it had been necessary for him really to go out on a limb. He had never failed to keep his word or make good on his promises.

Once or twice Tommy had seriously thought of turning legitimate, of honestly going into union work and making a career for himself. He knew that top national officers of the unions made big money. Made it legitimately. Everything else being equal, Faricetti was a man who would have preferred to make his money that way. To make it without risk and without the ever-present chance of ending up in criminal court.

He remembered the time he talked with Rafferty about it and what Rafferty had said.

They'd been out on a party together and it was late at night after they'd returned to a hotel suite they were sharing. Tommy was a little tight, which was unusual. He'd spoken to Rafferty as Rafferty was mixing a nightcap.

"You know, Jack," he said, "I've been wondering about something. What would you say if I were to decide to run for a district conference office—you know, maybe not President, but Secretary or something."

Rafferty put his glass down and turned and stared at him. "I'd say you were nuts, Tommy," he said.

Faricetti frowned. "Yeah? Why? Why shouldn't I? I been in the movement now for ..."

"Listen," Rafferty said. "Be sensible. You've got a criminal record as long as your arm. You've been in the rackets all your life. Do you honestly think that ..."

"A lot of guys who are going places in the unions have records," Tommy said.

"Sure—sure, I know," Rafferty interrupted. "But you don't find them holding office in the good unions. And another thing, the guys with criminal records who do hold high office didn't get their records the way you got yours. They got them fighting on picket lines, or because of their union activities. There's a difference."

"Then you're telling me that I wouldn't have a chance, that I wouldn't get the backing ..."

"You want the truth, don't you?" Rafferty asked. "I'll give it to you.

Tommy, you just aren't the right man for a big job in organized labor. I like you and I can tell you without betraying any confidences that several men a lot higher up than I am know about you and think you're O.K. But so far as running for a district office—that's out. The minute you raise your head, there are going to be about fifty guys around who are going to knock you over. As long as you stay where you are, handle things the way you've been handling them, everything is fine and you know you got friends in the right places. But if you do anything to embarrass those friends—well, Tommy, I hate to say it, but that's going to be the end of you."

And so he knew just where he stood; no longer entertained any wild illusions about his chances—at least with the ISU. He took it but he didn't like it and had it not been for the business which happened shortly after their conversation, a definite coolness could have developed between himself and Rafferty. But for once and all Rafferty had the opportunity to show his friendship.

The thing which happened was Tommy's own fault and he knew it. An accident, but still his own fault. He'd gotten greedy. The man ran a small car wash business out in Queens and Tommy had been shaking him down for fifty dollars a week regularly on the threat of giving him labor trouble. When he checked up and found out that the place was doing a booming business, he'd raised his demands. He wanted a hundred and fifty and the owner of the place squawked, so Tommy'd sent a couple of his boys around and they just about wrecked the establishment. The man called him up and offered to pay off. He had—with marked bills.

They picked up Tommy when he was making his first collection. The charge was extortion and they had him cold. One of the boys he'd sent around to do the wrecking was a junky and he talked. The district attorney had a cut and dried case. Tommy had a good lawyer, but there was nothing the lawyer could do. And so he took a fall—his third felony in New York State.

They sent him to Sing Sing for two to five years and he did three. When he came out he was broke, his organization had fallen apart, and he was desperate. Rafferty arranged to get him a job as a salesman in order for him to satisfy the parole board. And then Rafferty came to New York and saw him.

He laid it on the line.

"You did a stupid thing, Tommy," he said. "Real stupid. It didn't make me happy and it didn't make a lot of people happy. Including you, I guess. But what's done is done. Here's what we are going to do. Local 1670 is being run by a guy named Steve Kalleck. He's a weak sister but he's all right as a front man. You are going in—you'll be on the payroll as an organizer—but I want you to take the local over. Kalleck will understand your position. I want you to whip it together and build it up. And I want you to stay out of trouble. In a year or so, if everything is O.K., we'll put you in as Secretary."

He hesitated a moment and then said, "How do you stand on dough?"

"I don't," Tommy said. "If it hadn't been for my mouthpiece, I'd have lost my house and ..."

"Yeah, I know," Rafferty said. "Well, here's something to see you through until you get set again." He took out a roll of bills and peeled off several and handed them to him. "That's five grand," he said. "If you need more, yell."

Tommy had started to say something, to thank him, to tell him that he'd pay it back as soon as he got straightened out, but Rafferty quickly cut him off.

"It isn't a loan," he said. "Just a little token of appreciation. Forget about it."

That's the way it was between them and that's the way it continued to be. Rafferty helped him along and backed him up and he did favors for Rafferty. He'd always felt indebted and he always wanted to pay Rafferty back and finally he was given his opportunity.

It had happened a little more than six months ago and the minute Rafferty had called him from Los Angeles he knew that something important was in the wind. Rafferty had telephoned his house late at night.

"I'm coming into town tomorrow," he'd said. "I have to see you, Tommy."

"Good," Faricetti said. "Where will I meet you? At the office?"

"No, Tommy. Not the office. Make it the Commodore ..."

"What time, Jack?"

"I won't check in," Rafferty said. "Make it the men's bar. I'm only going to be in town long enough to see you and then I got to get right back."

"Fine, Jack, is anything ..."

"Five-thirty, the men's bar at the Commodore," Rafferty said, and the line went dead.

He'd known then that it was important.

Tommy was already there and waiting when Rafferty showed up.

"We'll take a walk," Rafferty had said. "I want to talk."

They'd gone outside and started up Madison Avenue.

"It's like this," Rafferty said. "I guess you know that the old man's in a little trouble. Income tax business. Several things have been going sour lately and we hear rumors that there's going to be some kind of Federal investigation into unions. They'll probably concentrate on the ISU."

"Yeah?"

"Yeah. But that isn't what I want to talk about. You know Claude Marks, don't you?"

Tommy nodded. "I've met him," he said, "that's about all." He knew who Marks was all right. He was an official in the biggest ISU local in the city, a long-time union organizer with an excellent record, but for the fact he'd been suspected of following a little too close to the Communist party line during recent years.

"Well, he's a troublemaker," Rafferty said. "He always has been. And he's fought us all the way down the line for a long while now. Recently he's been giving us a real headache. He plays footsie with a lot of people we don't like; he's been trying to oust Farrow from the presidency ever since the old man has been in office. He's a big mouth and he doesn't care who he talks to. He likes publicity and if there is widespread investigation, you can bet he'll play along with the government. Someone's got to shut him up before he can do any more damage."

Faricetti stopped walking for a moment and turned to Rafferty.

"Shut him up?"

"That's right. Marks is dangerous; he used to be nothing but a goddamned nuisance, but now he's dangerous."

"Is that the way Mr. Farrow feels about it?" Tommy asked.

Rafferty stared at him coldly for a second.

"It's the way I feel about it," he said at last. "I don't know anything about how the old man feels and it doesn't matter in any case. I'm just telling you how I feel."

"You mean, Jack," Tommy said, speaking carefully, "that something has got to be done about him? That there's no way of being sure …"

"I shouldn't have to draw a blueprint for you, Tommy."

For several seconds both men were silent and then Rafferty said, "It's pretty delicate. Marks is an important man. At least he is to the press and the public. It's something that you have to take care of personally. I wouldn't trust anyone else."

Faricetti looked at him and his surprise was obvious.

"Are you asking me, personally, to go gunning …"

"Don't be a damned fool, Tommy," Rafferty said with irritation. "No one has mentioned gunning. And by personally, I mean whatever is done, you have to arrange it and be responsible for it!"

"I see," Tommy said. Again he hesitated for a long time, and then spoke.

"You know, Jack," he said. "I've taken three falls already. One more fall and they throw the book at me. I'd sort of hate like hell to have anything happen …"

"You're not a child," Rafferty said. "You know how to handle things."

Tommy nodded.

"Sure," he said. "Sure, I know how to handle things. But Jack, just one question. Let's come right out with it. You want this guy rubbed …"

"Are you crazy?" Rafferty said quickly. "God no! I never said anything like that. I just said that he's a goddamned troublemaker and he's in my hair. He's already shooting his mouth off all over the place and he's going to keep right on shooting it off, unless someone stops him. I might add this—he doesn't frighten. It's been tried and it doesn't work. And you can't bribe him. That's been tried too."

"He don't scare and he can't be bribed, and yet you want him stopped. Is that right?"

"That's right, Tommy."

Faricetti slowly nodded.

"All right, Jack," he said. "If that's what you want, I can arrange …"

"Tommy, I don't want the details. I don't want to talk about it anymore. I know I can count on you, boy."

"You can count on me."

And he could.

Faricetti hadn't liked it; it was the sort of thing he'd avoided for a long time now. But a favor was a favor and so he'd gone ahead. He was as careful as he knew how to be. He gave the assignment to a cousin, a man he knew he could trust.

"It's like this," he explained. "I don't even want to know who actually does it. But it has to be done right. There's five 0's in it and I don't want you should hold out on the guy who throws the acid. He's to be scarred up and scarred bad, but he isn't to be knocked off. Under no condition is he to be knocked off. There is one other thing, I said I don't want to know who actually handles it. But one thing I want to be sure about. Don't use no punk and don't use no junky. I don't want this thing coming home to roost."

The cousin assured him that he could handle the assignment. He did, too. It went according to schedule except for one unforeseen factor. Claude Marks had a weak heart which neither he nor anyone else knew about and two minutes after the acid had been thrown in his face, he dropped to the sidewalk dead. The acid might have scarred him for life, but he didn't live long enough for anyone to find out.

The papers made a big thing out of it, riding hard on the police department. The police themselves had plenty of ideas, but they got nowhere. It was one of those things. A man leaves a movie, after the late show, and is on his way to his car. Someone steps out of a doorway and throws a flask full of acid in his face and turns and walks away. No one saw it; no one was around.

They questioned a hundred people and Tommy Faricetti himself was one of those questioned. They suspected him, but then again they suspected a lot of people. Claude Marks was a man who had made a thousand enemies.

And after a while the whole thing died down and the press forgot about it and almost everyone else forgot about it, except the widow, of course, and now and then Tommy Faricetti.

Even Tommy was beginning to forget it, when suddenly, out of nowhere, the whole thing blew wide open. It had happened only a month previously when the New York police suddenly picked up the cousin and charged him with first-degree murder. That was bad enough, but they also picked up a twenty-four-year-old punk who made collections for a policy ring on the lower East Side. They didn't charge him with having thrown the acid, but the press hinted that he had done it. The police held him on other charges and from various statements given out by the district attorney's office, it was a foregone conclusion that they figured he was guilty. They'd made no bones about tracing his connection with Faricetti's cousin. And finally Faricetti himself had been picked up.

They held him for forty-eight hours on suspicion and then indicted him. He made bail all right, but he knew he was in serious trouble. The district attorney had already announced that he was bringing the twenty-four-year-old policy-maker to trial first, as an accessory before and after the fact. And he wasn't talking when the press wanted to know if he had a confession or not. The prisoner wasn't talking either; he hadn't been able to get bail and no one knew what he might have been saying.

Rafferty had said only one thing to Tommy.

"Don't worry!" That was all, just, "Don't worry!"

Well he was worried and plenty worried.

Sitting there in the motel and watching Jack Rafferty's image on the television screen, he had every confidence in his friend and benefactor, but he was still plenty worried.

It was after six o'clock now, and Francis MacNammera had come in more than an hour ago and was nervously pacing the room as Tommy watched the television set.

"It's almost over," MacNammera said. "Another few minutes, Tommy, and it should all be through."

Tommy grunted.

"Sure," he said, "but that bastard Ames is back again asking him about me. Why the hell does he have to keep harping on me anyway? They had me there, didn't they?"

"Yes, they had you, Tommy. But you didn't talk. You took the Fifth. Rafferty's talking and so they're asking him."

"He's talking," Tommy said, "but thank God he isn't saying anything. But I still wish he'd have gotten in touch. I can't understand why he didn't. I can't understand...."

Once again Senator Fellows looked down at his wristwatch and once again he stood up, interrupting a question Ames was about to ask, to rap sharply on the table with the gavel.

"I don't believe that we will be able to finish this phase of the investigation until far too late," he said. "We will adjourn now for the weekend and I must request that the witness appear here on Monday." He hesitated a moment, and then said, "In view of the lateness of today's session, Monday's hearing will begin at two o'clock in the afternoon."

CHAPTER SIXTEEN

Martha Rafferty found the note where Ann had left it on the big, square kitchen table shortly after seven-thirty on Saturday morning. She had slept badly, tossing and turning most of the night and not falling asleep until almost daylight. But she had awakened as usual a few minutes after seven and gotten up at once. It took her fifteen or twenty minutes to wash and dress and by the time that she was ready to come downstairs and make breakfast, her mind was already made up. Finding the letter changed nothing.

For a moment or so as she stood there, after reading the few short lines and still holding the piece of paper in her hand, she was unsure, not knowing quite what to do. And then at last she walked across the room and found her bag and carefully folded the note and put it inside. She went to the telephone and called her brother in Seattle.

Steve Deheny arrived late that afternoon. They talked it over, argued a little, but at last came to an agreement. They wouldn't call the police and they wouldn't get in touch with Rafferty in Washington. But they did call the Abbot family. There was no answer.

At eight o'clock Martha packed a suitcase. Steve telephoned his own home and told his wife he would be staying on in Los Angeles for a few days. And at six o'clock the next morning, Sunday, he drove his sister to the airport where she boarded a plane for Chicago. She changed planes there and took the direct flight to Washington, arriving late Sunday evening.

The taxi driver suggested a small hotel not far from the center of the city when she asked his advice. Checking in, she told the desk clerk she would be there only overnight.

At ten o'clock on Monday morning she arrived at the hotel in which her husband was staying. She asked for his room number and when the desk gave it to her, she didn't bother to call from downstairs in the lobby, but went at once to the bank of elevators, giving the elevator operator the correct floor.

At five minutes after ten she was standing in front of the door of Jack Rafferty's suite. She raised her hand and knocked several times.

Jack Rafferty had left Washington in a union-owned Cadillac less than two hours after the hearing was adjourned on Friday afternoon.

He drove the car himself. He stopped at his hotel only long enough to pick up a bag, which he'd already had packed and waiting. He had sent Mort Kauffman up for the bag, and when the attorney asked where he was going and where he might be reached, he told him that he wanted a couple of days' complete rest and that he wanted it alone.

"Don't worry," he said. "I'll be back in plenty of time. You can reach me at the hotel any time after eight on Monday. But I need a rest and the only way I'll get it is to get away somewhere by myself."

"There are a hundred messages waiting for you upstairs," Kauffman said. "Don't you want …"

"No. I don't want to know who called. Right now I don't care. I just want to be by myself."

And so he had left, getting in touch with no one and seeing no one. He drove down to Virginia Beach and checked into a resort hotel under an assumed name. Friday night he went to bed immediately after dinner, neither looking at a newspaper nor turning on the radio. He spent most of Saturday and Sunday on the beach. He was careful to rub his body with suntan lotion, not wanting to get a bad burn. He just lay on the beach, periodically dozing off, and rested.

It was the first time in more than twenty years that he had been completely alone for an entire forty-eight hours; the first time in twenty years that for two solid days he did absolutely nothing but relax.

One thing kept constantly crossing his mind as he lay on the beach and baked under the hot sun. He tried not to think about it but it refused to go away.

"I've got to see them, see them and talk to them," he kept telling himself. But not until it was over. Not until it was over and done with. There was Martha, Martha and the children. He'd have to work out a story for them, something to set their minds at rest. But that wouldn't be too tough. He'd always managed to explain things to Martha; she could be trusted in turn to handle the children.

And there was Jill. He knew that she had left the proceedings and checked out of her hotel to return to New York. That reporter from the *News* had cornered him outside his own hotel, while he'd been waiting for Mort to bring the bag down. Had told him that he'd talked with Jill, but she'd referred all his questions to Rafferty himself, refused to comment on the relationship one way or the other. Merely told him that she was returning to New York and that so far as she was concerned, she no longer had any further interest in the hearings.

Rafferty believed the reporter was telling the truth; he was grateful that Jill hadn't opened up.

Yes, he'd have to see her, have to explain things to her also. But again it didn't worry him too much. Jill knew him and understood him and loved him. She'd always gone along with him, no matter what.

And there was Boswell—but no. He wouldn't have to see Boswell. Boswell was dead.

Faricetti. Faricetti was going to be a lot more difficult. Actually, he hadn't decided quite yet what to do about Tommy.

He knew of course that Tommy was in Washington, waiting even now for his call. Yes, he'd have to see him, sooner or later. But actually what *could* he do about Tommy? Really nothing. Nothing at all. It was one of those things. Tommy had taken a calculated risk and it just hadn't worked out. Anyway, it was just a case of time. Time would take care of Tommy Faricetti and all he had to do was sit tight and take it easy and things would work out.

And of course there was old Sam Farrow. Definitely, he would have to see Sam. Sam was still important. Still powerful. He really should have called him before he'd left. Talked with him. There was no point waiting until after the hearing was over so far as Sam went.

For a moment as he lay there on the sand thinking and trying not to think, he was tempted to get up and go in and telephone. But then he shrugged. Sam would probably be out of town himself for the weekend. But one thing he did decide. He'd call Sam the very first thing on Monday morning, as soon as he returned to his hotel. The old man would be upset and worried and it wouldn't hurt to calm him down.

And so at last he dismissed them all, the important ones and the ones who weren't so important. Dismissed them from his mind and stopped thinking about them and just lay there on the hot sand and made his mind a blank. God, it was really good to lie and rest and do nothing. Not even think. Maybe after Monday—and it should all be over by then—maybe he'd just come back to this place and spend a week or so. Lord knows he had a vacation coming to him. After what they'd put him through.

Yes, a few more hours and it would probably be all over. It would be time enough then to face his problem. And God knows, he had problems. It wasn't only the people; there was that matter of money, too. Mort Kauffman was expensive; everything about this hearing had been expensive. He was short, very short of money. Thank God for his foresight about that M-D Disbursement Company. At least he'd been lucky with that venture. And of course there was the hundred thousand dollars in securities and cash in the wall safe at Jill's apartment. But that, of course, was not to be touched. That was his insurance, the cache he had buried just in case sometimes he would be really desperate.

Yes, he had plenty of problems. But they could all be worked out. Everything would straighten itself out in the end.

Phillip Hunt took the receiver away from his ear and turned to the old man sitting slumped deep in the big red leather chair across the room. He held his hand over the mouthpiece when he spoke.

"It's Jack again," he said. "The third time now that he's called this morning. Do you still want me to tell him you're not in, Sam?"

Sam Farrow slowly lifted his eyes, staring half blindly at his companion, as though he heard the words, but didn't quite understand their meaning.

"Jack Rafferty," Hunt said. "He's on the phone again. This time he called himself. He's at the other end of the wire. Shall I tell him you are out?"

Farrow started to nod his head, and then suddenly he looked alert and quickly shook it back and forth.

"No, Phillip," he said. "No, don't tell him that I'm not here."

"Then you will talk to ..."

Farrow continued to shake his head.

"Don't tell him that I am not here," he said. "Just tell him that I don't want to talk to him. Yes, tell him that. Tell him that I don't want to talk to him, and that I don't want to see him. Not now or ever. Just tell him that, Phillip."

When he stopped speaking, he turned away once more, looking down at the pile of the heavy carpet under his feet, apparently not listening at all as Hunt spoke into the telephone. But he must have been aware of the words because he looked up again after Hunt had replaced the receiver. He spoke in a tired, old man's voice.

"I thought I had taught that boy everything that I know," he said. "Yes, I thought I taught him everything."

"Yes sir," Hunt said. "I'm sure that you ..."

"But there's one thing I guess I failed to teach him," Farrow continued, ignoring his companion's words. "One thing. Loyalty. Perhaps that's something that can't be taught. You either have it or you don't. And Jack Rafferty …"

His voice dwindled off and he was silent again, once more staring blindly at the carpet under his feet.

"See who that is at the door, Mort," Rafferty said, "and tell them to go away. My God, I thought I told the desk not to let anyone up here." He reached for the telephone as it started to ring and Mort Kauffman went to the door opening into the suite. As he opened it, Rafferty spoke into the mouthpiece of the telephone.

"No," he said. "No, damn it. I told you I didn't want any calls put through. Can't you understand? I don't care if it's California calling, and I don't care how important they think it is. I'm not taking any calls."

He slammed down the receiver and looked up as Kauffman pulled the door wide and that is when he saw Martha standing there.

"Hello, Jack," she said. She took a step or two into the room as Kauffman stepped back, staring at her.

"Martha. Martha—what in God's name are you doing here?"

He started to his feet, staring at her.

She said nothing, but walked farther into the room. For a minute there were no words and then he quickly recovered.

"My wife, Mrs. Rafferty," he said, turning to Kauffman. "Martha, this is my attorney, Mort …"

Kauffman quickly mumbled something, nodding and bowing. He edged toward the door then and spoke to Rafferty.

"Got to run down to my room for a few minutes, Jack," he said. "Have to be there for that call I'm expecting from New York. It's been nice meeting you, Mrs. Rafferty," he finished, rather lamely. A moment later and he closed the door behind himself.

"You had better sit down, Jack," Martha said, at the same time crossing the room and taking a chair herself at the cluttered-up table across from where her husband stood.

"Martha," he said. "Martha, what are you doing here? Where are the children? Why in the name of God have you come …"

"Sit down, Jack," she said.

"Listen," he said. "Listen here. What are you doing …"

"I came to see you, Jack. I have something to show you and I have something to tell you."

"Well of all the insane things. What have you done? Have you left the youngsters …"

He hesitated, seeing the expression on her face; she was looking at him as though he were a stranger, as though his words were meaningless. For the first time he realized what all this meant to her.

He'd been a fool not to realize it; not to understand how she would take it. The trouble was, he'd made it a habit in recent years to assume that she knew nothing of his activities and had no interest in them. But that business about Jill must have reached her and now she was here and he knew that he must do something.

Quickly he crossed the room and the old charming smile spread over his face.

"Why, honey," he said, "stop looking so grim. Hell, I'm glad to see you. Glad you came here. Only thing, you kinda took me by surprise. I wasn't expecting …"

He reached out, taking her by the arms and pulled her to him, attempting to kiss her as she turned her face away.

"Don't bother, Jack," she said.

He stepped back, looking suddenly hurt.

"What is it, Martha?" he said. "What's the trouble? Good Lord, you aren't letting anything that has been said about me upset you, I hope. You know how these things are; know how my enemies have been trying to blacken me and smear me? We've gone through this sort of thing …"

"That's right, Jack," she said. "We've been through it before. I guess it must be an old story to you. I guess …"

"Now see here, Martha," he said. "You know better than to believe …"

She looked at him rather sadly and half shook her head.

"Don't bother, Jack," she said. "Don't even try. I'm not upset, if that's what's worrying you. And none of it really came as news, you know. I guess I must have known all along, known for years now. It was just that I was too careless maybe, or too busy with raising children and taking care of the house and everything, to bother to open my eyes. But as I say, it no longer matters."

"Listen, honey," he said quickly. "Just be quiet and listen to me for a minute. I can explain everything. I know that you must believe …"

"It doesn't matter what I believe," she interrupted. "The thing that is important is that I don't care. I honestly don't care, Jack. It may hurt your pride, but I want you to believe that. So don't bother to try and lie to me and don't bother to charm me. I just don't care anymore. What I came here for is something entirely different in any case."

She opened her bag and drew out a piece of folded paper as she spoke.

"About the children," she said. "You'd better get a grip on yourself, Jack. Eddy has left. He left several days ago and has joined the Army. And I don't know exactly where Marty is. The last thing I heard was that he was on his way home. He'd quit the camp for the summer."

"The Army?" Rafferty said. "Good God Almighty. That boy didn't have to do his time yet. What's the matter with him? Why didn't you stop him? And Ann? Don't tell me you have come here and left Ann home alone?"

Without expression, Martha Rafferty held out the paper she had taken from her bag.

"You'd better read this," she said. "It will answer your question."

Staring at her, he slowly took the paper and unfolded it. Once or twice as he read it, he quickly shook his head.

He read:

Mother:

By the time you get this note, I will have left. Buddy Abbot and I have decided to get married. I know this will come as a shock, but after all, I am almost seventeen and it's time I started doing some of the things I want to do. Please don't try and stop us as it will be a waste of time. After all, Daddy has always done the things he has wanted to do and I think that he has been right to do them. I am sure that he would feel the same way about me. You won't have to worry about me as I am sure Buddy will give us a nice home. His family likes me and I know they will approve. I will get in touch with you and Daddy after we come back from our honeymoon.

Ann

The color drained from Rafferty's face as he finished reading the note. Slowly his hand opened and the paper dropped to the floor. He stared unbelievingly at his wife.

"What have you done?" he asked at last. "What have you done? Have you called the police? Have you gotten in touch with the boy's family? Why are you here? You should be home trying to ..."

"I haven't done anything, Jack."

For a second he stared at her, his mouth wide open.

"Haven't done anything? Good God in heaven! What do you mean, you haven't done anything? You know what kind of young snotnose that Abbot kid is. Are you out of your mind? Have you taken leave of your s—"

"No, Jack, I'm not out of my mind. And I haven't taken leave of my senses. To the contrary, I seem to have discovered my senses—for the first time in years."

"Martha! Martha, for God's sake what's the matter with you? Here my daughter ..."

"She says it in her note, Jack: 'Daddy has always done the things he has wanted to do.' And you have, haven't you, Jack? Well, so Ann is doing what she wants to do and I guess I can no more stop her than I could have stopped you."

"What in the hell has what I've done got to do with Ann?" Rafferty said, raising his voice so that he was all but yelling. "Jesus, we've got to stop this and stop it right now. I'll get the police to pick up that little bast—"

"They've been gone a couple of days now, Jack," Martha said. "Whatever has happened has already happened. I don't think I'd call the police now if I were you."

"All right. All right, I won't call the police. But I'll get a private detective agency on them. I'll find them all right. And when I do, I'll see that that boy ..."

"And suppose they are married?"

"We'll arrange an annulment. By God, Ann is just a child and she'll listen to me. She'll do what I ask."

Slowly Martha shook her head.

"No," she said. "No, Jack. I don't think so. I think Ann is all through listening to you. After the things which she has heard these last few days, I don't believe she'll ever listen to you again. I don't think any of us will."

As she finished speaking, Martha slowly got out of her chair. "And that," she said, "brings me to why I came here."

He looked up at her quickly, cocking his head.

"Why you came here?"

"Yes, Jack, why I came to Washington. I wanted to see you and look at you when I told you."

"Told me? What in the world are you talking about anyway, Martha? You didn't have to come here to tell me about Ann. I ..."

"It isn't about Ann. Ann is something else. What I came to tell you ..."

"Martha, will you please stop talking in circles! I swear I think you've …"

"I came to tell you, Jack, that we're through. All through. I'm leaving you."

For a moment he stared at her incredulously.

"Leaving me?" he said. "What do you mean, you're leaving me?"

"Just that, jack. We're through. Finished. I …"

He stood up quickly, his face suddenly red with anger.

"You *have* lost your mind," he said. "My God, as though I haven't enough to worry me, with this damned hearing and the business about Eddy and Ann taking off with that crazy hot rod idiot. And now you have to …"

"I haven't lost my mind," Martha said. "As a matter of fact, I've never thought more clearly before in my life. The only thing which makes me wonder is why it has taken me this long really to understand."

"Listen. Listen to me, Martha. I know you're upset. You're upset about the children and you've been getting a lot of hogwash from this goddamned investigation. But, honey, I can explain everything."

"There's nothing to explain," Martha said. "Nothing at all. Yes, I'm upset about the children, but that no longer matters. The children are like you, Jack. They can take care of themselves. Like you have always managed to take care of yourself. No, it isn't the children. And it isn't this hearing. Oh, I'll admit some of the things I've learned have surprised me. But really, that was my own fault. I shouldn't have been surprised; not at all. Not after these last twenty years. No, it isn't the children, or the hearing. It's just that I'm through. We're through. We've been through for a long long time now, only I never realized it before. Now I do. And that's why I came here to tell you."

She hesitated a moment and then walked to the door. "I'll be going now, Jack," she said.

"Goddamn it, Martha," he said. "Come back here! You can't walk out just like that. What makes you think— Listen, stop being a damned fool. Leave me? For God's sake! What do you think you will do, anyway? How will you live? What …"

She had reached the door now and she put her hand on the knob and twisted it.

For a moment she turned back to face him, half smiling.

"I'll manage, Jack," she said. "Oh, don't worry. I'll manage. You see, Steve came down Saturday from Seattle. He said that you were telling the truth on the stand the other day. That I do own three quarters of the stock in that company he manages. He said that the stock was registered in my name all right and that I can do anything I want with it. So don't worry too much about me. I'll be able to manage all right."

She opened the door then and half turned away.

"Goodbye, Jack," she said.

"Martha, Martha, now see here. I ..."

The door closed quietly behind her as his voice faded into nothingness.

For a moment he stood there, half tempted to run out after her. He took a step or two forward and then suddenly stopped. He knew. Knew then that there would be no point in it.

Five minutes later and Mort Kauffman was back in the room with him.

"And get on the phone," Rafferty said. "Get the best goddamned detective agency in California on the thing. Tell them to be quiet about it and keep it away from the papers. But I want them found. I don't care where they are, I want them found. And if that little bum has taken her across a state line, I'll have him ..."

"Right away," Kauffman said. "But Jack, it's going to cost something. The chances are they are somewhere in Mexico and if we have to send men down there, why ..."

"The hell with the cost," Rafferty said. "I don't care what it costs. Just get on the phone and ..."

"I'll do it from my room," Kauffman said.

As the door slammed behind the attorney, Rafferty looked at his watch. He saw that it was just after one o'clock. An hour to go until he was due once more before the Joint Investigating Committee.

"Money," he said, under his breath. "Goddamn it, always money."

He hesitated a moment, thinking, and then frowned. Damn it, he'd wanted to wait until after the hearing was over and done with, but now there wasn't time. They were forcing his hand. He had to do something and do it quick. It would have been better to wait and see her in person, but that couldn't be helped. The detective agency would be wanting cash. Kauffman himself had mentioned the retainer a couple of times and they were beginning to press him from all sides. Of course he could call Sam. But Sam had refused to speak to him. There was Steve, of course. Steve could always— And then he remembered what Martha had told him about seeing her brother.

He swore and reached for the telephone.

It took him several minutes to get through to the New York operator but at last he got a trunk line and he quickly gave the number of Jill's New York apartment.

He could hear the operator ringing the number and the seconds and minutes went by. He was about to hang up when he heard the receiver being lifted at the other end.

It was a man's voice.

"Is Miss Hart ..."

"I'm sorry, but ..."

"Is this Miss Hart's apartment?"

"It is. But Miss Hart is no longer with us. She ..."

"Who is this speaking?" Rafferty said. "This is Jack Rafferty and I would like to talk to ..."

"This is Mr. Friedman, the superintendent," the voice at the other end said. "I'm sorry, Mr. Rafferty, but Miss Hart is not here. In fact she had given up the apartment and I'm here seeing about ..."

"Not there? What do you mean, she's not there. Say, listen ..."

"Miss Hart's maid is here," Friedman said. "Would you care to speak to her?"

"Put her on."

The line was dead for a moment and then a woman's soft, Southern voice spoke.

"Yes, Mista Rafferty?"

"Is that you, Jane?"

"Tha's right, Mista Rafferty."

"Where's Miss Hart, Jane?"

"I don't know, Mista Rafferty. All I know is she came back las' Friday night an' tol' me she was givin' up the place. She give me the furniture an' I'm here now an' ..."

"Where did she go? You must ..."

"I don' know nothin', Mista Rafferty. All I know is I helped her pack an' Sat'dee mornin' I carried her suitcases down an' a limousine from the airplane company picked her up. That's all I know."

Rafferty swore.

"I'm sorry, Mist—"

"Listen, Jane," Rafferty said, speaking fast, "listen, do you know where the wall safe is in the bedroom? I want ..."

"I know where it is, Mista Rafferty."

"Well, Jane, go in and see if Miss Hart was sure that she locked it before she left?"

"I don' haf to go in, Mista Rafferty. It's locked all right."

Rafferty let the breath escape from his lungs.

"Fine, Jane," he said. "That's just ..."

"Yes, Mista Rafferty," Jane said. "It's locked all right, I closed it myself after Miss Hart emptied all her stuff out of it and packed it all in her overnight bag. Course there wasn't no reason to close an empty safe, but ..."

Rafferty dropped the receiver back on the hook, very gently, and sat there, staring at the phone with unseeing eyes.

He failed to look up a moment later when the door crashed open and Mort Kauffman entered, his face drained of color and his mouth trembling as he struggled to speak.

Sergeant Harold Comisky of the California State Highway Patrol replaced the receiver on the hook and turned to where the lieutenant sat across the double desk facing him.

"Still can't get hold of him," he said. "We are able to get the hotel, but Rafferty either isn't there or he isn't taking calls. Girl on the switchboard says ..."

"Well, we can't wait any longer," the lieutenant said. "I would have liked to reach him, but those boys from the press are outside and they are raising hell. I'm going to have to give it to them. They want to get the story on the wires and they also want to make the local afternoon editions ..."

"There's no doubt about it?" the sergeant asked. "No doubt about it's being the Rafferty kid? I hate to think ..."

"No doubt at all," the lieutenant said. "Just this minute heard from Feeney. He called in while you were on the phone. He was with the Abbot kid's old man when he was taken in to identify the bodies. It's the Rafferty girl all right. It was one of those freak things—the windshield almost decapitated her when she went through it, but for some reason her face was barely scratched. Feeney says the Abbot boy's father fainted dead away when he saw what was left of the kid, but then he came to and made a positive identification of the girl. God, they must have been doing well over a hundred miles an hour when that truck swung out"

"Well, I'd just hate to be in Rafferty's shoes when the story hits him," the sergeant interrupted. "I always feel that it's the parents who really ..."

CHAPTER SEVENTEEN

George Morris Ames looked at the plain gold watch on his left wrist, observing that there was still ten minutes before the hearing was due to begin. He turned to Senator Fellows, who had just entered the private chamber behind the room in which the hearing was to be held.

"Danials said he just saw Rafferty entering the building," he said. "I must say, I'm a little surprised."

Fellows nodded.

"Surprised myself," he said. "But I'm glad he decided to come. I think we can finish up this thing today—at least so far as he's concerned."

"We should," Ames said. "There isn't a great deal more. Mostly the business with Faricetti. I'm afraid that Mr. Rafferty's quota of bad news is not over ..."

Representative Ellison, approaching and hearing the last few words, interrupted.

"Horrible," he said. "I just heard the report over the radio. This thing should be postponed. It's inhuman to expect Rafferty to be here when his daughter is lying dead on a slab some three thousand miles away. He's had more than any man should have to take in one day. After all, I have a youngster myself. My girl's fifteen and I certainly know how I would feel; how any father ..."

"I talked with Rafferty myself fifteen minutes ago," Senator Fellows said. "He'd just received the news. Naturally I told him that we would be willing to postpone ..."

"And you mean that he didn't want ..."

"I mean that he said he would be here. I don't know whether he was in a state of shock or whether he has ice in his veins, but he insisted that he wanted to show up and finish things this afternoon."

"Well, we should have canceled the hearings in any case," Ellison said. "Rafferty must be temporarily out of his mind. He can't know ..."

"He wants us to continue," Ames said. "Senator Fellows has talked with him and I've talked with Kauffman, his attorney. They have agreed to go on. Kauffman says that Rafferty is shocked and upset, but that he insists we finish things. He's leaving right after the hearings for the Coast. Anyway, it's time. Shall we proceed, Senator?"

Senator Ormand Fellows nodded. Yes, he'd be glad to get it over with.

To see the end of Jack Rafferty. He was tired himself and he felt a vague sense of dissatisfaction and defeat. Somehow or other he felt that things weren't quite turning out as he had expected. It had been irritating, maddening in fact, when those others, Farrow and Faricetti and the Hart woman and all the rest of them, had taken the stand and then immediately resorted to the Fifth Amendment. It had been frustrating and the Senator, like all of the others, had believed that the very purpose of the constitutional provision was being misused and violated. And then Rafferty had taken the stand and had been willing to talk. Willing to answer the questions put to him by Ames and the others.

It wasn't that Ames wasn't doing an excellent job, young and slightly inexperienced as he was. And it wasn't as though the investigators hadn't turned up plenty of material. But somehow or other, the end results were disappointing. Oh, Rafferty had answered the questions all right. And his answers had frequently been damning. It was the end result, however, which counted. Somehow or other, without actually committing perjury, he always seemed to weasel out. The man's very forthrightness was, in a way, almost like a whitewash of his activities. And at the end of each day's testimony, in spite of the facts which had come out, there was a vague aura of sympathy for Rafferty himself—the villain in the drama.

And now this latest thing. It couldn't have happened at a more unfortunate time. Naturally the press would play it up. It was to be expected. And no matter how black a picture might be painted of Rafferty and his activities, once the public read the story about his daughter, well, there was no doubt of what their reaction would be. Rafferty, the man who sold his mistress down the river, who was unfaithful to his wife and his boss and his friends, would be forgotten, and the man who would be thought of would be the kind loving father who was in agony over the sudden death of his favorite child. God knows that the Senator himself felt deeply sympathetic with him on that score, but it was a shame it happened just at this time.

No, the whole thing was somehow disappointing. Senator Fellows was really a little more tired than he'd realized. The television cameras, the audience, the flash bulbs and the general confusion—all were beginning to wear on him.

Followed by Morton Kauffman, he walked down the aisle, pushing his way through the crowds, and except for the paleness of his face, he looked exactly as he had looked some seventy-two hours before when he had first entered the chamber. Jack Rafferty still retained the appearance of a man completely self-assured, self-contained. He glanced neither to right nor left but proceeded as swiftly as he was able to go to the witness table, where he seated himself. Once more the briefcase was placed within easy reach and once more he shifted a handful of papers on the flat surface of the wide oak table, moving the refilled water pitcher and the glass so that they too were within easy reach.

His youthful face was without expression and only the square muscular hands, occasionally nervously lifting this or that, betrayed him in the slightest.

While the members of the Committee were shifting and settling at the table facing him, he ignored the flashlight bulbs of the photographers and the television cameras trained on him.

Kauffman leaned close, covering his mouth with his hand. "You're sure, Jack," he said. "Sure you are all right? Want to go ahead ..."

Rafferty nodded, not turning his head, not changing expression.

All right? Yes, he was all right. As all right as a man could be who'd just had his heart removed without the benefit of anesthesia.

For a moment, as his attorney again started to lean toward him, he had a sudden almost irresistible desire to turn and strike the other man in the face. Goddamn him, why couldn't he shut up? Shut up and let him alone!

Why didn't they get on with it? All of them, sitting out there and staring at him. As though they knew what he was thinking and feeling and going through. As though they could or would help him, even if they did know.

What did they care? What did Kauffman or any of them really care?

They'd wanted his blood, hadn't they? Well, he may have bled, but it wasn't the way they'd wanted it and goddamn them, they weren't going to get what they wanted.

Yeah, he'd bled all right. And he was still bleeding. But it had nothing to do with them. The only thing that had to do with them was this hearing and they could go on with it and finish it and he'd still beat them. Still come out ahead. He'd never given up in his life and he wasn't giving up now. Now or ever.

In an hour or so, tonight, when that first sudden shock wore off, perhaps then the numbness would go and perhaps then he would ...

But he shook his head quickly and this time turned himself to speak to Kauffman.

"I'm all right," he repeated needlessly. "Let's get this over with."

It was four o'clock now and for the first time since he had started questioning Jack Rafferty, young Ames looked tired. His horn-rimmed glasses were pushed up on his brow and he ran a finger around the inside of his short collar as he spoke, his voice showing his weariness.

"All right, Mr. Rafferty, I have just a couple more questions and then I will be through. I just want to get a couple of things clear. You say then that you have had no contact with Mr. Faricetti for more than six months?"

"That is correct."

"You say that you have no knowledge of any of Mr. Faricetti's activities during this period of time?"

"That is correct, up to a point. I felt after reading about his arrest in connection with the Marks case, that Mr. Faricetti was no longer an asset to the ISU. The affairs of his local are out of my province, but I have always objected to anyone giving the union a bad name. I recommended that his charter be withdrawn."

"But you still feel personally friendly as far as Mr. Faricetti is concerned?"

"I do. Tommy Faricetti is my friend and has been my friend. I may not approve of what he does or may have done, but I don't desert my friends when they get in trouble. If I think a man is bad for the union I say so and I try to get rid of him. Friendship and loyalty are something else again. I may be wrong, but that is the way I feel about it."

"Thank you, Mr. Rafferty." Ames took his glasses off and laid them on the table and turned to Senator Fellows.

"I have nothing further to ask Mr. Rafferty," he said.

Chairman Fellows slowly got to his feet.

"At this time," he said, "we are going to introduce into the evidence two recordings from wiretappings made on Mr. Rafferty's private telephone wire in his Los Angeles office. Immediately after these records have been played and made a part of this case, we shall adjourn until further notice. The first recording ..."

Once more Kauffman was on his feet.

"This time," he said, and his voice was pitched high in anger, "I must really object. The Federal Government has firmly established that wiretapping ..."

"Please, Mr. Kauffman," Senator Fellows said. "We've been over all of that before and this Committee needs no lecture on wiretapping. This is not a criminal court, as I have said time and again."

"But Senator," Kauffman said, "the use of recordings from an illegal wiretap ..."

Fellows held up his hand.

"Your objection is overruled," he said tiredly. "I am handing a copy of the transcript of these recordings to the witness. The Committee members also have copies. We will proceed, if the audience will remain quiet so that we may hear the words. Mr. Ames, please."

Ames stood up.

"I would like to call Everett Barton to the stand. Mr. Barton."

A heavy-set man in a gray business suit pushed forward.

Ames nodded to the chairman and Senator Fellows at once swore him in. He asked, "Your name, address, and occupation, please."

"Everett Barton, Los Angeles, California. I am a private detective."

Senator Fellows handed him a copy of the recording transcripts and said, "Counsel for the Committee will take over."

"You made the wiretap from which these recordings were made, Mr. Barton?"

"I did."

"What wire did you tap and when?"

"The private telephone wire of John Carroll Rafferty in his office in Los Angeles. The taps were made less than eight weeks ago." He hesitated and consulted a slip of paper and then continued, "the first one at eleven fifteen on the morning of June ninth, to be exact. The second one on the same day at two o'clock in the afternoon."

"Will you now listen to the recording of these two wiretaps and tell this Committee if these are the tapes you made and whether they are exact reproductions of the conversations which you tapped in on?"

"I will."

Morris nodded to the technician sitting next to him and the man turned on his recorder.

There was the sound of a telephone bell ringing and then a man's voice.

"Yes?"

"Mr. Rafferty, Washington is calling. Will you take it?"

"Who's calling from Washington?"

"They didn't say. Said it was personal. It's a man's voice and I think ..."

"Don't think, put him on."

There was a pause and a third voice came on.

"Jack?"

"Yeah. How are things coming? Is ..."

"Jack, are you where I can talk to you?"

"Why sure, go ahead. Is anything wrong ..."

"Jack, I don't like what's happening. Have you read the papers this morning?"

"Yes. But what ..."

"About that Marks business. They're beginning to dig into it again and it's causing a stink. Now you know how I feel about it. It's a terrible thing and it should never have happened. We can't stand that kind of trouble and frankly, although I never liked Marks, it was a bad piece of business. I understand the police have questioned Faricetti about it."

"I believe they have. But he's in the clear. Tommy wouldn't ..."

"I want you to get rid of him, Jack. We're having enough trouble these days without thugs and hoodlums of his stripe being connected with us. You know how I've always felt ..."

"Faricetti hadn't anything to do with ..."

"I don't care, Jack. The police questioned him and they must have had some reason to do so. Anyway, you know what he is. We just can't afford to be associated with men like him. And right now, with all the bad publicity and with this Investigating Committee starting in on us, you just have to get rid of him. For once and for all."

"But Faricetti is ..."

"Don't quibble about it, Jack. He's your baby. You've always gone to bat for him but the time has come when he's got to go. Do you understand, Jack—I want him out. I don't care how you manage it, but get him out."

There was a long pause and then, "I see. But you realize he's done some good."

"He's given us just about the worst publicity we could get. God knows we have enough troubles without something like that Marks business ..."

"I said Faricetti had nothing to do with it. I know it was unfortunate, but ..."

"Just do what I say, Jack. For your sake as well as my own. Get rid of him. You can't afford, yourself, to be tied up with men like Faricetti. You know that. Think it over. Now, will you do as I say?"

Again there was a long pause.

"I'll do what you say."

Ames stood up as the recording ended.

"Mr. Barton," he said, "are you able to identify those voices?"

Barton scratched his head.

"The man who received the call was Jack Rafferty. I can positively identify his voice. I have heard it over the telephone at least fifty times. The other voice—well, I am not sure."

"All right, Mr. Barton. And now we will hear the other record." Once more he nodded to the man handling the recorder.

This time there were a number of preliminary squeaks and then finally a male voice, the same one which Barton had just identified as Rafferty's:

"Get me long distance."

"May I get the number for you, Mr. Rafferty?"

"No—no just get me long distance. And be sure to keep this wire clear. You understand? Another thing, Miss Harcourt. If the operator calls back and wants to know who made this call, you don't know. Have you got that clear? You *don't know*."

"I understand Mr. Rafferty. One moment, please."

Again there was a short pause.

"Long distance. May I ..."

"Operator, I would like to get Spring 7-1000 in New York City."

"What is your number, please?"

"This is Front 5-5200."

"Are you making a personal call to ..."

"Station to station. I'll talk with whoever answers."

"Thank you. One moment please."

During the next short pause there was a sudden stirring in the room, especially in the press box, where the telephone number had at once been recognized.

"Information Desk. New York Police Department."

"Please take this down. If you are interested in ..."

"Who is calling, please?"

"Never mind who's calling. And don't stall or I'll hang up. Just take this down. If you are interested in the Claude Marks murder, pick up a small-time hoodlum named Patsy Farmer. Also pick up Guiseppi Morelli. He is Tommy Faricetti's cousin. Farmer threw the acid and he will talk if you work on him. Morelli paid him off. Faricetti ordered the job done."

"Would you please repeat ..."

There was the harsh sound of a receiver being slammed down as the recording came to an end in a dead silence.

Tommy Faricetti stood up slowly, moving like an old man. He slouched across the room and leaned down and snapped the switch of the television set and then he turned and looked at his attorney, who stood across the room leaning against the window frame.

He didn't speak. He just stood there, an old man, tired and worn, his face dead and his eyes devoid of expression.

Francis MacNammera said, "Tommy, Tommy, I'm sorry. I just don't know what to ..."

He stopped when Faricetti shook his head. Moving slowly, Faricetti leaned down and lifted the television set and jerked it free from the cord which held it to the electric socket. He crossed the room and laid it on the bed on its side and then, still without speaking, he opened the back and retrieved the bills which he had taped to the side of the set. He stood up and held them out.

"I won't be needing them," he said. "I want you to see that the old lady ..."

"Look, Tommy," MacNammera said, "now don't just give up. We can still ..."

"There's nothing we can do," Tommy said. "Nothing at all. Just take these and see that ..."

"But, Tommy ..."

"Do what I say, Francis." He didn't raise his voice, just continued to hold out the money.

MacNammera moved forward and took the bills from his hand.

"Tommy, I'll do anything you want, you know that. But why ..."

"You got your car outside, haven't you, Francis?"

"Yes, but ..."

"All right. Just do what I say. Now. Get in your car and drive up to New York and go out to Brooklyn and see that the old lady gets the money. She's going to need it. Don't say anything more, don't hang around. I want you to go now. Right away."

"But Tommy, how about you? What ..."

"Francis, you are my friend, aren't you?"

"Of course I'm your friend. I just ..."

"Then don't say anything more. Don't even say goodbye. Just get in the car and do what I ask."

MacNammera hesitated a moment and then sighed. He reached for his hat and started for the door, but hesitated. Turning, he stepped back and threw one arm across Tommy Faricetti's shoulder and then once more turned and quickly left.

Three minutes later Tommy Faricetti himself left the motel. He wore a gray felt snapped-brimmed hat pulled over his forehead and a pair of dark glasses. He was driving the rented black sedan and he headed it toward the Arlington Memorial Bridge leading into Washington. The stubby black automatic lay on the seat next to him, under a folded newspaper.

Jake Meadows leaned against a pillar, at the bottom of the long flight of granite steps leading up into the building in which the Joint Legislative Committee for the Inquiry into Labor Practices had recently ended its latest session. It was after five o'clock and he stood there idly, smoking a stub of cigarette as he talked with Cartwright Minton, the AP man.

"What the hell are you hanging around for, Cart?" he asked. "It's all over. There isn't any more."

"I'm waiting for my wife," Minton said. "She's supposed to pick me up." He took a thin cigar out of his breast pocket and put it into his mouth, but didn't light it.

"Well, that's that," he said. "A lot of sound and fury and then nothing. He talked but he didn't say anything."

"Yeah, he talked," Jake said. "But what he didn't say was plenty. If a man ever proved himself a double-crossing son-of-a-bitch, Rafferty …"

"You're crazy," Minton said. "Rafferty came through stronger than ever. Suppose he did turn Faricetti in. Hell, it's a public service."

"Sure, sure. It also proved he had knowledge …"

"It proved nothing. It matters how you want to look at it. He wouldn't necessarily have had to know anything about the Marks business until after it happened. They can never prove anything one way or another. But at least the record is clear. He was responsible for the tip which will send Faricetti and his gang to the chair or at least put them away for a long, long time. Anyway, you can bet on one thing. This hearing hasn't hurt Jack Rafferty one bit. He's going ahead the way he always has. He'll be the next President of the ISU."

"You want to bet on that?"

"I don't bet," Minton said. "But …"

"Well, you might be right," Jake said. "However, I just have a hunch …"

"Say, what are you waiting around for, anyway?" Minton asked. "God, I should think you'd be only too glad …"

"Rafferty hasn't come out yet," Jake said. "He should be along any minute now."

"Sure," Minton said. "But so what? You've already filed your story and you know damned well that you won't get a word out of Rafferty. Rafferty isn't going to do any talking. Not today, especially. Have a heart. He's on his way to his daughter."

"You're right," Jake said casually. "By the way," he said, "that isn't your wife waiting across the street there, is it?"

Minton followed Jake's eyes over to where the black sedan was parked at the curb.

"Are you crazy?" he asked. "That isn't a woman in that car. It's a man. A man in a snap-brim hat wearing dark glasses. You need to see an oculist. You're a little blind."

"Yeah," he said, "I guess I am."

Turning, he looked up as the door of the building swung open at the top of the steps.

"Here comes Rafferty now," he said.

THE END

TO FIND A KILLER
Lionel White

To My Mother

CHAPTER I

1.

The time is very short and I should like to have it all clear in my own mind.

In thinking back to the moment I made that decision, it seems to me the complex motives behind it must have been building up over a long, long time—perhaps even from the very day I was born. But then again, the decision itself, was something which had to be made at one specific point in my life. I believe I remember the exact moment.

It is odd how we can entertain the vagrant fragments of an idea for months and years, and then some little, insignificant thing will happen and all the pieces will swiftly fit into the pattern of a complete whole. We suddenly have, crystallized in our hearts and minds, a very definite thing—a thing which up until that moment had only been haunting the fringes of our consciousness. It was that way with this decision.

Yes, that is the way it was. It is all very clear to me, now.

2.

The decision itself came sometime between five and six o'clock, on a Sunday morning, of the last week in August. I know I had returned to the small one family house in which Fern and I live, on the North Shore of Long Island, some twenty-five miles from Times Square.

I know now, also, that the decision itself was beginning to take form much earlier that evening. It is, probably, no coincidence that on that night the Billy Chamlers case broke wide open. Yes, the thing began to crystallize when Sal and I walked into the exotic, scented, apartment on East Sixty-first Street and I pushed a uniformed patrolman aside and looked down at the still warm body of the ridiculously beautiful nightclub singer. Somehow or other, even then, with the purple-red blood splashed over her white face and dripping onto the equally white pillow, she reminded me in a strange way of Fern.

The call had come to us directly from the captain's office—that would be Captain George O'Shea, in charge of the homicide detail at headquarters down on Center Street. It came around eight o'clock on a Saturday night, shortly after we had checked in and while Sal and I were playing a game of cribbage up in the information room. We were both quietly hoping it would be a slow weekend.

I picked up the interoffice phone.

The captain was very brief.

"A homicide at 560 East Sixty-first Street. Third floor. Precinct man reported it five minutes ago. Get going." That was all.

We went uptown in one of the department Mercurys and I drove. A recent department economic shakeup had left us without a chauffeur and I was just as glad. I made better time driving myself and I found it unnecessary to use either the siren or the red spotlight except when we ran through traffic signals.

"No hurry," Sal said once when I narrowly missed a Fourth Avenue bus. "Whoever it is, is already dead."

I slowed down to forty-five. Sal Brentano is as quiet and subdued as his appearance would indicate. He and I have been partners, on the homicide squad, working out of headquarters, for more than five years. He is, also, my best friend.

With his short stature and slight frame, his rimless glasses concealing the eyes of a tired priest, you'd never take Sal for a cop.

An ambulance squatted at the curb in front of the four-story, brownstone house, its engine purring like a sleek, fat cat. There was a second precinct car angled in front of it. Two uniformed patrolmen were keeping a curious crowd moving in each direction, past the house. A man I vaguely recognized as a plainclothesman from the local precinct, lounged at the opened doorway. He nodded as we climbed the granite steps.

"Ev'ning, Lieutenant," he said and shook hands with me. He nodded to Sal.

I tried to remember his name and couldn't. I asked him what it was all about.

"Some nightclub singer. Name's Billy Chamlers," he said. "Found by a guy named Sam Duffy. Her manager. She was supposed to be at the Velvet Room at the Maddox House at seven. When she didn't show, this Duffy came over to find out what happened. Said he phoned first and there was no answer. Then he got here and he walked in and found her dead. Head bashed in. The doc's up there now."

I nodded and we turned toward the stairs. There was a self-operated elevator, but we didn't bother with it.

The apartment took up the entire third floor. A beat patrolman let us in.

"Body's in the bedroom," he said. He gestured toward the rear.

I was in no hurry and looked around as we crossed the living room. It was something. The wall-to-wall carpet caressing our boots must have been three inches thick. It was powder blue. The walls themselves were a deep purple; that is, three of them were. The fourth was all brick and embraced a wide, flush fireplace. A baby grand piano stood in one corner, its exposed white and black keys grinning at a huge blonde combination television and record player in a second corner. A nine-foot sofa covered in leopard skin squatted in front of the fireplace.

The furniture was constructed mostly of a pickled wood; I believe they call it Swedish modern. Two or three water colors, originals, hung on the wall. And underlying the stale smell of cigar and cigarette smoke was the overpowering odor of perfume.

"Perfume," Sal said. "And expensive. Only too much of it."

"Nightclub singers do better than I thought," I said.

"They don't do this well," Sal answered, one slender hand vaguely indicating the lush appointments surrounding us.

We went down a long, narrow hallway and I noticed there was a half-opened door leading into a black tiled bath. Opposite, a second door shut off a kitchen and dinette. At the end of the hallway was the bedroom and that door, too, was open. The scent of perfume was almost overwhelming as we approached.

The fingerprint men were already there and a police photographer was setting up his equipment. Perhaps a dozen other men were crowded into the room and most of them I recognized at once as police. A pale, fat man with the ruined face of athlete gone to seed, sat hunched in a delicate wing chair and stared sightlessly at the bed. Sam Duffy, I figured.

The doc looked up as we moved across the room and several men stepped to one side.

"She's all yours," the doc said.

I edged close and looked down at her. It was then that I thought of Fern.

I had to push the uniformed patrolmen slightly to one side to get the full sweep of her body in my vision.

There was no doubt about what had happened to Billy Chamlers. She'd been lying there on the bed, stark naked, probably sleeping. And then something had awakened her and she had started to lift her head. Whoever it was who had disturbed her sleep had taken the crystal vase and hit her full in the face. The first blow had probably broken the vase. It had certainly broken that once beautiful face. Pieces of shattered glass were still buried in the macerated flesh. But I wasn't thinking of that.

After a while, after you have seen a great many dead bodies—bodies broken and bodies shot and bodies violated in every conceivable way man has discovered by which to destroy his fellow man—you become case-hardened. You look down at a dead person and you only wonder how he was killed, and when he was killed, and perhaps how old he was and in what sort of condition at the time death overtook him. It is a matter of cold mathematical calculation and the dead body doesn't really mean anything personal to you at all. It has to be this way if you're going to be a good cop.

But this time it was different.

The hair was the same. Even with the crimson brilliance of her blood streaking it, it still reminded me of Fern's blond loveliness—a loveliness which always seemed to form a sort of silvery nimbus around her beautiful face.

The face beneath the hair was nothing now. Probably it, too, had been beautiful. But the body below that shattered head again reminded me of Fern. The same slender column of throat and the same strong wide shoulders supporting beautifully formed, firm and not too large breasts. The same flat stomach and the swelling thighs and long slender legs.

This girl was probably an inch taller than Fern, and the delicate olive tint of her flesh was a shade or two darker, even in death. Fern was twenty-six and this one must have been about the same age. But this girl was dead, smashed into oblivion by the brutal hand of a murderer. Fern was home in bed, softly sleeping and waiting for my return. Or was she?

I shook my head to clear my mind and turned to Sal.

"How long, doctor?" Sal asked in his soft voice. The voice with the "bedside manner."

The police surgeon looked at his wristwatch.

"Well, it's almost nine-thirty now," he said. "Off hand, before an autopsy, I'd hazard a guess of three to four hours. Would make it around six." He reached down and casually pulled a sheet half across the body, partly covering that naked loveliness which so reminded me of Fern.

"She was probably hit once and she probably died within the minute. From the fragments, I'd say it was an especially heavy glass vase. Caved in the front of her skull. I'll give you a complete …" His voice dwindled to silence and he turned and began to close his little black bag.

I turned to the photographer.

"Get your shots," I said. "Then send down for the basket. Who's that?" I pushed a thumb toward the fat man in the wing chair.

"Name's Duffy," one of the plainclothesmen said. "He found her and phoned in. Waited till we got here. I kept him."

I nodded.

"Anybody …"

"No."

"O.K.," I said. I walked over to the chair.

"Come on," I said. "We'll talk."

Silently he followed Sal and me out of the room. I turned into the kitchen and the three of us crowded around a small breakfast table in the alcove.

"Let's have it," I said.

He looked up at me and his pudgy face was sick.

"God! She was like a daughter to me."

His voice was a whisper and he talked like a man who wasn't quite aware of what he was saying.

Sal nudged me and I knew that he wanted to take it. Sal, with that soft, sympathetic manner of his, is much better a lot of times than I am. He has a way with them; can take them out of fear or out of shock.

"I know how you must be feeling, Mr. Duffy," he said. "But you'll have to try and pull yourself together. There's nothing you can do about her now—except help us find who did it to her. Tell me, you have known her long?"

Duffy looked up at him and for the first time his yellow eyes seemed to show some faint trace of awareness. "Long? Yes, a long long time. I've known Baby for …"

"I thought her name was Billy?" I said.

The yellow eyes looked over at me.

"Billy was her professional name," he said. "She took it when she started singing."

Sal nodded.

"How long have you known her?" he asked.

He seemed not quite aware of us then, for a time, and his eyes again went blank. There was a full minute of silence and I thought he had gone back into his shock. But then he spoke and you could almost hear the sob in his hoarse, barely audible voice.

I'm used to that sob and it never fools me. It can mean anything. I've heard it when I've talked to men who have just lost someone who is the dearest thing in the world to them. But I have also heard it in the voices of men who have freshly strangled their wives. It only means that the person who has it in his voice is sick with heartbreak; it doesn't mean that he is innocent or guilty.

"Baby—Billy—is twenty-five. I first knew her when she was fifteen. I'm Sam Duffy. Theatrical agent. I've an office at 1660 Broadway. Been there for years. She came to me when I was running a deal to train radio and stage singers. When she was still a school kid. She's been like a daughter to me ever since."

"You came here tonight," Sal said, "and found her?"

Duffy looked up at him and his eyes were again glazed with misery. "Yes."

"You telephoned first?"

"Yes. At seven o'clock. She had planned to meet me a little earlier at the Velvet Room, and we were going to have dinner. She didn't show up, which was unusual as she always keeps her appointments. And so I got worried and I came over here."

"And then you rang the bell and ..."

"No," Duffy said. This time his voice was sharp and quick. He looked up at Sal, then at me, and there was intelligence and a trace of resentment in his face.

"No. The downstairs door is always open until ten at night."

"The upstairs door, that, too, was open?"

"No, you see I have a key."

Sal began to say something, but I cut in quick.

"How long have you been keeping her, Duffy?" I asked.

For a fat man he was amazingly fast. We each reached our feet in the same instant.

"You bastard," he said, and the hoarse voice melted into a thin, angry scream as though he were in pain. He started to throw a punch and Sal managed to get between us.

"The Lieutenant didn't mean it," Sal said and his tone was soothing and understanding. He turned to me. "I'll take it for a while, Lieutenant," he said.

Sal made the words sound as though I were a first-class son of a bitch. I shrugged and walked out of the room. It was an old act and we played it to perfection.

I was glad to get away. I didn't like Duffy; I didn't like whatever relationship he may have had with the dead girl. God knows it meant nothing to me, any more than she meant anything to me. Except that she reminded me of Fern.

Christ, I thought in disgust—have I reached a point where I can become jealous of women who have even a vague physical resemblance to my wife?

3.

Over a cup of coffee in the all-night restaurant at the corner, Bill Albright from the D.A.'s office briefed me on the other tenants in the apartment building and it looked as if there would be no help coming from anyone who was home at the time of the killing. The janitor who lived in the basement only remembered hearing the elevator at about seven-twenty.

"That was probably when Duffy showed up," Bill said.

I nodded.

"Killer sure picked his time."

Bill laughed.

"His time and his girl. Yeah. One thing I did get though. The tenants mostly mailed their rent into the agency. Except for the Chamlers gal. She always gave a check for her rent to the janitor and he would in turn give it to the agent, who made a practice of dropping around once a month with the janitor's own paycheck. "Well it just happened that the janitor got the check yesterday and was holding it until the first of the week, when it was due to be picked up."

Bill smiled wisely and took a notebook out of his pocket. He read from it.

"Two hundred and twenty-five dollars. Drawn on the Penn National Bank, North Philadelphia branch. Signed: K.V.D. Malcolm. And for the year and a half that the janitor—whose name by the way is Louie Panatelli—has been here, he's always received the same check, drawn the same way. Check was made out to Billy Chamlers, dated yesterday, and endorsed over."

I nodded. It fitted. I figured somebody must have been keeping her. I don't know why, but the idea made me mad.

Bill handed over the notebook and I wrote down the information.

"We checked the apartment," Bill went on. "Don't know whether anything is missing or not. She had some jewelry in a dresser drawer, but it's mostly junk. There's a colored woman comes in by the day, but this was her day off. We have her name and a vague sort of address up in Harlem. I got one of your boys trying to dig her up."

I said thanks.

"You probably noticed, the windows in the bedroom were open and one of them leads out onto a fire escape which runs down the back of the house and ends in an alley. No screens. Checked the lock on the front door and it doesn't look like it's been tampered with. Regular Yale snap lock."

"You thinking of prowlers maybe?" I asked.

"Thinking of everything," Bill said. "Whoever it was must have come in while she was sleeping. She started to wake up. And that was it. Could have been a prowler."

I nodded. It could have. I didn't think so.

I thought of her lying dead there on that bloodstained bed. And then again I thought of Fern. For some reason, which I'll never be quite able to figure out, I decided to go to the telephone booth in the corner and call my house out on Long Island.

"'Scuse me a second, Bill," I said. "I want to make a call."

It was the first time I had ever done it—in the three years of our marriage. And God only knows why I did it then. Fern certainly never expected me to call while I was on regular duty.

I could hear the bell ringing, and then a dead silence, and then ringing again. I looked down at my wristwatch. It was close to twelve o'clock.

I knew that if Fern had gone to a movie she would have been back by this time. I hung up and dialed over again and I got the same result. So then I put the dime in the slot again and dialed the operator and gave her the number. I waited while she told me three times that she was still ringing and that there was no answer.

I jammed the receiver back on the hook. I was annoyed and I slammed out of the booth without waiting for the return of my coin.

"Something wrong?" Bill asked when I got back to the table.

"Nothing," I said shortly. "Think I'll skip the second cup and get back," I added.

Bill said he'd be seeing me. After all, he wasn't actively on the case yet and he was just sort of filling in early details in case he might need them later. He had all the time in the world.

I stalked out of the lunchroom and headed back for the Chamlers apartment. As I approached, I was half-consciously aware that the ambulance had left, but my mind was certainly not on the case. I couldn't imagine where Fern was; why she hadn't answered the telephone if she had been home and where she might possibly be if she wasn't home.

4.

The cop on the first floor told me Sal was down in the basement talking to the janitor. I went down the inside staircase and pushed a few kids out of my way to enter the apartment. It smelled as strongly of garlic as the Chamlers girl's had of perfume.

Sal and Louie Panatelli were jabbering away in Italian. A folded check lay on the table between them.

Finally Sal looked up. He gestured toward the check.

"I know about it," I said.

Sal nodded.

"Louie here tells me he doesn't think anything is missing," Sal said. "It also seems several people had keys to the apartment. The maid, Duffy, some tall, thin, elderly guy who always showed up around the fifth and the twentieth of the month. Probably the guy who signs these checks. Louie says he would get his rent after the second visit. I'm afraid our gal was a bit of a tramp."

"How the hell do you know?" I snapped.

Sal looked up at me in quick surprise.

"What?"

"Sorry, Sal," I said. "I wasn't thinking. The fact is, I got a lousy headache. Feel crummy. I wasn't even listening to what you were saying."

Sal looked at me sympathetically.

"Look," he said. "Why don't you go on home and hit the deck. The precinct boys are doing everything that can be done for the time being. I'll stick around for a while and then we can really get started tomorrow, after some of the leg work is out of the way."

I nodded.

"Tell you what, Sal," I said. "We'll go back upstairs and see what's happening. If everything is under control, I'll just take you up on that."

But it was almost three o'clock before I finally made the break. There wasn't much new, just routine stuff. Duffy'd been sent along home and we had men going through the place with a fine-tooth comb. Sal himself wrapped up all the letters, bills and correspondence in the place. He was going to take them down to headquarters and study them over later.

I had to talk to the press for a few minutes and then at last I got away. I probably didn't make very good sense with the newspaper boys. My mind wasn't on Billy Chamlers. It was on Fern.

I left the official car for Sal and said good night. I told him to say hello to Mom for me. He told me to take care of myself. "And give my love to Fern," he said.

I took a bus to Forty-second Street and went down into the subway.

I dropped a token into the slot and climbed on a local. I'd bought a Sunday morning paper and first I read the comics and then turned to the sports pages. It was an hour's ride out to Flushing and by the time I'd got to the end of the line I was through with the paper. I can't remember a thing I read. My mind wasn't on it.

The parking lot was empty except for my five-year-old Buick coupe. I climbed in and began the last lap. The car was like an oven.

The garage doors under the rear of the house were open as they were supposed to be. There were no lights in the house, and I had expected none. If Fern were home she would be in bed. She had long ago given up the custom of our honeymoon days of waiting up for me.

I parked the car, cut the ignition and deliberately got out and pulled down the overhead door. I entered the house through a door leading into the kitchen.

5.

You'd think, after that telephone call which Fern hadn't answered, that the first thing I'd do would be to run upstairs and see if she was in. But I didn't. I can't explain just why, but somehow I just didn't. Perhaps, somewhere in the back of my consciousness, I was afraid she wouldn't be there. I don't know.

In remembering back, I do recall however, that it never occurred to me anything could have happened to her in the house. It's a strange thing and I guess I'm like a lot of other cops that way. I spend so much time putting my nose into other people's tragedies and troubles that it never enters my mind that I could have any of my own.

Usually when I come home late, I go to the icebox and take out some cold cuts and make myself a sandwich and have it with a glass of milk.

Instead, I took out a cold can of beer, punctured the top and sat at the kitchen table with it in front of me.

And then I took the letter from my pocket, the letter I'd received that morning at headquarters. The one from the friend of mine with the FBI down in Washington. I knew its contents by heart, but nevertheless, I sat there once more rereading it. The part I was interested in was brief; to the point.

> ... and we have been unable to find any record of a Fern Taylor. There is no such place as the St. Obisbo Convent. The fingerprints which you sent me, however, belong to a Joan Bronski, 26 years old, born in Portland, Ore., who served two and a half years in Tehachapi Reformatory for Women in California, after a conviction for grand larceny. She skipped parole after being released four years ago and no record has been had of her since that time....

The fingerprints belonged to my wife. She had written the name Fern Taylor on our marriage certificate when we had been wed three years ago.

I finished the beer, threw the empty can in the sink. I felt sick.

There was a full moon riding low in the eastern sky and it gave just enough illumination so that it wasn't necessary for me to turn on a light in the living room as I carefully crossed it and started upstairs.

Fern had, as usual, undressed in the bathroom, which I could tell by the pile of clothes which lay in a heap where she had dropped them beside the shower stall.

I took off my jacket and realized that it must be inordinately hot. The leather straps of my shoulder holster were damp and sticky. I laid the holster with the thirty-eight police special still in it, on top of the clothes hamper. Next to it I put my wallet and the blackjack and wrist chain which I carry attached to my belt. Also my badge in its leather sheath.

Then I loosened my tie and removed my shirt and ran a bowl of lukewarm water in the sink.

I had planned to take a cold shower before turning in, but I was very tired and didn't want to go to the trouble of digging up fresh towels.

So I compromised by bathing my face and hands and picked up one of Fern's discarded towels from the floor.

I opened the cabinet above the sink and reached for my toothbrush.

I groped for the toothpaste and it wasn't there.

A moment later I saw the twisted tube lying at the edge of the tub. The cap was off and nowhere in sight.

"Damn Fern," I said. "I wish she could remember to put that goddamned cap back on."

For some reason this irritated me extremely and I returned my toothbrush to the rack without using it. I picked up my jacket and shirt and tie and opened the door to our bedroom.

There was a dim reading light still on over the head of the double bed. An opened movie magazine lay on the scatter rug at the side of the bed. Fern had fallen asleep without raising the window and the fetid air in the room was stifling.

Unconsciously I reached over and pulled the linen sheet up so that it covered Fern's naked breasts. She lay flat on her back, in the very center of the bed, her arms spread wide. Her hair—long fine blonde hair which in certain lights looked almost like silver thread, and which reached well below her shoulders when she was standing up, was spread loosely over the white pillow case. Both pillows were under her head and her lips were partly opened as she breathed lightly. The line of her jaw was clean and sweet and she looked like a little girl.

It was hard to realize that we had been married for almost three years. It was hard to believe that letter from Washington.

I tripped over one of her mules as I walked around the bed to snap off the night light. And then I hung my clothes on the back of a chair and after stripping off my socks and shorts, went to the window and opened it all the way.

Fern moaned softly in her sleep as I crawled into bed beside her. She only weighed a hundred and ten pounds, but she was a dead weight as I eased her over so that I could find room to stretch out.

I must have lain there for a full half hour, unable to sleep. I was thinking of Fern and of our life together. The moon had disappeared, but the sun had yet to find the horizon and the room lay in darkness. There was no breath of air.

I turned on my side and the movement must have disturbed Fern.

Once more she moaned ever so gently. And then she, too, turned on her side so that she was facing me. One slender arm reached out and fell across my chest. She kicked out with one foot and the movement pulled the thin sheet from the upper part of our bodies. Her knees bent and her leg came close to my bare thigh and her body closed in so that it fitted into the curve of my own body.

She breathed a little more heavily and for a moment I thought that she had awakened. Her head fell back. I leaned forward and found her lips, which were still half opened.

Fern's arm drew tight around me as she pulled me over her.

It was like it always was. Beautiful.

Fern is the only woman I have ever known or heard of who made love in her sleep. Every subtlety, every delicious movement was there. But she never opened her eyes and she slept through it all. It was only at the very end, as I lay there panting and exhausted, that I could feel her lips move ever so slightly. I lifted my head and then I heard the words, very distinctly. She wasn't awake, that I knew. But it wasn't quite as though she were still fully asleep or were talking in her sleep.

She said, "Harry—oh Harry!"

It was right then, in that very second, that I made my decision.

Me, Marty Ferris.

I decided to kill my wife.

CHAPTER II

1.

I tried to ignore the sound of the telephone at the side of the bed, intermittently jangling, and was unsuccessful. The damned instrument kept ringing and so at last I opened my eyes. The room was bright with sunlight and I guessed at once that it must be near noontime. Fern, a good Catholic, undoubtedly had gone to church.

My right hand took the receiver from the hook.

"Marty Ferris speaking," I said.

It was Sal.

"You up yet, Marty?" he asked.

I grunted.

"The captain just had me on the phone," he continued. "Seems the newspaper boys have been after him for something on the Chamlers case. So far there is nothing to give them and he suggested we get to work."

"I'm working," I said. "I'm waking up."

"You're a dog," Sal said. "I haven't been asleep yet."

He laughed and his laugh was tired. "Suppose you meet me at the

Chamlers apartment in an hour. I'll wait for you and give you what we got so far, then I'll knock off for a couple hours."

I told him to make it an hour and a half and that I'd be there.

Sal talked for a couple of minutes more, sort of filling me in on everything which had been accomplished since I'd left. I was becoming more fully awake. And I was having a hard time following what Sal was saying. My mind was exactly where it had been when I had fallen asleep some five or six hours earlier. My mind was on Fern.

"O.K., Sal," I said. "O.K. Hold it and I'll be there as soon as I can make it."

I hung up.

I pulled myself out of bed and grabbed a dressing gown from the closet. I didn't bother with slippers. It was still hotter than hell. I went to the bathroom.

There were a couple of fresh towels added to the pile on the floor.

I couldn't help staring at my face in the mirror as I shaved. I thought, Jesus, can this be the face of a man who has decided to commit murder? And then I felt the fury rising in me and try as I might, I couldn't control it.

When I drew the razor blade down over my lean cheek, my hand shook and I cut myself. The blade was dull and I knew at once that Fern had used it for cutting something and hadn't bothered to replace the blade with a fresh one. I snapped the razor open and the blade was badly nicked. Looked like she'd been sharpening a pencil with it.

Christ, I thought, what the hell is wrong with her? Where was she brought up, anyway? And that question started it all over again.

Until recently I had believed that I knew my wife as well as it is possible for a man to know the woman with whom he is in love. And I had been in love with Fern from the very moment I had met her, exactly four months to the day from the time we were married.

She had been the only girl in my life; the only person I had ever accepted without question, without reservation. Of course now, in looking back, it seems almost insane that I could have taken the attitude and acted the way in which I did. I guess it all stems from my own background and my own personality.

You see, with me, everything has been different. I wasn't like other children, I wasn't raised like other children and I didn't think like other children.

It began one day, back when I was about eight years old. I had never remembered having a mother, and so one day I asked my dad about it. My dad was a cop, a good cop, and I worshiped him. I guess he thought I was old enough and so he told me the truth.

My mother had left him soon after I had been born. She'd run off with a musician. About six months later the two of them had been killed in an auto crash down in Georgia. The way Dad explained it, I didn't feel any special bitterness against my mother—I just thought that all women were bad. Bad and dangerous.

What happened to Dad a few years later hadn't helped matters much. He was a good cop, as I said, but he made one mistake. He raided a Bronx apartment where he had been tipped off that three bank robbers were hiding out. His mistake was in not taking any other cops along with him.

He killed two of them when they opened fire, but the third one got him with a submachine gun. Later, the killer was picked up and sent to the chair. But by that time my father was already a dead hero.

Sal—Sal and his mother, Mom—were probably the only ones who knew and still remembered the details of my childhood. For you see, Mom had raised me after my dad was killed. She and Sal's father had known him from the old days; they had known my mother also.

The death of my father, and the story he had told me about my mother, left me with a lifelong prejudice and a lifelong hatred. I always distrusted girls and women and I had a deep-seated, unreasoning hatred of all crooks.

Sal had argued with me about it often enough. And so have the captain and others in the department. Told me that there are crooks and crooks. Some better and some worse. But I look at criminals the way I look at women. Goddamn it, they're either crooks or they're not. Either good or bad. I don't see any shadings!

There's one thing I believe. I believe a man is guilty until he proves himself innocent. The hell with putting it the other way around. An innocent man should be able to prove it easily enough. There are a lot of boys in homicide who disagree with me, but the fact remains, I have one of the best records in the department for sewing up cases. When I work on a case, the D.A. gets a conviction.

Anyway, about Fern and myself. As I say, she was the first woman—outside of Sal's Mom of course—in my life. I had had no experience with girls at all. That is, no personal, romantic experience.

I met Fern by accident—literally an accident. In a way, it was a pickup. She'd been walking down the stairs in the subway station at West Ninety-sixth Street early one morning, in front of me, and she'd tripped and fractured her ankle. I helped her up. Then, after I'd called an ambulance, I carried her upstairs and checked her into the emergency ward at the hospital.

I don't know what it was about her, but from the very second I held her slight body in my arms, I was gone.

First I visited her in the hospital, and then, later, I saw her in the two-room apartment which she shared with another girl who worked with her in the office of one of the big insurance firms downtown.

The Lord only knows what we found to talk about, but it wasn't about our families. I never told her much about mine, only that I was an orphan. I guess that was one of the things which had drawn us together. Because she had told me that she, too, was an orphan, her mother and father having died during an epidemic when she was an infant. She said she had been raised by the sisters at St. Obisbo Convent in California. I had believed her.

Four months from the day I had first met her, we were married. She quit her job as I didn't want my wife working. Things were fine for those first two years. I guess we both had so much to learn, so many things to find out, that the time just passed. And then the change began.

At first it was nothing much, just an odd way Fern had of seeming vague and distracted. Almost secretive. Later, a couple of times, I caught her in small lies. She would tell me that she'd gone to a movie, and then not be able to tell me what was playing when I asked her about the picture.

I didn't say anything to her about it, but it worried me.

It wasn't until a couple of weeks previously, however, that things came to a head. At least, they came to a head in my own mind. I didn't discuss it with Fern.

That was when I came home unexpectedly late one afternoon and the phone rang. It was a man's voice and he started speaking the second I lifted the receiver.

"Get over here Kid, right away," the voice said. And then, when I didn't answer right off, the voice went on. "That's you Fern baby, isn't it?" he said.

I hung up. The next day I wrote my friend at the FBI. And I enclosed a set of Fern's fingerprints which I'd picked up off the toothbrush glass in our bathroom.

But I'm getting away from my story.

2.

Anyway, I finished shaving and I was still thinking about Fern. Somehow, when the phone rang a second later, and I picked the receiver off the hook, I wasn't surprised when I heard her voice.

"Mart?" she said.

"Who'd you expect, baby?"

Fern laughed. "Dope. How are you? Just get up?"

I said I had.

"I just left church," she went on. "And the funniest thing. I ran into a girl I used to know. Jill Bentley. She's some kind of an actress now; in a Broadway nightclub. Anyway, she wants me to have lunch with her. So if you don't mind...."

"Go ahead, kid," I said. "The captain put me on a tough one and I gotta meet Sal right away, anyhow. I'll call you later. You'll be home tonight?"

Fern gave a sort of half laugh.

"Of course, you crazy," she said. "Where'd you think I'd be?" She sounded surprised.

"O.K.," I said. "I'll call."

I hung up.

Jill Bentley. It was the first time in the years of our marriage that Fern had ever mentioned anyone from her past life. For some damned reason I was suddenly insanely jealous of this Jill Bentley. I determined to look her up; find out about her.

There was no coffee in the coffee jar and less than half a cup left in the Silex. I took two glasses of orange juice and called it a breakfast. I wasn't hungry anyway.

The garage doors were open and the Buick was gone so that I knew Fern had taken it. I damned a cop's salary which made it impossible to own a second car as I walked to the bus stop. It took me an hour to reach Grand Central, where I found a cab and directed the driver to the Chamlers apartment on Sixty-first Street.

I was out of the taxi and into the vestibule of the building before the group of newshawks across the street could reach me. The uniformed patrolman snapped the lock as the door slammed behind me.

I found Sal upstairs in the apartment. He looked tired.

"What's new?" I asked.

"Everything and nothing," Sal said. "Mostly that it could have been robbery. Seems there's some jewelry missing. A diamond and platinum wristwatch, which, from its description, must have been worth a couple of grand. It might have been given to her by Malcolm and we're checking on it. Tried to reach Malcolm, himself, through the Philly police, but he's out of town. Been gone several days. Also a pair of pearl earrings and a ring. Star sapphire set in platinum or white gold."

"You get the medical report yet?" I asked.

Sal nodded.

"Like we first figured. She was struck only once; killed instantly. No other sign of attack." He handed me a typed report which said the same thing in about three thousand words.

"About prints," I asked.

"A million," Sal said. "Of course plenty of hers. Then there were Duffy's, the janitor's, the maid's, a couple of sets which belong to Mrs. Panatelli, some which belong to the Panatelli kids. And probably at least ten or twelve which we haven't identified so far. Also a thumb and forefinger that belong to a guy downstairs, in the rear, name of Haverford—an advertising fellow. Sergeant Kelly talked with him."

Sal stopped for a minute and dug up some notes.

"Haverford is in his late twenties, a bachelor. Pretty much of a playboy, but he also makes money at his job. Clean record. He told us he knew the Chamlers girl and has had a couple of dates with her. Admitted he's been in the apartment, but not in the last week. Kelly got the impression that he was hot and bothered over her, but that he also plays the field. He's downstairs now waiting for you to talk to him."

"I'll get him later," I said. "What else?"

"Damned little. Haverford's alibi seems to hold up. The janitor could have been anywhere. All his wife and kids remember is that he was in and out all afternoon and early in the evening. Duffy cracked up and he's home now. Lives in one of those Broadway fleabags. The Milton Hotel on West Forty-sixth. We got a man on him. I talked to a Miss Rumson, a voice teacher, in the first-floor front and got nothing at all out of her. Except that she didn't seem to care for Billy Chamlers. Seems that she taught her for a while and there was an argument over money."

Sal pulled a sheaf of photos from a briefcase.

"Mug shots," he said. "Had 'em sent up from downtown. All of them apartment prowlers. Thought we might show 'em around in case there's anything to the robbery theory. If so, maybe the guy cased the place in advance and someone may recognize a picture. Personally, I don't buy the prowler idea."

I didn't either, but I didn't say so to Sal. There was a reason in the back of my mind that made the prowler theory particularly attractive to me, but it wasn't the kind of idea that I cared to discuss with Sal. In fact, it didn't have much to do with the Billy Chamlers case at all. I reached for the photographs.

"Anyone working on the Malcolm angle from this end?" I asked.

Sal nodded.

"It's covered and we expect a break sometime today."

3.

"Oke," I said. "Let's start at the basement." As we went out the phone was ringing and I picked up the receiver. It was Captain O'Shea.

"Gotta line on that Malcolm guy," he said. "He's back in Philly."

"They pick him up?"

"Hell no," O'Shea growled. "He's a big wheel in his hometown. Banker. Lives out in Paoli with his wife, who's social and got important connections. Two kids in college. Not the kind of guy you have picked up."

"Well …"

"The local boys are checking into his recent activities. They have to play it slow. We'll have a report by tomorrow morning and if it looks the way I think it's going to, I want you and Sal to go down and see him."

We talked for a couple of minutes more and I asked the captain for another man or two. He said he'd send them up and then hung up himself.

We took the self-service elevator to the basement.

Mr. and Mrs. Panatelli and four kids were in the kitchen and as we came in they all started to talk at once and then Sal said something in Italian which I didn't catch and they quieted down. I took out the folder of mug shots.

We were about halfway through them when Louie Panatelli grabbed one of the pictures and spoke rapidly to Sal. Mrs. Panatelli joined in and then a second later the children were looking over their father's shoulder.

I understand a little of the language, but they were talking all at one time and much too fast for me to follow. Sal waited until they'd quieted down and then turned to me.

"The milkman," he said. I took the picture and stared at it.

Wilbur Holiday. Age 24. Breaking and entering. The picture was taken seven years back. It showed a full face and profile of a slender man with a weak chin and watery eyes. A large nose curved over sensuous lips.

Sal took the photo and went into the front room where the telephone was. While he was gone I talked some more with the family. And then when Sal came back, he sent Mrs. Panatelli and the children into the other room and closed the door after them. He turned to the janitor.

"What kind of a woman was this Chamlers girl?" he asked.

Louie Panatelli gave an expressionable shrug.

"A woman," he said. "Who knows? She was always good to the kids. Gave us no trouble. Many people visited her. How should I say—she was the artist."

Apparently the janitor believed that artists were a special group of individuals and not to be judged by normal standards.

"Who was keeping her?" I said.

Again the janitor shrugged.

"She had many visitors," he repeated himself. "But she lived alone."

"This Duffy," I asked. "Did he come often? Did he stay over nights?"

"Often he was there. Staying—who knows?"

I wasn't getting anywhere and so I left Sal to continue the questioning. But I had learned one thing. Wilbur Holiday had been delivering milk at the apartment house for about four months. He seemed to have the concession for the entire house, but he always left all of the bottles at the janitor's door and stuck the bills in them once a week. As far as Panatelli knew, he never actually entered the apartment house proper.

But Wilbur Holiday had a record as a prowler. And he had done time.

They had a message for me when I got back upstairs. Headquarters had checked on Holiday's record and they said that he had been released from Sing Sing on parole some four months ago. They were able to get in touch with his parole officer and they had his address. The parole officer said Holiday was working for the Greater Boro Dairies as a delivery man and that he had, apparently, been going straight. He went to work at midnight and got off at eight in the morning.

I phoned back and told them to pick him up.

Sal came back upstairs and he looked dead beat. We left the

apartment house together and went down to the corner coffee shop. Sal ordered coffee while I horsed around for a few minutes, stalling the press. And then I joined him.

"Look, Sal," I said, "you go on home and hit the deck for a while. I'm going over and see Duffy. I think it's about time he had something to say. Plan to meet me down at headquarters at around eleven tonight. By that time they'll have picked up Holiday. If they haven't why we'll meet him at the dairy before he starts out."

Sal nodded.

"You still like that prowler idea?" he asked.

"I like it."

He looked at me for several seconds and his soft brown eyes blinked behind his rimless glasses.

"Bet you ten it was the guy in Philly," he said.

"You got a bet. Go on home now."

He took the Mercury and dropped me off at the subway. I got into a train going downtown.

4.

The clerk behind the desk in the first-floor lobby looked like a refugee from a tubercular camp. His shirt was silk and it was dirty. He didn't wear a tie. He was alone.

I leaned against the counter and looked at him.

"Oh God," he said, disgust heavy in his high-pitched voice. "Always cops."

"Look, Smelly," I said, "You got a guy named Duffy—Sam Duffy—living here. What's his room number?"

"One of your boys is already on his doorstep," he said. His voice was as unpleasant as his smell, which complemented the smell of the lobby itself.

"I didn't ask you that," I told him. "What room?"

He told me and I went over to the elevator. It was on the fifth floor and the desk clerk doubled as elevator boy. The cage rose as though it didn't think it would ever get there, but finally it did. He clanked the door open and I got out and saw a man from downtown leaning against the wall. I walked over and told him he could run downstairs and find something to eat. To kill about an hour and then come back.

"And Mr. Duffy will not be receiving any more callers for the afternoon," I said to the desk clerk, who was hanging out of the door with his ears flapping. The two went down in the cage and I banged on the door.

The night before, when I had first met and talked with Sam Duffy, I had thought he was probably one of these left-footed, North Irishmen. But when he opened the door a minute later I knew I had made a mistake. If he was Irish, then I'm a ballet dancer. I guess he'd tacked the Duffy onto his name to avoid some impossible mid-European handle which would have been a handicap in show business.

He needed a shave and the dark stubble stood out on his face in small, wily patches. His eyes were more yellow than ever and his flabby mouth looked as though he were about to cry. He was clothed in a filthy, brocaded dressing robe and his bare feet were thrust into ragged sandals. It made me a little sick just to look at him. He reminded me of a dyspeptic goat.

"You don't look well," I said. "Didn't you sleep?"

He made no move to invite me in.

"What do you want?"

"I want to talk, Mister Duffy," I said. "Just to talk. Do I come in?"

It was a sort of combination living-room-bedroom. Over against the far wall was an unmade bed, which looked as though it could be converted back into a couch. Next to it was an old-fashioned wrought iron ash stand filled with stale cigarette butts. One butt still smoldered and it added nothing to the fetid air in the small room.

In spite of the late August heat, the two small windows were tightly closed. There were a number of framed and autographed pictures on the walls. Most of them said "With love to Sammy," and from the unknown character of the signatures, I gathered they must have been mementos from his clientele. A faded Axminster and two leather chairs made up the rest of the furnishings.

An alcove to one side was half covered by a torn muslin curtain. From the smell, I figured it concealed a wash basin and an electric hot plate.

Sam Duffy sank down on the edge of the bed as I closed the door and went to one of the chairs. It was surprisingly comfortable.

"Duffy," I said, "my partner talked with you last night. Before you start, I want you to remember one thing—I'm not my partner. He has the gentle touch."

The fat man's ruined face went a shade whiter and he looked up at me with startled eyes.

"Yes," I said, "Sal takes a gentlemanly approach. I'm a little more crude. Keep that in mind when you talk to me."

"Am I under arrest?" Duffy asked.

"No pal," I answered, "you are not. And don't start yelling for your lawyer or demanding your rights. If you do, you'll end up defending yourself on a charge of resisting an officer—after you get out of the hospital. And you've been around long enough to know about that, haven't you, Sammy?"

The white complexion turned to a delicate shade of green and Duffy's hand shook as he reached out for the cigarette butt. We understood each other.

"I'll tell you whatever you want to know," Duffy said.

"I know you will, Sam," I said. "But don't only tell me what I want to know—tell me the truth. Now then, first about yourself. Let's just start say five years before you met Billy Chamlers."

"What you want...."

I reached over and sort of carelessly slapped him along the side of the face. Not so that it hurt.

"I ask the questions," I said. "Just start talking."

Sam gulped and then he started. I had to admit that he was pretty good, but then I guess he'd been questioned often enough in the past to know about what I would want.

The son of an East Side tailor, he'd quit school before he finished sixth grade. He'd become a hoofer. By the time he was twenty-five, he knew he'd never be any good and the combination of an inborn physical laziness and an avaricious appetite, made hoofing no longer even a bare livelihood possibility. So he had set himself up as a theatrical agent. He hadn't done too well. He'd had to branch out as a coach and voice teacher for potential Broadway talent.

It had been a tough living—and I guess it still was from the looks of Sam's quarters.

He'd had several brushes with the law. Nothing serious; just fraud charges when he'd made promises to pupils which he hadn't been able to deliver. He'd run a mail-order talent racket for a while, but the post office had closed him up. He met Billy Chamlers when she had answered an ad he'd inserted in a daily tabloid, seeking potential radio talent. He was thirty years old at the time.

I stopped him when he got that far. Just on a hunch.

"Sure that was the only kind of trouble, that post office thing, Sammy?" I asked.

He was on his fifth cigarette since I had entered his room. Sweat was pouring down his face and the sight of his obese body sprawled on the unmade bed made me sick at my stomach. His hand was shaking worse than ever.

"What do you mean?" he said.

I leaned forward and he drew away quickly.

"Well, the Chamlers girl was under age when you first met her. So were a lot of other girls who came to you, I guess. Didn't you ever get into any jams of any sort?"

I could tell by the way he reacted. God knows, I've questioned enough of them, that same sort of sixth sense lets me know. I didn't wait for Sammy to answer. I was too sure of myself.

"You dirty fat louse," I said, and stood up. "Tell me. Tell me quick!"

He let out a sort of half squeal and cowered. He spoke fast. "Yes. Yes. There was that one time with the Kolinsky girl. You know about that?"

"Tell me!"

"It was a rape charge. Statutory."

He was in such a hurry that he was sputtering. "But my God, I wasn't guilty. Even the judge said I had cause. That's why I got off on probation."

"And how about Billy Chamlers," I said quick. "How about her. Didn't you start laying her from the very first. When she was under age?"

His reaction was a complete surprise.

"You bastard," he screamed and he jumped from the bed. One pudgy fist shot out and I grabbed it in midair.

"You dirty bastard, you can't talk about her that way. She was clean—clean all the way through!"

Well, I got him quieted down at last. There was no longer any doubt of it in my mind. Whatever his relation with Billy Chamlers may have ended up in being, he had really loved the girl in his own peculiar fashion.

There were a couple of more things he told me. Billy had been under contract to him. Ten per cent for personal management and an additional ten for agency fee. She was getting two hundred a week at the Velvet Room, at the time she was killed. He had got her the job.

He started crying and getting sentimental about her. That's when I shot the question.

"How well do you know Jill Bentley?"

He stared at me for a second without expression.

"Who?"

"Jill," I said, "Jill Bentley."

"You mean the nightclub singer?"

I said I did.

"I hardly know her at all," he said. "She ain't no client of mine. I just know her name. What's she got to do with this?"

"I'm still asking the questions," I said. I got up and handed him an opened pack of cigarettes. He'd used up his own.

"I'll tell you what, Sammy," I said at last. "I think you've been leveling with me. Now I want you to do something. I want you to do it on the quiet and if you do a good job of it, I'll see to it that no one bothers you anymore.

"Get yourself up and dressed and get out on the street. I want you to find out everything you can about Jill Bentley. Everything there is. Where she lives, who she lives with if anyone, where she works, where she came from, who her friends are. Everything. And I want you to be sure no one finds out why you're getting this information. Very sure, Sammy, or God help you."

He nodded and he looked at me with a baffled expression. "Is she mixed up in this?" he asked at last.

"I can't tell you anything, Sammy," I said, my voice suddenly friendly. "Just do what I ask. Maybe I'll be able to do you a favor or so before we're through. But remember one thing, whatever you find out, you tell me and only me. No one else."

I left him pulling on his trousers.

The shadow was back in the hallway and I dismissed him. On my way downtown to headquarters, I stopped in a drugstore and called my house. There was no answer.

CHAPTER III

1.

Sal was waiting for me in Captain O'Shea's office. I came in while the captain was talking.

Captain George O'Shea is a truncated figure of a man in his late fifties. He is completely bald, his eyes bulge and his mouth is wide and loose lipped. He looks extremely stupid and when he speaks, even while in one of his few and rare good moods, his grating voice sounds like the bellow of a wounded steer. He fools everyone except those who have known him for a long time.

The Captain is one of the finest, and certainly the most honest, homicide detectives who has ever lived. He neither looks nor acts like the fiction version of a policeman, but he has a tremendous intelligence and he does his job exceptionally well.

"… and I say," the harsh, loud voice was saying, "you can forget all about a prowler or a burglar of any kind. It was almost sure to be one of the three of them, Duffy, Malcolm or that guy Haverford. Just in case I'm wrong there, then look for a boyfriend, a jealous woman or a discarded lover.

"I saw her pictures; especially the ones taken while she was alive. You can never make me believe a prowler would have killed her the way she was killed. Hell, man, she was alone in that place! The prowler doesn't live who wouldn't have tried to have her before he committed a robbery. And there was no sign of a rape or an attempted rape."

The Captain looked up and nodded to me.

"Don't waste any time," he said. "You aren't looking for no second-story man or cat burglar here. You're looking for a man or woman who committed a premeditated murder, motivated by either extreme hatred or jealousy!"

Sal started to say something, but once more the captain's harsh bellow overrode him.

"Marty," he said, "I was just telling your partner we have traced Malcolm's movements prior to the crime. He flew in from Philly last Friday and checked into the Waldorf Towers where he maintains a permanent suite. Friday night he spent with the Chamlers girl. Also

Saturday morning. As far as we have been able to determine he didn't get back to Philadelphia until midnight Saturday. We haven't been able to trace his movements so far, for Saturday afternoon and evening. He didn't actually check out of the hotel; we just know that he returned to Philly."

"Has he been questioned?" I asked.

"Not yet. We don't want to alarm him. He'll know of the murder, one way or another, by this time. You can bet that he will be laying low. Certainly, he won't return to New York and take a chance on being picked up for investigation. And he knows we haven't enough yet to extradite him on. That's why we've got to play it careful. The thing to do first is trace his movements for Saturday and Saturday night."

O'Shea stopped and lit the cold end of his cigar butt. "What about Duffy?" he asked.

"I just left him," I said. "First, his alibi doesn't mean much. Said he spent Saturday from four to six in a midtown movie. He could have; he knew what was playing and has seen the picture. But we haven't been able to find anyone to actually place him in the spot. Then he went to the Velvet Room at the Maddox House. Well, from five to seven that place is a madhouse, even on a Saturday afternoon. They have a sort of cocktail hour and the joint is always jammed.

"The doorman, a waiter and a bartender, all remember seeing Duffy around the place. But not one of them can swear exactly when he arrived and when he left. He is, more or less, a fixture around the dump and everyone is so used to seeing him, that they never really notice him at all. He's still wide open as a suspect. But my hunch is that he's in the clear."

"Why?"

"Well, the guy was nuts about the Chamlers broad. That I'm sure of. He's normally a greasy, overstuffed yellow-belly and is afraid of his own shadow. But make one crack about the girl, and he's ready to take on the U. S. Marines with bare knuckles. He claims his interest in the girl was strictly paternal. I'm inclined to believe him."

O'Shea grunted. He reached for his bottle of pink cough syrup which he drank like water in a futile effort to cure his chronic laryngitis. His face twisted into an evil mask as he swallowed half a wine glass of the foul stuff.

"All right, go to work," he said.

Sal waited until we were outside the office before speaking. "The Cap's right," he said.

"No Sal," I said. "No. This is one time I think he's wrong. We're going to see Holiday. I checked up on the way in and he hasn't been picked up. Did you bring the car down?"

Sal said he had. He gave me a strange look.

So we drove up to the Greater Boro Dairy and got there at exactly eleven forty.

I stopped the car in front of the large warehouse and turned to Sal, after I shut off the ignition.

"Sal," I said. "Let me handle this one. You can take care of the white-collar boys, but this guy is mine."

Sal nodded.

"Just take it easy, Marty," he said. "Remember, maybe the kid is going straight and maybe he is in the clear."

"He's a goddamned jailbird," I said. "They never go straight."

"Some do," Sal said in his soft voice. "Some do. Just take it easy Marty. Don't lose your temper."

I told him I wouldn't and we climbed out of the car. We had to ring a bell at the door to the office. The night dispatcher let us in and I showed him my shield.

"Wilbur Holiday check in yet?" I asked.

The dispatcher looked over a long-ruled sheet. He nodded. "Checked in five minutes ago," he said. "Why, is he in any trouble?"

"Not yet," I said. "But we want him for a while. Can you get someone to take his route tonight?"

The man nodded.

"Hope Wilbur isn't in any jam," he said. "He's been very steady so far."

"He's in no jam," I said. "Just go out and bring him in here."

Two minutes later, Holiday entered the office. He hadn't had a chance to change his drill uniform and peaked cap. A late Sunday night issue of a Monday morning paper was rolled up and stuck out of the coat pocket of his sharkskin suit. I saw enough of the headline to know that he had been reading about the Chamlers case.

Wilbur looked more than his thirty-one years. His face was prematurely wrinkled and resembled a sheet of yellow parchment. His hair was long and greased down on his narrow head. His tan shoes were highly polished and he wore green socks which matched the green handkerchief, neatly folded in his breast pocket.

I didn't like him.

There was no doubt about Wilbur being stir wise. He started right out before we had a chance to open our mouths.

"Law," he said. "I knew it. Jesus, why don't you guys let me alone? I'm goin' straight. Just ask. I been workin' ever since I got out. I'm payin' my own way. Give a guy …"

"Shut up, Wilbur," I said.

He shut up.

"I'm Lieutenant Ferris, from homicide," I said, "and this is Sergeant Brentano. We just …"

He cut in quick.

"God, I knew it!" He almost yelled it. "The second I see that story and the address, I knew someone would be around."

"If you're in the clear," Sal cut in, "you have nothing to worry about at all."

"No?" Holiday said, his voice almost inaudible. "No? I still got kidney troubles from the last time the cops questioned me and I didn't have nothing to worry about."

The milk truck dispatcher looked at us and there was faint loathing in his glance.

"We're not that kind of cops," Sal said.

"Never mind all that," I interrupted. "Just get your hat Wilbur. We're going for a little ride. We want to talk to you."

Holiday turned with a shrug of resignation. We followed him out to his locker while he got his hat. Then we left the warehouse through the office and told the dispatcher that Wilbur would probably not be back that night. We told him that if we needed him longer than that, he'd be notified.

I told Sal to get in the front seat and drive around slowly. I pushed Wilbur into the back and crawled in beside him. We'd done it often enough before and Sal knew the pattern. He headed downtown and cut into Central Park. He started circling in the park, keeping the speed down to around twenty miles an hour. I just sat silent and let Wilbur stew. Several times he started to talk, but I shut him up each time. I told him I was thinking. He lit each cigarette from the end of the previous one. It was getting on his nerves.

"You were crazy about her, weren't you Wilbur."

I made a statement out of it and not a question. And I threw it at him while he was starting to light up his fourth cigarette. He dropped the butt on the floor and burned himself and started to sputter. I reached over with my foot and put it out.

"Jesus, don't say that," he said, his high-pitched voice a thin scream.

"I never knew her at all."

"Never knew who, Wilbur?"

"Whoever you're talking about. I never …"

"Who am I talking about, Wilbur?"

I kept the tone of my voice low and friendly.

"You're talking about the Chamlers girl." Holiday said. "I knew the minute I saw her name and remembered that she was on my beat, you'd be around. The papers said jewelry was missing. But, my God, I been going straight. I never saw her in my life. Just left a quart of milk and a pint of cream for her every other day. I tell you I never saw her."

"All right, Wilbur," I said. "For the time being you never saw her. Next question. Where were you from four o'clock Saturday afternoon until seven o'clock?"

I let him take his time. I had all night.

I could feel his thin form shrink away from me as he huddled in the corner of the sedan. And then, after several minutes, he spoke and his voice was a hoarse whisper.

"I was in a movie."

I laughed.

It seemed that everyone was in a movie that Saturday afternoon. But I didn't say anything to Wilbur. I leaned forward and tapped Sal on the shoulder.

"Sal," I said, "this riding around seems to bother Wilbur's memory. He can't think clear. Take us over to the precinct."

Sal shrugged and pressed down on the throttle. Five minutes later we pulled up in front of the twin green lights of the station house.

"I'm taking Wilbur in and we're having a little talk, Sal," I said.

Sal began to get out of the car.

"No, Sal," I continued. "I can handle Wilbur fine, alone. You might drop back to the Chamlers place and have a talk with Haverford. Cover that end of it. I'll either see you there in a couple of hours, or call you."

Sal shrugged his shoulders and got back behind the wheel. "Oke, Marty," he said. "But just take it …"

"I'll be seeing you pal," I said, cutting him off as I pushed Wilbur out of the car in front of me.

2.

I said hello to the sergeant at the desk and told him I wanted a room for a while. He looked from me to Wilbur and then he winked.

"Upstairs, Lieutenant, or down?" he asked.

Upstairs were the detective's offices.

"Downstairs," I said.

Wilbur started to say something in a half cry and I took him by the collar of his coat and shoved him down the long hallway and to the steps leading down to the shower rooms. We passed a couple of uniformed cops on the way and they looked at Wilbur and laughed.

It was a rectangular room, about eight feet wide and twelve feet long. The walls were solid concrete except for a small iron barred window near the ceiling at one end, and the thick oak door. There was nothing in the room but a hat rack, a table, a flood lamp and a straight backed, wooden chair.

Wilbur Holiday had been in this room, or one very much like it, some time before. I could tell by the way he cowered as I shoved him through the door and closed and locked it after us.

"Take off your coat and tie, boy," I said. "Make yourself comfortable. In fact, take off your shoes."

For a long moment he stared at me, and then wordlessly he took off his coat and hat and carefully hung them up. He sat in the chair and unlaced his shoes and pulled his feet from them.

I hit him as he straightened up to loosen his necktie.

Not hard, just enough to tip him over backwards in the chair so that his head banged on the floor.

He was still silent as he carefully picked himself up and wiped a tiny trickle of blood from his lips.

"Now you two-bit little son of a bitch," I said, and my voice was still subdued and friendly, "just skip that 'I-was-in-the-movie' line of crap and tell me where you were."

"God, Lieutenant, I'm tellin' the God's honest ..."

This time I moved in and brought my heavy shoe down on his instep and at the same time I sent a short rabbit punch into the pit of his stomach. I slapped him twice in the face as he folded up. Then I pushed him out of the chair where he had fallen and sat down myself. I took my time lighting a cigarette.

When he had his breath back, he just sat there on the floor, half crying.

"Wilbur," I said at last. "You know I don't want to do this to you. It isn't as though I'm asking you to confess to murder. I'm just asking you to tell me where you were when it happened. Now tell me."

I stood up and started toward him.

"Don't," he said. "Don't hit me again. I'll tell you. But Jesus, it will mean I'll have to go back to the can."

I had a sudden sense of relief. I was getting what I wanted. "Talk fast," I said.

"I was with a dame."

"So? They put you in jail for that now?"

Wilbur really began to talk then.

"This dame—yes," he said. "Her name's Dolly. She's married."

"They still wouldn't put you in jail, Wilbur," I said and raised my balled fist.

"But I'm out on probation," he said. "And we're shacking up together. She's married. I been using a phony name."

"That's different, Wilbur," I said. "So she's married, eh? Who to?"

My voice was no longer nice and calm. Suddenly I hated this little man in front of me. I don't like people who shack up with other men's wives. I had a hard time keeping from really hitting him then. But I needed his answers.

"Her husband's Morris Gottlieb and he's doing time in the big house. He was my cellmate. She has a record herself and if the probation guy finds out about it, I'll be sent back to finish my term. They'll get me for consorting with known criminals, or adultery or something," he said. "And if I go back, Morris will hear about it and he'll kill me sure."

"He should kill you, you little bastard," I said. "But anyway, that's his business. Now just give me the facts straight."

He stood up and I let him have a cigarette and waited for him to light it. His hand was shaking badly and it took a little while. And then he told it to me.

Seems for the last couple of months he'd been keeping his room and paying rent and sleeping in it now and then. But most of the time he'd been living with his pal's wife in a furnished apartment down in Greenwich Village. That's why the cops hadn't been able to find him when I'd sent the flyer out on Sunday.

He claimed he was with this Dolly broad from noontime on Saturday until shortly after eleven o'clock, when he'd left to make his milk rounds.

I questioned him closely and he told me that they had stayed indoors the entire time. He had no other witness but Dolly. The way he told it, however, I believed him.

I felt fine. It was just the way I wanted it.

Then I went to work seriously. I took him apart and I did it with everything I had. But I was careful not to injure him. I just wanted to hurt him. When I got through, I pulled him into the showers and brought him to. And then I took him back and had him go over the story again from beginning to end. I had to be sure.

The second version was the same as the first, only more complete. I got Dolly's address and a lot of other incidental information. When we were all through, I patched Wilbur up and I sat him in the chair and I talked to him like a Dutch Uncle.

"You probably think I'm crazy," I said, "but I'm going to give you a break. I'm not going to turn you in. I'm not even going to hold you. You're going to leave here and go home—not to Dolly's but to that furnished room of yours. From now on you're staying away from Dolly. Get it? Completely away!"

Wilbur said he got it. He looked at me as though he didn't quite believe what I was saying. As though he suspected some trick.

"Not only that," I said, "but you're not going to repeat anything that went on in this room tonight—anything you've told me. Open up just one little peep and the best you can hope for is a ride back up the river and a chance to bunk with Morris Gottlieb instead of his wife.

"So you don't talk. You don't see Dolly and you don't talk. Get back on your job tomorrow night and stick to the job. And live between that job and your rooming house until you hear from me again. Get it?"

He got it, although he couldn't believe his good luck. We went upstairs and passed the same desk sergeant on the way out. He sort of cocked his head on one side and gave us a curious glance. This time, I winked.

Outside of the precinct house, Holiday turned and started to thank me.

"Get out of my sight, you crummy little pimp," I said. I gave him a shove that sent him halfway across the sidewalk. I swung on my heel and started for the hack stand on the corner.

3.

Instead of getting out in front of the Chamlers place, I paid the driver off at the corner. I went in and called my house. This time Fern's voice answered on the first ring.

"This is Marty, kid," I said.

"Baby! Where are you?"

Goddamn it, her voice did the same thing to me it always did. I was still crazy about her.

"I'm tied up on a case," I told her. "Probably be home very late. What you been doing all night?"

I made it sound casual.

"I got home about six and made dinner," Fern said. "Looked at television for a couple of hours or so and then climbed into bed. I wasn't able to sleep, honey, and have been lying here reading."

"Get some sleep, kid," I said and it was hard for me to control my voice. "I'll be along." I hung up.

Yes, I was crazy about her. Lies and all!

I walked twice around the block. My face was burning and my mind was seething with hatred and suspicion. She hadn't been there when I'd called around ten-thirty. Definitely she hadn't been there. Where was she? Where was she the night before? In fact, how many of those thousand nights of our marriage when I hadn't called and when she had supposedly been home, had she been out God only knows where?

Had she been with Harry—whoever Harry was?

Were there others beside Harry?

I began to shake with rage and knew that I would have to get myself under control. I gritted my teeth and made my way down the street to the Chamlers place. Sal was waiting for me upstairs.

"Jees, Marty," he said, when I came in, "you look as pooped as I feel. Let's call it a night."

I nodded shortly.

"You get anything?" I asked.

"Nothing that won't keep until morning," he said. "How about you? What's with the Holiday guy?"

"Nothing there at all," I said. "The Captain and you were right. He's in the clear."

It was the first time I had told an outright lie to Sal in all of the years we had known each other.

Ten minutes later we left the place. I took the car and dropped Sal off uptown and turned down his halfhearted invitation to come in for a nightcap. Then I cut across the Triborough Bridge and headed for home and Fern.

CHAPTER IV

1.

I had heard the words of that singular phrase at least a dozen times. Once they had been spoken by a brawny stevedore in the back seat of a squad car; again by an emaciated little Puerto Rican in the uniformed men's room down at headquarters. Other times by men in other places.

Some spoke in soft, perfect English, others used the language of the streets. But always they said the same thing and always, it seemed in thinking back, the men who spoke those words did it between sobs. Always I had believed they lied.

And now, sitting across the breakfast table from Fern, I began to wonder.

For although the words and the accents may have differed, the meaning was invariably the same.

"I loved her and so I killed her."

If you loved someone, you protected and took care of her. And if you killed someone, then you must have hated that person deeply. How could you put the two things together?

The ends of her honey, straw hair were still damp from the shower and she wore the Chinese silk robe I had given her last Christmas. Her small, delicately boned feet were thrust into a pair of open mules. I knew that she wore nothing else. Beneath the Chinese silk was that lovely, long-limbed body which had meant so much to me. There was a little wrinkled line just above her nose as she studied the bridge column in the morning paper, but her hazel eyes were clear beneath the smooth forehead. Just looking at her over the rim of my newspaper, as I reached for the coffee, brought a lump to my throat.

Yes, I loved her. Of this I was sure.

And then I thought of that letter in my wallet from Washington. I thought of the lies I knew she had told me. I thought of "Harry."

I hated her.

I hated her for the deceit and for having let me love her.

My hand began to shake and I put the coffee cup back in the saucer. I tried to keep the fury out of my voice when I spoke.

"Fern," I said.

She didn't look up. She half nodded and I knew that she was still working out the bridge problem, but also that she had heard me.

"Fern, I want to talk with you."

She looked up at me then and sort of half smiled, as though she wasn't really seeing me at all.

"Yes?" she said. And then went back to the paper.

I am not a violent man and I rarely lose my temper. But for some reason I suddenly saw red. I reached across the table and tore the newspaper out of her hands. I threw it down on the floor beside my chair.

"Goddamn it," I began, "I said I ..."

"Don't swear, Marty," Fern said. Her eyes were wide with surprise, but her voice was soft and low and there was no fear in it. "You must have crawled out the wrong side of bed," she said.

My own voice was tight with anger when I answered.

"It doesn't matter what side I crawled out," I said. "The point is, what side did you crawl in? And when? You told me you were home all night—but you didn't answer when I phoned at 10:30. Why?"

Her eyes opened even wider as she looked at me. For a moment she just sat there, her mouth slightly parted to expose the whiteness of her even teeth.

And then she laughed.

"Marty!" she said, "Marty, for goodness sake stop trying to make like a cop. It's me—Fern—your wife. If you want to cross-examine somebody, perhaps you'd better get out the rubber hose." She laughed.

I knew that the blood had left my face; that I was trembling. The strangest part of it was I was sitting there and silently praying that she'd have some sort of logical answer, something that would dispel the terrible suspicions I had and make everything come out all right. And then I thought of the letter and of "Harry."

There couldn't be any logical answer.

"So where were you?" I snapped, but this time there was control in my voice and I kept it level.

"I probably fell asleep for a few minutes and didn't hear the phone," Fern said. She laughed and stood up and in a second had rounded the table. Before I could move she'd thrown herself into my lap.

Her arms encircled my neck in a strangle hold and the softness of them was more confining than a steel chain. Her lips were inches from my own as she spoke.

"Honest," she said, "I do believe my baby's jealous."

And then she kissed me hard on the lips with her half-opened mouth.

That did it.

There was no Harry, no letter, no telephone call which hadn't been answered. No lies. Nothing but Fern, pressed close to me, her arms around my neck, her back arched as she half lay across me, her opened mouth drinking the strength of my fury and hatred. And also drinking my love.

I lifted her as I stood up and I carried her across the room and through the door and into the bedroom. She sighed as I laid her gently down on the unmade bed.

I hated her, but I loved her.

They must have been telling the truth. Those men who had used the words: "I loved her and so I killed her."

Afterward, while I showered and dressed and strapped on my holster and got ready to leave the house, I heard her soft breathing and knew that she had fallen asleep again. I didn't wake her.

2.

That afternoon, Sal Brentano and I drove down to Philadelphia and talked with K.V.D. Malcolm. It was the strangest damned interview with a murder suspect I had had in all the years I have been tracking down criminals. Captain O'Shea had briefed us before we left. It seemed Malcolm was willing to talk but only in his attorney's office. The New York Commissioner had put the okay on this. Malcolm had one hell of a lot of pull and we couldn't get away with dirtying him up if he wasn't guilty, but if we found out he was, we were expected to dig up enough evidence to throw him in jail. And the captain warned us that the press was to hear nothing of our trip or the interview.

Even with this briefing we weren't prepared for the session in the lawyer's office. We had a two o'clock appointment and we were kept waiting until about three along with Inspector Moran who represented the Philadelphia Commissioner. When we were finally ushered into the senior partner's office, there sat K.V.D. Malcolm, a man in his mid-sixties, dressed like Herbert Hoover in his heyday and he had about as much warmth to him as a ten-day-old corpse.

The lawyer ignored all our questions saying that the Inspector had checked Malcolm's whereabouts from Saturday morning until after the discovery of the body and would swear that he was completely in the clear. The Inspector himself looked pretty embarrassed throughout and when he suggested that he would tell me all about it in private, I blew my stack. I threw out a shot in the dark and asked if Billy Chamlers had been blackmailing the old goat. That really went home. Malcolm went white and the Inspector red—but with embarrassment, not anger. And that ended the interview. I was convinced that Malcolm had been keeping the girl and that she had been shaking the old buzzard. But I was pretty sure that he hadn't murdered her.

When Sal and I were on our way out of the building, the Inspector went along with us and tried to smooth the whole thing over. In a sense I felt sorry for him. I felt sorry for any cop who was trying to do his duty but worked for a department which was obviously controlled by a political machine.

3.

Back in New York, I told Sal to see the Haverford guy while I did some other things, and we agreed to meet at headquarters around nine o'clock. I called into the office and there were a couple of messages. One was from Fern but she had said not to bother to call back. The other was about an old case and didn't interest me. I started walking uptown toward West Forty-sixth Street. It was time I saw Duffy again.

I had to pass 1660 Broadway so on a hunch, I turned in and looked up Sam Duffy on the wall board. He was listed on the tenth floor and I took a crowded elevator up. If anything, the office was even dirtier and more depressing than the man's hotel room. There were the same photos on the wall of pretty much the same unknowns. The reception room was a little larger than the men's room in a gas station and smelled about like one. There was a long, hard bench, the photos, and a tiny square opening in the wall facing the doorway, covered by a half sheet of glass and nothing else.

A pimply faced, dark haired girl in horn rimmed glasses was in back of the window, cleaning her lacquered nails with an orange stick. She gave me what she undoubtedly thought was a glamorous smile.

"Duffy in?"

"Sick," she said. "He's home and I can't even put a phone call in. So you'll have to come back if you want to. Anyway, there's nothing casting now anyway."

I said that that was too bad and I didn't bother to answer when she asked who was calling.

The Milton Hotel was just where it had been when I last saw it. So was the desk clerk, but he was wearing a different silk shirt.

"Into your cage," I said, and he looked sour as he walked around the desk and stepped past me into the elevator. "What floor, Mister?" he asked.

I told him not to be a wise guy and he stopped at the fifth. He remembered me all right. I didn't bother to knock, just twisted the knob and walked in. I wasn't surprised that the door was unlocked.

It was a peculiar thing how each time I saw the man, he left me with a different impression. That first time, when he had sat dazed and in a state of shock in Billy Chamlers' room, he somehow had given the impression of an athlete gone to seed. And then, the other day, in this very room, he seemed to have shrunken in size and he merely looked like a little, dirty fat man with a bad complexion and a worse breath.

Now, he seemed somehow to have shrunken even more and he suddenly had taken on the appearance of not a middle-aged man, but an old man and a sick man.

The tiny yellow eyes were shot with red, as though he had been crying. The skin of his fat, jowled face was as dry and colorless as old parchment. It was intolerably hot in the closeness of the room, but the window was almost hermetically sealed. And yet he didn't sweat as he lay back in the old, overstuffed chair. He was smoking one of his endless chain of cigarettes, but I noticed that his hand no longer shook. The nails, however, were still dirty.

In spite of the heat, he sat fully dressed and with a bathrobe across his shoulders instead of a suit jacket. His feet were encased in a pair of cracked soled, felt slippers. He looked, this time, not only repulsive, but also, somehow, pathetic.

"I'm back," I said, and reached for a chair.

He nodded listlessly.

I took my time about lighting a cigarette. He seemed completely unaware of my presence. His eyes stared sightlessly at the floor and he made no move. For a moment I thought that perhaps he was drunk. Drunk or doped. But it was different. I'd seen plenty of drunks and not a few hopheads, but this was different.

"Well," I said at last, "what have you got for me?"

His eyes looked up and for the first time they seemed to come to life.

"Got for you?" he asked. "What have I got for you?"

"Yes, damn it," I snapped. "What have you got? About Jill Bentley? Remember—you were going to …"

It seemed to bring him to and he didn't wait for me to finish.

"Oh," he said. "Jill Bentley. That's right—you wanted to know about her." He even began to look somewhat intelligent.

He pulled himself to his feet and mashed his cigarette butt into the overflowing ash tray and then moved over to the bed and sat on the edge of it.

"She's doing a turn at the Shenandoah. That's a fancy spot up on the East Side. Comes on at four-thirty in the afternoon in time for cocktail hour and plays a little piano and does a few blue numbers. Then returns at eight-thirty for fill-ins in the evening show."

He stopped to light another cigarette.

"Anything else?" I asked," Is she …"

"She lives over in the Murray Hill section in a one-room apartment, alone," he went on. "I got her address here somewhere. She's a redhead, natural, about twenty-five or -six and came here from someplace out West about three years ago. I'm not sure, but I think she was married at some time or other and that Bentley wasn't the name she started out with. She's getting a hundred and fifty bucks a week. No boyfriends that I know about and seems to keep pretty much to herself."

He finished speaking and leaned back on the bed. At once his eyes lost interest.

"Fine," I said. "Have you talked with her yourself or did you just pick this up around?"

"I haven't talked with her," Duffy said. "Just got it here and there."

"You know the manager at the Shenandoah?" I asked.

Duffy thought for a second and sort of half nodded.

"Sold him a dance act about a year ago," he said. "That is if it's the same guy."

"All right," I said. "Then here's what I want you to do. It's just a little after six and you will still be able to catch her if you hurry. Get over there and get yourself introduced. Tell her who you are. And say that you got a good spot lined up for her in—say Toledo, for instance. A new night spot and that it will pay three hundred a week. That the owner of the joint is now in town looking over talent and that you want her to meet him."

Duffy raised a pudgy hand and stopped me.

"Jees," he said. "I can't do that. I'm a legit agent and ..."

"Shut up," I said. "You're going to do it. And then you're going to make an appointment for eleven o'clock tonight and you and I are going back together and you're going to introduce me. Except I'm not going to be Lieutenant Ferris. We'll stick to my first name—Marty—to make it easy. But make it Martin Crandall. And I'm from Toledo. I'll be back here at ten-thirty to pick you up."

I stood up.

Duffy again began to protest, but this time I stopped him quick.

"Listen," I said, "just do what I want you to do. Otherwise, you can get into your shoes and come on downtown. There are still a hell of a lot of questions you haven't answered in the Chamlers case."

The parchment face was suddenly red and he nodded his head quickly.

"You know what you're doing, Lieutenant," he said.

"That's right, Duffy," I said. "I know what I'm doing."

We went downstairs after waiting four minutes for the elevator and Duffy and I split out after we hit the street. He took a cab and I watched as it pulled away and turned the first corner going uptown. And then I re-entered the Milton Hotel.

4.

Silk shirt was back behind the desk, alone.

I went directly to the elevator and looked at him from inside the cage. For a moment he just seemed baffled, but then he shrugged and came over and walked in. He closed the door.

"You know everybody in this joint, huh?" he said.

I put my hand out and took his arm as he reached for the starting lever.

"No," I said. "Not everybody. Just Mister Duffy. And maybe you. And because I know Duffy, you're going back behind that desk and get a pass key and then you're going to take me upstairs and let me into his room. Then you're going downstairs and if you are smart you are going to forget all about it."

He started to give me some back sass so I decided to save time. I took my hand from his arm and got hold of the front of his silk shirt. With my left hand I slapped him hard across the face, backward and forward a half dozen times. I didn't hurt him but it brought the tears to his eyes and I knew that those eyes would be black in the morning. I don't like punks, especially fresh punks.

"Listen you cheap little pimp," I said. "If you think I don't know how you make your extra dough you're crazy. Now do what I tell you and do it fast. And one peep out of you and you won't be working here anymore. You tip Duffy and I gotta know it, so remember."

I released him and he staggered out of the elevator. A moment later and he was back with a key chain.

He didn't say a word as we rode up to the fifth floor and I got off.

"One other thing," I said as he started to shut the door. "Should Duffy come back before I'm through, you better warn me. Don't slip up."

The car started down as I entered the room.

The first thing I did was open the window to let in a little air. And then I started with the chest of drawers.

One of the things I have always disliked most about police work is going through another person's property. The dirty clothes, the old letters, odds and ends of junk, personal knick-knacks and things which people save over the years for no earthly reason—these always depress me.

With the possessions of Sam Duffy, it was worse than mere depression. God, what a filthy collection of worn-out souvenirs of a wasted and misspent life that was! The usual accruements of a bachelor's existence were there, of course. The dirty linen, the mismated socks, the worn-out glasses, broken fountain pens and the usual run-of-the line stuff which would have been better thrown away.

It wasn't, however, until I had opened the worn leather Gladstone which he kept under his bed, that I came upon anything which really interested me. The first item, I found in a collection of canceled checks. There were a number of them, all made out to Billy Chamlers. They started about a month back and ran over a period of years. A rapid calculation brought the amount into thousands of dollars. Malcolm may have been keeping the girl, but Sam was paying his share, too.

And then I found something else. It was a small package in oilskin wrapping and a thick rubber band had been twisted around it several times. I opened it and exposed half a hundred negatives.

I held one up to the light—and I guess I must have blushed.

At one time or another, in the course of my work, I have run into pornographic pictures, but I had never seen anything quite this bad. God, what kind of depraved mentality could take any pleasure in this sort of filth, I wondered. Apparently, as near as I could determine, the girl in each of them was the same. I took a half dozen from the collection and put them into my wallet. The others I carefully replaced in the oilskin and put them back.

It cast a new light on Sam Duffy's character.

In less than an hour I was finished. Outside of canceled checks and the dirty pictures, I had found nothing of significance. I went over to the sink behind the screen to wash my hands. I felt dirty all over.

I rinsed the soap off and started to reach for the towel, but it was black with dirt, and so instead, I jerked a half dozen sheets from the roll of paper beside the toilet. That's when it happened.

He must have had the stuff hidden in the recess in back of the roll, because, when I pulled, it jangled to the floor.

The watch was the size of a twenty-five-cent piece. It was platinum and encircled with diamond chips. The earrings were pearl tears; the ring a star sapphire.

The initials "B.C." were carefully engraved on the back of the watch.

It didn't prove that Sam Duffy had murdered Billy Chamlers. But it did offer conclusive evidence that he had taken the jewelry from her apartment shortly before her murder, or during her murder, or right after her murder.

Twenty minutes later, from a public pay telephone on Times Square, I was talking to Captain O'Shea at headquarters.

"So will you let Sal know I won't meet him as I planned, but will be working on another angle," I said.

"Then there's nothing at all new?" He asked, disappointment heavy in his voice.

"Nothing," I said, and hung up.

CHAPTER V

1.

I had a little better than two hours to kill. Usually, in a case like this, I would call Fern and she'd rush into town and we would have a late dinner together in one of the less expensive Italian or Armenian restaurants on the East Side. Sometimes we'd go down around Doyers and Pell Streets and get Chinese food.

These quiet, private little dinners, coming on the spur of the moment and never planned, constituted, oddly enough, some of the most pleasant times we had ever spent together.

Instinctively I went to a phone booth and started to dial. And then, in the middle of it, I hung up. I didn't want to see Fern. I didn't even want to talk with her. I left the booth and hailed a cab. I told the driver to take me down to Fourteenth Street, to Lüchow's.

During my life I have rarely been very happy or very sad. My emotions and my feelings run pretty much on an even keel. It is, however, a peculiarity of mine, that during those times I have felt either elation or disappointment, I have experienced a strange desire to eat good food and to be alone. These are the times also when I am indifferent to cost; normally I take the subway or a bus.

I had a good dinner and blew myself to a pony of brandy with my coffee, and a fifty-cent cigar. If I was going to masquerade as a wealthy nightclub owner, I might just as well start out feeling like one.

Before I left the restaurant, I called headquarters on the off-chance that Sal might still be around. They told me that he was back at the Chamlers apartment and I reached him there.

He had just left Haverford in his rooms on the first floor.

"The guy has something on his mind," Sal told me. "We had dinner at the Pavillon and he picked up the check. Boy must do all right for himself. I talked to the headwaiter when Haverford was making a phone call. Says the Chamlers dame, whom he remembers from her pictures in the papers, came there often with Haverford.

"He told me he only saw her once or twice. He's covering up something or else maybe he's just frightened. There's no doubt he was on the make for her."

"So she turned him down and he killed her," I said. I was being sarcastic, but Sal took it straight.

"I doubt it," he said. "My God, the guy smokes a pipe. You ever yet see a guy who smokes a pipe kill anything bigger than a rabbit with a sling shot. No, this boy is covering something, but I don't think it's murder. You better talk to him yourself, Marty."

"I will," I said. "You go on home now. See you in the morning."

He started to ask me something, but I hung up. I left Lüchow's and walked across Union Square to the BMT station. I took an express to Times Square, picked up an early edition of the morning paper, and started up Broadway to Forty-sixth Street. My wristwatch said ten twenty-five.

2.

The second Duffy opened that door I knew that he had checked the suitcase. He looked like a man who was sitting around waiting for them to come and put an electrode on his freshly shaved head. He didn't say a word as I pushed my way past him and slumped into one of the upholstered chairs.

He shut the door and then turned toward me.

"Honest to God, Lieutenant," he said, "I ..."

I cut him short.

"What's the trouble, Sammy?" I asked. "Isn't everything all set with the Bentley girl?"

For a moment he looked at me blankly. Gradually the color came back to his face, but there was a perplexed look about his eyes.

"Yeah," he said, "Yeah, it's all set. We ..."

"How'd she take it?" I asked. "Interested? Do you think she will go for the line?"

He fumbled around nervously for a cigarette and he kept looking at me peculiarly as he talked. He said that she was very interested. She was so damned anxious to get a three hundred a week spot, he said, that she wouldn't even wonder whether or not I was legitimate.

"She knows I'm legit," Sam added.

The way he kept looking at me, I knew exactly what was going on in his mind. He knew damned well that I had searched his rooms and had found the jewels. He suspected that I was holding out on him; attempting to trap him. And also, in another part of his mind, he was wondering if I was just going to keep the jewels and eventually fence them and make a nice piece of change for myself someday when the whole Chamlers thing was done with and forgotten.

That's the way Sam's mind worked. He figured I was a cop, I made a little better than a hundred bucks a week and that I was probably up to my ears in hock with the loan sharks and the bookies. As a matter of fact, in nine cases out of ten, he would have been right. Most cops, particularly the boys with wives and kids, are in debt from the day they join the force until the time their widow starts getting her pension.

Sam also probably figured that most cops wouldn't be above committing a little larceny on the side. In that he was wrong. Most cops, at least New York City cops, are honest. They might grab off a free drink at the corner bar and grill, or take a present now and then, but they don't steal. They don't take bribes. If they did, they wouldn't always be in debt.

But I let Sam Duffy go ahead and think what he wanted. Just so that he didn't know for sure and so that in not knowing, it worried him. I wanted to keep him worried.

Sam was looking at his watch.

"I told her we'd be there around eleven," he said. "It's eleven now, Lieutenant."

"Look, call me Marty," I said. "I'm supposed to be Martin Crandall, from Toledo, remember? I don't want you popping out with that goddamned 'lieutenant.'"

"Sure," he said. "Sure. I'll remember."

"Be sure you do," I said. "Another thing, do you think she's ever been in Toledo?"

"I asked her," he said. "She told me she hadn't, but that she once worked a stag date in Cleveland."

"Fine," I said. "Let's go. By the way, what's supposed to be the name of my club?"

"The Domino," Sam said. "Supposed to be a new joint, somewhere out on the Lake Front. I told her you were new in the business, too. That's so you wouldn't get caught up."

We took a cab to the Shenandoah. Sam Duffy surprised me; he insisted on paying the driver.

A subtle change had gradually come over him. He was beginning to lose the peculiar vagueness which had characterized his earlier behavior. Also his background of fear. Maybe it was the cab, I don't know. Some men are like that. They get in a taxi, give the driver an order, pick up a check, and they are different men. But with Sam, it was more complex.

His shrewd Broadway mind was beginning to work and he was figuring angles. He couldn't understand my interest in the Bentley girl, but I think he was beginning to figure reasons why I was using him to get a date with her.

In Sam's mind it went like this. I was just another crooked, carnal cop. I wanted girls and I wanted money. And so I was willing to overlook a few little things—like murder for instance—to get what I wanted.

The first time he called me Marty, after I had told him to, he was hesitant and shy. But then, as we entered the club, he turned to me and he said in a husky whisper, "You'll like her—she's hot, Marty."

It was very confidential and there was something slimy about it.

"Better than I like you, I hope, you fat bastard," I said, keeping my voice down. His lips tightened and his thick neck went red. The waiter nodded to Sam and led us to a table over in one corner of the nightclub. Sam had made a reservation.

Dim, indirect lighting and a low ceiling gave the small room a rather depressing atmosphere, particularly as the walls were done in deep purple and the floor, except for the small platform stage, was heavily carpeted in some dark material. There was no dancing.

The crowd was about what you would expect, although when we arrived, it was thin as the after-theater people hadn't yet showed up.

I ordered bourbon and water and Sam asked for cherry brandy. The master of ceremonies, a tall, thin, dark-haired man with a trick mustache and a tuxedo, if they still call them tuxedos, was just walking out on the stage and a girl in evening dress, who looked like a mulatto, was softly playing an old revival on a spinet. Two baby spots lighted the stage, but the girl was in the shadows.

I couldn't help but think that nightclubs, like hospitals, are basically designed for sick people. The way I felt, I was in the right place.

Sam started to talk, but I waved for him to be quiet. It was bad enough being with him; I didn't feel like companionship.

The place was crowded by the time Jill Bentley came on.

It is a peculiar thing, but the first moment I saw Jill Bentley, it wasn't as though I were looking at a person, or a girl, at all. It was like looking at a name.

Fern had run across an old friend—Jill Bentley, "a girl I used to know." And this was Jill Bentley, this tall, slender redhead with a deep, throaty voice, a sensuous, languid manner, a soft, almost delicate touch on the keyboard. What in the name of God, was my first thought, could this girl and my wife, Fern, ever have had in common?

She was about Fern's age, it is true. And she was good looking, yes, even beautiful, like Fern. But Fern was my wife, a simple, sweet girl who had worked in an office and whom I had married. There was a hardness about this Jill Bentley, a sophistication, a subtle worldliness in every gesture and connotation of her deep soprano voice which was completely alien to Fern and the world which I had believed was Fern's.

I looked at her closely as I listened to her music. They had the twin baby spotlights on her and it was almost as though I were standing at her side. Actually, I was no more than twenty-five or thirty feet away. The Shenandoah was small and intimate, as I have said.

Her heart-shaped face under the crown of dark red hair was almost bronze and it was completely unlined. She didn't appear to be wearing rouge. The eyes were very large and deep blue, almost black. Her lips were full and passionate under a small, upturned nose. The column of her throat fell away into a deep hollow between her breasts, half exposed by the low-cut evening dress.

The dress itself, a silk-like garment which clung to her flesh, showed a perfect figure, round, soft but with a strangely incongruous athletic look about it. She reminded me of a sleek cat. There was no sign of claws, but you were aware that they must be there, waiting.

She sang a semi-modern love ballad and if the words hadn't been heavy with sex and desire—which they were of course—her voice would have made them so.

"Knows you're here," Sam whispered. "She's giving it the works."

I nodded.

There was a subdued round of applause after she finished and she bowed and smiled. She didn't sing a second number. Instead, she left the stage and walked down the steps and directly to our table. She pulled a chair out and sat down as I started to get to my feet.

"How's Toledo?" she said.

Her eyelashes were very long and jet black; the eyes themselves, which I had thought were dark blue, were actually azure, like Fern's. The whites were not a pure white but a blue white.

She smiled as she spoke and I was surprised. I had expected a certain type of hardness in her. But her smile was open and friendly and unaffected.

"Toledo's fine," I said. "I'm Marty—Marty Crandall."

Sam started to say something and she put up a slender hand and waved it at him, sort of.

"You're the agent," she said with a light laugh. "You don't get to talk." She turned toward me. "Agents are a necessary evil," she said. "But hell, you don't have to chatter with them. This one tells me you're willing to overpay me to come out to your town and do my stuff."

She leaned a little toward me.

"You don't look like a guy who owns a nightclub," she said. "You look more like a cop, or a truck driver."

For a second it almost threw me. But then I made a quick recovery. Hell, there was no reason I shouldn't look like a cop. I was one. On the other hand, contrary to the general belief, people don't recognize cops just by their appearance, any more than policemen recognize crooks by the appearance. If the police went on appearance alone, half the people in town would be locked up every night. She just happened to hit on a lucky phrase.

"You do look like a singer," I said. "Also, having heard you, you sound like one." I smiled at her and she smiled right back.

"Well, I'm Jill Bentley," she said, "and this man here says you like my voice and want me to work for you."

Again Sam started to say something. This time I interrupted.

"Look, Sam," I said. "Now I have met Miss Bentley, we can go ahead and make our own arrangements. There's no reason for you to sit up any longer and lose your sleep. I'm sure Miss Bentley," I turned and smiled at the girl, "I'm sure she'll let you know all about any deal we make."

The waiter drifted by as Sam was getting to his feet and mumbling good night. He left and Jill Bentley ordered a dry sherry and I asked for another bourbon and water.

It was silly, but I found myself liking this girl, Jill Bentley. And there was a certain direct, unaffected manner about her, a forthrightness, almost a simplicity, which intrigued me. And then again I thought of Fern and I didn't like her at all.

We talked for a few minutes and she sipped her sherry. The spotlight swung over to the table, and the master of ceremonies called to Jill from the platform and made a smart remark. She stood up and said she'd take it from where she was. The room was sufficiently small that she didn't need a mike.

She sang "Danny Boy" and the mulatto girl on the stage tapped out the tune with one listless hand.

I listened to her and for those few moments I forgot all about Fern and all about the Chamlers case and all about everything except the words and the music of that sentimental Irish ballad.

She sat down after she finished and we had another drink while the master of ceremonies went on with his patter.

"I'm through for the night," she said as she lifted her glass.

"Good," I said. "Let's leave this dungeon. I don't think it's proper to talk to a girl about a new job while she is working on an old one. How about something to eat?"

She said she'd like something and told me to meet her in the lobby; that it would take her only about five minutes to change. I motioned to the waiter and asked for the check.

He told me Miss Bentley was taking care of it and so I got up and went out and got my hat and waited. She took exactly five minutes.

3.

She had suggested Lindy's but I was afraid of running into someone I knew. Instead I talked her into a place over on Third Avenue. They served good food and it was a hangout for cops and politicians. I knew that if I ran into anyone I knew there, I would be ignored when they saw that I was with a stranger. They'd figure I was working. Well, in a way, I was.

I wasn't hungry and so I ordered a bottle of cold beer. Jill Bentley had a steak sandwich and started asking me questions. She wanted to know about my club, about Toledo and a lot of other things. I was in trouble right from the first.

"I once worked Cleveland," she said at last. "Good town. Suppose you know the Goldstein boys? They have the Club Friday. Gets some of the best talent in the country."

"Sure," I said. "A nice spot. I want to model the Domino after it."

Carefully she put down her fork and she looked me straight in the eye.

"There is no Club Friday in Cleveland," she said. "And if there are any Goldstein boys, they are probably in the wholesale lingerie business."

She didn't sound mad, just curious.

"Let's get things straight," she went on. "Who are you and just what do you want? I didn't think you were in the nightclub business; you don't look the type.

"If you're a cop, I can save you a lot of trouble. There is nothing at all I can do for you. You probably know that I did a year in prison out in California—accessory before the fact—and I'm registered downtown. But I've been clean since. So don't bother me."

"I'm not a cop," I said.

I had a hard time controlling myself when she said that she'd done a year in California. That's where Fern, my wife Fern, under the name of Joan Bronski, had spent two and a half years. I felt a sense of elation as I realized I was beginning to get somewhere. The two must have known each other in prison. But Jill Bentley was still talking and I could see that she was getting madder by the minute.

"All right, you're not a cop then," she said. "But you certainly aren't any nightclub man either. Hell, you don't know the first thing about nightclubs. And I doubt if you know anything about Toledo. So what are you, mister? Looking for girls for your stable? If you are brother, keep right on looking. But get the hell and gone and away from me."

She was mad now and she was beginning to yell. I could see people at nearby tables turning and looking at us. A waiter hovered nearby, a worried look on his face.

"Look," I said. "Please don't yell. Just hang on to yourself and give me a second. I can explain everything."

"Can you?" she said, her voice lower, but still nasty. "Can you? Well then, start in explaining why Sam Duffy said you were a nightclub owner and you wanted to give me three hundred bucks a week."

She had me in a very tight corner. Normally, had she been just a girl I was questioning or investigating in a routine case, at this point I would have flashed my badge and got right down to hard rock. But this was different; this was personal. To find out what I wanted to know, I must at all costs keep my identity secret.

I started talking and I talked fast. I felt like the world's goddamndest fool, but I went ahead anyway. My face was brick red and I was fumbling around for words and I don't suppose I made very good sense. The fact that I did such a lousy job of it was probably the only thing which put it across. The story I gave her was so damned silly that it almost had to be true.

The one thing I did tell her which wasn't a lie, was that I actually was a cop. I showed her my badge. I figured if I did that, she wouldn't ask for further identification. I still wanted to be Marty Crandall and not Marty Ferris.

"You were right," I said, "I'm a cop. Only I'm not working at it. I first saw you at the Shenandoah when I paid a routine call. The department checks all the clubs periodically. Well, I saw you and I heard your act and I thought you were terrific. So I'm probably a damned fool and sentimental and everything else but anyway, I knew Sam Duffy, and I figured he could introduce me to you. Sam said that he didn't think you'd be much interested in knowing a plain flatfoot and it was his idea I pretend to be something else.

"I know, now, that it was stupid, and I'm sorry I worked it out that way. But I saw you, and heard you sing, and damn it to hell, I guess I must have half fallen in love with you. Anyway, it seemed to me that I just had to meet you."

You'll never know what it cost me to pull that line. I was sweating like a goat and I was redder than a beet. I didn't expect for a moment that she'd swallow it.

She just stared at me with her huge eyes, her mouth slightly opened. Then she put out her hand.

"Let's see the tin again," she said.

I took out the badge in the leather case and handed it to her. I thanked God that it had a number and not a name.

She looked at it for several seconds and then handed it back. Suddenly she started laughing. She doubled over and the tears came to her eyes. I thought for a moment that she was going to collapse in hysteria.

She looked up at me and she had trouble controlling herself. Finally she spoke and she had a hard time getting the words out.

"Well I'll be," she said. "Now I've heard everything! So you heard me sing and you looked at me and you wanted to meet me. Look, I really think you must be telling the truth. Nobody, but nobody, not even a cop, could make up anything quite so damned silly. All right, now you have met me. I'm a little disappointed that I'm not going out to Toledo at three hundred fish a week, but thanks for the dinner anyway."

"Look, Miss Bentley—Jill—I'm sorry," I began.

"You better order me a drink, flatfoot," she said. "Don't try to explain anything more. Just order me a drink. And then you can pay the check, call a cab and take me home."

She didn't sound mad, she just sounded tired.

This time she had bourbon and I had a sherry. For the life of me I couldn't think of a thing to say. I suppose if I had been some dumb bastard, like I said I was, who had fallen hook, line and sinker for her,

I might have acted the same way.

It was just before two o'clock when we finally left. We'd had a couple of more drinks and we'd talked a little. About nothing in particular.

Finally she had said, "Marty, you're a damned funny cop. You look like one, at times you even sound like one, but you're still a damned funny cop. Maybe it's because you're really telling me the truth. I wouldn't know. But in any case, you better take me home now. I can't drink and it only takes a few to throw me. You don't want a drunken gal on your hands."

So I got a cab and she gave me her address and I gave it to the driver. Fifteen minutes later the taxi pulled up in front of an old-fashioned brownstone building on East Thirty-fifth Street, just off Park Avenue.

I had sat at one side of the cab and Jill at the other. I hadn't made the slightest pass at her and we hadn't talked at all.

"You can come up and have a nightcap if you want," she said.

I paid the driver and followed her up the stone steps.

4.

In thinking back to that first time I crossed the threshold and entered Jill Bentley's apartment, it is very difficult to remember the various emotional reactions I experienced.

Fern, my wife, had been about the only woman I had really known. For three years we bad been married and I had been wildly in love with her and completely faithful to her. I had never as much as thought of another woman.

I was still in love with her, but I no longer believed in her. She had, I was sure, deceived and swindled me. She was not Fern Taylor, a pretty little, innocent stenographer, whom I had married and cherished.

She was Joan Bronski, ex-jailbird.

She was a woman who called the name of "Harry" in her sleep while I made love to her. And this woman, this Jill Bentley, had been her friend and knew her from the past.

All this was passing through my mind.

At the same time, I would be lying if I didn't admit that I was also experiencing another and vastly different set of emotional reactions. The man doesn't live, I don't think, who can follow a pretty girl into her apartment alone, after midnight, without sensing something of a thrill and a feeling of expectancy.

I had arranged my meeting with Jill Bentley with the single purpose in mind of finding out through her something of my wife's past history. I was prepared to beat it out of her, or trick it out of her, or make love to her and find out that way if possible.

By this time I didn't think I could ever trick any information out of Jill Bentley. I didn't believe I would be able to beat it out of her.

Jill went through the combination living-bedroom and into the small kitchen to knock cubes out of an ice tray. I crossed the room and dropped into a large, upholstered chair under a shaded reading light.

It wasn't a large room, but had been furnished with taste and it was comfortable. There were books on shelves along the wall and they looked as though they had been read. Magazines were scattered about and the place was immaculately clean. There was a large record player over against the far wall; a small studio piano next to it.

Jill came in with some ice cubes in a bucket, a bottle of inexpensive rye and a couple of glasses on a tray. She put them on the low table in front of me.

"You pour," she said. "I want to slip into something comfortable. Be right back."

She went through a door which I figured led to the bathroom.

Christ, I thought, this is just like the movies. She'll be back in a minute in one of those black lace negligees; a pair of mules on her bare feet.

But she fooled me.

She was back in five minutes and she was wearing a pair of long denim trousers and a man's shirt. No mules; bare feet. She had taken her hair down and it hung almost to her waist. She had also removed whatever makeup she wore. She didn't look glamorous anymore. She merely looked young and fresh and rather tomboyish.

"Never entertained a cop before," she said. "That is, voluntarily."

She laughed and reached for her drink.

She put a half dozen records on the record player and turned it low and then she poured herself another drink. I was still working on my first one. We just sat and listened to the music. By the time I was on my third drink, the bottle was more than half empty. It had been full when she had brought it in on the tray.

Jill wasn't paying the slightest bit of attention to me. She was holding her half-filled glass in her hand, looking over at the record box, and gently humming in time with the music. Her eyes were slightly misty.

I looked at her and then suddenly I had it.

She wasn't on the make. She wasn't a sharpshooter; I doubted if she had ever really been a crook. She was a lush. Plain and simple. A straight, out-and-out lush. And she liked company when she was drinking.

More than ever I wondered what she and Fern could ever have had in common.

At three-thirty the bottle was empty. Jill sat on the side of the couch and her eyes were glazed, but she still played the music and she still hummed softly. I stood up and walked over to her.

She was weaving as she got to her feet.

"You've been a good boy, Marty," she said and her words were thick. "A very good boy, indeed. Especially for a lousy damned policeman. Now you go home Marty, like the good boy you are, and Jill will tumble into her virginal bed. Drunk, but pure."

She laughed and suddenly sat down again on the couch. "Like a good little policeman," she said.

I reached over and picked up my hat.

I was at the door and had my hand on the knob when I was aware that she had once more reached her feet. She crossed the room and she was standing at my side as I turned the door handle.

"You are a good little policeman, Marty," she said, "and so Jill will kiss you good night."

She put her arms around my neck as she spoke and she lifted up her face to mine. Her lips were slightly open and her eyes were closed.

I leaned over and kissed her mouth.

My arm began to circle her waist and I was leaning close to her, pressing against her.

And then, a moment later, and she had twisted free. She seemed suddenly completely sober.

It was amazing.

"Good night," she said. "You're a cop, a self-confessed liar and probably a bit of a heel, but I like you. Call me soon."

She turned and went into the bathroom and closed the door. I could hear the click of the latch.

A moment later and I quietly shut the apartment door behind me. I walked down the single flight of steps to the street floor and let myself out of the building.

Unconsciously, I was wiping my lips.

A half hour later I was sitting in a Flushing subway car, reading the morning tabloid and cursing under my breath. I was so damned mad that I could barely control myself and I had completely forgotten Jill Bentley, and even Fern.

The story was on the second page, under the byline of one of the most reliable police reporters in New York. He hadn't pulled his punches. The lead ran:

> It has been reliably learned by this reporter that local police investigating the murder of glamorous Billy Chamlers, have cooperated with Philadelphia police in keeping secret the name of their top suspect—a wealthy clubman who is known to have been keeping the girl.
>
> In spite of the fact that this man, whose name is known to this reporter, has offered no alibi for the time the crime was believed to have taken place, and was also known to have been with Miss Chamlers shortly before her death, he has not been arrested nor has he been asked to explain his activities during that crucial period.

There was a lot more, but it was those two paragraphs which interested me.

I knew that when the Captain saw them, all hell would break loose. There may or may not have been a leak in the department, but it wouldn't matter. We'd be blamed anyway.

The hell with it, I said to myself, as the train approached Flushing. At least things will be in the open and that Malcolm character will have to come out from behind his lawyers and high-class connections and speak up. He was in for some plain and fancy mudslinging from the press.

I couldn't feel sorry about it.

When I got off the train, I unconsciously, again, wiped my lips.

CHAPTER VI

1.

Fern and I had breakfast together the next morning at nine o'clock. She looked as lovely as ever with the freshness of the new day in her face. I looked at her and then thought of Jill Bentley and I had a peculiar guilty feeling. With less than four hours sleep, I was still only half awake.

Then it occurred to me, what the hell was I feeling guilty about—she's the one who should feel guilt. She, Fern, my wife, a cheat and a liar and an adulteress. I began to feel the black anger coming over me.

Fern noticed me watching her face. She opened her mouth and was about to say something, when the shrill ring of the telephone cut the silence. I got up and went into the hallway and picked up the receiver.

A moment later I wished I hadn't.

It was Captain O'Shea and he was sputtering.

"You Marty," he said and his voice was a harsh yell. "Get your ass off of whatever you're sitting on and get down here. By God, did you see the morning papers?"

He didn't wait for me to answer.

"Another thing, don't ever again take the receiver off your hook when you go to bed. Who the hell do you think you're fooling. I've been trying to get you for an hour. Next time I'll send the beat man around. Get down here."

He slammed his receiver down before I could answer. He was really mad.

I hadn't taken the receiver off the hook. Fern must have done it when she got up before I did, so that I would not be disturbed. Damn it, it was one of those thoughtful little things she was always doing which had so endeared her to me.

I went in and gulped a half a cup of coffee standing up. "Gotta go at once," I said. "Hell's busting wide open downtown. The Captain ..."

"Is it that case of the murdered singer?" Fern asked.

I said it was, over my shoulder, as I went into the other room for my coat.

The Inspector himself was sitting in Captain O'Shea's chair when

I reached headquarters. The Captain and Sal Brentano were standing by the window looking glum. They were all there, waiting for me.

I said good morning and the Captain wanted to know what the hell was good about it.

"I suppose you have seen the papers?" the Inspector said.

I nodded.

"Just what the hell have you been doing, Lieutenant?" Captain O'Shea asked. I knew that when he called me Lieutenant instead of Marty he wasn't just being formal. He was burning.

"You're supposed to be working on the Chamlers case, you know. Here ..."

"I have been working on it," I said.

"Yes?" His voice was sarcastic. Sal interrupted.

"Marty was working on the Duffy and Holiday angles and I was covering Haverford," he interjected, trying to shift the conversation. It didn't work.

"Duffy—Holiday?" Captain O'Shea's voice dripped sarcasm. "Goddamn it, didn't I tell you that that punk Holiday was out of it? This is no prowler job. And what the hell's with Duffy. You got nothing there. What we want to know is what connection Malcolm has."

I blew up then.

"Jesus Christ," I said, "Malcolm! If the big brass would stop trying to protect him, maybe we could find something out. How the hell you expect us to ..."

The Inspector stood up and lifted his hand. His voice was calm and he didn't get excited. Which is probably one reason he was an Inspector.

"Take it easy, son," he said. "There's more to police work than just going off half cockeyed with an arrest warrant or a piece of rubber hose. You have to handle these things with finesse—with a certain amount of tact. We had to go slow with Malcolm. But after the stories in the papers this morning, that's all changed now. I've been in touch with the Philadelphia police and with his lawyers. We're through covering up for him. I told them that unless he shows up here this afternoon for questioning, we'll give the whole story to the papers and get out an extradition warrant. He's promised to be in on the two o'clock train."

It was news to Captain O'Shea and he suddenly calmed down.

"Good," he said. He pointed his short stubby pipe at me. "You and Sal be here. I want you to personally handle the thing. In the meantime, go out and pick up Haverford. It's time we started pinning him down."

"You mean hold him?" I asked.

"No, damn it, I don't. I mean question him."

"And suppose he doesn't want to play?"

"Listen," the Captain said, his face again red and angry, "do I have to tell you how to conduct police work? What the hell are you, a homicide lieutenant or a rookie? You know what to do; do it!"

The Inspector caught my eye and winked. A minute later Sal and I left the room. We stopped down the block, across from headquarters, and had a cup of coffee.

"The old man was in great form," Sal said. "I guess we better get going on this baby."

"We will, Sal," I said. "We'll get to the bottom of the Malcolm business this afternoon."

"Yeah," Sal said. "In the meantime, let's get up and see young Haverford. I think you'll find him interesting."

I hesitated a minute and then I turned to my partner.

"Listen, kid," I said, "I wish you'd go on up there alone. I have another angle I'm working on; something I'd like to clean up just for my own satisfaction."

Sal looked at me peculiarly.

"Holiday?"

I nodded.

"Jesus, Marty," he said, "I think you're barking up the wrong tree there. The Captain's right. That punk's in the clear. He'd have ..."

"Goddamn it Sal," I said, and for the first time since we'd been kids together, I was short and mean with him, "who the hell is in charge of this job? You do what I goddamn well tell you. And leave me alone—I know what I'm doing."

Sal blushed and didn't say a word. He looked away and a moment later I was sorry as hell that I'd snapped at him. I reached over and put my arm across his shoulder.

"I'm sorry, boy," I said. "I didn't mean to get rough. I'm just asking you to trust me, Sal. Let me play this one my way. I know what I'm doing."

Sal looked up at me with his quiet, thoughtful eyes. He smiled.

"Oke, Marty," he said. "You go ahead fella. I'll take care of Haverford. But you better meet me here about one forty-five so we get our stories straight."

He stood up and gave me a pat on the back. Then he left. There was a thoughtful expression on his scholarly face and although I knew that he had already forgiven, and I hoped forgotten, my outburst, he was wondering what had come over me.

Sal knew that I was much too good a cop to waste time with a guy like Willy Holiday on the slender evidence we had.

Of course there were a few things I hadn't told Sal Brentano about the evidence.

2.

I finished my coffee and after I paid the cashier, I took the slip of paper out of my pocket on which I had written the address Willy Holiday had given me—the address of Morris Gottlieb's wife, Dolly.

I got off the subway at Christopher Street and walked west on Fourth until I came to the house. There was a butcher shop on the first floor beside which was a doorway leading into a long hallway. There were a half dozen broken mailboxes, without names. At the end of the hallway, which smelled of a combination of garlic and stale cabbage, was a flight of narrow steps. There were two floors above the butcher shop with four apartments on each.

Dolly Gottlieb lived on the top floor, right rear.

I knocked on the door and I must admit I was curious to see what kind of a woman would have taken up with Willy Holiday.

Morris Gottlieb I remembered from the time he had been sent up. He was a cheap strong-arm boy, a product of the lower East Side, who had started with thieving and bootlegging back in the old prohibition days. His kind were a dime a dozen. Usually they married dull, drab females from their own environments; sullen, sickly women who raised their brood of brats and stayed in the shadowy backgrounds of their husband's lives. When they were flush the husbands played around with cheap floozies.

But Morrie's wife had been playing around with Willy Holiday so I expected something a little different. Probably a broken-down hash clinger with hennaed hair, somewhere in her mid-thirties. Or else a straight pro, a little too old to work the better call houses. The girl who answered my knock was a surprise.

She was in her early twenties and she wasn't pretty. Her weight was right and she had a fairly good figure, although she was short and in another year or so would be dumpy. Her hair was dark brown and combed severely back from her forehead and parted in the middle. She wore horn rimmed glasses, and although she was dressed in a plain, tailored suit, there was something a little dowdy about her.

More than anything else she looked like a librarian or a competent secretary.

She just stood in the doorway, which she held open about ten inches, and looked at me.

"Dolly Gottlieb?" I asked.

She nodded.

I took my shield out and showed it to her.

Well, I have met and talked with hundreds of gangsters' wives and women. All kinds. But this one took me right off my feet. Her first words were so completely contradictory to her appearance that for a second, I couldn't even get my breath.

"Get off my doorstep, you piss-faced flatfoot," she said, "or I'll spit right in your eye. You wanna talk with me, get a warrant!"

She started to slam the door in my face.

I got my foot in in time, but it almost broke a couple of toes. I didn't follow police college procedure for interviewing citizens. Shoving out with my right hand, I slammed the doorway wide open and the side of it caught her and sent her sprawling back on the floor. Before she could get to her feet, I followed her into the room, kicking the door shut with my heel. I reached down and grabbed her by both arms and lifted her up and threw her into a chair.

She started to gasp for breath, but before she could let out another string of obscenities, I spoke quickly.

"Don't get tough, sister," I said. "Willy Holiday sent me and you had better start listening. And one more foul word out of that dirty mouth of yours and I'll bruise it shut!"

I went over to the unmade bed and sat down and took a pack of cigarettes from my coat pocket. I took one from the pack and then tossed the pack into her lap.

Her glasses had fallen off and her eyes were wide. She stared at me, almost totally without expression, as she extracted a cigarette. I lighted mine and then leaned over and gave her a light.

For a moment neither of us spoke and I suddenly observed that without her glasses, her entire appearance was changed. Her eyes were very large and almost black. She had long, curved lashes. She wore no makeup, with the exception of bright magenta lipstick. The contrast of the lipstick and those dark eyes, with the pale olive skin of her small face, was startling. Had the eyes been slanted, instead of straight in her face, she would have passed for an Oriental.

She blew a cloud of smoke from her mouth, directly into my face. She started to say something.

Again I spoke quickly.

"Don't say it—don't say a word," I said. "Just listen. I know all about you and Willy shacking up. Willy's in trouble; he's the number one candidate for the hot seat in a very nice current murder. You're in trouble. Your old man, Morrie, may not know about you and Willy, but sister, he will. He will. Even you get the slightest bit out of line.

"And as you probably know, Morrie is due to get out in a very short time. Also, you have a record of your own and Willy's on parole. Among other things you and Willy have been doing, is consorting. It's an offense in this state, sister."

It was quite a little speech, but it did the trick. If her face hadn't been a dead olive white to begin with, I would have said she went pale. For several moments she just stared at me. I have seen the expression many times, on many faces.

She was a cop hater. You can always tell. One of those psychopathic personalities who just instinctively and without reason hate any cop, of any kind.

And then she spoke and I got my second surprise.

She laughed. It was a full-throated, completely open laugh.

"Consorting, eh?" she said. "So Willy and I have been consorting. My God, and all along I thought it was fornicating. Shows you what a lack of education will do."

She wasn't frightened; she wasn't annoyed. She was amused.

In spite of myself I had to laugh. This Dolly Gottlieb was something completely new in my experience.

She stood up and started across the room.

"I can't say I like you or want to talk to you," she said. "But here you are and here I am and there isn't much I can do about it. So let's have a drink and then you can get down to business."

She wasn't necessarily being friendly.

I made a quick decision. I had been prepared to be tough, but I knew instinctively that with Dolly's type, toughness would get me nowhere. I didn't kid myself that we could get friendly. She didn't like cops and she never would. But at least she might be willing to play ball if she figured that would be the best out.

"Drink sounds fine," I said.

There was a brand-new refrigerator in one corner of the dingy room and she opened the top, a freezer compartment. She took out a milk bottle and two jelly glasses with frost on them. She walked over to the card table and sat the glasses down and then poured from the bottle. She handed me a glass full of amber liquid.

"Martini," she said. "I freeze 'em in that gadget there. Cheapest and best tasting drink you can make. I use sherry instead of vermouth."

She lifted her own glass and drank and I drank mine. It was ice cold and surprisingly good.

"'Nother?" she asked.

"Later," I said.

She nodded, turned and put the milk bottle back in the freezer. She picked up both glasses, washed them in the sink and put them back on ice. Then she went back to the chair and sat down. Somewhere along the way she'd picked up the black horn rimmed eye glasses and put them on again. It completely changed her appearance and once more she looked like a plain little, slightly dowdy, stenographer.

"Shoot," she said. "What's the pitch?"

"You and Willy Holiday," I said. "I want to know all about it."

She looked at me through the thick lens of her glasses and it gave her a peculiar, owlish appearance.

"You must have a dirty mind," she said.

"Never mind my mind. Just talk."

"Well," she laughed again. "God, Will must really be in the grease. A lieutenant, no less."

I started to get up.

"All right, all right. Stop playing the heavy," she spoke quickly. "What exactly do you want to know?"

"Everything," I said. "When you first met Willy; how well you know him, why he's been shacking up here. The works."

She thought for a moment, and then started.

"Willy was a friend of my husband's; Morrie that is. Used to sell "packages" to him. When Morrie went up the river, Willy started seeing me. Then he just sort of moved in. He'd only been out on parole for a few days and at first he used to come up and just talk. Gave me messages from the old man.

"I don't work. I drink. Well, Willy got this job with the milk company through the parole board, he had a little loose money and he moved in. It didn't mean anything and it didn't hurt anybody."

"It might mean something to Morrie," I said.

She lost her blandness for a second and I could tell that the idea was not pleasant. Morris Gottlieb, as I remembered him, wasn't admired for his gentler qualities.

"Oh Willy's a harmless enough little pipsqueak," she said, a little too casually. "It don't mean anything. I'm alone, I got no money and Willy's just one of those guys. When Morris gets out I'll toss Willy back to wherever he comes from and just forget about him."

"When Morris gets out," I said, "Willy will probably already be back in—for good, or better than good."

She didn't say anything for a minute.

Then, "What's the rumble? You mean to tell me Willy killed somebody? I don't believe it."

"It doesn't matter what you believe," I said. "It's what a jury of twelve men believe. Let's talk about last Saturday. Just start say around ten or eleven in the morning and keep on going for the next twelve hours."

I could see her mind working. She knew that I must have talked with Willy; probably figured that we had him locked up incommunicado in some precinct house. She didn't have the faintest idea what he had done or what we suspected him of having done. She wanted to protect him if possible. At the same time, she wasn't sure just what to do. Anything she said might be the wrong thing. She decided to play it smart.

"I haven't seen Willy in more than a week."

3.

I stood up.

"Time for another drink," I said. "That's good news, Dolly, although Willy won't think so when he hears it. You were, up until a second ago, his alibi for the time of the Billy Chamlers murder. Too bad."

I started for the freezer compartment of the refrigerator.

"Hey," she yelled.

I turned back toward her. She was staring at me and taken off her glasses.

"Screwed again by a dumb cop," she said, as though she were speaking to herself. Then she looked at me and started talking, her voice terse and swift.

"Not so fast, Sherlock. Not so fast. You should make yourself clear. That is if a cop can ever tell the truth the first try. Sit down and I'll tell you all about it."

She was coming along nicely so I played it slow and hard.

"No rush," I said. "You already told me. Let's have the drink. I'll send a couple of bottles up from the corner liquor store on my way out. I don't want to seem a chiseler."

She didn't think it was funny. But she did get up and get the milk bottle out and poured us each another one. They were strong, but went down smoothly.

Then she started talking and I knew she was leveling. She'd lost her coy sense of humor and she was deadly serious.

"Goddamn it, you gotta believe this," she said. "Willy came here sometime shortly before noon on Saturday. He …"

"How do you know it was shortly before noon?"

"Because we sat here and doped a couple of horses and then I called Harvey, the bookie. We won the first race so I must have got it down in plenty of time. You can check."

I believed her.

"We sat here, right in this room, and played the horses over the phone all afternoon. Got the results on the radio. At the end of the day we were out so we went on playing, making bets on the west coast tracks. Around seven thirty we had some spaghetti I cooked up. Later we played two handed gin and I took a few more of Willy's dollars away from him. At about ten o'clock Willy took a shower and shaved and got dressed and then he left for work. Must have been about eleven."

"Anyone come in during all that time?" I asked.

"Nobody."

On instinct I played a hunch.

"You mean," I said, "you and Willy were here, in this room, from about eleven in the morning until eleven at night? And nobody stopped by at all who saw you? Nuts! How about the clerk from the liquor store when you ran out of gin?"

"There was no clerk," Dolly said, obviously suspecting a trap. "Willy picked up the bottle when he went out to square up with Harvey and get the meat for the spaghetti."

The minute the words were out of her mouth, she put her hand to her lips and her startled eyes opened wide. She looked at me as though I had suddenly grown horns.

"Nice going, Dolly," I said. "Very nice. I'll have another drink on that and I think you need one yourself. So Willy went out, did he? Then of course he wasn't with you during that whole eleven-hour period."

She started to say something but got mixed up between cursing me and trying to explain about Willy all at the same time.

"Sit down kid," I said and gently pushed her back into her chair. "We'll have another pour and then you can tell me all about it."

The milk bottle was down around the one quarter mark after I had filled the glasses.

"Now," I said, "I want you to start over. This is the third pitch and if you miss, you're out. Keep it in mind; you're out.

"There's a double penalty for being out. First, I'll be taking a little trip up to Ossining and having a talk with Morrie. Morrie Gottlieb, your husband. Second, we're going to put Willy in the chair for murder. Whether you like it or not. He's going to burn. And if you're out, then you're going to take a two to five ride of your own—as an accessory before the fact and after the fact. There's the thing about perjury, also, just in case you get smart at the trial. There are other things. You can't win if you miss, so don't miss. Now start talking."

For several seconds she just sat there and looked at me. The coyness was all gone now. She was thinking and thinking hard. And then she started to talk. I knew, that now at last, she was giving it to me straight. She knew I wasn't fooling.

The first part of it was the same. Willy Holiday had arrived at around eleven. He'd had to make a report to his parole officer when he had gotten off work that morning and so had been late getting there. He'd come home and stripped off his jacket and shirt and poured a drink and then he'd taken out the racing form and they'd started figuring the horses.

She even found the old scratch sheet in a wastebasket and it was marked up with both their initials and the sums they had bet as well as the results. She hadn't done as badly as Willy, but then I figured she was a lot smarter.

Somewhere around six o'clock they had run out of gin and Willy had put on his shirt and jacket and gone out. The bookie, Harvey, by this time was into them for a little and Willy decided to pay up before starting the bets rolling on the California tracks.

She couldn't remember exactly how long he'd been away and it didn't do me any good to pressure her. By this time she was so scared that she was sticking strictly to the truth. She didn't dare fake it any more.

"Maybe an hour, maybe two," she said. "It wasn't any longer than that. He had to meet Harvey at a bar over on West Tenth Street and he had a couple of shots while he was waiting around. Then he went down to Bleecker Street and got some hamburger."

"How come he didn't get it in the butcher shop downstairs?" I asked.

"Butcher's my landlord," she said. "I owe him dough for meat as well as a month's rent. He knows about Willy shacking up here."

Anyway, as near as she could figure it, he had returned before eight o'clock. She was willing and ready to swear to this.

It's a funny thing, but as she continued talking, I had a hard time following her conversation. My mind kept going to other things. I was thinking about Morris Gottlieb up in Sing Sing.

A goddamned crook; a no good, brutal louse.

But he was married and here was his wife, a woman who had shared his bed and shared his money when he was making it, calmly talking about the man she slept with while Morrie was doing time for getting that money and paying for the bed.

As I have said a dozen times, I hate crooks and I have no sympathy for them. But somehow or another, I felt a peculiar sense of sympathy for Gottlieb.

I thought, Jesus Christ what the hell am I worrying about Morris Gottlieb for? After all, who am I, Marty Ferris, to worry about that cheap crook and his bitch of a wife. I got a wife of my own. Fern. Or should I say Joan Bronski. Yes, a fine, beautiful wife.

And what's the difference between her and this Dolly? None that I could see. They both were liars; they both were adulteresses.

I should be feeling sorry for Gottlieb—hell. I should be feeling sorry for myself!

4.

I looked over at Dolly as she talked and I wondered what in God's name it was about women that made them liars and cheats. Morrie Gottlieb certainly wasn't much, but my God, compared to Willy Holiday he was at least a man.

"Get off your can and get me a drink," I said suddenly.

She couldn't have stopped speaking quicker if I had thrown a cold dishrag in her face. She looked at me oddly for a moment and then wordlessly stood up and walked over to the icebox. She began fixing up a Martini in the milk bottle, using cracked ice.

"What the hell could you see in a crumb like Willy Holiday?" I said.

My voice was bitter.

She took off her glasses and turned and looked at me in surprise. Her voice was soft when she answered.

"Nothing much," she said. "Except I got tired of living here alone; tired of waiting, tired of working. Willy isn't much, but he liked me and he was good to me. You get sick of sleeping alone."

"You better get used to it again," I said. "Willy's not going to be around anymore."

She poured the drinks into the glasses after rinsing them and then she walked over and she handed me one. She leaned down and I noticed that she looked at me curiously. Her eyes were just above mine as she leaned toward me and I saw that she had opened the buttons on her tailored jacket and that it hung loose.

She wore a white blouse underneath and it was cut so low that the line between her breasts showed deep and clean.

I stared at her, trying not to. I still couldn't understand what she might have seen in Willy, but it suddenly occurred to me what he saw in her. She no longer looked like a librarian. Not the type librarian I had ever seen.

I stared up into her face.

She was a tramp, a plain, out-and-out tramp. Not beautiful, not glamorous, nothing. I didn't even like her.

My hand reached up and I took her glass and carefully sat it next to the chair at my side. My other hand suddenly went around her waist and I pulled her quickly down so that she dropped to her knees, her slender body between my legs.

I reached in back of her head and pulled her face up to mine.

She was trembling and her mouth was hot and moist. I hated her.

My right hand reached up under her jacket and shirt and I felt the soft flesh of her straight back. And then, a moment later, as I kept my mouth crushed against her own, I felt the feverish activity of her own small white hands.

The bed was over under the window at the side of the room. I stood up and carried her over, never taking my lips from hers.

Later, she cried out and didn't want to let me go.

At twelve fifteen I left Dolly Gottlieb sitting on the edge of her bed, a drink of straight gin in her hand, a linen bathrobe over her naked body. She was staring at me with dull, unseeing eyes as I turned at the doorway and spoke to her.

"Remember," I said. "We'll be here tomorrow morning. Around ten o'clock. Willy and me. You know what to say."

She nodded and the robe fell partly open.

I opened the door and then slammed it shut behind me as I started walking down the mud-colored hallway.

I was filled with hate.

I hated Dolly Gottlieb.

I hated Fern. Somehow in the back of my mind I blamed her for what had just happened.

But mostly I hated myself.

CHAPTER VII

1.

I entered the restaurant at exactly one thirty. Sal was sitting at a table in the rear. He had a cup of coffee in front of him, but it was untouched. His hat was on the back of his head and he was tapping the end of a pencil on the edge of his saucer. He looked nervous, which in Sal Brentano was unusual.

"Glad you're early, Marty," he said. "Things are happening. Just talked to the Captain and stalled the interview with Malcolm until late this afternoon. O'Shea is going to keep him on ice until then."

I started to say something, but Sal kept right on.

"It's Haverford," he said. "Things are breaking wide open. I found out that our boy was with Billy Chamlers at five o'clock on the day she was killed. We have him cold. And they were fighting."

In a second I forgot about Morrie Gottlieb's wife, about Willy Holiday and about my own personal problems. Suddenly, I was once more all cop.

"Slow down, pal," I said, "and let me have it blow by blow."

Sal smiled; he was pleased with himself.

"One of those lucky breaks," he said. "After I left you this morning, I went up to Haverford's office. He wasn't in but was expected any moment. Well, I was sitting there waiting, when a girl walked in. She stopped at the desk and the receptionist said something to her in a low voice. A second later she came over to where I was sitting. She looked nervous.

"First she asked me to identify myself, and I did. Then she took me into a private office. She introduced herself. She was Haverford's private secretary and her name is Jane Cummins. A tall, good looking blonde.

"I saw at once that she was very nervous and that she had something on her mind. It took her several minutes to come out with it and I let her take her time. Then I got the whole story.

"Seems that she and John Haverford have been running around together for some time—maybe six months. I gathered they had been having an affair and that she was the one who had nursed the thing along. Also that she was anxious to tie it up with a marriage. About a month back, Haverford began to cool off. That's about the time he began making a play for the Chamlers girl. This secretary of his found out what the score was and she started taking a slow burn.

"Anyway, to cut it short, on the day that Billy Chamlers was murdered, Haverford left the office at around three-thirty. Told his secretary he had an appointment at Twenty-One with a client, but she knew he was lying. She figured he was seeing Billy Chamlers and she decided to have a showdown. She's pregnant, incidentally.

"So she went up to Haverford's apartment expecting to find him there. When he didn't answer the bell, she rang the Chamlers apartment. The latch clicked and she went upstairs. Billy Chamlers and Haverford were in the place together and there was quite a scene. She said she lost her head, announced she was Haverford's fiancée and that the Chamlers woman laughed and told them both to get out. Haverford asked her to go ahead and said he would meet her at her apartment after attending to some unfinished business with Miss Chamlers. But according to Cummins he never arrived."

I whistled under my breath. This new development certainly changed the complexion of things.

"What's this Jane Cummins' attitude now?" I asked. "Is she trying to get Haverford in trouble?"

Sal nodded.

"She's burned up all right," he said. "I think she'd like to put him in the middle. But the main thing is that she's prepared to swear that when she left the Chamlers apartment at around five o'clock, Haverford was still there. And that he and the Chamlers girl were fighting."

"You tell the Captain about this?" I asked.

"Yeah, I called him," Sal said. "I covered you—said you were still with the Cummins girl and he told me that we should follow it up and that he'd take care of Malcolm for the time being."

"This certainly changes the picture," I said. "She's got her boyfriend in a tight corner. Where's Haverford now?"

"He checked into his office a little before noon. I've got Kelly on his tail. The Cummins girl left just before he came in. Said she had a bad headache and was going home to rest up."

"Well, then, let's just jump over and pick Haverford up at his office. He has a little explaining to do."

"How about the girl," Sal asked.

"She won't be going anywhere as long as she's already told you the story," I said. We went out of the restaurant and signaled a passing cab.

2.

It was one of those fancy Madison Avenue office buildings and the reception room on the tenth floor looked a lot more like the entrance to a high-class gambling establishment than it did a business concern. The girl at the information desk could have been taken directly from the Atlantic City Beauty Pageant and the afternoon dress she wore could have easily doubled for a bathing suit. Her bare shoulders were cool and so were her manners.

She told us to sit down and that she'd send our names into Haverford.

"Send us in instead," I said, showing her my shield.

She merely smiled and again suggested we sit down.

We did.

If John Haverford had been expecting us, be couldn't have got out there faster. He was pulling on his light sports jacket as he came through the door.

He didn't bother to shake hands but he gave us what must have been his customer smile.

"Hot," he said. "Let's do it downstairs at the bar."

Sal introduced me on the way down in the elevator and Haverford gave my hand a perfunctory shake. His own hand was thin to the point of transparency and it had a nervous tremor. I watched his face as we rode down and while he talked with Sal. His voice was high-pitched and tense and the words escaped in a flood from thin, sensitive lips. His nose was large and aristocratic under a narrow forehead. The sandy hair was thin, but immaculately barbered. He seemed to have a lot on his mind.

There was a sort of semiprivate bar on the ground floor of the building and I gathered it was largely patronized by the advertising firms from the floors above. We took a table in a secluded corner at the rear and the waiter greeted Haverford by his first name. He ordered a double Scotch and soda and Sal and I each had a bottle of beer. We explained we were on duty and the information seemed to make Haverford even more nervous.

He tried to keep things on a friendly social basis, but I straightened him out at once.

"We should be having this conversation down at headquarters, Mr. Haverford," I said. "However, where we go when we leave here is going to be largely up to you. I might start out by saying that you have a great deal to explain. Particularly about your activities on the afternoon and early evening of Billy Chamlers' murder."

His tanned face suddenly went very white and he looked much older than the twenty-eight or thirty years which I had figured his age. He reached for his drink and then hesitated with it halfway to his lips. He started to say something, but, I interrupted him.

"Particularly, also, about how you happened to be in the Chamlers apartment around the time she was killed."

He knew at once what must have happened. I could see it in the guarded way he watched me from under his eyelids. When he finally spoke, his voice was so soft as to be barely audible.

"You've been talking with Miss Cummins," he said.

"We have."

He shook his head then, as though coming out of a daze. For a moment he looked me full in the face. His mouth lost its nervous twitch and his hand was steady as he reached again for the remains of his Scotch and soda.

"Am I permitted to call my attorney?" he asked.

"You are," I said. "But before you do, I'd like to give you a little advice. Your attorney will be interviewing you down at a cell in the Tombs. If you want it that way, you can have it. On the other hand, it's possible you can give us a straight story right here and now and save yourself a lot of embarrassment and trouble. You have a lot to clear up."

He leaned toward me then and he spoke in a clear unhurried tone.

"Jane—Miss Cummins—is hardly a fair witness," he said. "She has an axe of her own to grind."

"If we didn't know that," I said, "you wouldn't be sitting here. But axe or no axe, let's get back to you. Let's say we start at around three-thirty on the day of the murder. Take it from there. And this time, I must warn you, tell the truth. You won't have another chance."

He gestured to the waiter for a second round of drinks and began talking at once.

"There's just one thing I'd like to explain first," he said. "I lied before and I'd like to tell you why I lied. I was in Miss Chamlers—in her apartment—as you know. But if that story had come out, as well as the fact that Miss Cummins was also there, Jane would have been sure to have been fired. There is a good chance that I would have lost my own job as well. I couldn't see how it would have helped any if I mentioned it, and so I didn't. I wanted to protect both of us if I could."

"O.K.," I said. "I'll buy that for what it's worth. But now let's get down to cases. First, exactly what is your relationship with Miss Cummins; what was your relationship with Miss Chamlers? And I want to know about every minute from three-thirty until eight o'clock of last Saturday. I also want to know what was said as well as what may or may not have been done in Billy Chamlers' apartment while you were there. So let's start talking."

Right off he admitted having an affair with the Cummins girl.

"I didn't realize she was taking it so seriously," he said. He went on to explain the relationship and verified just about everything that Miss Cummins had told Sal. The only point on which they differed was his insistence that no thought of marriage had ever entered into the affair.

He told us he had first met Billy Chamlers when they entered the apartment house in which they both lived, together one evening, and she had misplaced her key.

There had been several dates and he admitted frankly that he had fallen pretty hard for the nightclub singer. He had been around a lot and he realized at once that somebody was probably keeping her.

The fact had made little difference in his feelings. Things had gone along fairly smoothly until Jane Cummins realized that he was making a play for the singer. His problem, however, had been with the secretary and not with Miss Chamlers.

"She is extremely jealous," he said. "At one point, she even threatened to tell the head of our concern about my past relationship with her. She did, in fact, call Billy Chamlers on the phone and tell her that we were planning to be married. That was just a few days ago.

"Billy was annoyed. The next time I asked her for a date, she told me she was busy. Then, when I persisted, she told me about Jane's telephone call. She said that she had enough problems of her own and didn't want any more.

"That's how I happened to see her last Saturday afternoon. I had called again and asked to take her to dinner. She told me she was meeting someone for dinner but that I could drop by if I wished. I left the office sometime after three-thirty and went directly home. I went to my own apartment first and freshened up, then I walked upstairs and knocked on her door."

"What were you doing in the office at three-thirty on a Saturday?" I asked. "I thought these places had a five-day week."

"We do," Haverford said. "Only right now we're in the midst of a big cigarette campaign and the whole staff is working on it. Everyone, almost, was here Saturday morning and most of us stayed during the afternoon."

I nodded.

"O.K.," I said. "So you went home and then up to Miss Chamlers' apartment. Anyone see you?"

"I don't believe so. She answered the door herself—it was the maid's day off. Billy hadn't dressed and we went back to her bedroom. She'd been lying down.

"Well, we talked for a few minutes and she told me that it would be best if I didn't see her again. Jane had sold her a real bill of goods and she was convinced that things between us were serious. It wasn't, you understand, that she would have objected to breaking in on anything. It was only that she didn't want to be bothered. I didn't mean enough to her, I guess."

"How much did she mean to you?" I asked.

Carefully he looked at each of us before he answered. He seemed to measure his words.

"That's a tough question. I liked her; liked her a great deal. For a month or more we'd been playing around and I still hadn't gotten to first base. Yes, I wanted her and wanted her badly. On the other hand, I knew she was being kept; I knew that she could never really fit into the sort of life I hope eventually to lead. I couldn't quite see Billy Chamlers settled down with the country club set in Westchester or Connecticut. I wanted her, but I didn't take her seriously. There was no question of wanting to marry her."

Haverford went on to explain that they were talking this very thing over when Jane Cummins showed up. He hadn't wanted a scene and he realized that the girl was overwrought and emotionally upset.

"You knew that she was pregnant?" I interrupted.

He looked up at me, startled.

"I did not," he snapped. "Furthermore ..."

"She says she is," I said. "She also says you are the ..."

"If she's pregnant I probably am," he said, with one of those strange about-faces which were characteristic of him. "On the other hand, nothing was said about it in the Chamlers apartment or at any time before or since—at least to me."

The way he said it, I was inclined to believe him.

"Go on with your story," I said.

"Anyway, I got her out of the place at once. Told her I'd meet her in a few minutes."

"And then what happened?"

"I talked with Billy for probably another ten minutes. I tried to reason with her, but she said she was getting bored with me. She'd be just as happy if she didn't see me again. I was a little sore and probably my pride was hurt more than anything else. Also, I was damned annoyed with Jane Cummins, although in a sense I did feel that she had some justification for acting as she had.

"Because of this, and because I realized that I was probably unreasonably bothered as a result of Billy's attitude, I decided not to see Jane at once. Instead, when I left I went to a bar and had a few drinks by myself."

"What time did you leave the Chamlers place?"

"As near as I can figure it must have been around five o'clock. I know that I arrived at the bar shortly after five. This bar that we are now in, to be exact."

"How do you know what time you arrived?"

"I don't for sure. Only shortly after five the boys from upstairs started drifting in for a drink or two before they took off for home. Most of them go to Grand Central and take a train up to Connecticut. They were coming in when I got here. In fact, I believe one of your men checked on me and can verify that."

I nodded.

"From here I went to the Pavilion and had dinner."

"We know," I said. "However, one fact remains. You were in Billy Chamlers' apartment at five. You were arguing with her. You could, possibly, have killed her."

If I had expected him to blow up at that, I was disappointed.

"I couldn't have and I didn't," he said. "According to the papers, she was murdered at six o'clock."

"That's a guess," I said. "You were the last person to see her alive."

"The last person except for her murderer," he said. "One doesn't go around bashing in the head of every girl who decides not to date you. If you're looking for a motive, I had a hell of a lot more reason to kill Jane Cummins."

Haverford waved again for the waiter, but Sal spoke up.

"I think," he said, "we better get downtown."

"We'll want you to come along," I said to Haverford. "I'd like to get your statement down and have you sign it."

He looked up, annoyed for a moment, and then shrugged. When the waiter brought the check, he insisted on signing it. We left and took a cab down to headquarters.

I left Sal with Haverford and a police stenographer and went into Captain O'Shea's office.

3.

The Captain was alone, his feet on the desk as he slowly sipped from a paper cup filled with his cough medicine. He listened while I told him about Haverford. When I got through talking, he took his feet down and leaned toward me.

"He's still far from in the clear," he said. "First place, about that business of going back to the bar. You know what that sort of setup is. That's the sort of place, from what you tell me, that Haverford and his associates hit every afternoon. Probably they drift in and out and some of them stay for a half dozen or more drinks. Place is probably jumping from about five o'clock until six-thirty or seven. They'd be so used to seeing him around that no one could say for sure just when he arrived or when he left.

"He could have come in at five-thirty or even later. On the other hand, he could have come in right after five, talked around for a few minutes and then gone back to the Chamlers place, killed the girl and returned. No one would have noticed."

The old man smiled grimly and began to doodle with a pencil on the scratch pad on his desk.

"He could have done it," he said. "As for the motive, right now it looks a little thin. But the guy's a liar on his own say-so and maybe something else will turn up."

"You think we should hold him?" I asked.

"Hell no. He can't go far and there's no point making an arrest until we have a case to go along with it. But I want you to make a thorough investigation—everything. His finances, his background, the works. I want to know all about him. In the meantime, I got a little news for you."

There was a pleased, almost smug smile on the old man's face. He let me wait while he took up his pipe and filled it. After he had it well lighted, he continued.

"I've just finished talking with Malcolm," he said. "And I think I have something for you. Malcolm's told me all about his relationship with the dead girl. The reason he's been playing it so cagey is because he was being blackmailed. Seems that somehow or other someone managed to get some pictures of him and the Chamlers dame. They are really something."

The Captain took a couple of snapshots from an envelope and tossed them across the desk.

I picked them up and I must have blushed. I blushed for two reasons. The pictures themselves were enough to make anyone blush. There were two people in them—Malcolm and Billy Chamlers. There was no question about either of them. There was also no question about what they were doing.

Yes, the pictures themselves brought the red to my face. It was just as well. Because I would have probably blushed anyway as the Captain stared at me. I suddenly remembered where I had seen a negative of one of those pictures. A negative which I hadn't mentioned to Captain O'Shea.

"It seems," the Captain continued as I tossed the prints back across the desk, "that somehow or other some guy got a hold of a full set of these and similar pics. The Chamlers girl was probably in on the thing. Anyway, Malcolm was sent these two in the mail. And then he started paying off."

"To whom?" I asked. "Billy Chamlers?"

"No. Says he used to mail the money to a post office box at the general post office. His instructions came to his office by mail."

"Had he talked with Billy Chamlers about it?"

"He says no. However, it's hard to say. After all, he'd been keeping her for some time, but he'd got tired of it and was trying to cut loose. She didn't want any part of that and had made frequent threats to tip off his family. He was in a tough spot.

"Furthermore, he spent the night with her and the morning of the day on which she was killed. Claims he left about three o'clock, but didn't go back to his hotel. Instead he said he picked up his car at a midtown garage and started back for Philadelphia."

"I thought he flew in from Philadelphia," I said.

"He did. But the car was here from his previous trip. We've checked that. Well he picked up the car all right. But he didn't go directly back to Philadelphia. In fact, the next check on him is when he put the car into a downtown Philadelphia garage around nine-thirty that night. So let's say it takes three hours at most to drive to Philly. He could have been in New York as late as six-thirty."

I whistled. "Any explanation …"

"None. All he'll say is that he has explained everything to the Philadelphia police. I threatened to hold him, but he still wouldn't talk. He seems a lot more worried about those pictures than he does about a murder charge."

"And where is he now?"

"I turned him over to the post office people. Convinced him that it would be best all around to try and get their help. I wanted him to take his mind off the murder for a while. Also, I'd be pretty anxious to find out just who was blackmailing him. Maybe it was the girl; if so there is every reason for him to have killed her."

"That may be," I said. "But I don't quite see him telling us about the blackmail if that was his motive."

"You may be right," Captain O'Shea said. "But in the meantime, let's see if we can find the original negatives of those pictures. If the Chamlers girl was the one who was holding him up, she must have them hidden someplace. Find them and prove that she had them, and I think you have your murder case solved."

"And how about Malcolm for now?"

"Let him sit. The post office people will keep him for the time being and it will give us a chance to work. Let's just keep him on ice while we find out everything we can on our own hook."

"All right," I said. "I'll get on it at once. And in the meantime …"

"In the meantime clean up Haverford. Let's for God sakes get someone out of the way. Either that or get them in jail."

I asked him if he wanted to talk to Haverford and he said that he didn't.

"You handle it," he said. "Also, you better check a little more on that Cummins dame. Jesus, she certainly had a reason."

I told him I would and then I left. I went back upstairs and I picked up my mail before I started again for the room in which I had left Sal Brentano and the police stenographer with Haverford. Leafing through the envelopes, I noticed the one from my FBI friend down in Washington.

4.

It's a peculiar thing, but for the last few hours I had completely forgotten my own problems; completely forgotten Fern. The sight of that envelope brought it all back to me.

The hell with Haverford, I thought. The hell with Malcolm and the whole goddamned Billy Chamlers mess. I had other things to think about. My own life and what had happened to it.

I ducked down the hall and went into the men's room. A moment later and I had locked myself into a toilet and was tearing open the envelope. My hand was shaking as I unfolded the single sheet of paper and spread it out to read.

After the first paragraph, I had a hard time focusing my eyes. But I finally got through it.

"I have been in contact with our San Francisco and Portland, Oregon, offices," my friend wrote.

> San Francisco's probation report on Joan Bronski shows that she was living with a man named Harold T. Woodlawn in 1946, which would have made her eighteen years old at the time. Woodlawn was indicted on a grand larceny charge early in 1947, but jumped bail while awaiting trial. It was in connection with this crime that Joan Bronski was later indicted and sentenced.
>
> Her part in the crime is vague, but from what we have been able to learn, it is believed she helped Woodlawn make his getaway and it was hoped that in convicting her, trace of the man might be found. He has never turned up. Woodlawn, now in his early thirties, had no previous criminal record. He is still wanted by California authorities.
>
> Portland informs me that Joan Bronski was born in that city in a charity ward at the Municipal Hospital in 1928. Her mother's name was Carol Bronski and she died giving birth to the child. The father is unknown.

The child was raised in a Catholic orphanage, from which she ran away at the age of sixteen. She obtained work as a stenographer and apparently supported herself for the next two years. No effort was made to bring her back to the orphanage.

She is believed to have met Harold Woodlawn in Portland and gone to California with him.

If necessary, I can forward you details of the grand larceny case in which she was involved.

The letter was signed by my friend and he had added a postscript asking if I wanted a new flyer put out on Woodlawn. He said that it was strictly a local case and that the FBI had not been called in on it.

Carefully I refolded the sheet of paper and put it back in the envelope. And then I just sat there.

I thought about it until I felt the top of my head would burst. God, I couldn't believe it, but I knew it must be true.

Fern. Fern, my wife. The woman I had lived with and loved. I didn't know what I had expected, once I had learned of her basic deceit, but this last news—the fact that she was not only a criminal herself, but had lived with one—completely took the wind out of me.

I felt the hatred growing in me. I tried to imagine what sort of man this Woodlawn might have been. What had happened to him? Where he was? And was Fern still seeing him?

Suddenly I found myself hating him, hating him more than I hated Fern.

A blinding fury was burning in my heart and I knew that I was rapidly getting beyond control.

I started to put all of the correspondence into my coat pocket when I noticed the letter from the bank. For a moment I stared at it, wondering why I was interested. And then it came to me.

Fern and I had a joint checking account and she handled all of the bills. I merely gave her my check on paydays and she deposited it. She kept track of accounts and all bank correspondence was sent to the house. It had been my custom to cash a check for twenty-five dollars each week for personal expenses.

I opened the bank's letter, wondering why they had written me in care of the Police Department.

It was a notice that our joint account was overdrawn by more than fifty dollars. The notice was signed by the vice-president of the bank and he wrote asking that I take care of the matter as he had already twice called it to our attention.

I couldn't understand it. Fern and I had always kept a minimum balance of five hundred dollars in the account, not only to give us a cushion, but also to save the expense of paying for checks that we wrote and deposited.

I got up and left the booth and went over to a washbasin and rinsed my face with cold water. I had a splitting headache.

Ten minutes later and I was talking to Sal Brentano in the hallway outside of his office. I repeated the Captain's information.

"Sal," I said, "I want you to take over alone for the rest of the night. I've got a bad headache and I feel like hell. Guess maybe I'm coming down with something. Anyway, I think I'll cut along home and get into bed. Probably be O.K. in the morning."

Sal looked at me and there was a worried expression around his eyes.

"You better see the doc, Marty," he said. "You haven't been right now for several days."

"It's just a headache," I said. "I'll be all right in the morning. Don't worry about me, pal."

He told me to go on home and said to say hello to Fern for him.

I said I would. I left headquarters five minutes later.

But I didn't go home. I went uptown as far as Grand Central and I went into the Commodore and had a couple of straight shots of Bourbon. I went into a phone booth.

I reached Jill Bentley just as she was leaving her apartment. She seemed the slightest bit cold and a little evasive. But she agreed to let me pick her up at the Shenandoah after the show.

Then I called my house out on Long Island.

There was no answer.

I went back into the Commodore Grill.

CHAPTER VIII

1.

At seven o'clock I was standing in the lobby of the Milton Hotel on West Forty-sixth Street. Silk shirt was at the desk. "He's in," he said, not looking at me.

I nodded.

"Take me up."

Sam Duffy was a different man when he opened the door. He was freshly shaved and his clothes were clean and pressed. Apparently he was just getting ready to leave as he had his hat on when he answered my knock.

He didn't look happy to see me.

"Hell, Marty," he said, the second I had entered the room and closed the door behind me, "you sure loused things up. Jill Bentley called and bawled hell out of me. Said that you ..."

"Lieutenant Ferris," I said. "Not Marty. And shut up and sit down, you fat pig."

His eyes opened wide and a sort of half hurt, half resentful look clouded his face.

"I was only ..." he began.

I reached over and took him by the lapels of his coat and pulled him toward me.

"I said shut up!"

I slammed him down and he half fell across the day bed. It was made up for a change.

I took my time as I sat down and brought out a pack of cigarettes. I took one and didn't offer Duffy the pack. The man made me almost physically ill and I had a hard time controlling myself when I looked at him. I would have liked to have messed him up.

For several minutes I merely stared at him. Once he looked up and saw my eyes on him and he quickly looked away. His mouth twitched nervously and he couldn't seem to keep his hands still.

"Duffy," I said at last, "it's about time you started coming clean."

"Why Lieutenant," he began "I ..."

"I said shut up."

He sank back on the bed and this time he looked directly at me.

There was fear in his eyes and there was something else as well. He looked like a man who, having figured out the score perfectly, suddenly finds out there are a number of factors he had forgotten to take into consideration.

"Yeah," I said. "You have a few things to explain. I gave you a break—a good break. But you've been holding out on me."

His face went yellow and once more he looked like a dissipated goat. I noticed his eyes dart unconsciously toward the door of the bathroom.

"There's something that you have of Miss Chamlers," I said, "That doesn't belong to you."

Again he looked at me and this time the expression was one of total fear. I knew what he was thinking. He was thinking about the jewels which he must have taken from her. He knew that I had found them before and at first he had been baffled when I hadn't mentioned it. Now he suddenly believed that I was about to bring it up and pin it on him. He probably figured that I had blown the introduction to Jill Bentley and didn't need him anymore.

Duffy looked like a very sick man.

"I can explain about the ..." he began.

Once more I shut him up quickly. The last thing I wanted was to have him confess taking the jewelry.

"I'll tell you when to talk," I said. "And don't explain anything. Don't say a thing. Just answer my questions when I ask them. That's all. Nothing else. The first question is, do you own a camera?"

He must have been still thinking about the jewelry. He looked up and the expression in his eyes was complete bewilderment. He hadn't made the connection yet.

"A camera?"

"Yes. A camera. And don't repeat my question. Just answer."

He was quiet so long that for a moment I didn't believe he had heard me. And then at last a semi-intelligent expression crossed his face.

"I did own one," he said, "but I sold it."

"When?"

He thought again for a moment.

"About a year ago."

I stared him straight in the eye and I knew that he was trying to look away but was unable to.

"Was it the camera," I asked, "that you used to take the pictures of old Malcolm and Billy Chamlers?"

And then it came to him. Up until that moment I don't believe he had the slightest idea of what I had been getting at. He knew that I had gone through his stuff, but once he found that I hadn't taken that package of negatives, he probably thought I had completely overlooked them.

I'll have to give him credit. At least he blushed. He started to stutter.

"You dirty pig," I said. "Get me those negatives!"

Once more Sam Duffy proved that he had had previous experience with the police. He didn't try to bluff it out; didn't try to stall.

I was relieved when he got up and pulled out the old suitcase. There had been a nagging worry in the back of my mind. If Sam, having missed the jewelry, had grown cagey and already got rid of the negatives, I would be in a spot. But he hadn't.

A moment later, without a word, he handed me the oilskin package. I took it; didn't bother to open it but held it in one hand and casually tapped it against my leg while I stared at him. He avoided my eyes.

"When did you take them, Sam? Better come clean with the whole story."

"It was Billy's idea," he said. "She …"

"I didn't ask you that."

He sort of half pulled away from me and started over again. "A little more than a year ago." His voice was harsh and wheezy again. He looked once more like the old Sam Duffy, frightened, sick and with an odd undercurrent of defiance.

"How and where?"

"In Billy's apartment," he said. "I got them one night when they—Billy and Malcolm—were half in the bag. I was in the closet off the bedroom."

"How about lights?" I asked.

Duffy looked at me and blinked. "That's the funny part of it," he said. "Malcolm used to do it with every light in the room turned on. I guess that was a part of his perversion. He liked to see what he was doing. And Billy had put in hundred-watt bulbs."

"O.K.," I said. "So you got the pictures. How much did you shake him down for?"

Again he started to tell me it was Billy Chamlers' idea and once again I stopped him. Finally he admitted that he had taken around twenty thousand dollars from the Philadelphian. He said that they had been playing it easy, setting it up for a final big kill. Billy hadn't wanted to make her big stake until she was ready and was all through with the old man.

Billy had denied to Malcolm that she knew anything about the pictures. She'd told him that someone must have snapped them from the fire escape.

Malcolm had half believed her at first, according to Duffy. It could have been done that way.

"She masterminded the whole thing," Duffy said. "She even got most of the money. I'd turn it over to her as soon as I got any."

I remembered the canceled checks on his bank, made out to Billy Chamlers. I had wondered about them as from what I had learned of Sam Duffy, he'd always been short of cash. This explained it.

"There's something else I got to tell you, Lieutenant," Duffy said. "I'd like to get it off my conscience."

But I held up my hand. I think I knew what he wanted to tell me. He wanted to tell me about the jewelry. He'd had time to get a story together and knew that I had found the stuff. But I didn't want to hear his story.

"Don't tell me anything," I said. "Only what I ask you. Right now you're in enough trouble; don't make it worse for yourself."

2.

For five minutes I sat and stared at him. Every now and then he would steal a look at me from under heavy lids. He fidgeted and his fat fingers were like nervous snails as they plucked incessantly at the covers on each side of the bed on which he sat. The pressure was beginning to tell on him and I knew that any second be would break down.

At last he looked up at me and then slowly got to his feet. He took a step toward me.

"Honest to God, Lieutenant ..." he started.

I looked up into his face coldly and he stopped talking and sat back on the couch.

"Tell me, Duffy," I said. "Why did you kill her?"

"Oh, Jesus Christ!"

He clenched his hands and the sweat was pouring off his saffron forehead.

"I didn't. God, I didn't. I tell you she was everything in the world to me. I'd a done anything for her."

"Yes? Well on your own testimony you collaborated with her in blackmail. Did you also pimp for her? Did you get her the men, too?"

He started to do it again. It was just like those other two times.

The pasty yellow complexion suddenly was suffused with red as the blood surged to his face. His eyes opened wide and there was hatred and fury in them. He came to his feet like a fat jack-in-the-box.

But he didn't go any further. Suddenly the wind seemed to go out of him and again he fell back on the couch. He looked down at the toes of his highly polished shoes. He didn't say anything for a minute. When he did speak his voice was so low as to be almost inaudible.

"You wouldn't understand," he said. "You wouldn't know how I felt about her."

There was no doubt about it. In spite of the other men, in spite of everything, in his own twisted way he somehow had loved the girl.

He was right about one thing. I wouldn't understand. For a moment it made me think of Fern.

I got up and flipped my dead cigarette into the wastebasket. I shook my head to clear it. Christ, I thought, I must be getting a little crazy myself. Fern and the dead Billy Chamlers may have had several things in common, but by God Sam Duffy and I certainly didn't. He may have loved her and I certainly loved Fern, but there it ended. I couldn't exactly see myself putting up with the stuff Duffy had put up with.

No, Duffy and I were of a different breed. It was because I loved her and because I wouldn't put up with anything, that I was planning to do what I was going to do.

I looked at the man in the room across from me and I felt like spitting on him. I despised him. God, what sort of man could he be. Here he was, ready to blow his top every time anyone said anything against the dead girl, and yet he had been perfectly capable of hiding in a closet and taking pictures of her while she went in for perverted forms of love with another man.

Sam Duffy made me sick to my stomach and I knew if I stayed in the room with him for another minute I would beat him to a pulp. I turned to the door.

"Maybe you didn't kill her," I said. "Maybe she meant too much money to you; I don't know. But anyway, unless I want you, stay out of my sight. They should burn men like you on general principle!"

I slammed the door behind me.

I put the package of negatives in my pocket and pushed the elevator button.

3.

The clock on top of the Paramount Building told me it was after nine when I reached the street and turned toward Broadway. My head was splitting and I had a foul taste in my mouth. A taxi pulled over toward the curb and I was about to wave him away. I felt like walking; I wanted some fresh air and I wanted to get the smell of Sam Duffy out of my nostrils.

But then I remembered what I had to do and I knew that I didn't have too much time, if I had any at all. I looked up again at the clock and turned toward the cab. The driver reached back and opened the door and I gave him the address up on East Sixty-first Street.

I was thinking of Malcolm as the cab wheeled through the Broadway traffic toward Fifty-seventh Street where it would turn east. Malcolm, a respectable, successful man with a wife and two nice kids in college. I wonder what made a guy like that tick. What in the name of God did he want with a tramp like Billy Chamlers? Why had he been willing to risk his home and his reputation to play around with a girl who was half his age and with whom he could have had almost nothing in common?

It didn't make sense. God knows, he had enough money to get all the women he wanted without bothering to get tied up in a serious attachment. I thought of the negatives in my inside breast pocket and in spite of myself I blushed. Serious attachment, hell, I thought. Malcolm may have been a respected pillar of society in Philadelphia—in my book he was a dirty old man and deserved anything that might happen to him.

For a moment I wondered if he could have killed the girl. Certainly he had reason enough. He must have suspected that she was involved in the blackmail plot. He must have known that sooner or later the demands would be too great and that the thing would have to come to a head. And he would have to lose. They'd either bleed him white or they would expose him. In either case he'd take the short end.

Malcolm was, I decided, a very likely candidate for the hot seat. He might not be the type to commit murder—although I know in my heart there is no such thing as a "type." On the other hand, to all outward appearances he couldn't be considered the "type" to take the male lead in that set of pornographic photography which I carried with me.

There was also the matter of his complete failure to produce an alibi for the time of the crime.

I found that in thinking about Malcolm, I was perfectly willing to see him go to the electric chair for the Chamlers murder. I didn't much care whether he had killed her or not.

Malcolm was, in a sense, like Duffy. They were different sides of the same coin. And it was a very dirty coin.

I smiled to myself and my smile wasn't pleasant. If Malcolm had killed the girl in an effort to get the original negatives and protect his reputation and his bank balance, at least he had failed in his objective, whether he was convicted of the crime or not. Within a very few hours the existence of those pictures would be public knowledge.

It would be tough on his family, but it's always tough on the families of sons of bitches.

4.

I rang Panatelli's doorbell and the janitor answered. He remembered me.

"Ah, Sergeant Brentano's friend," he said. "How is the Sergeant?" He gave me a broad smile.

"He's fine," I said. "Sends his best. I want to go up to the Chamlers apartment and have a look around," I explained. "You have the key?"

"You won't need a key, Lieutenant," he told me. "One of your policemen, a detective I guess, came an hour ago and is up there now."

I wasn't surprised. Captain O'Shea had probably sent somebody up to give the place a final going over. He would be wanting to find those negatives if they were around.

I took the self-service elevator and a moment later rapped on the door.

The voice said to come in.

It was Jim Gallagher, a first-class detective and one of my own men. He was stretched out on an easy chair, his feet on a hassock and he had an opened bottle of coke on the floor beside him. The record player was going, very low. He smiled at me.

"What the hell are you doing?" I asked.

"Captain O'Shea sent me over," he said. "Seems that the post office people are interested in this place and they're to meet me here. We're going to give the joint a real going over. The Captain didn't tell me what we are looking for, but I guess the man from the post office will know."

I grunted, pulled up a seat. I wouldn't have much time, but I didn't want Jim to get any ideas.

"When you expect them?"

"Oh they should be here any minute," he said.

"Where'd you get the coke?" I asked.

"Brought it in with me, with a sandwich," Jim said. "Didn't have a chance to get any dinner and I was just on my way home when the Captain nabbed me."

"I'm in the same spot," I said. "Except I haven't had the sandwich."

"Why don't you go out now while I'm waiting?"

I shook my head.

"I'm expecting a telephone call," I said. "Don't want to miss it. I wonder if you'd do me a favor, Jim? Run down and pick me up a couple of hamburgers and a container of coffee."

He got to his feet and yawned. He didn't have to put his hat on; he hadn't taken it off.

"Sure thing, Lieutenant," he said. "You know," and he started to lean against the wall.

I could see that he was about to start on one of his long drawn out stories and I stopped him quick. I knew that time was running out.

"Look kid," I said, "I'm starving." I walked over and opened the door.

"Sure—sure thing," he said. A moment later I closed the door behind him. I had to do some quick thinking.

I knew that the place had already been thoroughly searched. There wasn't even a slight chance that my boys would have missed any obvious spots. I had to find a place and find one fast. There was no time to open a mattress seam or anything like that.

I walked over to the baby grand and lifted the top. I took the package of negatives from my pocket and I dropped them down behind the sounding board and then pushed them over and out of sight. The doorbell rang as I closed the lid.

I quickly dusted off my fingerprints and then walked over and pressed the button which clicked the down stairs latch.

It was an inspector from the post office and I hadn't met him before. We introduced each other and showed our identification.

He was a tall thin man in his sixties and he smiled at me.

"I was expecting someone named Gallagher," he said.

"Yeah, I know. He just went down to get me a sandwich and coffee," I said. "I'm in charge of the case here and I just thought I'd stop by.

Those films—and I guess that's what you're here to find—are mighty important. Thought I'd better be here in case I could help at all."

He nodded.

"Well," he said, "they may be and they may not, from what I'm told. Looks like it might be a long job so I guess we better get started."

He wanted to begin in the bedroom but I suggested the room we were in. I wanted him to find the negatives, if possible. But I didn't want to waste any more time than I had to.

Jim Gallagher was back within fifteen minutes and he handed me the two hamburgers and the coffee. I offered some to the others, but both men refused. Jim started to help the post office man with his search and I took time out to eat.

By ten-thirty we were still working on the living room and had gotten nowhere. I must admit, however, that the postal inspector was thorough. We were about through and ready to move on. Jim himself had searched the piano. I had wanted one of the others to find the negatives, but I knew that they probably wouldn't. The next best thing was to have a witness when I found them myself.

I walked over to the piano as the other two stood nearby lighting cigarettes.

"If she had the films," I said, "you can bet they were well hidden."

I lifted the lid of the instrument and fumbled around. A moment later I looked up quickly.

"Got something here," I said.

I waited until they were behind me before I pulled the packet all the way out.

The postal man whistled under his breath.

"Could be," he said.

I let him open the package.

He whistled again and took out the two prints I had seen in the Captain's office.

"This is it," he said. "Jesus—some toots!"

Jim Gallagher looked away. I remembered that he was a family man.

"I'll have to take these in," the post office man said. "We'll probably have them printed up and then turn over the originals to you people. I understand they may be evidence in a murder case."

I said that they well might.

"Well I hope you beat the case. But we got our own problems. Malcolm was using the mails to pay off blackmail and we're going to try and get the man who was collecting. We have already found out that there was a man involved so the Chamlers girl wasn't in it alone."

"I hope you get him," I said.

Five minutes later and the three of us had left the apartment. Jim and I stopped at the restaurant and had a cup of coffee.

"What did you do, Lieutenant, change your mind?" he said. "The Captain said that Sal told him you were sick and went on home."

"I started to," I said, "but then I changed my mind. If you're going into report, you might tell the Captain you ran into me here. I'm still feeling pretty crummy and will go on out home now."

5.

The druggist gave me a pack of cigarettes and change for a dollar bill and told me that the telephone booth was in the back to the right. It was empty and I entered and dropped my coin in the slot.

Somehow, this time, I wasn't surprised when I didn't get an answer. I guess I expected it. The funny thing was, I wasn't sore. I wasn't anything. I just waited for the return of my coin and then left the booth.

It was still early and so I walked. I knew that Jill Bentley wouldn't be free for another hour or hour and a half.

The doorman nodded when I went in and the headwaiter treated me like an old customer. He started to show me to a table. Jill must have been watching because she reached us before I was seated. She nodded at the headwaiter and he smiled and left.

"Look," she said, "you don't have to hang around here. I won't be through for quite a while. We have a pretty good crowd tonight."

"I'd still like to see you," I said.

We had walked back toward the entrance.

She looked up at me and there was a curious expression in her large eyes. She had one thumb against her teeth and for a moment she reminded me of a small, slightly perplexed child.

Finally she nodded.

"All right," she said, "But there's no point in spending money in this dump. Pick up a bottle and go on up to the apartment." She reached into the small silver bag she carried and took out a set of keys.

"Wander around for a while and get up there about eleven-thirty. Not before. I'll be along by twelve."

I told her to make it as fast as she could and asked her what she wanted to drink.

"Tonight I feel like Scotch—Scotch and soda. I'm in my conservative mood." She smiled and patted the side of my cheek.

I said I'd get Scotch.

"Two bottles," she said and turned back toward the rear of the room.

In the light of the marquee I looked at my wristwatch. It was just a little after ten-thirty. Well, I'd have plenty of time to get the Scotch and get to her place before eleven-thirty or twelve. And then I remembered something. She had said not to get there before eleven-thirty. In fact she had emphasized it. It suddenly struck me as peculiar.

A cab was waiting just down the street, but I didn't take it. I walked to the corner and signaled a passing driver. I gave him Jill Bentley's address.

The Scotch could wait until later.

In thinking back about it, I don't know now what I really expected to find when I got to the girl's apartment. Certainly there was nothing definite in my mind. But there had been something odd about the way she had asked me—yes even ordered me—not to arrive before eleven-thirty. It wasn't that she herself would be there and possibly having an assignation with another man. No, she would be doing her turn at the Shenandoah.

I wasn't too surprised, as I was paying the driver in front of the building, to look up and see the lights on in Jill Bentley's apartment.

I took out the keys she had given me and opened the downstairs door. I let myself in quietly and then started upstairs. The place was very quiet and I figured that the janitor must live in another building in the neighborhood.

I went to Jill's door and for several seconds I stood outside and listened. I could hear nothing. I looked down at the floor and there was no crack of light showing, but this could mean only that the carpet in front of the door prohibited the light from escaping. I was sure that it had been her windows which had been lit up.

I waited a few seconds more and then I took the key and carefully inserted it in the lock. I held the handle tight and gradually began to turn it. When I knew that the latch and catch were free, I suddenly leaned forward and pushed the door inward.

6.

The blow caught me full in the face and even as I felt the hot blood burst from my nose, I crashed to my knees. His foot caught me neatly in the side of the head and I could actually feel the skin tear away.

It didn't quite knock me out and I instinctively lifted my arm to take the second kick.

But he was all through. He merely walked over and closed the door quietly and then neatly stepped over me and went to the couch and sat down.

It took me about a half minute to gather my senses. I was on my hands and knees and instinctively my right hand snaked for the shoulder holster under my left armpit. "I wouldn't if I were you," he said.

I looked up and it took a couple of seconds to get my eyes focused.

He must have been about six foot four; he was thin as a hound and had very wide shoulders. His clothes were immaculate and his shoes were highly polished Cordovans. He wore a white shirt with a tab collar and a conservative necktie. His hair was a shocking red and he effected a crew cut. The eyes were gray and lazy. One leg was carelessly crossed over the other as he slouched in the corner of the couch and his hands were crossed over his knee. He had a small automatic in his right hand.

"The next time," he said, "knock before you enter. And don't stand around doorways listening. It isn't polite. Get to your feet."

The voice was very soft; very smooth.

I got to my feet.

"Where did you get the keys?" he asked.

I shook my head and tried to clear it. I was still in a daze. "Who the hell are you?"

He ignored the question.

"I asked you where you got the keys," he repeated.

"From Jill," I said. "Jill Bentley."

"Yes?" He looked skeptical. "And who are you and what are you doing here?"

"Name's Crandall," I said. "I'm a friend of Miss Bentley and she gave me her keys and told me to come here and wait for her. I'm supposed to meet her here when she gets through at the Shenandoah."

He nodded then and suddenly smiled.

"That was careless of Jill," he said. "Careless. But it was even more careless of you. I'm sorry I hit you, but that was no way to enter a girl's apartment."

He smiled but I didn't like his smile. He put the gun away. "I'm Frank," he said, as though that explained everything. He stood up and I saw that I hadn't underestimated his height. He was still thin, but there was nothing anemic about him.

"You can sit down," he said. "I'm just leaving."

I started to say something then. In fact, I started toward him. I was so damned mad I couldn't see straight. But then, in a second, got control of myself. I didn't know what it was all about, but I couldn't afford to have any trouble. I wasn't here on official business and I couldn't risk a jam.

"You always carry a gun?" I asked.

He turned then and again he smiled at me, without humor. "Yes," he said. "I do. And do you?"

I didn't say anything. I was still bleeding badly from the nose and my head was splitting. I was still foggy.

"You better go in the bathroom and clean yourself up," he said. "Make pretty for Jill."

Once more I felt an almost indescribable urge to slug him and once more I resisted it. I just couldn't afford any sort of trouble. I walked over to the bathroom and opened the door. I went in and started the cold water.

My nose stopped bleeding and I got the blood off my face. I took off my coat and brushed it, but there wasn't much I could do about the blood on my clothes. I was thinking of the man in the next room. The man who said his name was Frank. I decided that someday—soon—I would beat him senseless. And then I'd kick his teeth down his throat.

When I came out about five minutes later the place was empty. He was gone.

Well, Jill had told me to wait until eleven-thirty before showing up and I hadn't followed her advice. I began to realize I'd asked for what I had got.

I thought again of Frank and I was aware of the fact that there had been something very familiar about him. I wracked my brains but I still couldn't place him. Certainly, if I had ever met that amazingly large man with the flamboyant red hair before, I should have remembered him.

Once more I shook my head to clear it and I started idly wandering around the room. It was then that my eye fell on the envelope. For a second I just looked at it, where it lay, torn open, on the end table next to the couch. For a second I couldn't make the connection, and then I got it.

It was a small gray square with a blue printed return address in the upper left-hand corner. There wouldn't be two like it and I leaned closer to read the print.

I was right.

It was one of Fern's. I had bought the stationery set for her on her last birthday.

I picked it up and it was empty. There was no address on it so it couldn't have been delivered through the mails or by messenger.

I could even detect the faint odor of Fern's perfume.

Suddenly I knew that Fern had been in that room. I knew that she must have been there while that tall lean man with the wide shoulders was there.

I sat down on the couch and for a few minutes I thought I was going to be sick to my stomach.

I was still sitting there when the doorbell rang an hour later. I pushed the clicker and opened the door and then went back and sat down.

A minute later Jill Bentley walked into the room.

She closed the door behind her and then stood and just looked at, me. Suddenly she laughed.

"A mess," she said. "A real mess, that's what you are. Well, I understand you asked for it. I just hope you didn't forget the Scotch."

CHAPTER IX

1.

"Are all your boyfriends mobsters?" I asked.

She didn't like it. For a moment she just stood there staring at me, and then she came all the way into the room. She took off the small cardinal's hat she wore on the back of her head and threw it on the couch beside me, along with her plastic pocketbook. Then she went into the kitchen without a word and a minute later was back with a pint bottle of brandy.

She poured two drinks and handed me one before sitting down.

"Look," she said, "I didn't ask for you. I even told you I didn't like cops. I also told you not to come here until after eleven-thirty. So you came anyway and you got yourself roughed up. I guess you aren't even a good cop."

"I'm a good enough cop," I said. "I didn't want trouble in your place." I was getting sore all over again. "Anyway, I just asked you a question. Are all your boyfriends gangsters?"

She looked at me for a long minute and her red mouth was pouted and her eyes were narrow and thoughtful. At last she shrugged.

"Not all," she said. "You for instance—you're just a dumb policeman. But anyway, what the hell. I shouldn't have expected you to be smart."

"If you call that long drink of water smart," I began. But she stopped me.

"Frank?" she said. "Don't be a damned fool, Marty. You've made enough bad plays for one night. Frank's my brother."

I got it then. I suddenly knew why he'd seemed oddly familiar. He was, actually, a dead ringer for her. Same features, almost the same general build with his tall thin frame and his wide shoulders. But there was one signal difference, outside of the fact that Jill's long thin frame was a lot more rounded and interesting. The difference lay in their individual expressions. Both had good-looking faces, cut and molded in the same pattern. But whereas Frank's face was essentially mean and sardonic, Jill's was pleasant and humorous and she exuded a sense of kindness and easygoing good will.

Quickly I decided that if I was ever going to get anywhere with her, I'd have to make my peace.

"All right," I said. "I'm just a damned fool. You're right, I guess I am stupid. And I'm sorry for the cracks. I'm also damned sorry I got here before I was supposed to."

She nodded, noncommittal.

"Oh, it's O.K.," she said. "Frank had a date and he was using the place was all. It was just that he wasn't expecting anyone to come barging in. After all," and she looked at me almost slyly as she said it, "after all, I don't usually give my keys to strange guys."

"Can I have another drink?" I said.

I wanted her to be doing something, not to be looking at me. I was having a little trouble getting myself under control.

So Frank had a date, I thought. And one of Fern's private envelopes had been laying there on the desk. Fern hadn't been home when I called. Also, Fern had known Jill Bentley in the past.

I was beginning to get somewhere, but I had a long way to go. This tall redhead pouring the shot of brandy, probably had all of the answers. I would have to get them from her, one way or the other.

"If you'll let me," I said, "I'll go out now and get the Scotch. I'm just a big goddamned fool I guess." I stood up and Jill put the brandy flask and the glass down. She came over and stood in front of me and she looked into my face.

"Just a dumb cop," she said, "but somehow I like you. All right, go on down and get it. With soda. There's a liquor store down on Thirty-fourth Street and I guess he's still open."

She reached up and her soft hand half caressed the side of my face where her brother's boot had taken the skin off.

"I'm sorry Frank was rough," she said. "He's impetuous."

Her hand drew down across my lips and I kissed it.

"Get going," she said. "I'll change and make up a Welsh rarebit."

I took my hat and went out.

The liquor store had closed, but I knew of a late spot a few blocks away. I got the two bottles and then picked up some soda. I got the soda in a drugstore and while I waited, I made a phone call.

This time Fern answered. Her voice sounded sleepy.

I didn't ask her where she had been. I just told her I was still tied up with the Chamlers case.

"Sal called a few minutes back," she said. "Seemed surprised when he didn't find you home."

I explained that I had started home and then run into something.

"I'll be late," I said. "You go on back to bed."

"Hurry home, honey," she said.

I hung up the receiver.

"Hurry home."

That's what she always said when I called. I'd always believed she meant it, too.

As I started back to Jill's apartment I wondered how I could have reached the age I had and still been so goddamned completely ignorant of women.

I hurried back to Jill's.

The phonograph was going and at once I recognized the voice. There were some of Jill's own recordings. She was stretched out on the couch, once more in denim slacks and an old sweater. Her feet and ankles were bare and she had taken down her long hair and it hung over her shoulders loose. She looked like a gamin and at the same time she looked very desirable.

I went into the kitchen and I made us each a drink. I made mine weak and hers very strong.

Several times during that next hour I started to talk. But each time Jill would shut me up.

"Listen," she'd say, "you're getting the benefit of my best records—for free. So keep quiet and let me hear the music even if you don't want to. I don't want to talk; I just want to lay back and drink and relax."

It wasn't what I wanted, but I knew I couldn't rush her. I decided the only thing to do was to get her drunk as fast as I could.

But I fooled myself. I guess when I made her the second drink she must have suspected I was making my own short. She smiled sweetly at me and changed glasses.

"You wouldn't try and get a girl drunk would you, Marty?" she said.

I told her that I certainly would.

"Then we'll both get drunk," she said.

We both did.

I can remember, sometime along two or three o'clock, taking off my coat and opening the collar of my shirt. Vaguely I remember kicking my shoes off and Jill and I dancing together in bare feet. The strange part of that was that I don't think I'd ever danced more than two or three times before in my life.

I remember the first bottle suddenly being empty and how surprised I was. I remember running out of soda, and then, later running out of cigarettes and Jill's digging long butts out of the overflowing ash trays.

Very vaguely I remember that I got sick and went into the bathroom and then coming back and Jill's saying something about putting the next shot in coffee and it wouldn't taste so bad. I also remember a couple of times when I started trying to lead the conversation around to her past life and each time Jill's shutting me up.

And then, suddenly, I didn't remember anything. Not until I woke up and saw the sun cutting crosswise through the thin white curtains.

2.

It was the strangest sensation.

I knew who I was, all right. I knew that I was Lieutenant Ferris of the New York Police Department. But that's all I did know for a long time. I just lay there and I watched the spot on the wall where the sun hit and for the life of me I couldn't imagine where I was or how I had got there.

My head felt as though someone had been using a baseball bat on it. My throat was congested and my eyes were half closed and I couldn't seem to force them open. I was aware of my own choked, heavy breathing. I was covered with sweat and I suddenly realized that I must be in a bed. The sheet over my chest was soaked. It was a bed all right, but there was nothing familiar about it, nor about the sunlit wall at which I looked.

It was then I became aware of the soft breathing next to me.

I was lying half on my right side and I made an effort and got my eyes wide open. Still nothing made any sense. And then I made another effort and lifted myself on one arm and I turned over.

That's when I saw her.

She was lying spread-eagled on her back. From the waist up she was completely naked. She still wore the blue denim jeans. Her dark auburn hair was spread in a willowy frame around her heart-shaped face and her lipstick was badly smeared. Her mouth was partly open and her eyes were closed. There were dark circles under them.

She couldn't have looked half as obscene if she had been completely nude.

I turned again and rolled myself over and then my feet found the floor. I stood up and tottered. Every bone in my body ached and I felt as though I had been beaten with leather straps. It was then that I became aware of the fact that I was, myself, completely naked.

A moment later I found my clothes over next to a chair, on the floor. I grabbed them up and went into the bathroom. I started to cough and then I leaned over the toilet and vomited. For a while after that I just hung my head over the washbasin and bathed my temples in cold water. After about five minutes I was able to get dressed.

I didn't look at Jill Bentley as I passed through the room and went into the kitchen. My own watch had stopped but the clock over the small electric stove said eight-thirty.

For a moment I thought of trying to make a pot of coffee, but then my eye landed on the two empty Scotch bottles and the empty brandy flask. I started to get sick all over again and I hurriedly went into the other room. For a minute or two I leaned against the wall to catch my breath.

At first I thought of a Turkish bath, but I'd never as much as been in one and wasn't in any shape to experiment. I knew I looked like hell and I certainly felt worse. I was afraid to go to a barbershop for fear I'd pass out in the chair. I was tempted to call a cab and go home. I had told the boys downtown that I was sick. Well by God I certainly was feeling sick.

But I had things to do. Important things and they couldn't wait.

So I went to a small midtown commercial hotel and took a room. The clerk at the desk looked at me skeptically but when I took out my billfold and paid in advance, he grudgingly called a bellhop and had me shown upstairs.

I gave the boy a couple of bucks and he went down to get me a razor and some shaving cream. I picked up the phone and got room service and ordered a double Bromo, some tomato juice and two pots of black coffee. Ten minutes later I was standing under the shower.

More than a hundred times I have heard drunks and alcoholics swear the next morning that they couldn't remember what had happened the night before. I'd never believed them. Well, I believed them now. To save my life I couldn't remember what had happened to me. Certainly I had no memory of having undressed, or being undressed, or climbing into bed. I don't even remember when I had taken my last drink.

The valet came up and got my clothes and for a couple of extra dollars said he'd see what he could do with them in a hurry.

At nine-fifteen I left the hotel. I still felt like hell, but I looked and smelled a lot better. My head was aching badly, but at least it seemed to be getting down to a normal size. I stopped in the lobby and went into a phone booth. I hadn't wanted to put the call through the switchboard.

Fern answered at once and her voice sounded worried.

"Gee, Marty," she said. "Where are you? Are you all right?"

I told her that I was all right and started to say something about not getting home. But she cut in again at once.

"Captain O'Shea and Sal have both been trying to get you since about six o'clock," she said. "They couldn't understand ..."

"What did you tell them?" I interrupted.

"Why I told them that you'd called and said you were working on that case of the murdered nightclub girl," she said. Her own voice sounded perplexed.

"I was," I said. "I'll call in right away."

"And Marty," Fern said, "try and get home and get some rest."

"Try and be there when I do," I said. I hung up, but not before I had heard Fern's slight gasp.

I left the phone booth and went to the street and hailed a cab. Hailing cabs was getting to be a bad habit with me, but I was in no mood for the subways. My stomach still felt queasy, although I had managed to keep down the tomato juice and a couple of cups of coffee.

While the driver was weaving in and out of traffic on his way down to the lower East Side, I thought about telephoning headquarters. I knew I should talk to Captain O'Shea. Or at least talk with Sal and give him a story for the Captain. But then I shrugged. The hell with it, I thought. After all, they got the Malcolm angle to work on, as well as Haverford. What I had to do had to be done at once. Time was running out.

I smiled to myself and it wasn't a nice smile. Well, I thought, when it's all over and done with, I'll be all right. In fact I'll be the fair-haired boy all over again.

I asked the driver for the time and he told me and I set my watch at nine-thirty.

3.

It was a narrow, one-way street and the block was crowded from curb to curb with small, broken-down trucks, taxi cabs, push carts and dozens of screaming, dirty-faced children. Fat, gray-haired women sat in the windows and old men stood in groups in front of stores and talked.

I got out halfway down the block and paid the driver. I could make better time walking than I could driving.

It was an old-law, red brick, six-story tenement, almost at the corner. The usual complement of idlers and bums were standing around the stoop. I was about to push my way through when I caught sight of a car sitting at the curb.

My head began to pound and I felt a sudden hollow sensation in the pit of my stomach.

It was the department Mercury and I knew at once that it was the car assigned to myself and Sal Brentano. I turned and started toward it and as I did I heard a slight commotion behind me. A second later and there I was facing Sal.

"Jesus, Marty," he said. "I been looking all over hell for you."

For a moment I just stared at him.

"How'd you happen to be looking here?" I asked at last.

Sal shrugged.

"Come on," he said. "Get into the car. We can talk on the way downtown."

I followed him and he climbed under the steering wheel. I waited until he had driven to the corner and turned down the avenue.

"Pull over to the curb, Sal," I said then.

Sal looked up at me for a second, curiously, and then he did as I asked. After he'd pulled on his brake and switched off the ignition, I spoke.

"That house you came out of," I said. "That's where Willy Holiday rooms. How'd you happen to be looking for me there?"

For a moment Sal looked at me and there was a strange expression in his eyes.

"What's with your face, Marty?" he asked. "My God you look …"

"Sal," I said sharply. "Tell me how you happened to be around here."

"Why Christ, Marty," he said. "Everyone in the whole damned place is looking for you. We tried everywhere. I knew that you had been working on the Holiday angle and I thought it might be just possible you were here."

I nodded.

"And was Holiday in?"

"Yeah, he was in. But my God, Captain O'Shea …"

"Never mind the Captain, Sal," I said. "Tell me about Holiday. Did you see him? What did you ask him and what did he say."

Again Sal looked at me curiously before answering. His voice sounded hurt when he did speak.

"Hell kid, I didn't ask him anything. You don't think I'd ask a punk like that for anything, do you? No, I just told him I was expecting to meet you at his place. He said you hadn't been around and he hadn't seen you. He seemed damned nervous, but I guess that was to be expected. I had to wake him up. He'd just got in from work and was already in bed."

"O.K.," I said. "Then what?"

"So I waited around a few minutes and then told him I'd go on downstairs and see you when you arrived. You can imagine how surprised I was to see you when you did show up."

He still looked surprised.

"All right, Sal," I said.

I turned and reached for the car door handle.

Sal quickly put his hand on my arm.

"Marty," he said. "Listen Marty. Hell's popping downtown. I don't know where you've been or what you've been doing, but my God you gotta get down and see the Captain. He's about ready to break you as it is."

I pushed Sal's hand from my arm.

"Screw the Captain," I said. "Damn it, didn't I just get through handing him the Malcolm negatives? Haven't I been working on this goddamned case all along? Don't I usually work on my cases? What the hell's the matter with him anyway? I got a right to run this thing the way I see it, haven't I? What the hell's he want from me anyway?"

I was sore, legitimately sore.

"All right, Marty," Sal said. "All right. Take it easy boy. I'm just telling you what's going on. The Captain's all right—he just wants to know what you're doing. What's going on."

I calmed down a little.

"Well tell him," I said, "that I'm busy. Tell him we're going to crack this thing and crack it damned soon. Just remind him that I usually do crack murder cases."

I tried to smile at Sal and I patted him on the shoulder.

"Just let me play it my own way for a little longer, Sal," I said. "You go on now and get back. You can tell the Captain you ran into me—say at Holiday's if you want to. Tell him I know what I'm doing. And in the meantime, let's clear up the Malcolm angle. Let's find out for sure if he has got an alibi and just what it is. If the Captain is getting racked from higher up, why hell, toss young Haverford in the clink for a few days. It will take the pressure off, anyway."

Sal nodded, but he didn't look happy.

"When will I tell him you'll be in?" he asked.

"This afternoon for sure," I said. "Say around three o'clock. No later."

Sal nodded again. He reached over and opened the door. "I'll be there," he said. "Take care of yourself, Marty."

I told him I would and I got out of the car. He put in the clutch and slowly pulled away from the curb. I turned and started back toward the tenement where Willy Holiday had his room. I still felt like hell, but my headache was almost gone. Christ, I thought, I need about twenty hours sleep.

That wasn't all I was thinking. It came to me then that I had very little time left. Things were beginning to close in and if I were to do what I planned, I would have to get into action at once.

The Chamlers murder case and the solution of my own problems ran a parallel course; I couldn't let one get ahead of the other. Sal's seeing Holiday had been a close and risky thing. Only luck had kept it from completely wrecking the thing which I had to do.

4.

It was a typical old-fashioned railroad tenement, a high stoop going up to the first floor and then a long hallway the length of the building. On each side was a series of rooms making up an apartment and at the end of the hallway was a lavatory, used by all tenants on the floor. I'd been in similar buildings any number of times and I knew that they had no bathtub. I wondered how the inmates kept clean.

Willy Holiday had a single room which he rented from a family named O'Brien on the top floor to the right. The air inside the building was ten degrees hotter than that on the steaming streets and it was heavy with the odor of stale food and the smell of too many people living in a confined space. I was sweating heavily as I reached the top floor.

Holiday had told me his room was the last one down the hall to the rear and he had a separate door leading off from the hallway itself. I walked toward the back and stumbled over a pile of old newspapers half concealed in the shadows. I cursed and wiped the perspiration from my forehead. I lifted my hand and knocked on the door with a closed fist.

For a moment there was complete silence, and then I heard movement on the other side of the thin panel. A moment later the door opened and Holiday was standing in front of me, silhouetted by the light streaming through the dirty pane of the single window at his back.

He was covered only by a pair of striped blue and white shorts; he needed a shave and his eyes were bleary. A dead cigarette dangled from one corner of his mouth. He didn't seem at all surprised to see me.

Without a word he stepped back and I passed him and went into the room.

A white iron, single bed on which were a pair of grayish, dirty sheets, stood under the window. Next to it was a straight-backed kitchen chair which he used as a sort of night stand to hold a cheap alarm clock and an overflowing ash tray. On the worn linoleum which covered most of the floor, next to the bed, were half a dozen comic books. A round deal table with a scarred top stood in the center of the room and there was an electric coffeepot, a dirty cup and saucer, a half-filled container of milk and another, overflowing, ash tray on its grimy surface.

In the far corner of the room was a clothespress. Beside it was a half opened, cardboard suitcase which spilled out a collection of dirty linen.

Neatly folded over the back of a second straight-backed chair were a pair of linen trousers. Socks and a white silk shirt lay on the seat of the chair and under it were a pair of lavender suede shoes.

A clothes hanger hung from a nail on the wall next to the clothespress. It supported a coat which matched the trousers folded over the back of the chair. Willy was a neat dresser.

He had closed the door and stood with his back to it. The black, narrow eyes had lost their sleepy, bleary expression and I could tell by the sudden play of the muscles around his mouth that he was fully awake and alert.

"The other one just left about five minutes ago," he said. "He was here looking for you."

"I know," I said. "I saw him."

I went over to the chair next to the bed and flipped it up, spilling the clock and the ash tray to the floor. I sat down and carefully crossed my legs.

"Get dressed, Willy," I said. "We're taking a walk."

The black eyes were suddenly alarmed and the pointed, receding chin fell and he started to say something.

"Just a walk, Willy," I said. "Get dressed."

Willy went over to the chair on which he had hung the trousers. He started to reach for his socks and then he turned to me. His face was white and his hands had begun to shake.

"Look, Lieutenant," he said. "Honest to God …"

"Willy, get dressed."

I stood up and took a step toward him. He turned back to the socks quickly and I sat down again.

He had his underwear and socks and shorts on and was lacing the suede shoes. He had been stealing glances at me as he pulled his clothes on. He was worried, but he was becoming curious as well.

"Can I get washed?" he said. "I just got in from work a while ago."

"Yeah, get washed."

"The basin's in the can at the end of the hall," he said.

"O.K.," I said, "get washed."

He fumbled around in the suitcase and took out a comb and a brush. Reaching into the clothespress he pulled out a folded Turkish towel. And then he turned and went toward the door. There was a perplexed expression around his eyes and I think he was waiting for me to say something; he probably thought I would warn him not to take off.

I didn't open my mouth as he pulled the door open and went into the hall. The door swung half shut behind him and he didn't bother to close it all the way. A moment later I heard the bathroom door at the end of the hallway open and then bang closed. I thought I heard the sound of the latch.

It took me a second. My left hand had gone to my upper inside jacket pocket. I had the white, bulging envelope in my hand by the time Willy had reached the end of the hallway. And then I was crossing the room and I leaned over the half-opened suitcase. I was careful to dig down well under the pile of dirty linen and I planted the envelope on the opposite side from which Willy had taken his comb and hairbrush. I was sitting in the chair, lighting a cigarette, when Willy returned five minutes later.

He put on the white shirt and then he reached for his coat. Carefully he lifted the shirt collar so that it lay outside the coat collar. He turned toward me and his hand went into the coat pocket and came out with a crumpled pack of cigarettes.

"Jesus, Lieutenant," he said, "I ain't had much sleep. I thought everything was all cleared up."

"It is all cleared up, Willy," said. "That is if you've been telling me the truth."

"I told you the honest to God truth," he said. "About everything. God, would I lie at a time like this? Jees, I appreciate what you done for me. Why ..."

"All right, Willy," I said. "Let's go." I stood up.

His face was drained of color. He stood still and stared at me.

"Can you tell me where we're going?" he asked.

"You don't have to worry, Willy," I said. "I told you everything was all right just so long as you told me the truth. You said you did so you got nothing to worry about. So let's get going." I moved toward the door.

For a second he hesitated and then he shrugged his thin shoulders.

He tried to pass it off, but I could see that he was still considerably worried.

He preceded me down the staircase and we walked out onto the high stoop of the building. A tall, heavy-set youth in an army uniform, with a corporal's chevrons on his sleeve and a Korean service ribbon over his left breast, stood leaning against the iron railing. He looked up as we passed and nodded to Willy. His eyes were completely without expression as he stared at me.

Willy didn't acknowledge the greeting.

We walked down the block to the corner and stood there for several minutes until a cab passed on the far side of the street. I whistled and the driver nodded. He went to the corner and made a U turn and swung back on our side of the street. He stopped and I opened the door.

Willy climbed in first and then I followed him. He sat as far to the left as he could get.

"Where to, Buddy?" the driver asked.

"The Village," I said. "Christopher and Fourth Streets."

I wasn't watching the driver as I gave the directions. My eyes were on Willy Holiday. This next second or two would be of vital importance. I had to know whether or not Willy had seen Dolly Gottlieb since I had talked with her. And I had to guess from his actions in that next moment.

There was no doubt but what he was startled at my words. He seemed to lean slightly forward in his seat, but his eyes stared straight ahead. Then he sort of sank back and there was a peculiar, subtle expression of relief on his face.

"She'll tell you I was telling the truth," he said. "She'll tell you I was with her."

I looked over at him but he didn't meet my eyes.

"Then you have nothing to worry about, Willy. By the way," and I lowered my voice so that the cab driver wouldn't hear me, "by the way, Willy, you didn't go against my orders and get together with her and get your stories straightened out, did you?"

He turned to me and there was no doubt about the sincerity of his words.

"My God no, Lieutenant," he said. "I been staying strictly away. I did just what you told me. You can ask her; she'll tell you. She'll tell you I been playing straight with you."

"Good, Willy," I said. "I will ask her."

He sat back and he started to clean the nails of his left hand with the thumbnail of his right. There was an almost self-satisfied smirk on his lean face.

Christ, I thought, he's sure got confidence in her. I was positive that he hadn't talked with her since I had warned him to stay away.

Willy Holiday was due for quite a surprise.

CHAPTER X

1.

The butcher was standing in the doorway of his store as the cab pulled up and stopped. I got out first and handed the driver a five-dollar bill. Willy followed me to the street as the cabbie made change. The butcher saw him and walked over toward us.

"Listen," he said, "how about the money for ..."

Willy looked at him and there was a nasty expression in his eyes.

"You'll get your money all right, you ..."

I pushed my way between them.

"He'll pay you," I said.

"What have you got to do with it, mister?" the butcher asked. "I'm getting tired of these cheap crumbs ..."

But Willy had turned and started into the hallway beside the store and I followed him as the butcher continued to grumble. He went ahead of me, knowing very well where we were going. When he got in front of the door to Dolly Gottlieb's apartment, he started to reach for the knob. I pushed his hand away and knocked on the door.

Dolly Gottlieb was a better actress than I would have figured. When she opened the door she just stood there, surprise heavy on her face and a questioning look in her eye. She was dressed the same as she had been when I had seen her the day before. Except that the shoulder length brown hair was loose and tied back with a red ribbon. She still wore no makeup except for the magenta lipstick. Today her eyes were more of a deep brown than black.

"Hi, kid," Willy said. He pushed his way past her and into the room. He had a proprietary attitude.

She didn't look at me as I followed him in.

Willy went over and sat on the edge of the bed. It was neatly made up and covered with a blue and red checkered spread. The whole place looked clean and neat.

I noticed at once that there were no signs around of Willy's having lived in the place.

Willy turned to the girl the second she had closed the door behind me. His voice was smooth and I could tell at once that he was feeling confident and sure of himself.

"This is Lieutenant Ferris of ..." he began.

I cut in.

"I'll handle the conversation," I said. "Sit down, Mrs. Gottlieb."

She walked over by the new refrigerator and stood looking at us. Her expression was completely blank.

"Holiday here," I said, "has told me a certain story. I'm a police lieutenant and I'm just checking up on a few facts. Nobody has anything to worry about."

Dolly Gottlieb nodded and Willy was completely at ease. "I want you to remember back to last Saturday, if you can," I said. "From about eleven o'clock on."

"Tell him," Willy said, "tell him I ..."

I turned to him quickly.

"Shut up and let her tell it," I said. "Don't start putting words in her mouth."

Willy began to protest that he was only trying to prove what he had done and where he was, but I shut him up. I turned again to the girl.

"Was Holiday with you?" I asked. "If he was, when did he arrive and when did he leave? That's all we have to know."

For a long minute she looked at me and then she looked over at Willy. I watched his face as she started to talk, in a flat monotone, completely without expression.

Willy was looking almost smug.

"Willy came in around eleven o'clock," she said.

"How do you know it was eleven?"

I wanted to make it good. I wanted the surprise, when it came to come with a complete shock.

"Well, we started to play the horses and we looked over a scratch sheet and we put down a bet soon after Willy got here. I phoned the bet in and they gave me time on it, which they always do. I remember it was shortly after eleven o'clock."

I nodded and I still watched Willy. He had taken out a cigarette and was lighting it and his hand was steady. Willy figured he was in.

"And then what happened?" I asked.

"We had some drinks and we played the races until about four or four-thirty."

Willy looked up quickly and there was a sudden surprised expression on his thin face. But he didn't look worried.

"We played all afternoon," he said.

"Let her tell it," I quickly interrupted. "Go ahead with your story, Dolly. And then what?"

"We ran out of gin and Willy decided to go out and get some."

For a second Willy stared at her as though he couldn't quite believe his ears. But he still didn't look worried and he had no idea of what was coming.

"Listen, kid," he said quickly, "you got it wrong. I ..."

This time I walked over to him and I reached down and grabbed him by his shirt front. I pulled him up off the chair and held him close to me.

"One more goddamned word out of you," I said between my teeth, "and I'll slap you silly."

I threw him back on the bed.

He wasn't even looking at me. His eyes were on Dolly Gottlieb. They were wide with surprise and anger.

"Willy went out for gin," I said. "And then what?"

"Well he wanted to meet the bookie and pay off," Dolly went on, in the same dead monotone. "The bookie hangs out in a bar and I guess Willy had to wait around for him. He probably had a couple of drinks while he was waiting. I remember I was getting sore 'cause I wanted a shot myself."

Willy started to get to his feet. His face had suddenly gone very pale. He stared at the girl and there was complete bewilderment in his eyes. He still didn't get it.

"Yes?" I said.

"So he got back here around seven-thirty or eight and we ..."

Willy Holiday's scream of anguish cut her off short.

"Jesus! Jesus Christ, Dolly," he yelled. "You got it wrong. Don't you remember? My God, tell the truth. You remember I was ..."

This time I slapped him hard across the side of the face. I could tell as he fell back on the couch, his eyes never leaving the girl, that he still didn't get it. He figured she must have forgotten, or been drunk, or was just excited and making a mistake.

"How do you know it was around seven-thirty or eight?" I asked Dolly.

Willy looked at me for a second and there was almost a thankful expression on his face.

Dolly's next words did it.

"Why because," she said. "Because, don't you remember, Willy, you wanted to get down on the fourth race out at California and it was too late. And the fourth goes off at seven-fifteen?"

For a moment there was dead silence in the room. And then it happened.

2.

Willy was stupid, but he knew a frame when he saw one. Particularly if he was the one being framed.

He was off the bed like a shot and I didn't have a chance to even stop him. Not that I would have. What happened next, I wanted to happen.

He was screaming as he reached the girl and his right fist shot out and caught her full in the face. She began to fall to the floor and he struck her a second time as she was halfway down.

"I'll kill you," he yelled. "Goddamn you, you bitch, I'll kill you!"

He was almost frothing at the mouth and I knew that he had completely forgotten that I was in the room. He was intent on only one thing—he wanted to murder the woman who was double-crossing him.

I let him hit her twice more and then I reached him and pulled him off her. Her mouth was a mass of blood and she was choking, but she was conscious. She lay huddled on her hands and knees and the blood dripped onto the floor. She was crying and for a moment she didn't look up.

For a minute or two I had my hands full. Willy was like a madman and he was surprisingly strong. He was still mouthing obscenities as I got him back on the bed. I had to smash him a half dozen times, hard in the face, to quiet him down. And then, a second later, I had my hands full again.

She'd gotten to her feet and she'd reached over to a drawer and taken out a knife. She was almost across the room when I looked up and saw her.

She wasn't screaming or hysterical and she spoke in a dead calm voice through her broken and cut lips.

"You've killed one woman, you bastard," she said. "This time, goddamn you, I'll get you before you do it again."

She lunged for him and I just caught her knife arm in time. I didn't want to hit her and it took me a couple of minutes to get her over to the other end of the room and calmed down. She was breathing heavily and half crying.

"Get in the bathroom and get a cold towel on your face," I said. "I'll take care of this son of a bitch all right." I pushed her toward the bathroom door.

"Get me a drink," she said.

She opened the bathroom door and a second later I heard the water running. I turned back toward the bed.

But I didn't have to worry about Willy Holiday. All the fight had been taken out of him. He sat there, his thin face between his hands and he stared at the space between his feet through puffy eyes. He looked very much like a man who was suddenly struck by lightning. He wasn't hurt, but he was thoroughly licked.

Walking over to the refrigerator, I opened the top compartment. The milk bottle was there, three quarters filled with Martinis. There were two empty jelly glasses, frosted on the outside. I took them out and half filled them. I walked over to the sink, took a third glass, filled it and took it to Willy.

He didn't see it and I kicked his leg. He looked up at me blankly for a moment and then looked at the glass. He started to shake his head, as though he couldn't quite figure it out.

"Take it, chum," I said. "You need it."

Listlessly he reached for it, but he just held it and didn't put it to his lips.

Five minutes later, when the bathroom door opened and Dolly Gottlieb reentered the room, he didn't even look up at her.

She'd wiped the blood off her face and her mouth was badly cut and swollen but no longer bleeding. One eye was turning a nasty purple. She looked at Willy Holiday and there was loathing and hatred in the glance.

Women, I thought. Jesus Christ. She's just framed the guy for the electric chair and instead of hanging her head in shame, she looks like she'd like to murder him where he sits. And this is the girl who's been shacking up with him for the last month or so.

Dolly took the drink I handed to her, without expression. She drained it in two gulps.

I drank the contents of the glass in my hand, but Willy still held his. He looked like a dead man.

Dolly went to the refrigerator and took out the milk bottle. She poured us each another drink and she drank her own quickly. I put mine on the sinkboard and she came over and stood beside me. She stared at Willy.

He was watching us with blank, unseeing eyes.

"Put the dirty rotten bastard in the chair," she said in a low, tense voice. "Burn the lousy little woman killer."

Her slender right arm went around my waist and she leaned close to me. Her other hand sort of half caressed me.

Willy looked straight at her and suddenly he began to cry. His face was still without expression, like that of a man in a somnambulistic state, as the tears coursed down his cheeks and dropped to the floor.

I gave Dolly Gottlieb a pat on her cheek and carefully brushed her forehead with my lips. I wanted Willy to know exactly where he stood. Then I gently pushed her away.

"I will," I said.

I walked over to Willy and lifted him to his feet by one arm. "Let's go, brother," I said.

I pushed him out of the door in front of me.

He slumped far over in one corner of the cab and I don't think he even heard me when I gave the driver the address of the tenement where he roomed. His eyes remained completely without life until we had once more pulled up to the front of the house on the teeming lower East Side.

The Korean veteran was still on the stoop, surrounded by a group of wide-eyed kids in dirty, castoff clothing. I paid the driver, through the window, and then pulled Willy's arm. He looked up at me blankly for a moment, and then hunched over and started to crawl out of the door behind me. I stood on the curbstone, waiting for him.

For the first time, as he looked up and saw the tenement building, a glimmering of intelligence crossed his face. He seemed mildly surprised.

He was wondering, I guess, why we were not downtown at headquarters.

I had to half push him to get him upstairs and into his room. He went over to the unmade bed and sat down. He was beginning to come to a little bit.

In about five minutes he suddenly looked up at me. "Oh Christ," he said.

For a second he just stared at me and I was afraid he wasn't quite ready yet. But then he started. He talked fast in a hysterical voice, frequently mispronouncing his words and slurring them.

"You gotta believe me, Lieutenant," he said. His voice was like that of a small child and he was almost crying. "You gotta believe me. I don't know why she's doing it, but she's lying. Lying like hell. My God, I was with her; with her all day and most of the night."

He went on and on and I just let him get it out of his system. I didn't say anything, one way or another.

"Lieutenant," he said, "you wouldn't want to frame me. You wouldn't want an innocent man to go to the chair while a killer gets away? Jesus, you ..."

"Why did you kill her, Willy?" I asked suddenly.

"Oh Christ!"

He turned and put his head in the pillows and I thought he was going to bawl again.

I waited a couple of more minutes and then I went over and pulled him upright.

"Let's take a look around, Willy," I said. "Maybe you got the junk you took off the Chamlers girl here. Maybe, but I don't think you'd be quite that stupid."

He looked at me, surprised for a moment. And then his face suddenly lighted up.

"My God yes, Lieutenant," he said. "Look around. You won't find anything. Nothing at all. You'll see that I didn't do it. I couldn't do it!"

"You could do it all right, Willy. Easy. Hell, less than half an hour ago you tried to kill Dolly Gottlieb. You've done a lot of pretty rough things in your time. Peddled junk, burglary and what not. Yes, you could have done it all right."

"Maybe I could," Willy said. "But I didn't."

"We'll just take a look around," I said.

Willy got off the bed and for the first time he seemed a little more alive. He was beginning to realize that he wasn't where he would normally have expected to be. In the back room of a police station trying to explain things. He was baffled, frightened, but he was also beginning to regain a fragment of hope.

He pulled the stuff out of the clothes closet and there was nothing there but a lot of old suits and a couple of pairs of shoes. There were a few letters and personal effects, but I didn't bother with them. Next he picked up the suitcase and carried it over to the bed and turned it upside down and dumped out the contents. He started to pry through them and I watched his face. He was beginning to look a little more sure of himself.

And then he found it.

For a second, as his hand collided with the envelope, which was concealed by a pile of dirty clothes, I could see a strange, surprised look on his face. Suddenly his eyes went furtive.

Quickly I reached over and grabbed his wrist. I pulled out his hand and in it he had the white envelope I had planted. He opened his fingers and dropped it as though he held a rattlesnake.

His eyes were staring at me, wide open and shocked, as I took the small package and opened it.

A ring, a white gold wristwatch and two earrings fell to the bed.

If I had expected Willy to go into another trance, I was due for a surprise. He didn't even scream. He just suddenly sat down again on the edge of the bed and his eyes never left my face. Willy knew at last what was happening to him.

"Oh my God," he said. "Oh—my—God!"

3.

We just sat there then for about five minutes. Willy stared straight into my eyes and his own never wavered. For the first time in my life I found I had to look away. I'm tough, but I wasn't quite tough enough to stare him down. Finally I spoke.

"It looks like you're it, Willy," I said.

He blinked a couple of times and kept staring at me.

"I'm it," he said at last and his voice was barely a whisper. "But don't look for a confession. You won't need it anyway. The frame is too perfect."

I nodded.

"You're right, Willy," I said. "We won't need a confession. It's cut and dried."

Suddenly he laughed. It was the sort of laugh I never want to hear again. He doubled over and the tears came to his eyes. It took him about six or seven minutes to get over it. It was a silent sort of laugh and it ended in a long sob.

"Jesus," he said then, "I should have known. I should have known I'd never have a chance. Don't you want to ask me why I did it? How I did it? Don't you want all the bloody details?"

His voice now was high-pitched and on the borderline of hysteria.

I leaned over and slapped his face, back and forth, several times. I didn't hurt him, but I brought him around. I wanted him to listen to me—closely.

"Willy," I said, "listen to me. Does anything strike you funny about this whole thing?"

For a second he just stared at me.

"Yeah, funny as all hell," he said. "But then again, I'm me and you're a cop—so it isn't really funny at all. It's natural. You had to have a patsy and I'm your boy. So go ahead and take me in, lock me up, hang me. It couldn't be simpler."

"It's not that simple at all," I said. "I'm not going to take you in—at least just yet. And maybe you won't be locked up at all; maybe you won't even go to trial."

His black eyes suddenly widened and his mouth fell partly open. For the first time I noticed that he had a gold cap on one of his lower teeth. It gave him a peculiar, almost clownish look, which was oddly contradictory to his normal wolfish expression.

"No," he said. "No?"

"No. That is if you just sit tight and listen to me for a while. You will admit, though Willy, that we have just about as tight a little case as we can get?"

"As tight a frame," he said.

"All right, as tight a frame, if you want it that way. It doesn't much matter what you call it. You're a dead pigeon no matter how it's cut."

Willy nodded, but he still stared at me, and the expression in his eyes was gradually changing from complete desolation to one of bewilderment. He had no idea where I was going.

"You don't have to be locked up at all, Willy," I said. "In fact," and I waved one hand at the jewelry which I had spread out on the bed, "in fact all of this can be forgotten. And Dolly Gottlieb—well we could forget about her too."

A quick, smart look came over his face and for a moment he watched me sharply. He didn't quite believe it, but he was beginning to get an idea. And then, suddenly he again looked down at the floor and he half shrugged his shoulders.

"I got something like twelve bucks in cash and another seventy in the Bowery Savings Bank," he said.

I stuck a finger under his chin and jerked his head up so that he had to look at me. He cringed and thought I was going to hit him.

"You got me wrong," I said in a very soft voice. "Dead wrong. I'm not shaking you down—for money."

He continued to stare at me.

"At this point, Willy," I said, speaking very slowly and making quite sure he followed every word, "at this time, you have, to all intents, committed a murder. You've killed a woman. There is enough evidence to put you straight into the electric chair. You have a record; you got no alibi for the time of the crime. You could have cased the job. The motive is right here," and I pointed to the jewelry on the bed.

"You wouldn't have a hope in hell."

He half nodded.

"Except maybe," he said, "the guy who really did it might slip up somehow. Might even confess. Maybe *he* wouldn't stand to see an innocent guy framed."

"Wrong, Willy," I said. "It happens I *know* who killed Billy Chamlers. He's not the kind of man who would ever confess. And as for slipping up—why Willy if I'm smart enough to put a man in the chair who didn't do it, I'm certainly smart enough to protect the man who did. Especially as he wants protection."

"He must have more money than I got," Willy said. This time he sneered outright. He wasn't afraid any longer. I guess he figured he didn't have anything else to lose. It's an odd thing about Willy's type of criminal. As long as they're dealing with a cop who they figure isn't on the make—who's honest—they scare easy. They worry about dishonest cops—but they're not frightened of them. Willy no longer believed I was an honest cop. He hadn't the slightest idea of what the angle was; he just knew that I must be crooked.

"Don't try to figure it, Willy," I said. "It won't be necessary. I'll give you the blueprint. But there's just one thing."

This time I had his full attention. And I could see that his twisted mind was completely alert. That's the way I wanted it. That's the way it had to be.

"It's like this Willy. Believe me or not, I can get you the full treatment for a murder that, let's say, you didn't do. And another thing, Willy, while I'm talking …"

I wanted to take the smugness out of him again.

"Another thing. Just remember that we happen to be alone now. If you got any idea of repeating this conversation—forget it. No one in the world would ever believe you. Even Dolly Gottlieb, the dame you were laying won't back you up. So just listen and don't get fancy ideas. So getting back. I can put you away for good for a murder you didn't do. You can completely believe that."

Watching him as I talked, I could see that he did completely believe it. Well, he should have; it was true.

"By the same token, Willy," I said, speaking very slow and careful, "I can arrange for you to commit another murder and I can absolutely guarantee that you will get away with it—clean."

I stopped then to let it sink in.

It took him several minutes. I could almost see his mind working. He tried at first to figure out every angle but the obvious one. But at last it came to him. When it did he just looked at me for a while as though he couldn't believe what he had heard. Finally he spoke.

"Are you asking me to commit a murder?" he said at last.

"No Willy," I said. "I'm not asking you. I am only telling you that unless you want the hot seat for the Billy Chamlers job you are *going* to commit a murder. The only difference is that instead of going to the chair for a murder you didn't do, you are going to actually do a murder for which there will be not the slightest chance of your going to the chair."

4.

Well, it took about another three quarters of an hour to get it all clear and through his thick skull. Of course he made the usual protests; said he couldn't commit murder if he wanted to. Said there wouldn't be a chance of getting away with it.

I reminded him that the guy who'd knocked off Billy Chamlers was getting away with it. I also reminded him that as far as could or couldn't—it would be a lot easier, he'd find, to actually murder someone than to burn for not having done so.

It wasn't as tough as I thought it would be. Willy was a criminal; a born crook and an instinctively anti-social human being. All along, it turned out, his only real prejudice against murder as such was the personal danger of being caught. He had no moral scruples to break down.

Once it was completely clear in his mind that this one was being played in reverse—that the danger lay in not committing murder, he switched around fast enough.

I can't say he ever liked it, that I ever had too much confidence in him. But I counted on two things, two terribly strong facets of Willy's character or lack of character: the fact that he was a dyed-in-the-wool crook and the fact that he'd do anything to save his neck.

His not trusting me was the biggest stumbling block. He figured I would probably double-cross him at the end—that he'd go up for two murders instead of just the one which he really hadn't done—that was the hard point to overcome.

So at last I played my trump card. I told Willy who it was he had to kill.

"The victim, Willy," I said, "is going to be my wife. So you can see I'll probably have to go on protecting you—that I won't be able to double-cross you without putting myself in the chair right along with you."

Up until that point Willy's attitude toward me had gone through a number of sequences. First there had been the hatred and physical fear, when he'd first been picked up for questioning. Then later, when he figured I was framing him, bitterness and plain simple hatred. After that he couldn't conceal his almost sneering condescension.

Now it was different and something new. From the minute I told him that I planned to kill my wife, he looked at me as though he were sitting opposite some strange monster. I don't think he ever again thought of me as sane or even human. I wasn't any longer just a venal, crooked cop to Willy: I was something not quite normal.

"Oh God," he said, "I'll never get away with it. You'll never get away with it, yourself."

"You're wrong as usual Willy," I told him. "You will get away with it and I'll tell you why. You will because there is only one type of killer who ever gets away with it. I know; I'm one of the best homicide detectives there is. And I've seen it happen a hundred times.

"Yes, there is only one murderer who is never found out. Only one type of killing. One single pattern.

"It's when a complete stranger, runs into a second complete stranger and suddenly takes a gun and shoots that second stranger dead. He has no motive; no reason in the world for the crime. And of course there can be no witnesses. Then he just walks off and the police have nothing—nothing at all. Nobody saw it; there was no reason for it. That's what this is going to be.

"You never saw my wife; you didn't even know I was married until I told you I was. There isn't the slightest reason in the world anyone could figure that you'd want to shoot a woman that you didn't know existed.

"When it's going to happen, and where, which I'll explain in a few minutes, will be at a time and a place where you are guaranteed no one will be around. Not even by accident. I'm even taking care of accidents. After it's done and all over, why you just walk off. No one will see you; no one will ever know. Only me. And I won't be able to talk. No more than you'll be able to talk, Willy. Because this one—this one we're doing together."

Willy just stared at me. "I haven't even got a gun," he said at last.

"You got seventy bucks in the Bowery Savings Bank," I said. "Buy a gun. You know how to do that, I'm sure. And when you're through with it, for once in your life play it smart. Go out on a party fishing boat out of Sheepshead Bay and when the boat is about six miles offshore you must drop it overboard. Before the boat's moved another fifty yards the gun will be buried in a couple of feet of mud. God himself wouldn't be able to find it. That's all; don't try to resell it, don't dump it in an ashcan or throw it in the East River or try to hide it. Get rid of it for all time."

"And about nobody seeing; nobody being around?" Willy asked.

"That's the easiest part," I said. "Tomorrow is Thursday. Tomorrow night my wife—she does it each Thursday without fail—goes to a bridge club. It's a neighborhood affair. She leaves about five in the afternoon and there are about seven other women. Most of their husbands work nights, which I usually do myself. So they all have dinner together in one of the women's homes. Then they play bridge. Until ten-thirty. They always break up then as two or three of their husbands get in before midnight.

"At eleven o'clock you can expect my wife home. I'll make sure she'll be on time as I'll arrange to meet her there myself. Except it will be you Willy, that will meet her.

"You're to go to the house—I'll give you the address and all the details—and be there waiting. You'll have to memorize the number and the floor plan. Anyway, you'll get in through the garage which I'm going to leave open. After you get in it's around in the back off an alley and no one could possibly see you enter—after you get in, you must leave the garage door open as you found it. Then, while the house is dark, you're going to jimmy a downstairs window. I want this to look like a burglary. And I don't have to tell you how to make it look like one. You've had experience.

"You're going up to the bedroom then and pull open a couple of drawers in one of the bureaus. Just enough to make it look right, but not too much. You're going to time it so you'll have about a fifteen-minute wait. You probably won't hear Fern when she drives into the garage, but you won't have to. I know what she always does. She flips on the light in the hall downstairs and she comes right up at once to the bedroom. She goes through the bedroom into the bathroom and takes off her makeup and washes her hands and face. She always does it.

"You're going to be in that bathroom, Willy, and the minute she opens that bedroom door, you see her through the crack. That's when you're going to shoot. You're to do it with one shot, if possible, but in any case you're to be sure it's a complete job."

Willy's mouth was hanging open again as he listened to me. He didn't look quite intelligent.

"Suppose someone hears the shot?"

"They won't, Willy," I said. "They can't. Once, by accident, I fired a shot in that room while I was cleaning a .38 police special. That's a heavy gun. My wife and a friend were on the lawn at the side of the house. They didn't hear it. The bathroom has a small window and it's going to be closed. So will the bedroom windows."

"And the getaway," Willy said. "No one is to see me? How do you ..."

"You go downstairs after it's all over and you look out the front windows. It's a wide, tree-lined street and there are no houses on the other side for an eighth of a mile in either direction. If there's no one on the street—and the chances are a hundred to one there won't be at that time of night—you open the door and walk out. You are going to have a car waiting a half block away. It had better be a hot car, Willy. That shouldn't be any problem."

5.

For the next hour, we went over details. Willy had a thousand objections and questions, but I could tell by his very curiosity that it was no longer a question of whether he'd do it or not. He was going to do it all right.

One thing he did bring up. He didn't like the hot car idea. It left too much to chance; the possibility of a cruising police car coming along and spotting it; the bare chance of being picked up when he took the car.

His idea was better. He'd use a rental car. I told him it might be traced; someone might accidentally see the plates and remember. He laughed.

"Hell," he said. "Don't worry about that. I'll rent it, but the plates will be hot ones. I can get them easy enough. When I return it the right plates will be back on it."

So we went over the details again; every fine point. He had it all clear in his mind. He knew what he had to do.

I finally stood up and I scooped the jewelry off the bed. "One more thing," I said. "When it's all over, go on into work at the usual time. And don't slip up; don't make any mistakes. Do just what you're supposed to do. If everything goes right, you'll probably read in the paper Friday morning about the guy who is being charged with the Chamlers murder. That should take quite a load off your mind."

I turned and left Willy Holiday sitting on the edge of his bed. He just stared at me wordlessly.

The door into the lavatory on the third floor was open and I walked into the tiny cubicle. The smell was overpowering and I kicked the door shut and sat down on the toilet seat.

I thought for a second I was going to be sick to my stomach. It wasn't the smell of the room either.

For a moment I considered taking out my service revolver and putting a bullet through my head.

I didn't even know that I had been crying until I stood up and saw my face in the cracked mirror over the stained enamel washbasin.

CHAPTER XI

1.

I heard the radio broadcast at one o'clock on Wednesday afternoon. I had gone across town to a bar and grill on Lower Broadway and was sitting in a booth having a sandwich and a cup of coffee. I had wanted a chance to pull myself together before seeing anyone after I left Willy Holiday.

It was a newscaster from one of the smaller New York stations and he mentioned the thing in passing. I'd been sitting there idly listening in an attempt to get my mind off the Chamlers case and my own problems for a few minutes.

It hit me like a ton of bricks.

"Less than half an hour ago," the voice said, "John Haverford, New York advertising executive, was arrested in connection with the weekend murder of glamorous nightclub singer, Billy Chamlers. It is understood that a newspaper reporter this morning interviewed Mr. Haverford's fiancée, also believed to be his private secretary, and that she placed the youthful businessman in Miss Chamlers' apartment at the time the crime took place. The woman's name is Jane Cummins and her own version of the affair is being printed now for release in an afternoon newspaper. Police were quick to act after getting wind of the story. At the present time it has not been learned what, if any, charge has been placed against Haverford. Lieutenant Martin Ferris, in charge of the homicide detail assigned to the case, has not been available for comment."

That was all and it was plenty.

I didn't finish my sandwich but got up and grabbed my hat. I hailed a cab and told the driver to take me to headquarters.

They were all there. The Inspector, lean, gray-haired and his conservative business suit as immaculate as ever, once again was sitting in Captain O'Shea's chair. His legs were crossed and he seemed completely at ease. If it hadn't been for the slight nervous twitch at the corner of his mouth, I might have been deceived.

The Captain stood over by the file case and he didn't look up as I came into the room. But I knew at once that he was aware of my entrance. I could tell by the way his heavy, red-veined face, suddenly went almost purple.

Sal was talking with Sergeant Kelly over in one corner and Bill Albright from the D.A.'s office was talking to a plainclothes man from my own detail in another corner of the room.

"We were hoping you'd get in," the Inspector said, staring at me completely without expression.

Sal looked up and winked, but there was nothing humorous about the wink. He was warning me to expect trouble.

I could hear a rumble start in the back of Captain O'Shea's throat and I made a sudden quick decision. The best defense would be an offense.

"Goddamn it," I said, "I understand that some damn fool has had Haverford picked up. Of all the stupid ..." The rumble became a full-grown bellow.

"You don't like it, eh?" the Captain said. "Well by God and by Jesus if that ain't one for the books. And just where the hell have you been for the last day or so? Who the hell is supposed to be running this investigation anyway? What goddamned goose chase have you been off on anyway?"

The Inspector cut in and the Captain's voice died off in a deep grumble.

"The fact is, Lieutenant," the Inspector said, "we haven't been able to get hold of you. And then when that damned reporter dug up the Cummins woman—or anyway, once she'd gone to him and spilled her story, why we had no option. We had to do something before it hit the newspapers. Not quite knowing just where we're going in this case—and we don't know largely because of your own secrecy—there was no intelligent statement we could release. So the only thing to do was pick up Haverford. He's being held on a short affidavit until we know where we're at."

"Haverford's no more guilty than I am," I said.

O'Shea glared at me.

"Who the hell said he was?" he asked. "But that's all beside the point. Nobody's guilty until we have a case wrapped up against them. So what have you been doing about it? Huh? What!"

"By God," I said, "I've been working. Working along my own lines and I think I'll have this thing wrapped up for good within the next thirty-six hours."

The Captain looked at me and there was nothing of friendship in his expression.

"Ferris," he said and this time his voice was quiet and dripping sarcasm, "Ferris, just what the hell do you think you're doing? Who the hell do you think you are anyway? A detective in the New York City police system or a goddamned Ellery Queen? This department is not a one-man organization; we don't go in for grandstand plays. We got an organization. Why even your own partner, Brentano, doesn't know what the hell you've been up to."

Once more the Inspector interrupted.

"It isn't that we don't have every confidence in you, Lieutenant," he said. "But this is a tricky case and right now it seems wide open. I feel that we should all be pulling together on it. Perhaps you'd like to explain your own point of view."

I looked around and with the exception of Sal, I found no sympathy. For a second I hesitated and then I started talking. I kept my voice low and controlled. I didn't want to get into arguments if I could help it.

"Well," I said, "Let me just give you a rundown. I think I can explain what I've been doing and why I've more or less had to play it alone.

"To begin with we can start with Malcolm, our Philadelphia friend. If you recall, I was the one who turned up the evidence that he was being blackmailed because of his connection with the Chamlers girl; probably blackmailed by the girl herself in as much as the negatives of the photos used for the blackmail were found in her apartment. Secondly, Malcolm has still to establish an alibi for the time of the murder. Apparently he refuses to do so.

"Malcolm is to be considered a serious candidate for the chair in this case. But we still haven't got a case against him. Because of his connections and influence, I have been ordered to go slow with him. I'm not even allowed to question him. I've been stymied at every turn. If we should arrest him, we have no reason to believe that he may not turn out to have an absolutely waterproof alibi. We'd just make fools of ourselves. It is my personal conviction that he has such an alibi; otherwise he'd have long ago come up with a phony one.

"There's Haverford. He could have committed the murder; possibly he had reason to. However, I doubt it. It just doesn't fit. You've arrested him, but now what? Do you think we have a case?"

Bill Albright cut in.

"Case hell," he said. "All you've got so far is a possible false arrest suit to defend."

"He has no possible suit," I said. "After all he lied to us in his first statement and we have the right to take him in for examination. But as of now, we have damn near nothing to go on as far as pinning the thing on him.

"Anyway, to move on. We have Duffy. Sam Duffy, the girl's agent. He definitely could have done the job; at least it would have been possible as far as the time element is concerned. However, we have found no motive of any sort. We know that over a long period of years he had a strange sort of relationship with the girl—a sort of combined business agent and father confessor. As far as we have been able to determine, he treated her like, and thought of her as, a daughter. He had nothing to gain from her death; no reason for killing her.

"There are several other persons we have investigated and questioned. The janitor, who had the opportunity of committing the crime, Miss Rumson, the music teacher from the floor below. In each case, however, we have been unable to establish a motive or a reason.

"Then we have the milkman, Willy Holiday, an ex-con with a record for burglary."

Once more the Captain interrupted.

"Hell, you told me yourself, Ferris, that you checked his alibi for the time of the crime and that he's in the clear. Anyway, I've told you all along that this was no accidental kill by a break-in artist."

"That's right," I said. "I did check his alibi and he did seem to be in the clear. On the other hand, I have gone just a little further. I know you didn't like him as a possible suspect, Captain," I said, "but after all, I'm supposed to be in charge of this case. I double checked on that alibi and it begins to look as though it's a phony. There is, in my own mind at this time, a feeling that Holiday is very far from being in the clear. If so …"

"Well then why in the hell don't you bring him in here and let's kick the goddamned truth out of him," the Captain said.

"Captain," I said, "you can bet I'd do that very thing if I thought it would work. But this is murder and an important murder—at least from the standpoint of the newspapers. I have no doubt but what I could get a confession out of Willy Holiday. None at all. On the other hand, when the D.A. takes this case into court, we don't want some smart shyster for the defense screaming about police brutality and third-degree methods. With a crumb like Willy Holiday, you've got to have an open and shut case. And that's what I'm trying to get."

Once more Bill Albright spoke up.

"Lieutenant Ferris is right," he said. "My God, a punk like Holiday would have one of those smart publicity wise lawyers in his corner in five minutes. This case will make plenty of headlines at the time the trial—if there ever is one. We are going to have to have evidence and very concrete evidence."

"All right then," the Captain said. "So you think maybe Holiday did it, even if I don't. So what's all the goddamned mystery about? Why not take the rest of us into your confidence? Why the lone hand?"

I talked to the Inspector directly when I answered Captain O'Shea.

"There is no mystery at all," I said. "I've had Sal and the boys working on the other angles—on Malcolm, Haverford and the others. Because I have felt all along that Holiday was far from in the clear, and because no one else seemed to agree with me on it, I went ahead and covered that angle myself. Also, I felt that in this particular case, I could probably do a better job working alone. The Captain knows, as well as Sal and the rest of you, that I'm not looking for any glory nor am I trying to be a prima donna. And I certainly am not trying to steal the show.

"I've worked on a good many murder cases and if I say so myself, I've done a good job on most of them. No one has ever yet seen me trying to grab off any headlines or any medals."

Captain O'Shea walked over toward me and there was a slightly embarrassed expression around his eyes. He said it grudgingly, but he said it.

"Lieutenant Ferris is right, Inspector," he said. "He's certainly no publicity hound. The only thing is, I just wish he'd sort of kept a little more in touch with me. And I must admit frankly that I think the Holiday angle is a lotta crap. I just don't see it."

"Captain—Inspector," I said, "I just wish you'd let me play this my own way for a little longer. After all, the case is still only four days old. If either Malcolm, or Haverford, or any of the others so far involved, are guilty, we're going to find it out and find it out soon. In the meantime, they will all keep. None of them are going anywhere. But I'd like just about thirty-six hours more. I have a feeling I can wrap the whole thing up by then."

The Inspector stretched and uncrossed his legs. He stood up and walked toward the door.

"It's your case, as you know, Lieutenant," he said. "On the other hand, Captain O'Shea is in charge here and he's your superior. Work it out any way you want to, gentlemen. But for God's sake work it out and let's get this one cleaned up."

He closed the door softly as he left the room.

For a minute no one spoke and then the Captain pulled over his chair and sat down. He looked up at me.

"Marty," he said, "I've known you a long time. You've done some mighty fine work for this department. Go ahead if you want and play it your own way. Take Sal with you if you want. But for God's sake don't let me just sit here without any answers. I'm the one that the Inspector asks the questions of; I'm the one who has to see the press. And what the hell am I supposed to do with young Haverford in the meantime? There are going to be a couple of lawyers in here with habeas corpus papers before you can turn around."

"Hold him as a material witness," I said. "Hell, he was the last person to have seen the girl alive. Get him out to one of the outlying precincts and bury him for twenty-four hours."

I looked over at where Sal and Kelly still stood by the window.

"Sergeant Kelly can handle it," I said. "I'm going home and get some sleep. Goddamned if I've seen a bed for the last couple of days."

"O.K.," the Captain said as I started for the door. "But for Christ sake spend a dime and call in once in a while. I get lonely."

Sal dropped me at the subway station and I told him I'd keep in touch.

"But tonight," I said, "I'm just going home and take it easy."

He wished me good night and I turned away and started into the station. The minute the car was out of sight, I walked back and went over to a drugstore on the corner. I called Fern and she was home. I told her I was on the way out.

"Good Marty," she said. "I'm tired of being a widow."

"I'll be along soon," I told her.

Then I called the Club Shenandoah.

It was hard to talk to Jill, but I was still worried about that blank I'd drawn in her place. I still didn't know what had happened and it bothered me. She recognized my voice at once and her words came as a surprise. I was amazed at the odd tenderness in her voice; it didn't sound at all like Jill.

"Well, sweety," she said. "I was wondering when you'd call. How are you feeling?"

"Terrible," I said. "Jees, I'm sorry …"

She didn't let me finish.

"Honey," she said, "You're something. You really are something. My God!"

I must have blushed and I started to stutter. I didn't even know for sure what she meant.

"When am I seeing you again?" she asked. "Tonight maybe?"

I told her that I'd be tied up: And yet I wanted to see her. There was something about the tone of her voice. I suddenly knew that I had her where I wanted her. I knew that at last she was ready and that she'd be willing to talk; to tell me what I wanted to know.

"Look," she said, "I'm going to be off tomorrow night. Have to go in for an hour around five-thirty, but I have the night off. Let's pick it up where we left off? What do you say, Marty, lets …"

I said that would be great. I had a quick flash of inspiration. I not only wanted to talk to her; it would also be a good idea to be with her for the early hours of that next evening. It would fit perfectly. I told her I'd be at her apartment at seven o'clock.

"You're a doll," she said. And then she said something else that made my ears burn and I felt myself reddening. I still didn't remember what had happened during that time I had drawn the blank, but I was getting an idea.

I hung up and went back across the street and climbed the stairs and took the train out to the North Shore.

2.

Fern was just finishing a cup of coffee as I walked into the kitchen.

"Marty," she said. "Oh Marty—what in the world's happened to your face?"

She stood up and started toward me, a worried look in her eyes.

"Sit down Fern," I said. "Sit down and don't worry about me or my face."

For a second she looked almost as though I had struck her. Then the hurt expression was replaced by one of bewilderment. But she turned and went back to her seat, never taking her eyes from me after she once more was sitting in front of her coffee.

"What is it, Marty?" she asked. "What's the matter, honey?"

"Maybe you better tell me," I said. "Is something the matter?"

I didn't wait for her to answer. I reached into my pocket and I took out the letter from the bank and I threw it across the table.

"Take a look, baby," I said. "Maybe you can find something the matter with that."

She reached for the envelope and she pulled the folded sheet of stationery out. Her eyes still watched me and I noticed that they were wide and that the azure was now gray.

She looked down and I saw at once that she blushed. I probably should have waited for her to say something, but I felt the anger coming over me. I didn't want her lies.

"What have you been doing," I said and my voice was harsh and bitter. "Taking it out to spend on your old girlfriends—or maybe it was the old boyfriends?"

She looked up at me then and her face was suddenly white. "What did you say, Marty?"

"I said what have you been doing, spending it ..."

"You better not say it after all, Marty," she said. "You're not yourself. You're tired, Marty. I think ..."

"I'm tired all right," I said. "Tired of harlots and tired of liars and cheats."

She started to say something then and there was an expression almost of pleading in her deep eyes. Her chin began to quiver and she half reached out toward me.

"You're like all of the rest of them," I said. "Every goddamned one!"

It was then, suddenly, that the expression changed. A stubborn look crossed her face and she quickly got to her feet. The color rushed back into her face again. She stood up very straight.

"Maybe I am," she said, speaking very slowly. "Maybe I am like all the rest of them. And I'm tired, too. Tired of a policeman's narrow, bigoted mind. Of a policeman's manners."

Before I could say another word, she was out of the room. I could hear her half sob as she went through the living room and started up the stairs.

For a second, then, I started to get to my feet; to follow after her. But my eye fell on the letter lying on the table, and I dropped back. The hell with it, I said to myself. Follow her, apologize? For what?

It would be too easy. It had always been too easy. I knew only too well. I'd forget the letter and those other letters. I'd forget about Joan Bronski; I'd forget about the envelope I'd found in Jill's apartment. I'd forget about the information from Washington; about Harry and everything else. All I'd remember would be Fern and the three years we'd had.

Those were the years which I must forget.

I made myself a sandwich and got a bottle of beer out of the icebox and opened it, at the sink.

Fern was in bed by the time I got upstairs. She lay as she always did, in the middle of the bed with a white sheet half pulled across her naked body. On her back. She was breathing lightly. She looked as innocent as a newborn baby.

I felt the old desire coming over me as I watched her in the dim light of the shaded reading lamp.

I tried to hate her. I tried to remember all of the things which had happened and which I had learned in the last week.

It was very strange, but suddenly I began to think of Jill Bentley and then, a moment later I thought of Dolly Gottlieb.

I walked over and carefully pulled the sheet up so that it covered her nakedness. I was careful not to awaken her.

I was trembling but I didn't have to fight the desire which was tugging at me.

I felt dirty all over and even the shower and the rub down didn't help.

Later, I went downstairs again and I curled up on the couch.

It was hours before I managed to get to sleep.

CHAPTER XII

1.

She had wanted to talk to me but I hadn't let her. I didn't want to hear her lies. I didn't even want to hear her tell the truth. The truth would be even worse than the lies.

So I had told her that I'd have breakfast on the way into the office. I told her that I'd be home that night about the time she got back from the bridge club and that if we had anything to say to each other we could say it then.

"We've got to get things straightened out, Marty," she said. "We've got to ..."

"I've got to go to work," I cut in. "I'll be home at eleven o'clock tonight. If there's anything to say, we can say it then."

She just looked at me as I went over and got my coat and put my arms in the sleeves. I turned then and went to the door.

It was the first time in the three years of our marriage that we hadn't kissed each other good-by.

I left the car for her, as I always did on Thursday.

There was nothing new downtown when I got there and the Captain wasn't in yet. Sal was on his way down from the Bronx. I left word that I'd be in touch and then I went out to the street and started walking north. I walked all the way and it took me a little more than a half hour.

Willy Holiday was lying flat on his back, on the unmade bed, fully dressed, when I entered his room without knocking. He was just lying there, staring at the ceiling.

He didn't look up or make any move.

I closed the door and pulled a chair over.

"You're all ready for tonight?" I asked.

He half nodded.

Then, still without looking at me, he spoke.

"I never killed anyone before."

"You were never facing the electric chair before, either," I said.

He lifted the upper part of his body and twisted over and reached for the cigarettes on the chair.

"Right," he said.

He was all right. I could see that he was all right. Nervous maybe and worried, but he'd go through with it.

He told me he had the gun and that it was a .32. He repeated all of my directions.

"Don't worry," he said. "I'll be there, waiting. Eleven o'clock."

I left him then. I was sure that he'd be there.

I began to walk uptown again. I had all the time in the world. There wasn't a thing to do but wait. I almost wished that I hadn't told Jill I would see her that night. I didn't feel like seeing anyone until it was all over. But then, there was the other thing. The thing I wanted to find out and make sure of. Before it happened I wanted that last single verification. The sure knowledge. And Jill was the one who could give it to me. Jill had known her in the past. Jill had known Harry, too.

My mind went back once more to Willy Holiday. In another twelve hours he'd be dead and the Chamlers case would be washed up. Somehow, I couldn't feel sorry for Willy. By that time, by the time he was dead, he would be a murderer. A paid killer.

I realized that my timing would have to be perfect. Willy would be there, crouching in my own bathroom, at eleven that night. Fern would walk into the house and up the stairs and open the bedroom door.

It wouldn't be Fern Ferris, Lieutenant Ferris' wife, whose body would slump to the floor with a lead slug from Willy's gun in her breast. It would be Joan Bronski, ex-con and ex-mistress of a criminal.

And when the bullets from my own gun cut Willy Holiday down two minutes later as he left my front door, the man who would lie there dead would be a killer who had come looking for the man who was putting him in the chair for the Chamlers murder. That's when the evidence, the stolen jewels, would come out. That's when the whole story would come out. And the only person in the world who would be able to find any fault with the story would be the dead man himself. And he wouldn't be in a position to do any talking.

Yes, in another ten or twelve hours it would be all over.

I didn't want to think about it anymore. So I went into a double feature movie up around the Times Square district. I sat there and I tried to watch the screen. I tried to forget everything.

A couple of hours went by and I left. I never did remember a thing about the picture.

It was only three o'clock and I still had time to kill. I went over to a bar on Third Avenue and I sat on a stool and had a beer and I watched the afternoon ball game on the television screen. It was as meaningless as the motion picture had been.

I tried not to think of what was going to happen, but I couldn't help myself. I found that the whole thing kept going around and around in my mind. I tried to find flaws, and I couldn't find any.

Willy? No, Willy would go through with his end all right. It was the only way in the world he would be able to escape the rap on the Chamlers job.

Dolly Gottlieb? After all, what did she know? Nothing. Willy *could* have done the Chamlers job while he had been out that afternoon. And Dolly knew nothing of the actual frame-up. Nothing of the planted jewels.

Of course there was Sam Duffy. Duffy had taken the jewelry. Probably taken it that evening when he walked in and found the girl's dead body. But Duffy didn't *know* that I had taken them from him. He might guess, but guessing wasn't knowing. And certainly Duffy wouldn't talk. He'd be the last one to say anything.

No Sam Duffy and Dolly Gottlieb would be safe enough. And Willy Holiday would be dead. There were no flaws. Captain O'Shea would have his case all neatly wrapped up and the D.A. wouldn't even have to worry about a trial.

And I'd be back where I was three years ago. A good homicide detective who had only one interest in the world. His job.

I left the bar and went back across town to a restaurant and ordered a steak and some French fries and a salad. But I wasn't hungry. I killed another couple of hours though, over three or four Scotch and sodas.

Before I knew it it was seven o'clock and I was on my way downtown again.

Jill Bentley answered my ring at once.

2.

The double feature hadn't been able to do it and the baseball game hadn't been able to do it. But somehow, the second that tall girl with the wide shoulders and the flame red hair opened her door and I looked into those green eyes of hers—the eyes of a sleepy kitten—I completely forgot everything. Everything but Jill Bentley.

The blue jeans must have been hanging in the closet because she was dressed in a short pleated skirt and a sweater. Her feet and legs were bare as usual.

She didn't say a word. Just pushed the door shut behind me and then turned and in a second her long, beautifully rounded arms were around my neck and her face was lifted to mine and then her half-opened mouth met my own. She pressed her body hard against me and I could feel one leg as she twisted it between my own. I was conscious of the twin indentations her firm, pointed breasts made against my chest. Her eyes never closed and my hands went behind her and cupped and held her close and then raised her to her toes.

We held it for a couple of minutes and then she began to moan.

I started to push her gently away and her eyes flickered and she pressed tighter against me.

"Now," she said. "Now, Marty!"

I carried her over and I sat her on the couch.

I stood back and looked at her.

"Listen," I said. "We got all night."

She looked up then and she pouted. She wasn't really mad, though.

"You're a bastard, Marty," she said. "A real bastard. Anyway, baby will play along. I don't know what's got into me; I seem to have fallen for you. My God!"

Then she stretched like a cat and half yawned.

"Yep, I've fallen for a dumb cop," she said. It wasn't nasty; just a sort of casual comment.

"Liquor's in the kitchen," she said. "Take off your coat and let's have a drink. Maybe we better take it slow. The way I feel, you wouldn't last an hour."

I winked at her and went into the kitchen. The ice tray stuck and it took me a little time, but when I came back I carried two tall iced drinks.

She was curled up on the couch and looked happy.

"How did you feel yesterday?" she asked as she took one of the glasses.

"Dead," I said.

"You should have been."

We drank.

At nine o'clock Jill called the Chinese Restaurant, a couple of blocks away, and had some food sent up. She went into the bathroom while we waited and took a shower and meantime, I got dressed.

It was while we were eating and I was trying to figure a way to get around to asking what I wanted to know, that she said it.

"Marty," she said. "Marty, I don't think I'm going to see you anymore. I'm beginning to like you too much."

I thought at first that she was kidding, as she always did, or that she was half drunk. But then I looked at her and I saw that she was dead serious.

I had to be very careful.

"I like you too, Jill," I said. "I like everything about you. That is except one thing. I don't like your brother. I think your brother's a crook, a racket guy, Jill."

For a second her eyes went yellow and I thought she was going to blow up. But she didn't. She just stared at me for a moment and then she half laughed.

"Always the cop, eh, Marty?" she said. "God, how could I go for a cop? But you're wrong, you know. Frank isn't a racket guy as you call him. He's not even much of a crook. The only trouble with Frank is that he's a little weak and probably no damned good. He just picks on women—let's them take care of him."

I decided the time was right.

"Women like my wife?" I asked. "Like Fern Ferris?"

She had a glass of water in her hand and it dropped on the table and then spilled over onto the floor and broke as the name left my lips. Her eyes went wide open and she stared at me for a full half minute. She looked at me as though she were seeing a ghost.

Her face had gone completely white and it took her another minute before she could speak. Her voice was very low, then, and the words came as though she couldn't quite believe them.

"You're Ferris? You're the husband—the cop she married?" She still didn't quite believe it.

"I'm the cop she married," I said. "And apparently your brother's the guy she's keeping on the side."

She began to half shake her head, as though she still couldn't quite make it all out.

"Well I'll be damned," she said. And then suddenly her expression completely changed.

Now she was mad. She was no longer baffled; she was burning up.

"Oh, you fool—you stupid, damned ridiculous fool." She cried out the words and stood up as she spoke. She stared right into my eyes.

"You godforsaken idiot," she said. "Your wife isn't keeping anybody. I told Frank he shouldn't have done it. I knew ..."

"Done what?" I said, my voice suddenly cold and deadly. "Told

Frank he shouldn't have done what?"

Again she just stared at me for a minute.

"God," she said at last, "I don't know why I bother to even talk to you. I don't know what there was I ever saw in you."

I started toward her and she must have seen the half mad expression on my face.

"Told him he shouldn't have done what?" I said.

She backed up a little and then spoke quickly.

"He was shaking her down," she said. "He knew her in the old days and he knew she was married to a cop now and so he was shaking her down. I tried to get him to stop."

For a second it took me back on my feet. It explained one thing; it explained the money taken from our joint account. It might have explained the envelope laying on the desk that day I knew she had been in Jill's apartment with Jill's brother. It might have explained the telephone calls when she hadn't been home. But it still didn't explain a lot of other things.

"How about Harry?" I shot out. "I suppose he was shaking her down, too? Did you try to get him to stop?"

"Harry?"

For a moment she just looked at me blankly.

"Yeah—Harry," I said. "He's probably another friend from the old days. The days you knew her as Joan Bronski."

Her eyes widened when I said Joan Bronski. Now it was all out; now she knew that I really knew who my wife was.

"Harry," she said, in an almost inaudible voice, "Why Harry was her husband."

I grabbed her then by her shoulders and my fingers dug into her soft flesh. I felt like shaking her, shaking her until her teeth rattled.

"I'm her husband, goddamn it," I said. "Me, Marty Ferris, I'm her husband!"

Suddenly I let her go and I went over and sat down on the couch. I held my head in my hands.

"Tell me about Harry," I said.

For a minute she didn't say anything. She went to the table and poured herself a drink of straight Scotch and she drained it in a gulp.

"You never knew about Harry?"

She began to speak in a slow, careful voice. As though she were weighing her words.

"Harry," she said, "was Harry Woodlawn. Harold C. Woodlawn. He married Joan—Fern—secretly in Mexico, when she was seventeen or eighteen. Joan was a good kid but she didn't know much. Harry was a crook. He pulled a job out on the Coast and that's how your wife happened to be arrested. They thought she knew something about it—but she didn't. She didn't even know Harry was a burglar. You probably know that's when I met Joan—while she was doing time."

I just stared at her blankly. It was coming too fast and I couldn't quite take it all in.

"You mean," I said, "that Fern, Fern, my wife, was married to somebody named Harry Woodlawn? That she went to jail for something she didn't do?"

Jill nodded.

"Sure, I mean it," she said. "Why, didn't you know that she couldn't possibly have been a thief. My God Marty, you're married to her. Married to one of the sweetest kids ..."

"Where's Harry Woodlawn now?" I asked suddenly. "What's happened to him?"

"He's dead," Jill said.

"Dead? How do you know he's dead." I suddenly remembered that the FBI didn't even know that.

"I know because he was a friend of Frank's—of my brother's. Frank was with him in Mexico when he was killed."

Jill went on talking. I heard her say, "God, Marty, you're sweet, but you're really awfully dumb. Like all cops, I guess, just plain dumb."

But I wasn't listening to her. I was thinking about something else.

For the first time in weeks I believe that at that particular moment I suddenly regained a part of my sanity. I suddenly saw myself—not through my own eyes, but through the eyes of the rest of the world. I realized then, for the first time in my life, that I had been wrong all along. That the world, and people, were not at all what I had thought. That I had been wrong about everything.

But most of all, I had been wrong about Fern.

I had been jealous of a dead man, a man my wife had known when she was a child. I had condemned her for a criminal when she had committed no crime. At the same time I had been threatening to put an innocent man in the electric chair for a crime that he hadn't committed. In my heart I had accused her of infidelity while I was actually committing adultery myself.

I had been wrong at every turn in the road.

It was at that precise moment, I believe, that I first really loved my wife, Fern, for what she was—not what I thought she was or wanted her to be.

I would have to get home and tell Fern what I had discovered. What I knew about my love. I would have to be there when she got home from her bridge party.

I suddenly remembered, then, who would be there to meet Fern when she got home.

It was like emerging from a nightmare. In that next split second my mind became crystal clear. Even as my eyes went down to my wrist and I saw the small hand almost at ten and the large hand at five minutes before the hour.

I was shaking so that I could barely handle the knob as I reached the door.

I remember Jill calling something, but I never knew what it was.

I had to get home, I had to get into that house and into the bedroom before Willy Holiday got there. Before death walked in through the opened garage door and climbed the steps to the second floor.

I must have looked like a wild man, running down the street and half screaming. The first cab driver looked at me over the door and suddenly put his foot down on the gas. I could have shot him then and there.

But I slowed down and tried to gain control of myself. I had to get control.

The second cab stopped.

The man was a fool and I had a hard time explaining to him. But at last, after he insisted on seeing my badge, he believed I was a policeman and he stepped on the gas. He still drove as though he were going to a funeral.

We were stopped once out near the airport and I wasted a precious three minutes telling a story to the speed cop. Then he wanted to go ahead of us and clear traffic, but I didn't want that.

It was just ten-forty when the driver pulled up a block away from the house. I knew by now that Fern would be safe. But I still had something to do. I prayed that Willy Holiday was not already there; not already in that bathroom, waiting, with the gun cocked and ready.

Quickly I paid the cab off and then ran up the street. The house was dark and a hundred yards from the front door I turned and circled to the rear. I went down the alley at the back and it was with a sudden sense of deep relief that I saw that the garage doors were still opened.

Walking as swiftly and silently as possible, I entered the building. Just to be sure, once in the garage, I took out my service revolver and held it ready. Carefully then I crept upstairs. A moment later and I had thrown the bedroom door open. It was as I expected.

Willy had not yet arrived.

I knew that he would be around any second now, so I didn't turn on the light. Carefully I closed the door and walked into the bathroom. I left the door open a crack, but I still didn't turn on a light. I waited.

It seemed like hours and I knew that the sweat was rolling off my forehead. I couldn't understand why he hadn't come. I wanted to look again at my watch, but I didn't dare show a light. He might, even now, be soundlessly making his way up the stairway.

I remembered how slow time can go when you must wait in the dark.

And then I heard the slight noise. The sound of footsteps.

I opened the bathroom door a little wider and I held the gun steady in my right hand. The muzzle pointed directly at the bedroom door.

I heard the creak of the floor boards outside the door. I heard the knob turn. And then the door quickly opened.

I fired, three times in rapid succession, as the figure loomed in silhouette.

I reached then for the light switch just outside the bathroom door and a second later the room was flooded.

For just that one fraction of a minute, while her eyes were wide and she looked into mine, I saw everything. I even heard the words as they struggled to get through her blood congested throat.

She said, "Marty. Oh Marty."

It was then I started to scream.

Later, they told me I never stopped, not even after the doctor gave me the hypodermic and they tried to pry Fern's dead body out of my arms.

CHAPTER XIII

1.

As I said in the very beginning, the time is very short. In less than an hour now I shall be walking down the narrow green hallway. I will be going first and the other one will follow me fifteen minutes later. I just want to be sure it is all clear in my own mind.

In one sense, both of us, that other man and myself, are innocent. On the other hand, we are also guilty. I am certainly guilty of the murder of my wife, Fern Ferris, whom I loved and whom I killed. Of course I hadn't meant those bullets for her; those leaded slugs were for Willy Holiday, the man I had bribed to murder my wife.

By now of course, everyone knows what happened. You've read all about it in the papers. You have read about how my partner, Sal Brentano, had become worried when I didn't show up, and went around looking for me. How he stopped by Willy Holiday's room to see if I might be there and how he started questioning Willy when I wasn't and then found the gun on him. Of course he arrested Willy and took him downtown and booked him.

I didn't know about that until too late.

No, when I fired those fatal shots, I thought I was firing at Willy. But I wasn't. I was firing directly at the one woman I truly loved. I killed that woman.

I didn't mean to do it and in a sense it was an accident. But in my heart of hearts I consider myself guilty of my wife's murder and that is why tonight, just before I am to die for that crime, I can say that at last my mind and heart are at peace.

It is a rather odd thing that the man who follows me to the chair tonight should be the man who killed Billy Chamlers. Odd because of the peculiar way in which the Chamlers murder was so closely related to my own particular tragedy.

And in a sense, it isn't odd, because, in many ways this other man has suffered the same sort of thing which I have suffered.

That fat, shoddy, rather disgusting man, Sam Duffy.

He was in love with a woman, too. And he killed the woman he loved. He killed her because he loved her. Not because he couldn't have her, but because he loved her. He just couldn't stand to see what she was doing to herself. And so he killed her.

Why did he take the jewels? He took them because he had given them to her, on her various birthdays. Somehow, to him, they represented the sweetness of the sentiment that he had felt and he wanted them back to remember her by.

I told Sal all about Duffy once I had regained my senses sufficiently to think straight. I told Sal a lot of things.

To the very last I had to fight Sal—my friend and my partner. He wanted me to plead insanity; he wanted me to tell the true story about Holiday.

I think, though, I have finally convinced him. I convinced him that I'd have no peace until I had paid for the crime I committed. I think he finally understands that it isn't a matter of much importance that it was my gun that killed Fern and my finger which pressed the trigger.

It was my lack of faith in her love that killed her.

I was a good cop, but I was a poor human being.

I didn't understand love.

THE END

www.ingramcontent.com/pod-product-compliance
Lightning Source LLC
LaVergne TN
LVHW021221080526
838199LV00084B/4302